For the average Joe

The reason birds can fly is that they have faith,
For to have faith is to have wings.

–Sir James Matthew Barrie, Peter Pan

Flying Blind

A cropduster's story

LUANNE OLEAS

i

Flying Blind: A cropduster's story
Published by Sand Hill Review Press, LLC

www.sandhillreviewpress.com,
1 Baldwin Ave, #304, San Mateo, CA 94401

ISBN: 978-1-949534-09-2 paperback
ISBN: 978-1-949534-10-8 case laminate
ISBN: 978-1-949534-11-5 ebook

Library of Congress Control Number: 201939537
© 2019 by Luanne Oleas

SHRP
Sand Hill Review Press
1 BALDWIN AVE, #304, SAN MATEO, CA 94401

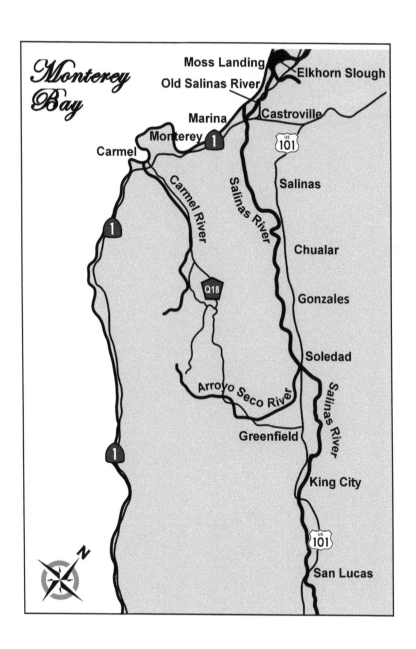

Flying Blind
A cropduster's story

LUANNE OLEAS

Goodbye, Texas

LIFE MADE SENSE when Tony was alone in the cockpit. He slowed the plane on approach. His gloved hand nudged the stick, he pressed the rudder pedal with his boot, and the plane banked. He cocked his head to follow the horizon. The plane leveled out, and he straightened his neck. The narrow airstrip centered in his windscreen had a single hangar at the far end.

The shadow of the plane passed over the boss's pickup. It was racing up the dirt road that connected the airstrip to a singlewide mobile home. Seeing the pickup surprised Tony. Velma Lee had told him that R.J. wasn't supposed to be back from Dallas until tonight. Tony tapped his shirt pocket, then remembered his pack of Kools on R.J.'s nightstand.

"Shit," he muttered. He hoped Velma Lee had thrown them out with the vodka bottles and the Polaroids. He pushed those thoughts aside. He knew distractions and landings didn't mix.

Tony picked out his touchdown spot. It was halfway down the airstrip, near the company sign that boasted: "R.J.'s Cropdusters, Beaumont, TX — Two planes to serve you better." Only 10:00 a.m. and he had polished off the last load on a 600-acre rice job. That was almost $250. In 1972, at 28, that felt like getting rich. Should he get a new car? A round waterbed? At least some expensive booze. He brought the Weatherly in for a picture-perfect landing with the words to *Satisfaction* (and not getting any) drumming in his head.

The wheels of the low-winged monoplane kissed the ground. Landing was bittersweet. He liked doing it well. He hated returning to earth. The tailwheel touched down, the horizon disappeared behind the engine, and he began the familiar bumpy roll down the runway. The right rudder pedal wilted beneath his foot. No brake.

"Oh shit!"

Tony steered using the tailwheel while he had speed. The aircraft slowed and he jabbed at the dead brake pedal over and over. The end of the runway approached in slow motion.

"Not the fucking hangar," Tony groaned. The tin structure and the plane parked beside it grew larger.

Tony sucked on his dark, thick moustache with his lower lip and rolled on helplessly at five miles per hour. The plane was a breath away from the building and he was just along for the ride. The landing gear hit a small rut. The craft veered left. The wingtip snagged the corner of the hangar and turned the plane.

R.J.'s other plane sat dead ahead. Tony's spinning prop chewed into the wing of the other plane with the noise and fury of a giant can opener. Tony listened and winced. Seconds later, finally at a standstill, he scowled at the pool of brake fluid on the cockpit floor. He unlatched his seat belt, and the clicking sound broke the menacing silence.

Tony popped open the canopy, pulled his long body out of the plane, and climbed out to stand on the wing. The pungent smell of gas hit his nose and crawled down his spine like electricity. Was there fire? It was always his first thought after a sudden stop. But there was no smoke, no open flame. The fumes rose from the severed gas tank in the shredded wing of the other plane.

He exhaled, snagged the helmet from his mop of black curls, and shielded his blue eyes from the sun. R.J. wouldn't be happy. The curled propeller blades were tangled in the half-eaten wing of the other plane.

"These two are history," he said. He wanted to brush it off or fix it. He couldn't stand the sight of a plane that couldn't fly.

Trembling spread through his body to his fingertips and toes. He threw his scuffed white helmet halfway to his ragtop '67 Mercury Monterrey. Twenty minutes ago, sulfur dust had swirled behind the single-seat Weatherly. The landing gear had skimmed over shuddering blades of rice. Tony had felt safe in the yellow plane, even flying fence-high at 100 mph.

R.J. always assigned the worst fields to Tony. The one he just finished had been a damn obstacle course. Trees, standpipes, a shed, barbed wire fence, power lines. For Tony's first day on the job, R. J. had made him fly that field. Later, R. J. had slapped him on the back and called him "a pilot's pilot." R.J. had even admitted he couldn't put the plane under the low wire on the south end. His boss probably wouldn't remember that now. Tony just hoped he would remember that pranged aircraft were part of cropdusting.

Tony stood on the wing and looked back at the tangled mess. This would come out of his paycheck. Hell, it was an accident. The only thing that could make it worse would be if R.J. found out Tony was doing his wife. The sound of rubber squealing against asphalt made him look over his shoulder. The quick stop of R.J.'s pickup caused a cloud of dust to envelop Tony's boss's truck. R.J. threw open the driver's door.

Maybe R.J. wouldn't call the NTSB. Tony didn't want to deal with the National Transportation and Safety Board again if he could avoid it. They could separate the two planes, and Tony would offer to work on the mangled wing for free, just to keep it all off his record. He raised his hand over his head, signaling to R.J. that he was OK. The next thing he knew, R.J. had a shotgun propped on the truck door's open window. Both barrels were aimed at him.

Shotgun pellets peppered the fuselage. *Holy shit!* Tony jumped from the wing and ran behind the hangar. He kept his back pasted to the hot, corrugated tin building. Two seconds of silence prompted him to peek around the corner. He saw R.J. break open the weapon and empty a box of shells on the front seat of his pick-up. Damn, he was reloading.

"It was an accident, R.J.," Tony yelled, venturing from behind the building, but not far. "Fluid leaked from the cylinder. I didn't have any right brake."

R.J. took aim again. Tony stepped back, spun around, and lunged behind the hangar just before R.J. started yelling.

"Bang my wife." KA-BOOM! "Wreck both my planes." KA-BOOM! "I'll kill you, Tony Damascus." KA-BOOM! KA-BOOM!

Tony dashed behind the conjoined planes, the blasts following him. He snagged his helmet from the ground and dove headfirst into the front seat of his car. The gear shift stabbed him in the ribs.

Damn. A shot hit his windshield. Shit. Shit. Shit. He yanked off one glove and fought to remove his keys from his pants pocket. Another shot. He fumbled with his keys. His shaking hand struggled to make the key penetrate the ignition switch.

"Come on, come on," Tony urged the key.

The key cooperated and Tony turned the ignition switch, pushing the accelerator pedal with his hand. He drove away, lying low. Roadside bushes scraped the car doors. He crossed the railroad tracks and sat up. Even then, R.J. blasted another round in his direction.

Tony turned left onto highway FM 1193, headed west. He didn't look back. No need. The trunk of his faded yellow car held most of his possessions. Velma Lee would know he wasn't coming tonight.

He would miss little things about her. The way she always came into that blistering hot hangar, wearing shorts and asking him if he wanted ice cream. Telling him she was lonely. Tony knew why too. R.J. was always bragging about his other women when he was lining out the day's work or while they waited for the wind to shift.

Texas, flat Texas, passed. Tony had trouble keeping his focus on the road. He had dealt with other jealous husbands, but the shotgun was a first. Worse than the knife in Mississippi. Worse than the pitchfork in Arkansas. Not as bad as the guy in Oklahoma, whose only comment was, "You're welcome to her."

Ten years ago, Tony had left California, escaping Jealous Husband #1, his foster father. He'd heard the old man was dead. It seemed as good a time as any to go back. His foster mother might still be alive. Well, fuck her if she couldn't take a joke. Hell, he had, and, um, no, she couldn't.

Four burgers, ten beers, and a whole goddamn day later, he took a whiz on the sign that said: "You are now leaving Texas." He popped another brew to salute the "Welcome to New Mexico" sign. He did the same at the "Welcome to Arizona" sign before pulling into a roadside flophouse for the night. Tony stood in the narrow door of room 17 and stared across the empty parking lot, feeling too hot to sleep, too tired to drive. Would life always be like this?

He noticed a car pulling into a driveway across the road at twilight. A family emerged and headed into the house, Mom and Dad first. The kids bounced in behind them, looking happy to be home. Some people were lucky enough to go home.

He had heard his real dad say once that Tony had a brother somewhere, but he was pretty sure his father had been lying. The old man always had tried to sound like a real stud. Maybe that's why Tony was such a fuck-up. Maybe things like that ran in families.

He grabbed the molding above the door jamb and stretched. Too many hours in the car. He rubbed his eyes, glanced down at the motel office, and stretched again. At least he had managed not to flirt with the proprietor's wife when he registered. Twenty-four hours without touching another man's wife. Not much of a record. He wasn't good enough for a woman to want only him. So he had been told. So he believed. He looked over his shoulder at the empty bed and decided to call it a night.

Tony woke in the middle of the night, dreaming about Velma Lee. He couldn't recall the dream, but he could remember lying in bed with her after sex. She would play with his little finger. He liked that about Velma Lee. She didn't want to snuggle or get too close. She would just pick up his hand and bend his little finger back and forth. He had always tried to stiffen his finger, so she couldn't move it. But no matter how hard he tried, she always could.

He had probably stayed with Velma Lee too long. Two or three weeks used to be enough with any woman. A month tops. Lately though, things had been different. For some reason, he wasn't as interested in the chase as he used to be, and the thrill of getting caught was becoming more of a drag. Maybe it was age, although 28 wasn't that old. At least he wasn't 30. Tony kicked off the covers and rolled over, but it took him a while to go back to sleep.

FOURTEEN HOURS LATER, he stopped and bought three gallons of water and a 12-pack of Coors before crossing the California state line. He nursed the convertible's tired engine across the desert with the water, but saved the beer for himself. A real meal would have to wait until he landed a job.

Tony checked all the cropdusting hotspots in the state's wide Central Valley—Needles, Buttonwillow, Tranquility, Firebaugh, Dos Palos. Each one told the same story. "Got all the pilots I need," the boss would say. It was probably true, since climate in California offered year-round work. He turned west, passing through Los Banos and over the Pacheco Pass. He followed the setting sun, making stops in Hollister, Gilroy, and finally Watsonville near the Pacific Ocean. His rotten luck was holding. That night, he'd be sleeping in his car.

Lesson One

TONY ANALYZED SALINAS from the freeway overpass. The city seemed to be laid out with all the forethought of a cow pissing on a flat rock. The Salinas Valley sprawled between two ranges of rolling hills, the Gabilans for the sunrise and the Santa Lucias for the sunset.

Tony guided his yellow convertible off Salinas' last freeway exit and pulled over for a cheap fill-up. He unfolded his cramped legs and his empty wallet. The view from the gas pump consisted of an airport and endless rows of crops beyond the city limits. He shacked up at the Overnighter Lodge by the Fast Gas at the end of the runway. The next day, he told a few believable lies and landed a job as a flight instructor.

By the end of the first week, he began wondering why he had been hired. Business was slow at the flight school. He cruised down the barren road toward Salinas Municipal Airport, not worried about returning late from lunch. The black interior of his faded car, top down, baked in the Indian summer sun. Marvin Gaye's latest, "Let's Get It On," blared from the radio. Tony nodded in rhythm, knocking back the last of a brew.

He spun the ragtop in a dusty circle, parked, lifted his shades and peered into the rearview mirror. Crackling blue eyes framed by long, dark lashes beneath jet black eyebrows stared back at him. An attempt to smooth his moustache with the palm of his hand failed. He stepped from the car and studied his image while strolling past the windows of the terminal building. The wind played with his full head of black curls. Not a grand physique, just a long and lanky guy whose jeans were hanging a little loose these days. Maybe if he ate more regularly. Maybe if he drank less. Never happen.

Tony stashed his beer can in the planter box and headed for the flight school's rear entrance. The rolling growl of a 600-horse, radial engine called to him. He shaded his eyes and stared up at the Stearman bi-plane on approach. Ah, baby. . .

Tony stepped away from the door to watch the plane, lacing his fingers through the cyclone fence. Gripping the metal reminded him of hanging on to a cyclone fence that once had surrounded a big backyard. Back then, he would point at the sky and the smiling woman beside him would say, "Airplane, Tony, airplane." When she picked him up and twirled him around, he felt like he was flying through the lilac sweet air that always surrounded her.

Then, he remembered her lying on the kitchen floor. Long black hair hid her face. He sat down beside her, cold linoleum pressed against his bare legs. He cried until he couldn't make any noise, but she didn't open her eyes. He was too little to understand words like "aneurysm," "alone," and "abandoned." He squeezed the soft hem of her dress in his small fist and lay down beside her. He must have fallen asleep. He must have let go. He released his grip from the fence outside the flight school. For a moment, he thought he saw a blue-and-white floral pattern on the palm of his hand.

The memory hit him like a blow to the stomach. He grabbed the cyclone fence with both hands and remembered the day his real father had left him at an airport. Tony's new foster family had taken Tony to the airport to watch his only remaining family member go away. His small fingers had remained entwined in the cyclone fence, long after the commercial airliner had left. This time, he wouldn't let go. His foster father had pulled him off the ground, but Tony wouldn't let go. His foster mother had to loosen Tony's fingers one at a time.

Tony pushed himself away from the fence, wiped his hands on his jeans, and glanced over to the spot where he just had left his beer. There were a few sips left in the bottom of the can. Better not. After a deep breath, he yanked open the back door to the flight school and stepped inside. The wind slammed it closed behind him.

Louise Bandini, secretary and co-owner of Skyways Unlimited, was talking at the counter with a small man in a pale green shirt. Tony could hear her brassy Brooklyn accent beyond the crooked room dividers. He collapsed into a chair behind a worn desk. Her fried, dyed hair always reminded him of his ex-mother-in-law. That marriage had lasted all of three months.

"How about a demonstration flight?" Louise said to her clean-cut client. "Due to a cancellation, we have a flight instructor available." Her eyes darted in Tony's direction.

"Cancellation?" Tony mouthed and rolled his eyes.

A rattling fan pushed hot air around the cramped room. That noise and Tony's bum hearing made it easy to tune out Louise's sales pitch. His upper ranges were gone forever, thanks to all his hours behind a radial engine. Tony could still diagnose engine trouble by sound, but he figured that had more to do with rhythm and feel than hearing. Ladies' voices were the hardest for him to understand.

He turned the squeaky swivel chair toward the window and stared at the Stearman landing. His boots on the desktop exposed the nail heads in his worn heels. Tony possessed neither the patience nor the desire to instruct, only an aching need to fly. The cash was a necessary evil, and though he would never admit it, his starving heart would pilot a plane for free.

"Let me think, let me think," the little man at the counter said, gathering his papers. He paced across the stale lobby, out of earshot. He wandered between a worn, orange couch and some office space for lease, vacated by the latest commercial liner to go broke in Salinas.

"He sounds Italian," Louise said under her breath to Tony, pushing his feet off the desk. He let them drop with a thud.

"Italian?" Tony echoed, and gave her a wink. "Great. We'll stay on the ground and sing a chorus of O Sole Mio."

"Guys like that pay your salary, toots," Louise said with a wagging finger.

"Lucky me."

She looked like she had more to say, but the phone rang. Tony's boots went back on the desk. He was watching another plane taxi toward the runway. His elementary school teachers had reprimanded him for daydreaming, but others hadn't been so gentle. Some men prayed. Others stared out windows.

"Excuse me." It was the man who had just talked to Louise. "Do you work here?"

"Some," Tony answered.

"Do you know anything about flying airplanes, instructing, that kind of thing?" The customer spoke with a thick accent and a staccato rhythm. The heel of his hand bounced on the countertop. Despite the heat, he looked cool in khaki slacks and an open collar shirt.

"Wha . . . ?"

"Do you teach flying lessons?" the man rephrased his question.

"Some."

Just then, Tony caught a flash of daylight from the back of the room. It signaled the return of Louise's husband, Frank. The boss had ridden Tony's ass earlier that week about his lack of enthusiasm. "Damascus, I'm not thrilled with your attitude," he had said. Tony unglued himself from the chair. He picked up a registration clipboard and slid it the length of the counter toward the customer. Leaning forward, he locked eyes with the small man.

"Bet you wanna learn to skywrite."

"Not at first," the man answered.

"What do you know about airplanes?" Tony asked.

"They go up. They come down. They fly like a bird without flapping." A grin and dancing green eyes accompanied the customer's rapid response.

"Hell, you don't need lessons," Tony said. "Just buy a plane."

Louise's turkey-necked husband entered the room. Frank's presence made the hair tingle on the back of Tony's neck. Tony could bullshit Louise all day, but Frank was a hard-nosed cuss. He'd warned Tony that if he didn't like working for the flight school, unemployed cropdusters were a dime a dozen. Tony cleared his throat. "Have you flown before?"

"Some," the Italian parroted Tony.

"Often?"

"Every time I go home. It's too far to swim."

"Left seat?" Tony asked.

"Left seat? No, no, no. Window or aisle."

"Terrific," Tony said. He was pretty sure it was pointless, but he initialed the form on the clipboard and prepared to fill it out. "Ever had lessons? Wait—is this cash or credit?"

"Cash—"

"You qualify. Name?" he asked, his pen poised on the first line.

"Roberto Guiseppe Ferentini."

"Yeah?" Tony raised a black eyebrow, glared at his customer, and scratched beneath his piles of black curls with the blunt end of the pen.

"Use Robert, if it's easier," Roberto said. Tony printed the name in the first box on the form. "Ah, such beautiful handwriting. What is *your* name?"

"Tony," he answered, moving to the next box on the form. "Age?"

"Tony Age?"

"No, Tony Damascus," Tony said without looking up. "I need your age."

"Fifty-six."

"Fifty-six?" Tony repeated, his eyes scouring the man's youthful face. "Hell, I look closer to that than you do."

"You need proof?" Roberto asked.

"No. Why would anyone say he was 56 if he wasn't?"

Tony continued to fill in the form. The customer produced a transcript from the local college where he had recently completed ground school. Tony ignored it.

"Business address?"

"I work out of my home," the man answered. "Counseling mostly."

"That's about it," Tony said, giving the form a last look before focusing on the empty wall hook. "Where the hell are the keys for 2-6?" A set lay sprawled on Louise's desk. Tony pocketed them, headed toward the end of the counter, and hit the waist high swinging door with his hip. It opened with a bang. Tony stepped into the airport lobby and headed for the terminal fire exit.

"Follow me," he snapped without looking back.

Both men crossed the apron in silence. Tony took advantage of his long legs to swagger ahead of Robert. The smaller man caught up after 20 paces. Tony watched Robert from the corner of his eye. The older man trotted beside him, chin high, his head bobbing at Tony's shoulder.

Tony led Robert to a green and white Cessna on the flight line ahead. It was a dog in Tony's eyes, but a reliable old plug compared to the boss's flat-spinning Yankee skywriters. Tony unhitched the tie downs and freed the wings. He flung the chocks away from both wheels, opened the cockpit door, and reached inside.

"First thing you always do is check the master switch and drop the flaps," Tony said. "Then—"

"Check the fuel," Roberto said. Roberto, standing tiptoe, unscrewed the gas cap from the top of one wing, stuck his finger in the gas, and replaced the cap like some student straight from ground school. "What next?"

"You don't fucking know if there's gas in this sucker," Tony roared, slapping a flat palm against the fuselage.

"But I felt—"

"You want to risk your ass on a wet finger? Fine. But if I'm going up, I want to see gas, smell gas, and hear it hit the pavement."

Tony reached beneath the wing and opened a small valve. Fuel splashed on the hot tarmac with a pungent sizzle. He smiled at Robert's shocked expression, knowing he had his student's attention.

Tony had trained with an ex-military flier. The son of a bitch had whittled away Tony's flaws with angry criticism and had made sure that Tony had finished each lesson in a sweat-soaked shirt. He'd once overheard his instructor say that a student as gifted as Tony comes once in a lifetime, but to his face, the asshole had only said Tony was a worthless sack of shit who wouldn't amount to squat. This wasn't a news flash to Tony. He remembered his foster father yelling the same thing. Roberto was staring at Tony. The guy seemed to know Tony's mind had wandered.

"Use every sense you've got, uh, Robert," Tony said, changing his tone, but stumbling on the man's name. "And maybe a few senses don't know you have. Think about what you're planning to do in this machine."

Tony dragged Robert's hand over the leading edge of the wing and the prop during the pre-flight. They both walked all around the Cessna, and Tony insisted that Robert kneel and check the landing gear.

"Do you do this every time you fly?" Roberto asked, standing, and then dusting off his slacks.

"You're damn right I do," Tony said. He would tell the same lie to anyone starting a steady diet of Sunday flying.

They entered the cockpit and sat shoulder to shoulder. Tony let Robert sit on the left to entice him with the pilot-in-command seat. Robert used the instrument checklist and ticked off varying pressures, temperatures, and gauges. He flipped open his side window, shouted "Clear," and reached for the ignition switch.

"What the hell are you doing?" Tony asked, snatching the key from the panel.

"Starting the motor."

"Like hell you are."

"I check everything," Roberto said, slapping the checklist.

"Slow down!" Tony said, noticing his student's fractured grammar.

"Why?"

"Because, if you don't, you'll plant yourself face down in this mother, and they'll use your ass for a bicycle rack."

To Tony's surprise, Roberto smiled. Tony tried to stay stern, but Robert's steady gaze got to him. Tony looked away. He didn't like some stranger staring into his soul.

"Go on. You tell me. What I miss?" Roberto said in rapid, stilted English. "Name one thing—"

"What are you bitching about?" Tony asked, turning his good ear closer.

"What did I miss?"

"Who knows?" Tony answered, buckling his seat belt. "You went so damn fast. Now, go slow—and point to every instrument when you read it. That way, you really look at it and know exactly where the fuck it is in an emergency."

"Do you do it every time you fly?"

"You better believe it," Tony answered, but he didn't look Robert in the eye when he said it.

Tony let the plane roll to the taxiway before he slipped on headphones with an attached microphone. He braked and ran up the engine. The vibration rattled every window and loose part on the instrument panel. It would feel good to be back in the air. On takeoff, he saw Robert peer out the side window and gasp as the ground pulled away.

"It's not like the big jets," Roberto said, eyes wide. "I can see every pebble. So glorious."

"Breaking ground," Tony said over the engine noise. "It's like an orgasm."

"Or a miracle," Roberto answered and gave Tony an irritating smile.

Tony shrugged, not sure what Robert meant, but he lived for the sensation. Gravity gave up and nothing could hurt him. That wasn't something he thought or believed or knew. It was something he felt, and he felt it every take-off. Nothing was more reliable. Not popping the top on a cold one, not sex, not driving fast. Everything in his life that had ever been the real thing always felt like that blast of freedom that passed through him when he broke ground.

Tony grabbed another headset from a hook above the windscreen, and dropped the tangle of wires, earphones, and microphone into the older man's lap. Robert gave Tony a quizzical look, and Tony motioned for him to put it on. They exited the flight pattern, heading south and gaining altitude. The plane's shadow slid over the wide, brown Salinas River, which snaked down the valley from Castroville through Salinas to King City and beyond.

"This *is* a demo flight, so I'll do most of the flying," Tony said, his voice piped into Robert's ears. "We'll start slow and easy with some S-turns."

Tony dipped one wing, and the plane slid one way. The other wing dropped, and the aircraft slithered the opposite direction. Playful flying always made Tony smile. The slippery back-and-forth motion prompted Roberto to murmur a few words and sign himself.

"You want to talk to God?" Tony asked and rapped his knuckles on the windscreen. "Just knock. You Catholic?"

"Yes," Robert answered. "You?"

"Nope," Tony said, twitching his black moustache. "Flying's my religion. This," he pointed to the sky, "is church. Or maybe heaven."

"Perhaps it is purgatory," Robert answered, smiling.

"What the hell is that anyway?"

"What the hell is purgatory?" Roberto said, repeating Tony's response with a chuckle. "It depends. I once heard it described as a place for people who didn't learn to love as children. I hope it is. Don't you?"

Tony scowled, but didn't answer.

"My mother, she could never love me," Roberto said, sounding a little too personal. Tony rolled his eyes. "When I was young, my little sister died in a kitchen fire that I had started. I suppose not loving me was my mother's way of pushing me away, in case something happened to me too."

"Yeah, right," Tony answered, looking out the window and waiting for the guy to shut up.

"She told relatives I was ugly and scrawny," Robert continued. "She wished I had died instead. My parents sent me away to semin— Catholic school when I was 13. My father couldn't afford to support eight children between the Great War and the Great Depression. It was for the best."

"For the best?" Tony asked with a side glance. "And *you* do counseling?"

"You don't understand."

"I don't have to," Tony said. "I'm a pilot, not a therapist." Tony lifted his hands from the controls. "Here, you take her. Keep her straight and level."

Roberto grabbed the yoke with both hands. Tony could see sweat starting to form across the other man's forehead and smiled.

"But my mother—" Robert tried to continue.

"Use your left hand," Tony said, taking a swipe at the Italian's white-knuckled grip and knocking his hand away. "Your right's for the throttle."

"A mother's love—" Roberto started again.

"Leave that crap on the ground when you fly," Tony said. He'd had enough. "Emotions are deadlier than fire in a cockpit."

"A mother's love is hard to explain," Roberto persisted.

"Not really," Tony fired back. He hadn't gotten through to Robert, so he decided to try another tack. "My mother died, but my foster mother made her love real clear. When I was four, she took me into her room, stripped naked, and told me what made her feel good. My foster father always watched, and then expressed his disapproval. I still can't stand leather belts, locked closets or lavender perfume." Yes, he had Robert's attention. "See? You're losing altitude."

"I'm sorry . . ."

"We'll both be sorry if you stick this baby into the side of a mountain," Tony answered, regretting his tactic. Why had he said that? He had never told a living soul.

"Forgiveness is powerful," Roberto said, battling to control the aircraft.

"If you are bored, we could do some turns." Tony had stayed home from school on the bad days, when the bruises were too noticeable. It helped to imagine flying through the blue sky beyond the closed drapes. In those days, his collection of pencil-drawn airplanes grew thick, and while friends had memorized batting averages, he learned to tell Messerschmitts from Spitfires. Curtiss Orioles from Travel Airs. Years passed, and he survived.

"I hope there was someone you could talk to," Robert said.

"What for? You just dropped 100 feet while gabbing."

"But no one ever stopped them?"

"Watch your heading," Tony said. "And mind your own damn business. Give it some right rudder. Keep the nose up. Follow the river."

Robert shut up, his eyes darting between the gauges and the river. Tony flipped off his own headset, just in case the old guy started yapping again. He was beginning to regret returning to California. Something about being back in the state had stirred up memories about growing up in the hot Central Valley. He wanted to leave them buried. Fords had flames back then. He kept his cigarettes in the sleeve of his tee-shirt and wore his curls greased back. "Piano Tuner" had been his nickname in high school because he fixed engines by sound. And swearing and drinking beer. Back then, frying in an oily driveway and fixing cars was better than going home. He wished the flood of memories would stop, but they continued.

He would go home at night. When had his foster mother started locking the bedroom door instead of inviting him in? And why? Sure, it wasn't everyone's idea of maternal love, but he had forced it to work. The one morning he wanted to forget was when he grabbed her, thrown her on the couch, and torn off her clothes. He kept her there for hours, naked. He could still remember the click of the latch when his foster father opened the front door. Tony was so angry by then, he slugged the old man. The son of a bitch swore he would kill

Tony and had him arrested the next day. Tony walked out of jail two weeks later and made the decision to never go home again. Why had he come back to California? He shook his head. Robert's mouth was moving, and Tony switched on his headset to hear him.

"Huh?"

"How did you learn to fly?" Roberto asked again.

"It wasn't easy."

He'd lived like a hangar rat for a while, sleeping in the bushes by the control tower and washing airplanes. Hours of work had been traded for minutes of flight time. It probably sounded strange to some people, but Tony had liked it a lot better than where he'd been. It was tough but he had gotten his commercial license. That was almost ten years ago. He'd dusted in six states, but—

"I never forgave," Tony said. "Sounds too much like forgetting."

"It's not."

"Purgatory," Tony said. Avoiding Roberto's eyes was easy with Roberto struggling to control the plane. "A place for people who didn't learn to love in childhood. There'd be some sweet trollops there."

"That's not exactly what God intended," Roberto said, sounding a little too certain about it for Tony.

"Look, this is a flying lesson, not Sunday school," Tony said, taking back the controls.

"It's a demonstration ride," Roberto answered.

"Yeah, right," Tony said, slipping the plane left and right with an easy rhythm. "Notice how I move the controls. Feel her. OK, you try."

Robert moved the yoke, and, by the look in his eyes, Tony could tell the plane's reaction shocked Robert. The novice pushed one pedal, then the other, moving the controls with no purpose.

"Hold it, for Christ's sake," Tony said, taking back the controls. He brought her straight and level again with ease. Robert's lost look told Tony that he was losing confidence, and that meant the flight school was losing a customer, which wouldn't go over well with the boss. But Tony was sure he could sweet talk anyone when it came to flying. "Now, put your hand over mine lightly and just the tips of your toes on the pedals." Roberto did, and started to smile. "Feel her move?"

"Like dancing together in the sky," Roberto said. "So effortless."

17

Right. Tony smiled, but didn't say what he was thinking. It was effortless, if you didn't count the years he had sunk into learning how to fly like it was effortless.

"Now you do it," Tony said. He handed over the controls, half-knowing what would happen. Roberto tried to duplicate Tony's smooth maneuvers, but his motions were too anxious. Tony took over again.

"You got to feel it right here," Tony said, wiggling his butt. "In the seat of your pants. It's not like fucking. It's like making love with a beautiful woman. You know how you both move so perfectly?"

"Not exactly," Roberto answered.

"What do you mean?" Tony asked, slipping the plane left and right.

"Is there some other way of explaining it?"

"Maybe, but I don't know what it is," Tony answered.

"Try," Roberto said.

"Why?" Tony asked. Robert was getting on Tony's nerves. First, he reminded Tony of his fucked-up childhood. Then he questioned Tony's sex life.

"Because I never did that," Roberto said.

"Never did what?" Tony asked. He kept the plane turning in a tight circle, concentrating on the conversation more than the flying.

"Made love with a beautiful woman," Roberto admitted.

"How about an ugly one?" Tony said, glaring at Robert. His palm felt wet against the yoke. He didn't like where this was going.

"No," Roberto answered with a laugh.

"You queer?" Tony found himself checking for an emergency landing spot.

"No, I'm a priest."

"Fuckin' A."

"Maybe it's like praying," Roberto suggested, his blank stare trapping Tony.

"I don't know," Tony answered, looking away. "I never did that."

An uncomfortable silence settled between them. It only dissipated when Tony resumed instructing, so he focused on that. They flew the length of the Salinas Valley and back. As much as Tony liked flying, it felt good to land and get out of the cockpit, away from Robert.

18

Star Wars Bar

TONY CROSSED THE AIRPORT LOBBY and cruised into the Skyport Bar and Grill at five past five. It was a typical Friday night at an airport bar with ex-WWII tanker fliers and obsessed private pilots flying bar stools at the SkyBaG. Amazing gestures accompanied their wild stories. Hands orbited drinks with palms down, extended fingers served as wings. One man rehearsed an aerobatic routine, walking in circles behind a clenched fist and leaning backward to indicate inverted flight. Tony lowered his shades at a passing waitress, exposing his sky blue eyes and an arched eyebrow. He followed up with his "how about it, honey" smile.

Tony knew airport bars. For the past ten years, events in bars like the SkyBaG had filled his life with tall tales, dumpy waitresses, and stiff drinks. Smoked glass above dark booths separated the SkyBaG cocktail lounge from a worn out restaurant with its burnt coffee and sticky tables.

"Screwdriver, Paul," Tony said. Only one week at the flight school and he was already on a first-name basis with the bartender. Paul hadn't said "the usual"—yet. He placed the drink in front of Tony and said, "Enjoy." No need to belabor the obvious. Tony relished the promise of the first sip, from the chill of the ice cubes to the flavor dripping from his moustache. Life was good again.

The nearest booth was occupied by a young pilot named Bill. Tony had already talked to him twice. The first time, Tony had thought Bill looked like a local and asked him where he could get an oil filter. Bill knew the area and had been nice enough to help. The second time, they had met again in the SkyBaG after work. They had started talking and ended up closing the joint. Mostly, they had discussed flying, but there were times in the conversation when Bill sounded as if he had been raised on a different planet from Tony. Just certain phrases Bill had used made Tony cock his head. Home movies. Savings account. Library book. Vacuum cleaner. Still, when it had come to flying, the great equalizer, they were in sync.

Tony didn't recognize the guy sitting with Bill in the booth. Still, when Tony's drink arrived, he wandered over to the two men.

"You fly today, Billy boy?" Tony teased the younger one after a sip.

"I wish," Bill answered. Square, gold-rimmed glasses framed Bill's sea green eyes. His sensible haircut had grown out and sprouted rebellious dark blonde curls at his ears and collar. "My chance might be coming though."

"How so?" Tony asked, knowing dreams of flying bred like fleas in airport bars.

"Bart munched one of the Stearmans today," Bill answered with a smile. Tony knew that Bart was chief pilot where Bill worked, but he hadn't heard about him going down. "We hauled it back to the hangar before the Feds found out."

Bill gestured with one thumb over his shoulder, pointing beyond the picture windows and past the flight line to an arching metal building. The peeling paint above a set of wide, sliding doors spelled out "AirRaid Ag."

"Unfortunately, he wasn't hurt," Bill added.

"Too bad," Tony said.

If poor Bart had broken two arms and a leg, Bill and Tony both would've sent him flowers and then applied for his job. Both wanted and needed it. Bill knew the area, but Tony knew the business and had the flight time. Tony would scare up something, just like he did in Texas, Idaho, and Mississippi. After six months, Bill still didn't have any real flying time. They both knew cropdusting seats were hard to find, especially in California's coastal valleys where the flying and the paychecks lasted year round. Tony hated seasonal work that forced him to drive truck or flight instruct in the winter.

"How'd Bart go down, anyway?" Tony asked. Preventive measures were half the lessons he had learned in airport bars; the other half were about how to lie.

"He was hungover, and it was 5:00 a.m."

20

"So?" Tony asked.

"He got turned around in the fog." Bill's hand went up, fingers extended for a visual aid. "The old bologna slicer clipped a sand dune. Then the tail went over the top. It slid down the sand dune upside-down. The open cockpit filled with sand. He was yelling for help when we got there."

"What a bitch if she'd caught fire, huh?" Tony said with a cringe.

"He wasn't pinned in," Bill answered with a chuckle. "He forgot to release his seat belt."

Tony laughed and leaned against the planter box, making a mental note to unbuckle his seat belt in an emergency. He finished his drink and straightened up to hunt down a waitress.

"I've heard turning upside-down is strange," Tony said and looked around. "I know a guy who flipped a bi-plane. He wasn't hurt in the crash, but he broke his shoulder when he popped the seat belt and fell out onto the runway."

"Oh, shit," Bill said, and Tony sensed Bill making a mental note of that mistake.

Bill chewed at his moustache, fair and sparse at age 19. Tony knew that flying into the sun had creased the corners of his gentle eyes sooner than years could. The lines had helped Bill pass for 21, Tony figured, and allowed him to drink in the airport bar. Bill had told Tony that his mother tried to discourage her only son from flying. He also said that his father knew him well enough to know he couldn't talk him out of it.

"Tony, do you know Patches?" Bill asked, nodding to the balding man beside him with the wiry, gray goatee.

"Patches?" Tony asked, not trusting his hearing.

"Ed Pacheco," the older man said, offering his hand. "They call me Patches since I'm such a snappy dresser." A faded denim shirt and worn jeans hugged his short, fit body. A wide forehead and worn face suggested he was around 50. His vise-like grip and coarse palm surprised Tony.

"You a pilot?" Tony asked.

"Never had a chance," the older man sighed. "Always wanted to be. Still do. First, it was the war, then the divorce, and now the bills. One of these days—"

"Need another?" Tony asked, rattling the ice in his glass.

"Not yet," Bill answered.

"None for me," Patches said, pushing his empty glass aside. "I'm driving down to Arroyo Seco."

"A what?" Tony asked.

"Arroyo Seco, down by King City," Patches said and slid out of the booth. "The name means 'dry canyon.' I'd better hit the road. I'm running a drag line in King City tomorrow."

Tony said good-bye to Patches but saved his smile for the waitress. He caught her eye, lifted his empty glass, and winked.

"She could sit on my face any day," Tony said to Bill and took Patches' abandoned seat.

"Della?" Bill asked, following Tony's gaze. "Forget it. She's married."

"On the job training."

"That doesn't bother you?" Bill asked under his breath before she walked toward them.

"Not if it doesn't bother her." Tony's smile broadened as she approached.

"Another drink, sugar?" Della asked with a fading drawl. Black mascara dotted the puffy skin around her dull brown eyes. Tan make-up on her boxy face created a mask above her short, white neck. Her clingy white blouse rippled over lumps of fat, and her short black skirt fit too tight to be flattering.

"I'll have another screwdriver," Tony said. "Heavy on the *screw*."

"I can arrange that." She bent forward to replace his damp cocktail napkin. Her stiff hair brushed his curls.

"I hear you're married," he whispered to her cleavage.

"I've heard that too, darlin', but you wouldn't know it when I'm home in bed," she purred in his ear before heading back to the bar.

"Um, um, um . . ." Tony said, biting his lip and watching the extra wiggle in her rear end. She glanced back, and Tony gave her his best wicked smile. She wrinkled her nose, smiled, and turned to place his order.

"You can't be serious," Bill said. "Could a lady like that make you happy?"

"Two things, Billy boy," Tony answered, lifting one finger and looking Bill in the eye. "One, she ain't no lady." He lifted a second finger. "Two, never wait for someone else to make you happy."

"You'd go out with her?" Bill asked, leaning forward and staring at Tony in disbelief.

"I'd go anywhere with her providing there was a bed nearby," Tony answered and leaned back in the booth with a knowing smile.

"You think she's sexy?" Bill asked, looking first at the waitress's station, and then back at Tony.

"I think she's horny," Tony answered, folding his arms.

"But aside from that?"

"There's something aside from that?"

"I hope so," Bill answered, shaking his head.

"God, I hope you're right, Billy boy," Tony said. "But you couldn't prove it by me."

Lesson Two

"You teach him," Tony said, following his boss through the flight school on Tuesday afternoon.

"Do you want this job or not?" Frank asked, heading past the room dividers.

"Frank, he's a pr— He's a walking accident."

"You're supposed to be flying, not walking." Frank ducked into his office with Tony on his tail.

"Maybe you don't care about your aircraft, but it's my butt up there," Tony said, pointing to the ceiling.

"Maybe if you took your brains up there, you could teach the old goat how to fly," Frank said. He dropped into the chair behind his cluttered desk and massaged the back of his skinny neck. "Reading his paperwork isn't helping this headache."

"He's not an old goat. He's a pr—" Tony started.

"He's 56 and fresh out of ground school," Frank said and dug through his desk drawer. "Old fools like him pay the rent."

"It's not that."

"Then what the hell is it?" Tony's boss asked, firing an empty aspirin bottle into his metal waste basket.

"It flat can't be done. I'll take the next two old farts that come through the door, but I don't want him," Tony said, pounding his finger on Robert's forms. "He hasn't got it."

"Look, son, no one who comes through here has it. If they do, they leave."

Tony felt he could push Frank a little without the risk of being fired. They'd flown together the day before. Frank had told his new hire during the flight that he was impressed by how Tony handled the plane. His boss even reminisced that when he was younger, he had had something extraordinary too, before becoming an old goat and the last skywriter in the West.

"He's a priest, for Christ's sake," Tony said.

"So pray for a miracle," Frank answered. He rolled backwards in his chair, put Roberto's paperwork in the file cabinet, and slammed the drawer. "He'll be here in five minutes. I suggest you go outside, cool off, and do a quick preflight."

"Fuck," Tony said, exhaling, rolling his eyes, and then storming out.

Tony slumped against the wall outside and took a Kool from his crumpled pack. He cupped his hand around his match, lit his cigarette, and forced smoke to stream from his nostrils. He took two long drags before throwing it on the walkway. His boot heel ground the butt into the pavement, and he headed toward the plane. All too soon, Robert was strutting across the apron toward him. Tony folded his arms and waited.

Religion hadn't been the cornerstone of Tony's upbringing. Once, when the county had threatened to remove Tony and his foster brothers due to neglect, his foster father had had the bright idea of showing up at the social worker's church on Sunday. Tony could remember it was stifling hot and too quiet in the packed hall. His foster brothers, Rusty and Ray, started fighting. Rusty stepped on Ray's shoes and scuffed them. Ray could be a real priss about his clothes. Ray whined and Rusty slugged him in the chest, knocking the wind out of him. For some reason, Tony started laughing and couldn't stop. His foster parents dragged all three of them out of the church. Back home, Rusty and Ray dashed into the bathroom, locking Tony out to face their angry foster father alone. Tony, the youngest, hadn't stood a chance against the old man.

"Tony! Good to see you," Roberto said with his irrepressible grin. "Glorious day. Glorious day. This is the day the Lord has made. I shall rejoice—"

"Did anyone ever tell you that you talk too damn, oh shit— too fast?" Tony said and turned to open the cockpit door.

"All the time, all the time," Roberto answered, standing behind Tony and looking at the gas cap on the wing. "So, what's first? Fuel check?"

"I did it," Tony said, climbing in and freeing the controls.

"Great. Leading edge?" Roberto asked, still standing on the tarmac.

"Handled it," Tony said over his shoulder.

"You what?"

"I checked it."

"Everything outside the plane?" the priest asked with a pleased smile.

"Yep."

"Let's go," Roberto said, rubbing his hands together. He walked to the other side of the plane and opened the door.

"You trust me?" Tony asked, looking at Robert through the open door. It was one of the most vital things he would teach the priest. He repressed a smile, thinking 'this is where the lesson begins.'

"Of course," the priest answered, gripping the hand rail, ready to pull himself into the cockpit. "You know more about airplanes than I do."

"What if I forgot something?" Tony gave his student a dark stare that stopped Robert cold. "What if I'm lying?"

"You would lie to a priest?" Roberto asked with a twinkle in his eye that bugged Tony.

"I would lie to my grandmother to make her a better pilot."

"O-o-o. Bless me Father, for I have sinned," the priest said, making a cross in the air.

"Cut the crap and do the preflight."

Roberto made quick work of the outside preflight before climbing into the seat beside Tony. He sailed through the checklist of gauges, reading and pointing to each one. Tony swallowed all praise. His dark soul knew overconfidence killed new pilots.

Tony helped Robert radio the tower. Tony got the plane off the ground and handed over the controls to Robert. He directed the priest north, away from the long valley. Roberto wobbled into a banking turn against the hills and headed toward the sea. The thrill of breaking ground didn't keep Roberto quiet for long.

"How am I doing?" Roberto asked, never looking up from the instrument panel. "Could we fly over the convent? I told the sisters I was going up and—"

"Keep her level and watch for traffic," Tony said.

"Traffic?" the priest said, his head popping up. "No traffic. Tell me, how can you fly an airplane with your pants."

"What?" Tony wasn't sure he heard Robert right.

"I woke up at two in the morning thinking about it. You said, 'feel it in your pants,' like making love to a beautiful woman."

"Forget it," Tony said and laughed. He had to admire the priest's spunk, but he was beginning to think the old boy was nuts. "That's obviously not going to work for you."

"How do you know?"

"Call it a wild guess," Tony said, giving Robert a frank stare.

"Because I am a priest?"

"Yeah," Tony said and nodded. It was going to be a long lesson.

"I'm still a man," Roberto answered, returning Tony's glare.

"Look, this isn't a sex ed class," Tony said with a sneer that he hoped Robert would notice.

"It was your idea," the priest continued. He seemed happy to ignore Tony's look. "You said like making love to a beauti—"

"I know what I said," Tony said, adjusting the trim on the plane. Why couldn't he just behave like a normal student?

"Sometimes I stand at the front of the church for a wedding," Roberto said, not bothering to watch where he was heading. "A beautiful woman walks up the aisle in a long, white dress. She glides like a swan. Her father at her side seems like a weight."

"Don't start—" Tony said, hoping the priest would listen but somehow knowing he wouldn't.

"When the groom takes her arm, they move toward me like one person. When you make love to a beautiful woman, do you both move like one person?"

"Shit, I don't know," Tony answered. "I guess." He really didn't want to discuss it.

"Can you fly like you are one with an airplane?"

"I try," Tony said, more comfortable. At least they were talking about flying.

"And do you make love to lots of beautiful women?"

Tony stared at his co-pilot. He wasn't going to answer that. He reached up and flipped a switch. The engine died. An alarm sounded, followed by silence.

"You've just lost power," Tony said with a cocky nod out the window. "Where are you going to land this sucker?"

"I don't know how to land this 'sucker.'"

"Never, ever fly without looking for somewhere to land," Tony said, repeating advice he'd found as handy on the ground as in the air. "Find a spot. You're losing altitude."

Looking down, Tony's co-pilot searched the landscape. Below them, there were highways, beaches, and bare fields. Roberto surprised Tony by choosing another tack.

"Hail Mary, full of grace, the Lord is with thee."

"What the fuck are you doing?" Tony asked, his frustration piercing the silence.

"Praying."

"Why?"

"Because it works," Robert answered with a simple confidence that Tony didn't get. "Blessed art thou among women and blessed is the fruit of thy womb, Jesus."

Tony flipped the switch, and the engine sputtered to a start.

"Praise your holy name, Father," Roberto said, looking toward heaven and smiling.

"What if there was no miracle?" Tony asked, sighing and shaking his head. He had only taught a few people to fly, but he'd never had these kinds of problems before. He wanted to smack the guy. But he was a priest. And an asshole. Tony would have to try something else. "What if God or I didn't start the engine? Then what would you do?"

"Die."

Tony smacked his forehead and wondered at the crazy man in the command seat. He didn't admire his faith. It was foolish. He assumed Robert was too old to learn disbelief, just like he was too old to learn to fly.

"You wanna know how ordinary mortals handle that situation?" Tony asked, remembering his paycheck rode on teaching the clown how to fly.

From 3,000 feet, Tony pointed out the back roads and flat spots. He reminded Roberto that in desperate situations, he should land parallel to the rows of crops, not against them. And there would be time. The plane would glide even after the engine stopped. Robert seemed to be listening. Maybe he did want to learn to fly after all.

Watch the horizon, Tony instructed. Follow a true heading. He knew Robert was overwhelmed, and probably wouldn't remember to compensate for the wind or magnetic deviation. After a while, flying over the coastline, it was obvious Robert was going to get them lost, or worse. Tony took back the controls and made a diving turn. He started chasing a sea gull, skimming the plane just above the waves.

Out Tony's side window, blue-green water darkened the edge of the white, tidy-looking beach. They flew just high enough to prevent seeing the garbage left along the shore. Tony handed the controls back to Robert, directing him to gain altitude and head back to the airport. As the priest flew, Tony looked down and felt at peace flying over the well-ordered world below them. He always felt safer in the air, surveying miniature rooftops, sidewalks, and backyard swimming pools in neighborhoods linked by endless, ant-trail freeways. Before long, the airport came into view.

Father Robert's first landing was terrible. Tony wondered if it was just his age or all that talk about sex with beautiful women.

Doping the Wings

"YOU SEEING DELLA again tonight?" Bill asked. His disembodied voice rose from beneath a disconnected wing propped across two sawhorses.

"As soon as she leaves her other job," Tony answered, resting a beer can on his knee. He sat on a stool by the workbench in AirRaid Ag's paint room where Bill was working.

"She works somewhere besides the airport restaurant?" Bill asked from under the wing.

"Yeah, at a massage studio."

Tony smiled even though he knew Bill couldn't see him. Bill was focused on spreading dope on the underside of a freshly repaired wing. The thick glue would stiffen the canvas fabric, then Bill would paint it and remount it on the Stearman that Bart crashed last week. Tony felt comfortable talking to Bill in the walled off section of the hangar where they did repairs. The door had to remain shut even though it was warm outside. Dope spread more easily when it was warmer, and Tony didn't mind inhaling the intoxicating, trapped fumes.

"You've seen Della every night this week," Bill said and stood up. He adjusted his glasses and gave Tony a funny look. "What's her husband think?" To Tony, it sounded like Bill had wanted to ask that question for a while.

"Mr. Long-Haul Trucker?" Tony said, lighting a cigarette. "Haven't asked him."

"Hey, watch it," Bill said, focusing on the lit end of the cigarette. "Are you trying to blow us up?"

30

"You worry too much," Tony said, taking a drag. "Look, the dope won't set right unless you put it on evenly."

"If you know so much, you do it," Bill said, wagging a goopy brush in Tony's direction.

"It's not that tough," Tony said. He found another brush buried in the clutter of the workbench, mashed his cigarette on the floor, and opened two beers. "First, you need one of these," he said, handing a can to Bill.

Together they spread the dope smoothly over the coarsely woven fabric, each with a brew in one hand and a brush in the other. Bill lay on his back on the ground, wearing denim overalls. Tony stood to coat the topside of the wing. He noticed that Bill worked hard enough to create damp circles under both armpits. A loud and flashy polyester shirt was more Tony's style, which is what he was wearing on lunch break from the flight school. They both did the same job but with a different approach. Tony could reach farther with his long arms but admired Bill's methodical, crisp brush strokes that coated every thread. Tony knew they both fantasized about flying with that wing and were careful to leave no drips on the leading edge.

"The old man is going to can Bart's ass for this," Bill said, flicking his finger against an uncoated portion of the taunt fabric.

"He should," Tony said with a hopeful smile.

"Why?" Bill asked, sounding suspicious. "So you can get his seat?"

"You want me to lie and say 'no'?" Tony asked, attempting to peek over the wing but unable to see Bill's face.

"Why you?" Bill asked, stopping work for a moment. He moved from under the wing so he could look up at Tony.

"Because I can fly hung-over and Bart can't," Tony answered. He wet the finger of one hand, touched it to his ass and made a sizzling sound. "I'm just talented that way."

"What about me?" Bill asked, pointing to himself with the sticky brush.

"You can probably fly hung-over too," Tony said, after sucking on his beer. They had flown together the week before, and Tony had noticed that Bill's gentle touch at the controls had made the plane perform without stressing it. "Billy boy, you're a good pilot, but

31

everyone here knows you too well. All pilots lie about their actual flight time to get their first job. Stay here and you can't get a job because you don't have the time."

"And I can't get the time because I don't have a job," Bill answered, summarizing his dilemma and spreading dope again. "I heard about this school with Stearmans in Arkansas. They'll sell me time. I've saved a grand already, and my dad has offered to match it."

"Bitchin'" Tony said, abandoning his brush in the bucket and watching Bill work. "Shit, you'll make it. Someone believes in you. Now, I hope I make it. I can't take many more lessons with that priest."

"He still wants to fly after his last landing?" Bill asked.

"Yup," Tony said, downing half his beer. He would need it to teach Robert to fly. Anyone would. "He's coming back today. I scheduled him for a cross-country so we don't have to shoot touch and goes. He wouldn't have blown that landing so bad if we hadn't been talking about sex."

"I suppose you told him about the mile-high club," Bill said, pushing the bucket of dope ahead of him as he worked. A silly chuckle floated up from under the wing, a direct effect of the intoxicating fumes. "Did he believe you could make it with some chick at 5,280 feet?"

"Hell, no. I was just talking about sex in general," Tony said, putting his beer aside, lighting a cigarette, and picking up the brush again. He worked and talked with a lit cigarette clenched in his teeth. "Making love, actually. There's a diff—"

"What?" Bill asked, half-sitting up on the concrete floor. "You can't talk to a priest about that stuff. I know. I used to be Catholic."

"He's a man, isn't he?" Tony asked, remembering Robert's claim.

"He's a priest," Bill answered in disbelief. "For God's sake, Tony, those guys don't even have impure thoughts."

"You don't think so?" Tony asked, and he had to laugh. Bill was just young and clueless. "Hey, speaking of impure thoughts, I got a tart for you."

"If she's anything like Della, forget it," Bill said, refilling his brush and lying flat again.

"Nah, Della's a sleazebag," Tony answered. But then, sleazebags were easy and easy worked for him. He didn't think that type would fit Bill. "This girl works with Della. She's kind of . . . wholesome."

"Wholesome?" Bill asked with a laugh. "At a massage studio?"

"Really," Tony answered, making two more swipes with his brush before heading to the glue pot for a refill. "And she's not bad looking either."

"Great!" Bill said, coating the wing. "You date her."

"She's more your type," Tony said, watching Bill's face.

"What is my type?"

"You know," Tony said, enjoying the teasing. "Wholesome."

"Forget it," Bill said, turning red. "I'd have better luck with twenty bucks and a streetwalker."

"Only because you don't give women what they want."

"I don't have that kind of money," Bill said. He stood up and began covering the topside of the wing near the far end. "I'm not a pilot yet, remember? I'm just a swamper."

"I'm not talking money," Tony said, lying down. He began to coat the underside of his half of the wing, near where it would connect to the plane. His words floated up on the fumes. "You got to eat pussy."

"Cut me about ten feet of slack," Bill said with 19 years of disgust in his voice. "You do that for Della?"

"All the time, Billy boy," Tony answered, smiling while he thought about it, and smiling even more at Bill's reaction. Maybe it was the dope, but it struck him funny.

"What's it like?" Bill asked. He didn't seem to be moving the brush anymore.

"Like eating an old tuna taco," Tony said with a sigh. He peaked over the wing, cocked his head, and gave Bill a resigned look. "But then, that's Della."

"Ack! You're making me gag," Bill said, convulsing with laughter against the windowsill.

"It makes me gag too," Tony said, chuckling at Bill. "But it puts her through the roof."

"No lie?"

"Would I lie to you?" Tony asked. His black curls reappeared from under the wing, and his smile gave Bill the answer he needed. Bill dropped his brush into the bucket and threw his hands in the air.

"You're a pervert," Bill said.

"Of course I am," Tony answered, half surprised that Bill hadn't realized that before. He stood up, dropped his brush in the bucket and stared at Bill. "Come with me tonight to the massage studio. You need to meet this chick. Eat her pussy and she's yours."

"Oh, sure," Bill said, stepping back and folding his arms. "I'll say, 'Hello, my name is Bill. Care to step in the other room?"

"That should work," Tony said without blinking. "There's nothing but rooms with beds there. She's really nice and—"

"Wholesome, I know," Bill said, sipping his drink.

"And built," Tony continued, holding his beer and outlining an hourglass shape with both hands. "Tits like battleship guns."

Bill looked at the wing, half coated, and the bucket of dope, still half full. He took another sip of beer and then checked his watch.

"What time should I be there?"

Lesson Three

"HOLY FUCK!" Tony said, yelling at Robert through the headset. "You take off like we're in a jet." It was all he could do not to take the controls. He stared across the cockpit at the side of Robert's head. "Next time, I want a slow, steady rate of ascent."

"Slow and steady, slow and steady." The priest repeated Tony's words in his quick and ready style.

Tony twitched his moustache and watched for traffic. Roberto flew with a death grip on the yoke, circling the tower and staring straight ahead.

"Get out of the flight pattern," Tony said, complaining before they were two minutes into the session. He searched the skies around them, checking left and right, above and below. "Pilots on approach can't honk to move your ugly ass out of the way."

"It works in Italy," Roberto answered.

"Yeah, well, we're not in Italy."

"It looks like it sometimes," Robert said, attempting level flight.

The priest peeked out his side window and Tony looked out of his. So, this is what Italy looks like. Cauliflower clouds floated in the hot, blue sky. In the distance, rounded hills turned to jagged pinnacles where Tony had noticed the tortured landscape marking the San Andreas Fault. Straight below, giant quilt squares of deep green broccoli, pale head lettuce and brown earth covered the flat valley floor. Long parallel lines of grapevines ran for miles, following the contour of the foothills. Tony imagined there were lots of drunken cropdusters in Italy.

"The vineyards here are bigger than in Italy," Robert continued, "but they still remind me of home."

"People drink a lot of wine over there, don't they?" Tony asked, settling in for the long ride to another dusty farm town at the end of another long valley. It wouldn't be easy to relax with Robert for a co-pilot.

"Ah, vino is mother's milk," the priest answered with a laugh. "A lot? It depends on what you consider 'a lot.' I'm a priest. I drink every morning at seven o'clock mass."

"You drank this morning?" Tony asked, sitting up straight.

"Of course," the priest answered, his sparkling green eyes squinting in the sunny cockpit.

"It's eight hours from bottle to throttle," Tony said, knowing Robert couldn't even fly when he was sober. If the priest had been drinking, Tony could only imagine how this lesson would proceed. "Even a small amount can affect your reflexes, especially at this altitude."

"It's the Blood of Christ," Robert answered with confidence. "I'm sure God will forgive me."

"Yeah, but what about the FAA?" Tony asked, already calculating the fine in his head.

"You drank this morning," Father Robert said, ignoring Tony's question.

"The hell I did," Tony said, looking away. Eight feet from bottle to throttle was more Tony's motto. "What makes you think that?"

"I have my sources," the priest answered, nodding upwards and grinning.

"Who exactly?" Tony said, trying not to look up as well.

"Oh, angels."

"Oh, right," Tony said, turning toward the priest. "Are you saying that some flying baby with a pie pan behind his head told you I had a drink this morning?"

"Angels don't look like babies," Father Roberto said, and he sounded serious. "They look like strong men, body builders, maybe eight, nine feet tall."

"Great," Tony said, throwing up both hands. "I'm up in the air with a nut who thinks he sees angels." Tony looked once around the cockpit and laughed. "So, where do you see them?"

"Everywhere," Robert answered, sounding calm about it.

"In church?" Tony said. They could be there, and Tony would never know.

"No, hardly ever in church, unfortunately."

"Are there any here?" Tony asked, sweeping his hand around the plane.

"Oh, they're here," Roberto answered without looking.

"Yeah,. right," Tony said. "So's my mother."

"Probably."

The pain in that possibility shut Tony up. She died so long ago, he couldn't remember what she looked like. In his dreams, she was always in the distance. He could never see or hear her clearly.

"Feels like we're riding a roller coaster," Tony said, changing the subject. He wasn't about to start another walk down memory lane with Robert. "Keep your altitude and speed constant. You need more trim."

Tony dished out six reprimands during the first leg of their cross-country, and Robert rewarded him with a lousy landing. On the ground, Tony grunted one-word answers unless Robert asked him about flying techniques. He endured coffee and donuts in silence with the priest in the remote airport restaurant. Back in the air, Roberto rambled on about the beauty of nature and the wonders of God's creations until Tony was ready to puke.

"You should've decided to be a park ranger, not a priest," Tony said, cutting him off and adjusting the trim for him.

"Oh, I didn't decide to become a priest. My mother did that. I was only 13 and—" Robert's statement surprised Tony, and he stopped fiddling with the radio.

"You never wanted to be a priest?" Tony asked.

"Being a priest isn't something anyone really chooses to do," Robert answered. Tony noticed that the priest started to use hand gestures while talking and shot him a dirty look. Both hands gripped the yoke again. "It's something most of us can't escape."

"Like the draft?"

"Not at all," the priest replied.

"Then what is it?" Robert struggled to make his point, and Tony wasn't about to make it any easier for him. Let him squirm, he thought, folding his arms and leaning back in his seat.

"Some of us are born for certain things," Roberto said, speaking in a halting voice. "They come easy. They feel natural. Even when they're not easy, they are what we want."

Tony understood what he meant in a heartbeat, but he wasn't about to let on. He could tell Robert wasn't sure he had made his point, and Tony raised both eyebrows as if he didn't understand.

"When did you decide you wanted to be a pilot?" Roberto asked.

"I don't remember," Tony answered right away. Robert was heading for memory lane again, and Tony wasn't about to give him any details. "I always wanted to."

"See? Some of us are called to certain professions. In my work, I want to teach people to know God. You want to teach them to fly."

"You're wrong there, padre," Tony said, shaking his head and tapping the altimeter, which showed they were losing altitude. Robert made a graceless correction.

"You don't want to be an instructor?" Roberto asked.

"Hell, no," Tony answered, not mentioning who had confirmed his decision. "I'm a cropduster."

Their plane cleared the mountains and dropped back into the valley south of Salinas. Robert was so engrossed in their conversation that he forgot to watch the instruments. They were headed west, not north. Tony decided not to mention it, just to see if his student would notice that they were off course.

"Cropduster?" Roberto repeated. "That's a dangerous profession. Are you crazy?"

"You see angels and I'm crazy," Tony said. "I like that."

"Have you done it before?" Roberto asked, looking at Tony from the corner of his eye. Maybe the priest didn't believe him. "That cropdusting kind of flying?"

"I've been doing it for the past eight years. This pussy job is just a filler." Tony longed to be back at it, and just about anywhere other than in that Cessna with Robert. However, when it came to talking about 'dusting, he was a hopeless case. "Watch your heading." Roberto made another violent correction.

"Does it scare you to fly so low?"

"All the time," Tony answered, surprising himself with the truth. "Anyone who says otherwise is crazy or doomed. Probably both."

"What is it like to go under a telephone wire?" Robert asked, lost in their conversation. Tony knew the plane would miss the approach for the Salinas airport if his student didn't start paying attention.

"It's hard to explain," Tony answered, looking over his shoulder. "You really need to consider making a turn."

"Is it like sex with a beautif—" Robert started.

"Better." Tony cut him off. "I'm sorry I brought it up. Now, what's your heading?"

"If I don't ask you about cropdusting, how will I ever know what it's like?"

"You won't," Tony said, and his frank answer brought a scowl to Robert's face. "You really need to—"

"But I want to know what it's like."

"No, you don't," Tony said. He was shaking his head and fighting to hide the smile at the corners of his mouth. It would be so sweet to really show Robert what it was all about.

"Yes, I do." Roberto's face said he meant it. His prodding was more than Tony could resist.

"Gimme the controls," Tony said, taking over and starting a sharp descent. Hell, they were off course anyway. The engine's snarl swelled when Tony added power.

"What are you doing?" Roberto asked, eyes wide.

"Hang on to your socks, Father." Tony almost coughed when he called Robert that. Father was too weird. He'd never do that again. "You're gonna feel it now."

Tony put them into a falling swoop that was both sickening and exhilarating, like dropping 30 floors in three seconds. At the last moment, he brought her level and approached a lettuce field with the ground flashing by just beneath the wheels. He hopped a fence. A telephone wire bisected the view from the windshield. The wire shaved over the canopy, and Roberto ducked. Tony laughed and dropped the tail even lower. He hoped he wouldn't return to Salinas with leaves in the landing gear. It would be a dead giveaway.

Flying a field was definitely against policy, but Tony couldn't stop himself. The crops passed below them, and Tony thought, 'Have a thrill on me.' Poor jerk. He would never have sex. Tony just hoped he didn't have a heart attack.

Huge eucalyptus trees with droopy leaves lay dead ahead at the end of the field. Roberto tried to speak. Tony applied power and scaled the tree line. The force sucked both men deep into their seats. Just then, a large hawk surprised Tony by deserting its nest in a tree-top. Feathers flew from its wide and frantic, flapping wings. Tony banked right, and the bird fell off to the left. The quick maneuver left them pulling G's that made Tony's stomach feel as if he had driven over a hilltop at a high rate of speed. He hoped Robert wouldn't toss his donut and coffee.

The near miss left Tony's heart in his throat. Hitting the hawk could have brought them down, but he wasn't about to admit that to Robert. Besides, those "almosts" tended to happen on a somewhat regular basis when cropdusting. Being able to fly while scared half to death was just part of the job. Tony made a lazy turn and brought the plane around again. Heads of lettuce lined up in straight rows before them like parallel strands of leafy green pearls.

"Ready?" Tony asked.

"Ready," said a squeaky voice to his left.

Tony thought the priest sounded game, but he didn't have time to check the expression on his face. The plane was already descending into the field, making the next pass. He pulled up again at the edge of the field, splitting the air between a fence and a phone wire.

"Enough," Roberto gasped. Tony broke away, gaining altitude.

He turned to the priest and noticed that he looked a little green around the gills. Tony didn't press it. It was best not to talk if airsickness was coming on, and he didn't need a mess in the cockpit. Tony was scheming about how to keep his pupil from revealing what he'd just done during the ten minutes it took for a normal color to return to the priest's face.

"I'll fly," Roberto said, taking the yoke again.

"Look, sorry—" Tony started, putting both hands in the air to indicate that Robert had control.

"So that's what it's like?" Robert asked. His head began to nod, and a small smile crept across his lips.

"That's it," Tony said, nodding in return. Could he con his way out of trouble? "So, it's probably better if you don't mention—"

"Is that what it's like to make love to a beautiful woman too?" the priest asked. Tony laughed out loud.

"It's as close as you'll ever come," he said, raising one eyebrow and giving Robert a surly look.

"Is it as close as *you'll* ever come?"

Tony clenched his fists and worked the muscles in his jaw. That asshole didn't know shit about his sex life, yet his comment had hit home. It was true that Tony tended to stay away from the beautiful ones. They expected more than he could give. At least he thought they did. Something beyond sex and a good time. Something like love. And how the hell would he know anything about that? And, it wasn't like it was any of Robert's business anyway. Tony wanted to belt him, but he would wait until they were on the ground. The priest kept his eyes on the instrument panel. Tony's humor didn't improve when Roberto blew his first approach to the airport.

"Bad approach, bad landing," Tony said, then snarled under his breath. "Bring her around again."

On the second attempt, the priest recited the Lord's Prayer at least ten times. Tony wouldn't admit that his approach was perfect that time. He wanted Robert to rely on skill, not bum luck or miracles or whatever the fuck the priest wanted to call it.

"I'll bet you decided to be a priest before you ever saw a naked woman," Tony said when they were two feet from the ground.

His comment distracted the priest just enough to make the bottom fall out of his landing. Roberto started to pull back on the power.

"No-o-o, damn it," Tony said, pushing the throttle forward. "Never pull power on a bad landing. You'll stick this baby like a dart in the middle of the runway."

They bounced past the first and second exit, and used the whole runway before she was stable enough to make the turn-off.

"You think anyone saw that?" the priest asked. Tony looked past him, noticing that every window of the airport restaurant faced the runway.

"Everyone sees a bad landing," Tony said, focusing on the flight school. The boss's Venetian blinds dropped so fast, he could almost hear them slap the windowsill.

Harmony Lane

TONY DROVE BILL over to the Harmony Lane Massage Studio and parked across the alley by the Chop Chop China House restaurant. They arrived just as the Friday evening shift was ending. Tony winked at Della, who was writing a receipt for the last customer. She shooed him and Bill down the hall. They went to the back lounge where Della's coworker, Cindy, was waiting. The three of them drank red wine from white Styrofoam cups.

"What a case," Della said to them from the lobby. She turned off the blinking neon hands in the window, locked the front door, and wandered toward them. Her long skirt skimmed the red shag rug that lined the white, cinder block hallway. Tony liked her "uniform," which matched Cindy's. They both wore tight, white body suits and long, black wraparound skirts. He liked to think of it as easy access. Della approached them, passing four identical rooms, each with a massage table in the center. Tony poured her some wine but didn't hand it to her when she sauntered into the back lobby. She shot a glance behind her. "Geez. A 300-pound man with a big black car and a three-inch dick." Della flopped into the red director's chair next to Tony.

"What did he want?" Tony asked, holding the cup of wine just out of her reach.

"Everything, sugar," Della answered, squeezing his thigh. "And he wanted me to sing Rock-a-Bye Baby while I gave it to him."

"What did you tell him?" Bill asked in amazement. He folded his arms and took a quick look at the front door.

"I told him I couldn't sing."

"What did you give him?" Tony asked, feeling uncomfortable and curious at the same time. She snagged her drink from his hand.

"As little as possible," Della answered, lifting her cup. "After all, sugar, a girl's got to make a living."

"Doing what?" he asked. Her "clients" hadn't bothered him in the past, but seeing the guy made it more real. Della didn't answer him, and Tony turned to Cindy. "What does she do in there?"

Cindy shrugged and looked away, glancing at Tony's friend standing next to her. Bill shoved his free hand in his pocket.

"How about a cup of coffee?" Bill asked Cindy.

"I suppose," she answered, sounding embarrassed. She turned to Della. "Can you wait? I need a ride home."

"Take your time," Della answered, sending a sly look in Tony's direction. "I can't take him home with me, and I hate that sleazy hotel he's staying in."

"It doesn't matter where we do it as long as we do it," Tony said, grinning. It struck him funny that he could make Cindy blush and look away with so little effort.

"You're worse than my old man," Della said, giving him a shove.

"You said I was better."

"We shouldn't be gone long," Bill said.

"We'll be here," Tony said with a wink, and Della climbed into his lap.

BILL AND CINDY CROSSED Harmony Lane and headed for the back entrance of the Chinese restaurant. Faded red paper lanterns hung above every table. They slid into a booth near the back door. The worn red seats were the sort that sat too low. Bill like the way Cindy flipped her long sandy hair away from her friendly face. They waited for coffee and he watched her calm blue eyes study the soy sauce container between them.

"Are you and Tony good friends?" she asked.

"I've only known him a few weeks," Bill answered, trying not to stare at her tight shirt. Tony hadn't lied about one thing. Well, two. "He's a little depraved but—"

"A little?" she said with a hearty laugh. She studied his face to see if he was kidding. Her eyes now staring into his made his heart jump.

"OK, maybe a lot," Bill added, sitting back to allow the waitress to pour his coffee. It was true. Tony was downright immoral, but he had a trait Bill found almost magnetic. He seemed to grab a hold of every moment and find something fun in it, even when it didn't seem possible. The waitress left and Cindy leaned forward to talk to Bill.

"Della's married, you know," Cindy said in a soft voice. He could tell she didn't want to be overheard. He liked how she passed on that information in a secretive way.

"Yeah, I know," Bill answered, smiling. "Kind of strange, huh?"

"Yeah, but everything about that place is strange," she said with a glance in the direction of the massage studio. "It's sad really. So many people, well, men, come in just to be touched. Maybe they're old or lonely or just unattractive. They pay just to feel your hands on their back."

"Is that all you do?" Bill asked, looking into his coffee and avoiding her eyes.

"That's all *I* do," Cindy said, sounding a little offended. He hoped he hadn't said the wrong thing. She seemed like someone he would like to get to know a little better. "I can't say what others do. I wouldn't be doing that much if I could sell my paintings."

"You're an artist?" Bill asked, his head popping up. "Tony never mentioned that. Are you from Salinas?"

Cindy's cheerful answer dwelt mostly on family, music, and friends she knew from school. Bill liked her easy smile. He felt more comfortable looking into her blue eyes and not just at her tight body suit.

"Tony said you're a pilot."

"Yeah," he answered. He tried to sound humble, but he felt proud. "I want to cropdust someday, but it's hard to break in. Maybe I could take you up sometime."

"How neat!" she said, and he laughed. "What's so funny?"

"Oh nothing," he answered, shaking his head. She wasn't what he expected at all. Wholesome, Tony had called her. "I can't believe you're Della's friend."

"That's OK," she said, seeming to understand. "I can't believe you're Tony's."

Bill was relieved that they could converse with such ease. No long awkward silences. They finished their coffees, and he held the door for her with a funny grin on his face. She smiled, and he blushed. She'd caught him staring at her tits.

Bill and Cindy entered the massage studio in time to see Tony and Della slip naked into the steam room in the back. Their angry conversation traveled through the building.

"You're making it with everything in pants, and I'm supposed to ignore it!" Tony's accusation traveled up the hall. Bill looked at Cindy and winced. Tony's rant continued. "I'm not some wimp like your old man."

"You sure sound like him," Della answered, sounding peeved.

"Look, baby, whatever you want to do is your business," Tony continued, his voice softening in an artificial way. "Just tell me about it."

"Why? Della asked, teasing him. "Does it turn you on?"

The sounds of their fighting ended at that second. Bill and Cindy were left standing in the entry, avoiding each other's eyes in the awkward silence that followed. Cindy walked over to use the phone. Della started moaning. Bill preferred the silence.

"Della's supposed to give me a ride home," Cindy said, too embarrassed to meet Bill's eyes. "I have to call my folks."

"Sorry," Bill said, leaning against one wall and trying to look nonchalant. Fact was, he had never stood around and listened to someone else getting it on. He should have never come with Tony, however, he did like Cindy. It wasn't her fault that Tony and Della were so crude. "I'd give you a lift, but I rode with Tony."

Bill moved, bumped a picture of a naked lady painted on black velvet, and then stepped away. The phone book sat on one corner of the reception desk. He opened it and pretended to read it, hoping he looked interested. Cindy mumbled into the receiver, and then hung up. The door of the sauna opened in the back, and Tony chased Della into one of the massage rooms.

"They'll probably be busy for a while," Cindy said, straightening her skirt.

"Probably," Bill said, turning to the yellow pages. If he had brought his own car, he could have driven her home. He would have liked that. It would be easier than the approach that he and Tony had discussed.

"Since we have to wait, would you mind if I . . . practice on you?" she asked with a red face.

"Practice?"

"You know, massage."

"I guess not," he said, and the phone book fell from his hands. He felt like such a jerk.

"If it bothers you—" she started.

"No, no, it doesn't bother me," Bill said, scooping the directory off the red shag rug. He tried to place it back on the desk, fighting with its numerous pages. "What do I have to do?"

"Nothing, really," she said, watching him with a smile. "Just go into a room, take off your clothes, and lay face down on the table. Is that OK?"

"Fine," he answered, shoving both hands into his pants' pockets and then pulling one out again. "This room?" he asked, pointing to the first door.

"Any of them, really. Well, except, you know, the one where they are."

"Yeah, right, of course," he said, laughing more than he should have.

TONY DROVE BILL HOME after midnight with the top down on his drafty old convertible. "Maggie May" came scratching through the speakers just when he turned on Bill's street. Tony pulled into Bill's apartment complex and turned down the volume.

"Hey," Bill objected.

"So, was she good?" Tony asked, putting it into park. He liked "Maggie May" too, but he wanted to know if Bill scored.

"Cram it," Bill said, reaching for the radio. "I don't ask you that shit about Della, do I?" He switched the song on again.

"You like her," Tony said, laughing and turning down the volume. He probably should have disguised the cynical tone in his voice.

"What's it to you?" Bill asked. Tony shrugged. "You don't know how I feel."

"Sure I do, Billy boy," Tony answered, feeling confident. He dropped his hand from the ignition and rested his elbow on the open window of the driver's door. "If you didn't like her, you'd be like me. I'll tell you anything you want to know about Della. Hell, I'll lend her to you. I don't care that much about her. I like to fuck, and she's easy."

"Gee, I didn't realize it went that deep," Bill said with a laugh, half turning toward Tony from the passenger seat.

"It isn't deep," Tony answered. "Deep" wasn't his strong suit. Never had been. "But when you score and won't talk about it, watch out. We're talking the L-word, and I don't mean lust."

"For Christ's sake, Tony, I've only known her for four hours."

"When's the wedding?" Tony asked with a quick lift of his chin. Teasing Bill was like picking on the little brother he never had.

"You're nuts," Bill said, getting out of the car. He shut the door and changed the subject. "You working tomorrow?"

"Yeah, I got the priest again."

"Happy landings."

"Don't remind me," Tony said, raising his hand to the ignition key, then letting it drop. "Funny thing. He isn't half bad for a priest. He's a regular guy . . . almost."

"I guess they are just people too," Bill said, staring at something in the back seat. "What's that?"

"What?" Tony asked, following Bill's gaze. "This?" He reached back and pulled a piece of wood from the rear floorboard. He had bought it back in Texas, hoping to have done something with it before now. "Someday, it will be a rifle stock."

"Let me see it." Bill held the hunk of wood with the dramatic, striped grain toward the carport lights. "What's it for? A zebra safari?"

"I don't know," Tony answered, taking back the wood and dropping it behind the passenger seat. "It won't matter if I don't get a job spraying. You know how much it costs to mount a barrel on one of those suckers?"

"Couple hundred, I guess."

"At least," Tony said, glancing into the back seat. "It's such a beaut."

"You think so?" Bill answered, looking down and adjusting his glasses. Tony could tell by the look on Bill's face that he didn't agree. "Well, hang in there. I still think the old man's gonna axe Bart."

47

"I'm ready," Tony said, throwing his car into reverse and squealing the tires. He used his rearview mirror to watch Bill walk to his apartment. Bill wouldn't get Bart's job. He lacked the flight time. Tony just hoped he could land it for himself. It was only fair. After all, he had set Bill up with a nice girl with great tits.

Lesson Four

BILL PHONED TONY to tell him that AirRaid Ag's owner Sam O'Malley had taken Bart out for coffee at 6:00 a.m. and had come back alone. He also told Tony that by 6:30, Sam had turned Bill down for the job.

"Sam, that asshole," Bill said. Even over the phone, Tony could tell he was still hot about it. "You know what he said? 'Pilots are all over, but good swampers are hard to find.' Damn!"

The call ended with Bill vowing to call an ag flight school in Arkansas and buy some time. His friend hung up and Tony slammed down the receiver.

"Hot damn," he said, slapping the side of the pay phone at the Flea Bag Hilton.

The brew back in his room, opened in preparation for the priest's lesson, was now downed to celebrate Bill's call. With Bart's seat available, Tony could loosen his purse strings. After a couple cigarettes and a shower later, he prepared to check out.

"I'll get an apartment," he said while stuffing his suitcase. "Better yet, a house. My own den of iniquity."

He took the stairs two at a time. Roberto's lesson that day would be a bummer. Tony toyed with the idea of quitting the flight school, but he didn't have Bart's job yet.

"I'll be mad as hell if that dago busts my butt today," he said, slamming his key on the reception desk and waking the night clerk.

Tony indulged in a greasy breakfast at the Skyport Bar and Grill, then waited beside the plane. The priest crossed the tie-down area, approaching Tony minus the usual spring in his step. He acknowledged Tony with only a nod. Robert's uncharacteristic silence continued through the preflight and shaky take-off. They flew in silence for the first five minutes, following the Salinas River to Castroville where it met the sea. At first, Tony had appreciated the quiet, but it soon started to get on his nerves. Something was up.

"Bring her around and shoot some touch and goes," Tony said, feeling brave or crazy for suggesting it.

"What for?"

"What do you mean, 'what for?'" Tony answered, twisting in his seat to get a better look at Robert's face. "To practice landing and taking off, that's what for."

"The up and down part doesn't interest me," Robert answered, sounding distracted. "I just like making holes in the sky."

"Look, I don't want to seem like a hard ass here, but if you don't learn to take off and land, you might as well quit."

"You're right," the priest answered, staying his course.

"The airport is over there," Tony said, pointing back over his shoulder.

"I know, I know," Roberto answered, heading out to sea. "I just like flying over the water."

"You don't care if I lose my job?" Tony asked, not really caring himself. The priest seemed to always make things more difficult than necessary.

"Lose your job?" Roberto asked.

"These aren't sight-seeing tours," Tony said, raising his voice. "If a student can't make a decent landing by the fourth lesson—"

"Tell them it's my fault."

"This isn't church," Tony said, slapping the padded instrument panel in frustration. "I can't tell my boss 'He didn't want to land today so we just dicked around.'"

"It's my last lesson anyway," Roberto answered, still looking at the horizon. "I'm being assigned to a new parish."

"What for?" Tony felt insulted when he knew he should have felt relieved by Robert's news. Maybe it was something about the way he had instructed the priest. Maybe the new parish thing was bullshit.

"God's will," Roberto answered with a sad smile.

"Right," Tony said, pressing his moustache flat with his hand. "Like He called you this morning? And try to keep it straight and level, would ya?"

"Almost," Roberto answered, looking into Tony's eyes at last. "The bishop called."

"You don't sound too thrilled," Tony said, trying to read Robert's face. "Did you tell him that you didn't want to go?"

"*You* are obviously not Catholic, Tony," Robert said with a sad chuckle. "No one tells a bishop— What I mean is, I prayed over the decision and I believe it is a good one. We don't always know the mind of God."

"Why not?" Tony asked in an indignant tone. His guess was if a priest didn't know the mind of God, no one did. Maybe there was nothing to know.

"What?" Roberto said, showing his first real smile.

"Look, you work for Him," Tony said, giving two quick nods upwards. "Did you ask Him why you have to go to, um, wherever?"

"King City," Roberto answered, filling in the blank.

"Oh, sweet," Tony said, looking back over his shoulder, south, in the little town's direction. "The armpit of the valley. Did you ask Him why?" Tony continued, turning back to face Robert.

"Yes."

"What did He tell you?"

"Nothing." Roberto's answer didn't satisfy Tony.

"This is the same guy who won't allow sex, right?" Tony asked, staring across the cockpit at Robert.

"No, that's the Pope," Robert added, shaking his head. Tony didn't like his amused look.

"I'd work somewhere else," Tony said, turning to look out the window. "Hey, don't take us out to sea. Even you can't land on water."

"Are you sure?" Roberto asked.

"Follow the coast, wise guy."

Father Roberto flared out the plane with a smoothness that surprised Tony. They flew along the beach, and Tony looked to his right, where white sand dunes encircled some two-story condos. Each building had two long windows that stared like blind eyes out to sea. A solitary man walked a black dog at the edge of the unending water.

"Sex is OK with Him?" Tony asked, twitching his moustache. He might as well ask how God felt about sex as long as Robert was leaving.

"Of course," the priest said, his green eyes twinkling. "He made us in His image. He knows what a man's body is capable of. That's why He created the sacrament of marriage."

"Yeah, but He's not married," Tony said, feeling smug. Memories of his first wife made him glad he and God were in the same camp on this.

"He's married to us all in Christ."

"That's not marriage," Tony answered, not satisfied. "Who takes out the garbage? Who goes to bed with Him?"

"You're thinking of an earthly marriage," Robert said, giving Tony the all-knowing look that he hated. "God's marriage is spiritual. Besides in heaven, there is no garbage."

"Are there beds?" Tony asked without bothering to suppress his smile.

"For what?"

"Only you would ask," Tony said, rolling his eyes. He sat up in his seat and watched the waves below them breaking on the beach.

"But you have no body—"

"You mean, no sex?" Tony said, exaggerating the disappointment in his voice. Actually, for some reason, he had suspected that all along.

"I don't know," the priest answered.

"You know what I think?" Tony asked, leaning back in his seat. For a moment, he paused. Had he ever given spiritual life a thought before he met Robert? Not much. He turned and looked across the cabin at Robert's right ear. "I think maybe heaven isn't all it's cracked up to be."

"Is sex so great?" the priest asked. Tony groaned in response, but Roberto pressed on. "You took me flying fast and low. Better than making love to a beautiful woman, you said. Coming together spiritually is infinitely more fulfilling than sex."

"How would you know?" Tony asked, staring out the window and feeling bored. Robert's voice piped into his ears via the headset wasn't making much sense. "What are you talking about?"

"I've done it."

"You've had sex?" Tony asked. That comment jerked the slack out of Tony, and he sat up and looked at Robert.

52

"No, no. I've joined with someone spiritually—and it's better than flying fast and low."

"How did you do this joining?" Tony straightened up. To him, this seemed weirder than the angel stuff.

Father Roberto hesitated. For once, instead of harassing him, Tony felt sorry for him. How could some foreign chump explain religion to him, a guy whose only frame of reference was great sex and great flying? It wouldn't be easy. It might be impossible. It certainly wasn't prudent. Tony glanced down at the breakers pounding the rock cliffs below them. Foamy fans of salt spray shot skyward. The drumming engine and rushing wind created a comfortable solitude in the plane.

"God does the joining," Roberto said, his words sounding measured in Tony's headset. "Not me."

"Who do you 'join' with?" Tony asked. "Angels?"

"No, no," Robert answered, sounding hesitant. "Just people."

"Women?" Tony continued. Robert had his attention now.

"Sometimes."

"Are they women you know?" Tony was trying to pull the details out of Robert like it was a game of charades. Next thing, he would be asking how many syllables or what joining sounded like.

"It's not what you're thinking."

"Are they women you know or are they imaginary?" Tony persisted.

"They are women I know," Roberto said, and nodded, watching the sea.

"What does it feel like?"

"It doesn't feel like anything," Robert said, shaking his head. "It's not a physical act."

"Is it enjoyable?" Tony scrutinized his student's face. The priest smiled. "It is," Tony said, laughing and slapping his hands together. "You sly dog. When does it happen?"

"Never when you expect it," Roberto said. He took a deep breath and looked away. Tony was losing him.

"Morning, noon, or night?" No answer from Robert. "Morning, noon, or night?"

"Mostly nighttime. But I think you have the wrong impression."

"You're probably right," Tony said. He hid his smile and let his fingertips trace the outline of the yoke on his side of the plane. If Robert knew how interested he was, he probably would cut him off completely. Still, Tony couldn't keep one black eyebrow from rising at the thought. "I always suspected there were hidden benefits to a job like yours. I mean, the pay stinks and the nuns are nothing to write home about."

"Some things are more important than money and good looks."

"You're right. Flying, sex, and more money," Tony answered, stretching his arms out toward the front windscreen and focusing on the controls. "Hey, do you want to learn something different today?"

"How different?"

"A loop."

"What is this loop?" Roberto asked, turning toward Tony with a curious look.

"It's an aerobatic maneuver. I usually reserve it for the later lessons, but seeing how—it's like a back flip in an airplane."

"Is it hard?" Robert asked, sounding intrigued. That was all Tony needed.

"Piece of cake," Tony said, rubbing his hands together. "Watch this."

Tony took the controls and started a steep descent. Streaking downward, he pulled back on the stick and raised the nose. He pushed the throttle forward before he broke the horizon. They headed straight up and the engine noise increased. Tony leaned his head back to watch for the horizon coming up behind them, and the priest let out a war whoop. Upside down, Tony felt himself floating and noticed that Roberto was grabbing onto his own seat, which made Tony laugh. For one long moment, the sea seemed to be above the sky. Tony pushed her over the top and eased back on the power. They resumed level flight, the engine noise grew quieter, and the priest's stunned look turned into a silly grin.

"You could teach me that?" Roberto asked.

"After a few more lessons," Tony offered with a smile. Was he out of his mind? He had just suggested more lessons for possibly the worst pilot in the world. With any luck, he wouldn't be around to teach them.

"I don't have a few more lessons," Robert sighed. "What else could we do?"

"I don't know," Tony said with a shrug and a devilish grin. "Maybe a roll."

"Do one."

"You sure?" Tony asked.

"Of course, of course," Robert said, showing his game side. "It's my last chance. Show me anything."

Father Robert's words were too tempting, and Tony soared off without looking back. He rolled the plane, wingtip over wingtip twice. Roberto was still smiling. Tony pointed the plane straight down, heading straight at the beach and spinning the plane. The sand and the sea traded places faster than the priest could bear to watch. The color faded from Roberto's face, and Tony pulled out of the maneuver.

"Time to head back?" Tony asked, skimming the waves.

Roberto nodded, and Tony kept her straight and level. He adjusted the microphone attached to his headset and radioed the tower, thinking it would have been better if he had stopped after the roll. To his surprise, the plucky priest straightened himself in his seat.

"What happened to the gyro?" Roberto asked. The floating compass on the dashboard resembled a dead goldfish.

"Nothing," Tony said, hoping it would suffice. "Tell me, was the spin better than joining?"

"No, but it's better than flying fast and low, which is better than making love—"

"Take her," Tony said, releasing the yoke and lacing his fingers behind his head. Robert grabbed the controls with both hands just before the airport came into sight.

"I can't do it," Roberto said, trying to line up on the runway.

"It's the last time you'll get to try," Tony said, knowing he still had time if it all went south on them.

Roberto's focus remained on the airport, and he started to pray.

"Hail Mary, full of grace, the Lord is with—"

"Don't do that," Tony said.

"Prayer moves the hand of God," Roberto said, staring at his target straight ahead and talking faster. "Blessed art though among women and blessed is the fruit . . . "

The priest's near perfect approach and flawless descent amazed Tony. He was pretty sure Robert's method of landing only worked for priests. God's little compensation for no sex, like the spiritual joining Robert tried to describe. Tony's next thought popped out at the wrong moment.

"Have you ever joined with a man?" Tony asked, and the priest pulled back on the power right before they touched the ground.

"Mama Mia," Roberto said. A bounce launched them back into the air.

"I'll fly," Tony said, grabbing the yoke. "You pray." It may have been his skill. It might have been Robert's mumbling. Somehow, Tony managed to bring her down before he ran out of runway.

Job Interview

TONY STEPPED OUT of his car at sunset, and the wind at the airport styled his black curls. It was Friday, and he had cashed his final paycheck from the flight school. The roll of bills bulged in the front pocket of his tight jeans, pressing against his thigh like a wad of confidence. He swaggered toward the terminal building with his logbook jammed in one pocket of his denim jacket with the fake sheepskin collar. His reflection in the glass door reminded him to remove his sunglasses.

"It's show time," he said in a sly whisper. He entered and headed into the dark bar, taking the first seat by the door. His penetrating eyes adjusted to the dim lighting, and the establishment's fixtures and occupants came into focus. A craggy voice sounded from across the room.

"This beautiful blonde comes in one night and sits right there," Hartley Bolger said and pointed to Tony's bar stool.

Most Friday nights, Hartley flew the next to last bar stool at the far end of the SkyBaG's counter. He was fat and feisty, five-foot-five, and his face reminded Tony of one those dried apple dolls. Bill had said Hartley was a fighter pilot in WWII. Now, he was head mechanic at AirRaid Ag. Bill stood by Hart, buying him one for the road. The regular crowd seemed to only be half-listening to his familiar story.

Tony looked from the storyteller to a nearby table. Sam, the old boy's boss, was gabbing with Patches. He looked fairly happy for having just fired a pilot. Was he in the mood to hire another? Tony hoped so, feeling for his logbook even though he knew he had it.

"She had chi-chis like grapefruits and a neckline split to her navel," Hart continued after a sip. "A doctor was buying her drinks while a lawyer lit her damn cigarettes. So I bets Sam she'd walk away with me, didn't I, Sam?"

"Bet one gin, no ice," Sam said, without looking up. He looked more interested in stirring his drink.

"Did she?" Bill asked, knowing the answer.

"I hope to shit in your flat hat on Sunday morning," Hart answered.

"O-o-o-o. . ." Tony said, leaving his stool with a fresh screwdriver and approaching Bill and Hart. He could feel a tall one coming on. He'd heard enough to know.

"I looked at them two city boys and said, 'But, can you fly an airplane?'" Hart's gravelly chuckle led to a cough that required a long sip from his drink. "Then the blonde says, 'Can you really fly?'"

"Like hell she does," Tony said, moving closer to the storyteller.

"Like hell she doesn't," Hart said, sounding like he enjoyed a little disbelief in the crowd. "I offers her a ride and she can't get off that bar stool fast enough."

"Oh, sure," Tony said, half turning away.

"We walks out to the flight line," Hart said, "and I stuffs that tart between my legs in a one-holer Stearman. Each of those high-class palookas steps up on a separate wing and grabs a strut, like they's daring me to take off. At the end of the taxiway, I gives 'em one last chance to let go."

"But they don't," Bill said with a smile. Tony thought it sounded like a line Bill had said before.

"That's right," Hart said. The wheezy laugh that followed prompted an even worse cough. "I don't know how she ever broke ground with those two fools on the wings, but—"

"Like hell she did," Tony said again.

"Like hell she didn't," Hart answered. "Sam saw the whole thing, didn't you Sam?"

"Yep," he answered, disinterested but on cue. Tony tried to read the expression on Sam's face, but he was more discreet than a veteran poker player.

"How did you do it?" Bill asked Hart. Tony could tell Bill loved this story. He liked that about Bill. "Did you have a head wind? Did you go full power?"

"You know, son, I don't really know," Hart answered, shaking his head. His jowls wiggled in response. "I might've had a few that night. No one counted back in those days," he said, jingling the ice cubes in his waning drink. "Stearmans are just that kind of plane. You ask 'em to perform and they do. Every pilot has his dream plane—"

"Mine's a Buchmeister Jungman," Bill said, smiling at the thought.

"Mine's a Waco," Sam added from his table, proving he was aware.

"A Great Lakes," Tony said, imagining the agile biplane known for its twitching tail.

"And mine's that homely old Stearman," Hart said, thumping his chest. "But thanks to this old ticker of mine, I'll never fly one again."

The room grew still. Tony knew Hart had busted his medical years ago, but the old boy seldom mentioned it. Something like that, if it happened, would be too painful for Tony to talk about too.

"I'll rent a plane tomorrow and we'll go up," Bill said, lifting his drink to seal his promise.

Tony looked at Bill, knowing his young friend couldn't afford flying time for himself. Giving it to some old geezer with a sorry heart was crazy, Tony thought, but right on. The rest of the patrons sensed it, and the chatter resumed.

"I just might take you up on that," Hart said with a melancholy smile.

Tony wandered past the retired ace and put his drink down beside Bill's on the bar. His wary eyes stayed on Sam, and his cigarette dangled below his full moustache. He picked up two dice cups and handed one to Bill.

"High man buys," Tony said, already shaking the dice.

"Just one round," Bill said, ever careful of his pennies. It was a trait Tony admired but didn't possess.

"One round," Tony answered and winked.

Bill shook a full house, fives over twos. Tony slapped his cup upside-down on the counter and lifted it half an inch for a peek.

"Son of a bitch," he said and scooped the unseen dice back into the cup.

"What was it?" Bill asked, trying to peer around Tony's hand.

"Two fours," Tony lied and dropped some bills on the counter. Bill didn't need to know the truth. Flight time for Hart wouldn't come cheap. "Hope that doesn't indicate my luck tonight." Tony pushed the cup away and spoke to Bill in a whisper. "Bart's out for good, right?"

"Yeah," Bill answered under his breath.

"What are my chances?" Tony asked, keeping his voice low and nodding at Sam.

"Fair," Bill said, adjusting his glasses and giving a quick look at the boss's table. "He's nicer after he's had a few, like now. He gets mean after ten or so."

"I'm going in," Tony said, grabbing his drink and starting toward Sam's table. He looked back at Bill and said, "Cover my ass."

Bill nodded and gave him the thumbs up.

"Can I buy you a drink?" Tony asked, approaching Sam. His heart was in his throat, like it was when the hawk flew out of the trees at the end of the spray run he flew with Robert. Like then, Tony knew he could mask his nerves. He counted five swizzle sticks on the table and a sixth in the glass in front of the big man.

"Depends," Sam answered in a deep voice. He smashed out his cigarette with a burly hand and raised his thinning head of hair. His lined face, down-turned mouth, and big features spoke more than his words. He scrutinized Tony with one eye narrowed to a slit. "Why would you want to buy me a drink?"

"I'm feeling generous," Tony said. He slipped one hand in his front pocket to feel his money. It helped him relax. "You want one or not?"

"I got one, but I'll take another if you twist my arm," Sam answered, nudging Patches and giving a dirty laugh to his partner, who had his own pile of sticks. "Have a seat."

Sam probably hadn't bought a drink all night. Tony knew that any operator of a cropdusting business who needed a pilot was in the catbird's seat in an airport bar. Bill had told Tony earlier that Sam had talked to two potential pilots already. He also let Tony know that Sam had put out feelers to ask other operators some questions about

Tony. Bill had overheard Sam tell Patches what the rumors were. The operators had described Tony as a cocky cropduster-turned-flight instructor who could tie a knot in the tail of an airplane but couldn't keep his business in his pocket.

"I hear you have an opening," Tony said. He dropped a twenty on the waitress's tray with a wink and took the chair opposite Sam. "One for me and one for my friend here," he said to the waitress, then turned his focus back to Sam. The sweat on the back of his neck started creeping down his spine. "I have experience in your type of aircraft."

"How much?" Sam asked, sounding skeptical.

"Enough," Tony said. "I can fly rings around anyone in this room . . . except him." Tony nodded toward the bar where Hartley sat.

"I don't need rings," Sam grumbled. "I need someone who can do the old turn-and-squirt without thrashing my equipment."

"I can spot a bad mag within three minutes of take-off and drag the tail through the crop until the farmers come in their pants," Tony said. He felt anything but relaxed. Still, he leaned back in his chair to fake it. "And I can do it hungover."

"Not in my aircraft."

"In anyone's," Tony shot back. "I'll drink you under the table tonight, fly my ass off in the morning, and never cut a wire."

Sam put down his drink and eyed Tony. Tony gave him a no bullshit glare, then BAM, he slapped his logbook on the table.

"What do I want with that pack of lies?" Sam asked, poking the book with a swizzle stick.

"Just a formality," Tony said. Their drinks arrived, and Tony took a quick sip. "I've got the time, and I've got the experience."

"I've seen some shitty landings in that flight school plane," Sam said, eying his fresh one with a disgusted look.

"You've seen some great recoveries, too," Tony said. If that fucking priest blew this for him . . .

"You familiar with sulfur dust?" Sam asked, making Tony believe he might be interested.

"Very," Tony answered. He could ace this one.

"If you've got 450 pounds of dust for a 93-acre field, what setting do you use on the spreader?"

"I look at the sacks of dust, I look at the field, and I make it fit," Tony answered, forcing a smile. "I never run short or long, unless you ask for it."

"Why would I ask for it?" Sam said, his attempt at honesty a poor one.

"Robbing Peter to pay Paul," Tony answered. He'd been in that situation before. One farmer was short of chemical, and, what a coincidence, the next job ran long. How convenient. "Or just saving a little for the wife's flowers. I can talk to you all night about flying, but so can he," Tony said, glancing at Bill. "We both know you've got to see me fly. Reading this," he said, knocking on his logbook, "won't tell you anything."

"Tell you what," Sam answered, meting out his words with care and looking at his watch. "You load for me for a week—"

"Load?" Tony said, almost losing his latest swallow.

"If you fuck up as a swamper, I'm sure not going to put your ass in a seat."

Tony wanted to dust right away but he half-expected Sam's response. The area was lousy with telephone wires, and most of the fields were small and hilly. Some fields would be easy, but some farmers would be assholes. Some loaders could be trusted, some county inspectors couldn't.

"That's my offer," Sam said. He picked up the drink Tony bought him and saluted Tony. "Take it or leave it." Sam took a long drink, swallowed, and let out a refreshed sigh.

Tony picked up his drink and logbook, and walked away. That son of a bitch. He paused after two steps and looked back.

"I'll take it."

Federal Offense

TONY TOOK UP RESIDENCE on Bill's couch until the big money started rolling in. Every night demanded a party and every morning, a hangover. Della, Bill, and Cindy were sucked into the whirlwind of his lifestyle. Tony liked that better than being alone.

Work proved monotonous however. He and Bill worked together at AirRaid Ag, loading chemical, but Tony never flew. His frustration with Sam built, but Bill's friendship sustained him until one Friday evening at the airport bar. Bill entered the SkyBaG with Cindy and announced he was moving on.

"Give me one for the road," Bill said, waving a piece of paper and holding Cindy's hand. "I'm going to Arkansas."

Tony, Della, Patches and Hartley lined the bar, turning their heads toward Bill in unison. Only Sam stared straight ahead.

"What?" Tony said in disbelief. The thought of losing his new friend felt like a punch in the gut.

"I'm going to an ag flight school," Bill said, wrapping his arm around Cindy. She lifted a mascara-smudged tissue to her sad blue eyes.

"You practically grew up here," Patches said, shaking Bill's hand. "The 'port won't be the same without you." He tugged his goatee before lifting his glass in envy. "You're doing what I never did, and always wish I had."

"I remember your first drink," Hartley Bolger said with a smug grin. "I ordered it for you."

"One gin, no ice," Sam grumbled to the bartender, then continued under his breath. "Smart ass pup."

"And another for Billy and me," Tony said, sneering at the cheap bastard. Tony would celebrate Bill's decision, though he didn't feel like it, if it would annoy that asshole, Sam. The guy was losing a great loader in Bill, and Tony knew Sam would never admit it.

"Hey, I was planning to drive to Arkansas, not fly," Bill said, now with two drinks in front of him thanks to the bartender.

"How long does the ag school take?" Tony asked.

"Eight weeks, maybe longer," Bill answered, glancing at the letter. "It depends on the student."

"For you?" Hart said, showing his feelings for Bill. "Eight weeks tops."

"Eight weeks?" Sam said in a low voice. "How much time can you get in eight weeks?"

"More than I've had lately," Tony answered, shooting a hard glare in Sam's direction. Sam heaved a grumpy sigh, picked up his drink, and wandered off to a distant table. Tony leaned on the bar and watched him until he was out of earshot. He turned back to look at Bill. "I might have blown my chances, but, at this point, ask me if I give a shit."

"It won't matter," Bill answered. "When I told Sam I was leaving he said, 'Good riddance. I've got Tony for a loader now.'"

"That son of a bitch," Tony said, launching off the bar stool after Sam.

"Wait," Bill said in a low voice, grabbing Tony by the arm. "I know of a job for you . . . maybe."

"Where?" Tony asked, still leaning in Sam's direction. He'd deck him.

"Lopes Air Care," Bill said, talking faster. "Their strip is by the mouth of the river in Castroville. It's a father-son operation. The old man wants to retire, but he isn't sure the kid can handle it alone. Next week, he's going to Hawaii on vacation. They need someone to fill in, at least temporarily."

"Why aren't you going for it?" Tony asked, questioning Bill's motive. If Tony knew of an open seat, he wouldn't tell Bill about it, as much as he liked him.

"I tried already," Bill answered, sounding sheepish. "But they know me. Said I need more hours." His believable admission made sense to Tony.

"How long'll the old man be gone?" Tony asked, letting go of his anger for Sam for the moment.

"Two months—" Bill said.

"Oh—" Tony couldn't hide the disappointment in his voice. The expression on Bill's face told Tony that he had heard it. Still, the idea of dusting for two months, and then going back to work at the flight school was a sorry situation to be in. His gaze shifted back toward Sam.

"Hey, you fill in now," Bill explained, moving into Tony's line of sight. "If the old man still wants to hang it up when he comes back, you're in."

"You think so?" Tony's eyes left Sam and focused on Bill. Was he leading him on?

"Beats loading for the next two months, doesn't it?" Bill asked, looking Tony square in the eye.

"Sure as hell does," Tony answered with a nasty glance at Sam. He turned around, lifted his drink, and took a swallow. "It sure as hell does."

Tony, Della, Bill and Cindy kept drinking that evening at the SkyBaG and tried to have some fun despite Bill's news. An hour later, Sam and Hart rolled out the front door, and Della and Cindy went to the ladies room. Patches stopped by the table where Bill and Tony were nursing their drinks.

"When are you leaving?" Patches asked Bill.

"Sunday," Bill answered, patting the letter in his coat.

"Tell you what," Patches said, pulling a key from his pocket. "You can use my cabin for the weekend. You know where it is?"

"Arroyo Seco, just north of King City," Bill answered. "How far up the canyon is it?"

"All the way." Patches drew a map on a napkin to accompany his piss poor directions. "It's nothing fancy, but the scenery is great, and it's a dry place to sleep."

"Thanks, Patches," Bill said. "I'll miss you."

"We're gonna miss you 'round here," Patches answered, slapping Bill on the back before he walked out.

"Speaking of places to sleep, I better find somewhere to flop," Tony said after Patches left. Tony knew everyone thought of Bill as the kind of guy you could trust. No one would ever have handed Tony the keys to anything.

"There's two weeks left on my apartment," Bill said. "It's yours, if you need it."

"Great," Tony said, then lowered his voice. "Hey, don't tell the landlord, Billy boy."

"Why not?"

"Well, he—" Tony paused, looking in the direction of the ladies' room. "He caught me banging his wife in the laundry room. I don't think he—"

"You never told me that," Bill said, sitting back in his chair with a look of disbelief.

"I forgot," Tony said with a shrug. It hadn't seemed important.

"How could you forget something like that?" Bill asked.

"She wasn't that memorable, I guess." It wasn't her fault so much, Tony thought to himself. Laundry rooms just ain't that comfy.

Tony ordered another round. Bill saw Della and Cindy returning and changed the subject.

"My only regret is that I never got to fly Sam's Stearman," Bill said, when Cindy and Della sat down with them again. Cindy gave Bill a sad smile, and Della squeezed Tony's leg under the table.

"You ought to fire up that mother and take her around the pattern once before you go," Tony said with a gleam in his eye. There might be hope for this night after all.

"Are you crazy?" Bill asked. "That's a federal offense."

"Only if you're caught. Look, you work there—"

"I used to work there," Bill said.

"The boys in the tower don't know that," Tony said, pointing to them with a swizzle stick. He leaned forward and told Bill his plan. "They'll think you're running up the engine for Hartley. Only this time, you lift off and take her for a spin."

"You *are* crazy," Bill said, folding his arms. "In the first place, I need a key for the damn thing."

Tony twisted in his chair and dug into his pants pocket. He slapped a milled piece of nickel silver on the table in front of Bill. The key flickered in the glow of the candle in the red glass vase on the table.

"For the Stearman?" Bill asked, looking from the key to Tony.

"Doesn't fit my ragtop," Tony said, using the swizzle stick to edge the key closer to Bill.

"I don't know," Bill said, but Tony didn't hear any conviction in his voice.

"G'won, hon," Della said.

Bill adjusted his glasses and chewed on the fringe of his slight, blond moustache. He ignored Tony's questioning leer and turned to Cindy. She answered his look with a subtle grin and a nod. Bill pushed his Manhattan aside, took a quick look around the bar, and then scooped up the key.

"Hot damn," Tony said, plucking his half-full bottle of beer from the table and heading for the door with Della. "Time to count the stars, Billy boy."

Tony led the way across the parking lot with his usual swagger and the bottle of beer. The four of them rounded the far corner of the hangar to see the silent aircraft waiting with her nose pointing at the moon. Tony wanted to steal a plane ride himself. His thick moustache started to twitch at the thought of flying the biplane.

"Ever fly open cockpit?" Tony asked Bill, approaching the plane.

"Not yet," Bill answered. He stepped up on the wing and crawled into the aircraft.

"No sweat," Tony said with a laugh. "Just don't look back at us."

"Why not?" Bill asked and strapped himself in.

"You'll see," Tony said, and stepped toward the prop with a knowing grin.

BILL TRIED TO IGNORE Tony's warning, but that wasn't his nature, even if he was excited and drunk. It was foolish, but he found himself slipping the key into the ignition and trying the engine. She wouldn't turn over. This was his opportunity to turn back.

"Sit tight, Billy boy," Tony said, already in place at the front of the plane. "I'll prop her." He grabbed one blade with both hands and kicked out one leg for counter balance. With a practiced, rhythmical swing, he pulled down on the propeller, and the big round engine went from a sputter to a roar.

"Clear!" Tony and Bill yelled at the same time.

The vibration of the plane came through the seat, up Bill's spine and out to every nerve ending. Bill checked the rudder pedals and flipped the ailerons. Below him, the prop wash battered Tony's curls. Cindy's long blond strands flew about her face, but not a lock moved on Della's over-sprayed hair. Bill took a deep breath, pushed in the throttle, and the noise level fell off a decibel. She felt good, and the grin on his face wouldn't go away. He would have loved it even if he wasn't sticking it to Sam in the process.

"Should I do it?" Bill yelled down at Tony. It was lost in the rumble of the engine. Tony gave him a thumbs up, even though Bill was sure he hadn't heard his question.

Bill started to roll down the taxiway, still doubting if he could go through with Tony's plan. Bill had run up the engine for Hartley after repairs dozens of times and warmed up the engine at dawn for Bart. Sam always gave him hell if he rolled her fast enough to pick up the tail wheel. He couldn't imagine letting the landing gear leave the ground.

Let the boys in the tower throw a fit, Bill thought and then realized, he had been living Tony's life too long. The controller would know that the old duster lacked a radio. She spent most days at an outlying strip, coming into the airport only for maintenance. On those occasions, Bill had seen the tower signal landing instructions at the plane with a red or green light.

She picked up speed, and the once familiar plane felt foreign to Bill. A thousand warnings were firing in his head. They ranged from what would his dad say ("You did *what?*") to the words of his last instructor ("Keep your head."). He whirled her around at the end of the taxiway and pointed her into the wind. The landing lights stayed off, making him less visible, and Bill studied the starry sky for other aircraft. There were none. His face tightened in the prop wash and cold night air. The next voice in his head belonged to Hartley.

"There are old pilots, and there are bold pilots. But there are no old, bold pilots." He pushed the throttle and stick forward, vowing to himself that he would only go once around the patch.

Bill roared past Tony and the girls. The wheels left the ground, and another surge of adrenaline overwhelmed him. He turned to look back at his friends and give them the thumbs up. The pressure of the wind in the open cockpit locked his head facing sideways. Bill couldn't see where he was going, and panic rose up from his stomach. On the ground, he watched Tony put his hand to his own cheek and push his head to one side. In an instant, he understood Tony's gesture. Bill placed his own hand on his cheek and forced his face forward again.

The big engine growled, and wind rushed by his cold ears. All the books he'd read, all the WWII movies he'd watched, and all the dreams he'd dreamed hadn't prepared him for the sheer rush he felt flying that plane. She had more horses than anything he'd ever flown. Her wide double wings and Hartley's stories had convinced him she'd do anything he asked. His own conservative nature told him not to ask too much. It took every ounce of discipline he had to set her down after flying once around the pattern. He parked and chocked her in a rush. Tony and the girls were in the ragtop with the engine running. Bill scrambled toward the car, crawled over the trunk and into the back seat beside Cindy.

"Do you believe that?" Bill asked, trying to catch his breath. He draped his arm across Cindy's shoulders. It would be hard. He would miss Cindy, and Tony too, but now he knew that going to Arkansas was something he had to do.

"LET'S HIT IT," Tony said, roaring away with squealing tires. His car hit the freeway, and they headed for the cabin. Tony kept checking the rearview mirror, waiting for sirens and flashing red lights, but all he could see was the stupid-ass grin on Bill's face.

"That was right on!" Bill said from the back seat, still breathing hard.

"Why do you think it's a federal offense?" Tony asked with a laugh, then cranked up the radio when *Bad, Bad Leroy Brown* came on.

In another week, Bill would be in Arkansas. Tony was going to miss him, but at least some day, Bill could tell Sam that he flew his fucking Stearman. Tony just hoped he could be there to rub it in.

Tony, Della, Cindy and Bill rode to Patches' cabin, sharing two six-packs and a joint. Tony switched the radio station in time to hear the announcer talk about a comet that had once passed through the constellation Taurus. According to the voice on the radio, every

November, the fiery remains of a meteor shower entered Earth's atmosphere. To Tony, the magical display of shooting stars was all one big, happy accident.

They turned off the paved road to a dirt one. The further they went the worse the road got until Tony began to worry that the potholes and rocks would tear the muffler off his car. They descended one last, brutal grade and entered a wide flat area.

"I hope this is the place," Tony said. He killed the motor where the rutted dirt road ended in a narrow ravine. "That last slope almost munched the undercarriage."

Crickets chirped and a stream rushed beyond the skinny birch trees. In the darkness, the water sounded as if it was running right next to where they parked. Tony stared at the dark cabin caught in the headlights.

"Patches built that sucker himself," Bill said. "For his mother."

A rough wooden door sat dead center with smaller ones on the far right and left, one for each room. Tony spotted the limb of an old sycamore growing through the redwood planking of the front wall and out through the tin roof. Water-worn stones formed the bottom third of the cabin's walls. A chimney of the same river rocks climbed the peach colored adobe side wall. The hooded pipe of a pot belly stove stuck up from the low ceiling on the left and multi-paned windows bordered either side of the front door.

"What a place, Billy boy," Tony said, leaning his head back on the driver's seat. It was cold, but the top was still down on the convertible. He stared up at the glittering sky between the canyon walls. Sometimes, it just felt good to be alive. At that moment, a streak of light shot across the sky. "Hey, did you see that?"

"I saw it, sugar," Della said with a hoarse laugh. "Gimme a sip of your beer."

"How come you always call him 'Billy'?" Cindy asked with a choked voice and passed the joint to Tony.

"Because he's my brother," Tony answered, taking the glowing reefer from Cindy. "He's the brother I never had." That wasn't true, exactly. But it felt true. Ray and Rusty were his foster brothers, but they never seemed like family to him. It was hard to admit he felt closer to Bill than maybe anyone in his life. He pondered his answer to her, took a deep toke, and stared up at the sky again. Della plucked the joint from his hand, calling him a bogart. He held his breath as long as he could, then exhaled into the night air, making smoke rings and watching another shooting star cross the sky. "Fuck! Did you see that one?"

"I did, I did," Bill and Cindy said together, from the back seat.

Lights continued to whiz across the black sky, and the conversation deteriorated to periodic oohs, ahs, and the occasional 'all right.' They were all spellbound by the galactic display, and Tony shook his head at their good fortune.

"We got us a cabin in the woods," he said and laughed. "How do you like that shit?"

"I'm cold, hon," Della said with a long look toward the cabin.

"Go inside and build us a fire," Tony said, half-hoping she would.

"I'm not going in by myself," she answered. "Come with me, Cindy."

"Not yet," Cindy said, warm and comfortable beneath Bill's arm.

"Ton-ee . . ." Della whined.

"Don't nag me, wench," Tony answered with a wink. "Damn, that Sam, son of a bitch. All operators are like that, Billy boy. Every last fucking one of 'em."

"So quit," Bill said.

"Can't," Tony said with a chuckle. "I love the chems."

"Let's go inside," Della said again, nibbling Tony's ear.

"Oh, all right," he said, opening the car door and looking in the back seat. "What about you two?"

Bill looked down at Cindy, who snuggled a little closer.

"We'll wait," Bill said with a soft smile.

"Suit yourself, Billy boy," Tony said, lifting one eyebrow. The boy had it bad. Tony could tell by the sappy look on Bill's face. "That means we get the best bed."

"Whatever," Bill shrugged. Tony leaned into the back seat and looked Bill in the eye.

"L-word," Tony said, trying to warn him.

"Cram it," Bill said.

Tony straightened up again and walked behind the car. Bill was a hopeless case. Tony opened the trunk and removed a sleeping bag. He unrolled it and threw it over Cindy and Bill. Della and he walked away, but Tony could still hear their whispers in the back seat.

"I'll miss you, Bill," Cindy said.

"I'll be back," Bill promised and sealed it with a kiss.

Tony shook his head and led Della inside. It was better for him that his relationship with Della wasn't like the one Bill and Cindy had. He didn't need the complications. Just the sex. At least that's what he told himself, and he was more than willing to believe it. He built two fires that sent smoke billowing from the chimney and the stove pipe. They made the deserted cabin just warm enough for business.

Soon Della was naked on the double bed by the stone fireplace. Tony liked the way Della's animal-like moans rose through the cold, night air. It made him laugh out loud. She was so damn easy, he thought. She liked the same things that his foster mother did. Tweak her nipples, put a vibrating forefinger on her clit, and she was gone. She didn't complain when he did her fast and hard, which was fine by him. Her annoying urge to snuggle afterward always bothered him. He never was one for playing spoons.

His pack of cigarettes lay on the nightstand. He grabbed it and some matches and headed out the door. The stream gurgled past in the dark somewhere, and he stood naked, cupping his match from the wind. Bill and Cindy had gone to bed in the other room, and as he had warned, were left with the worst bed. Tony blew smoke rings, thinking they were probably cramped together in the lower bunk bed by the pot belly stove. Probably playing spoons. Love might work for Bill and Cindy. They both had real parents, not foster ones. Some people could ruin it for you. Their rapport didn't involve suspending disbelief or pretending to care. Tony shook his head and watched another star fall from the sky.

King City

FATHER ROBERTO POURED CREAM into his morning coffee and watched the liquid turn caramel-colored with two quick stirs. He set his cup on a heavy wooden table, sat in one of its mismatched chairs, and looked around the room. A dying ficus plant, a small crucifix, and some dry shafts of wheat in a Mason jar did little to enliven the faded walls of the rectory's dining room.

"The 'establishment' of King City has invited me to be the sacrificial lamb. . . again," Father Roberto said over his shoulder.

"Che? What?" A disembodied man's voice, speaking half Italian, half English, floated into the room from the direction of the kitchen.

"It's always the same," Roberto answered in English. "They fatten me up with a good lunch, then they tell me how to run the church."

Father Carlo carried a steaming mug of coffee into the room and dropped his copy of Homily Weekly on the table. The thin man slipped into the chair opposite Roberto.

Roberto's quick green eyes gazed at the man across the table. Carlo's dark eyes, tired and puffy, rested behind the dirty lenses of his wire-framed glasses. They both wore the same style black shirt and white collar, but Roberto focused on the worn black cardigan that hung from Carlo's rounded shoulders. Roberto smoothed the bright red pullover that fit snugly over his own compact frame. Carlo stirred two teaspoons of Parmesan cheese into his coffee.

"Why do you do that?" Roberto asked in frustration. He had watched his housemate do that every morning for the last three weeks.

"I was in Columbia for 22 years," Father Carlo said, struggling in English and giving a weak smile. "We get no fresh cream but always Parmesan cheese."

Roberto already knew that two decades in South America had left Carlo with little Italian, no English, and a dialect of Spanish not spoken in California. He also knew that "an incident" had prompted Carlo's immediate removal from that assignment, although he didn't know any details. Roberto knew it didn't take much to be reassigned. Something as minor as holding a differing opinion from the local bishop could set the wheels in motion. That had happened to his predecessor in King City.

"Where were you Saturday night?" Roberto asked. "After I finished the English mass, I had to do the Spanish mass for you."

"I drive to Los Angeles," Carlo answered in broken English.

"That's over 200 miles away. You could have told me."

"Sorry," Carlo said in a humble voice, offering no further explanation.

Another dream was dissolving for Roberto. His first three months in King City had been hectic, overwhelming, and lonely. The small parish needed at least two priests to serve both its Hispanic and white parishioners. Three weeks ago, this paisano, his own age, had bumbled up the front steps of the rectory to share the workload of St. Peter's Catholic Church.

The communiqué that Roberto had received from Father Carlo Vizzini's former bishop had been brief. It alluded to the fact that Carlo's missionary past had left him ill-prepared for his brief assignment in Los Angeles. Carlo had been shuttled to the smaller parish in King City for damage control. His presence assured Roberto that God truly did work in mysterious ways, especially in King City. Father Roberto ran the parish, asking only that Carlo perform the Spanish language masses and visit the sick, the two tasks that Roberto dreaded most.

"The Spanish mass was a circus," Roberto said, hoping Carlo might listen. "Parents slept with their noses in the missalettes, while their children raced up and down the aisles. At the consecration, two men came up the center aisle on their knees. Why?" Father Roberto asked, throwing his hands into the air.

"To be worthy of—" Carlo began, looking up from his cereal.

"Worthy?" Roberto interrupted. "Worthy of what? Does a child crawl to his father to beg him for candy? That's not faith. It's Christianity by coercion. It's nearly as bad as the Saturday night English mass."

"There is music for Saturday night," Father Carlo said.

"You call that music?" Roberto asked, pushing his empty breakfast plate aside. "I call it blasphemy. The organist is never on key."

"But her family donated the organ to St. Peter's—"

"Yes, she told me," Roberto said, irked to be reminded. "Fanny White is older than half the statues in the church and twice as deaf. She either plays the right song at the wrong time or the wrong song at the right time, or no song at all, which is almost a blessing. She haunts me like penance unsaid."

Roberto paused, realizing he too was slipping into the bad habit of many priests. He spent too much of his time giving homilies in church, where he became too accustomed to talking for long periods of time without being interrupted. It was a trait he noticed in other priests. He found he too tended to expound instead of converse, yet he continued. "I tried locking her out of the choir loft once."

"Roberto, no!"

"Yes," Roberto said, smiling at his own confession. "Did you know she has her own key? Last Saturday, I finally said, 'Mrs. White, don't ever play here again.'"

"What did she say?" Carlo asked, running a nervous hand over his thinning hair.

"She said, 'Thank you, Father. I thought so too,'" Roberto said, throwing up his hands in frustration. "She's deaf. She didn't understand a word I said."

"Thanks be to God."

"She's as bad as those people at lunch," he said.

"People at lunch?" Father Carlo asked. He looked bewildered, and Roberto knew his companion wished he would speak Italian. Roberto wouldn't oblige him. Carlo could never be an effective minister, or help Roberto, unless his English improved. Even now, drinking milk from his cereal bowl, Carlo seemed more like a child than an adult.

"Each one acts like he owns a pew here," Roberto said, folding his arms. "As soon as the meal is over, they start. 'We know you mean well, Father.' 'We do things a little differently in King City, Father.' 'You should play golf on Wednesdays with the Catholic Men's League, Father.'"

"Do you play golf?" Carlo asked, a drip of milk falling from his chin.

"Of course I don't," Roberto answered, looking at the bottom of his empty coffee cup. "Dogs chase balls. And if I did play, I wouldn't do it on Wednesdays. They actually asked if we could go back to saying the mass in Latin. Hell, they think the changes of Vatican II were my idea."

"You did help to write it," Carlo added, still not wiping his face.

"I helped to type it," Roberto said, correcting him. "There's a big difference. That was almost ten years ago. Will they ever accept the modernization of the Church?"

"In more time," Carlo answered.

"And the altar area— Have you noticed how dark it is?" It bothered Roberto that the area that should provide enlightenment looked so ominous and haunting. He had put in higher wattage bulbs, but it hadn't helped.

"It's just the dark wood—"

"The moment I saw it, I knew it was the perfect place for a stained glass window."

"So much money," Carlo said, shaking his head.

"Oh, no—" Father Roberto said, glancing at his watch and popping up from his chair. "Daily mass is in 30 minutes, and I haven't unlocked the church."

Roberto raced down the empty hall and out the front door of the rectory. He slipped through the side entrance of the adjoining church, his heels clicking over the hard flooring of the side aisle. A gentle pull opened the wide, double front doors, and the church filled with daylight. He hoped the light breeze and clear blue sky promised a better day. Maybe today his heart would accept his new assignment. Maybe today he could cast off the feeling that he had been saddled with a hopeless mission.

The wide building seemed bright from the rear. He walked toward the front of the building, passing beneath stained glass windows that lined the long, side walls. Three similar windows glowed in the choir loft above the main entrance behind him. Roberto genuflected at the head of the center aisle, his knee not quite touching the cold linoleum. He signed himself in front of the darkly paneled altar and rose again.

A huge crucifix loomed above the altar. His eyes gazed at it for a moment. He had been a priest for years before he questioned what Jesus looked like. His involvement with the enlightening documents of Vatican II had affected him. He had come to believe the concept, suggested by the finest Catholic minds of modern times, that knowing God could be a personal experience. It had inspired him to take his first trip to the Holy Land and see for himself.

His tour bus had traveled the miles and miles that Jesus once walked. Roberto had followed the steps to Golgotha Calvary where Christ had walked before he was crucified. A small man like Roberto could never have carried a cross that distance after days of torture. Small men weren't strong enough to preach all day from a boat or a mountain top. Roberto had returned to the United States, and, to satisfy his curiosity, had attended a meeting of the local carpenters' union. There, he remembered his suspicions had been confirmed. The hall had been filled with burly men. Christ, Roberto had decided, was not a small man like himself, though he doubted he could ever convince anyone in King City of that.

He turned right and bustled around in the sacristy behind the altar, preparing the church for mass. Roberto finished lighting the last candle and looked up. Maria Consalvo entered and knelt in the first pew. It was the fourth straight day he had noticed her coming to mass early, wearing the same long scarf of black lace over her hair. The pretty senorita's lips moved in the noiseless fashion of pain he had seen before. Long black rosary beads dangled from her hands, slipping through her fingers as she prayed.

Roberto moved in silence about the church, wondering whether to approach her. He wished he felt more spiritual. Some days it oozed all over him. But today, between the Spanish mass, Fanny White, and flack from the 'old guard,' spiritual intuition evaded him.

He thought Maria was the kind of person, like so many in King City, who believed that small towns shouldn't change. Every year, King City held parades at Christmas and for the Fourth of July. Kids swam in the city pool during sweltering summers. In spring, folks showed their roses at the county fair, and local salesmen hawked shiny new tractors. For fifteen years, no one had murdered anyone. Then, it happened twice last week. It had to happen now, while Roberto was the parish priest. He couldn't believe his timing.

"How are you, Maria?" Roberto asked in English, sliding into a seat in her pew. He hoped she would understand and answer in the same language.

"The police are making a big mistake," she answered, speaking English with a thick accent. "They are not looking for other reasons. They are only thinking Hector was a thief."

Recent headlines in the small town's daily newspaper had contained clues about Maria's distress. Early in the week, Roberto had read the bold lettering that screamed "Mendoza Arrested for Beabot Rape, Murder," followed by a story about the first murder. Two headlines later, the words "Richardson Kills Consalvo in Shooting Accident" spread across the front page. The "Consalvo" in big print referred to Maria's brother, Hector.

"Losing your brother so suddenly—" Roberto started, leaning forward and holding the edge of his seat with both hands.

"Hector was drunk," she said, clinging to a wadded tissue. "It was his birthday. He was only 23. That Anglo staying at the Motor Court had no reason to shoot Hector. If Hector was a robber, he wouldn't just walk in Senor Richardson's front door. All the rooms at the Motor Court look the same. Hector picks the wrong door, and he is shot dead."

"It's a tragedy," Roberto answered, keeping his voice low and steady in an effort to sound understanding.

"The policia are discriminating only because my brother is Mexican." Her anger surfaced, and her English suffered. "When Raoul Mendoza kills an old lady two days before, they arrests him right away. How come? Because Mendoza is a wetback, and she is white."

"We don't know what happened exactly," Roberto said, shifting in his seat and trying to reason with her.

"Father, I must go to confession for all these bad thoughts," she answered, her brown eyes locked on the floor.

"I understand, and I absolve you of your sins," he answered, making a sign of the cross in the air.

"No, I must have a real confession." Maria pointed to three narrow doors beyond the empty, honey-colored pews. "Over there."

"If you wish . . ." he said with a sigh. He wanted her to know that forgiveness was not some magic act that happened only in a confessional booth. How he hated those cubicles. They were hotter than hell in summer and just as uncomfortable in winter for both priest and confessor. He wished he could avoid the mystique that surrounded the whole ritual.

Roberto accommodated Maria, as he had others. He knew that most Catholics clung to the sacraments during turning points in their lives. Weddings, funerals, and last rites helped the Catholic mind comprehend what the heart couldn't believe.

FOUR HOURS LATER, a ritual of a different sort took place in the church office. Father Roberto dozed off and on in his recliner, half-listening to the conversation in the next room. Two volunteers, both widows, were preparing the Sunday bulletin. Emma was the typist. Virginia was a cut-and-paste specialist, slaving over the hot copier.

"It's the only way to be safe now," Emma said. "Shoot first. I know I won't hesitate." Her remark filtered through Roberto's sleepy haze and seemed an odd sentiment for white-haired Emma.

"Neither will I," Virginia said. "Not after what happened to Esther." Roberto knew Virginia referred to the murdered Mrs. Beabot, of recent headline fame. He hadn't known that the incident had impacted members of his parish. Virginia's voice carried a concern he could almost imagine on her over-powdered face. The tall, grandmotherly southern belle had jet black hair, which Roberto had always presumed came from a bottle. He knew she had lived in California for decades, but her accent was still strong.

"Land sakes," she continued, "a body isn't safe in her own home these days. Just remember to shoot them inside the house. If they're outside, you could go to jail." She paused, and he heard paper rustling. "Oh, this is a nice article on the new stained glass window. Do you think the Catholic Men's League will donate to the fund-raising?"

"I don't know," Emma answered. Roberto shifted in his recliner on the other side of the wall. Her lack of enthusiasm bothered him, and, more irritating, she dropped the topic all together. "You know, my brother Eddie says it's best to drag them inside if they happen to fall outside after you shoot them." Roberto could imagine her wagging finger and the jiggling, wrinkled flesh of her generous upper arm. He couldn't imagine her dragging a dead body anywhere.

"Isn't this just precious?" Virginia asked, commenting on something. "Where do y'all think I should put this?"

"I think it would look nice on page two," Emma said with a smile in her voice.

"Oh, perfect," Virginia said. After a short pause, she let out a quick scream. Roberto lifted his head. Then she added, "Oh, it's you."

"Excuse me," Sister Mary Teresa's voice entered the conversation. Roberto recognized the nun's distinctive Indian accent and settled back into his chair. Her sudden appearance must have frightened Virginia. "It's just me," the sister said, sounding a little perplexed.

"It's just the recent news in the paper, Sister," Emma said, explaining her coworker's reaction. "We're all on pins and needles. You know, it's not good for you to be in the convent alone. Not after all that's happened lately. Poor Esther. The Hospital Guild won't be the same without her."

"I wish I had known her better," Sister Mary Teresa answered. "I only met her once before her funeral."

"Such a beautiful service," Virginia said, and then added, "*even* if it was at a Baptist church. Lord knows I couldn't have cried any harder if it were my own." Roberto smiled at her comment.

"Esther was such a dear," Emma said. Roberto could tell she was walking back and forth across the room. Her voice and footsteps grew louder, and then faded when she moved away from the open door. "Let me take those, Sister. Esther was always volunteering at the hospital gift shop or working at the polls on Election Day. Sister, if you insist on staying in that big building alone, I hope you take the proper precautions. That's what Police Chief Alvarez said at that special safety meeting. Keep all doors locked and buy a deadbolt, especially considering what happened to that Mexican boy at the old motel by the highway."

"It's just a different culture," Virginia added. "You do have a deadbolt, don't you, Sister?"

"Well, no . . ." Sister answered. Roberto should look into that. Later.

"Y'all really should have the locksmith install one, if you can," Virginia said over the churning copier. "He's been very busy ever since Esther's murder. It's just horrible. They say she screamed."

"To be stabbed so many times with a screwdriver," Emma said. Her comment surprised Roberto. His eyes flashed open and stared at the ceiling. She continued, "I, for one, am glad they caught that Mendoza boy."

"At the meeting, Chief Alvarez said Mendoza was a burglar," Sister Mary Teresa said.

Roberto didn't realize Sister had attended the town meeting, or that she ever met Esther Beabot. Maybe he should have attended the meeting, but it was too late now. However, Sister was doing well with her cooler-heads-prevailing speech. There was something about entering a room full of estrogen that always made him uncomfortable. He avoided it whenever possible. She carried on talking, and he relaxed in his recliner again.

"The chief wasn't sure what was used as the murder weapon," Sister Mary Teresa said with authority. "Or if Esther really screamed."

"Oh, he was just being reassuring to keep everyone from panicking," Virginia said. "You know, our friend Louise's brother's boy has one of those special radios that picks up all the police calls. He heard them say it was a screwdriver. Right, Emma?"

"A Phillips," Emma added, over the slicing sound of the paper cutter.

"Mr. DeVries at the hardware store told me the weapon was probably a knife," Virginia said. "I declare, they all carry knives."

"Who?" Sister Mary Teresa asked.

"Why, Mexicans, of course," Virginia said. "Like I said, it's just a different culture."

"They just don't value human life like we do," Emma said, with a sigh. "What do you think? Should we have the stained glass story next to the new baptisms?"

"No, I think it should go by the schedule of masses," Virginia answered. "What do you think, Sister?"

"I think they value human life just as much as we do," Sister Mary Teresa answered. Roberto felt a gust of air and heard the front door close.

"My, my," Virginia commented after the sound of her footsteps faded. "Sister seems upset."

"It's probably all this talk about murder," Emma explained. "I know it has had me on edge."

Roberto was more inclined to believe it was the volunteers' attitudes about Hispanics that upset Sister Mary Teresa, but he was too tired to say anything. After a lull, Emma's typing started again, and he fell asleep to the rhythmic shoop-shoop of the copy machine.

Counsel on the Mount

Father Roberto and Pastor Stewart Fowler had arrived in King City and had joined the local, established prayer breakfast meeting at about the same time. They were the only two who showed up on the third Wednesday in March at King City's only decent restaurant.

"Just us?" Father Roberto asked the young pastor when they met in the restaurant foyer. Roberto had always felt comfortable with the young Baptist pastor. He reminded Roberto of himself, back when he was young and idealistic. Customers brushed past them, walking from the busy dining room to the gift shop.

"We're the only ones today," Stewart said, stuffing both hands into his pockets and stepping back toward the restroom doors. The slight young man's worried face seemed to add years to his pale eyes. Stewart's fair, thinning hair always gave Roberto the impression that the young pastor pulled it out by the handfuls on a regular basis.

"Not worth a table," Roberto said. The hostess was eyeing them. "Most mornings, I like to get up early and walk in the hills."

"Sounds good to me," Stewart said, looking toward the door. "Would you be opposed to a little company?"

"No, no," the priest answered. "Not at all. There's a trail up a canyon west of town. It's only few miles."

"May I seat you in the dining room?" asked the frazzled hostess.

"Not today, after all, thank you," Stewart said in a kind voice before both men headed out the door.

Roberto drove them both up the winding road into the foothills. Fog covered the valley floor but dissipated when they gained altitude. The warmth of the morning sun streamed into the car.

Roberto's fingers drummed against the steering wheel. He was starting to feel uncomfortable about the silence growing between them. Maybe he was driving too fast. He knew he had a tendency to do that.

"Where did you pastor before King City?" Stewart asked.

"Let me think, let me think," Roberto said. "Italy, Chicago, Montreal, Vancouver, Milwaukee, San Jose. . ." Roberto could tell from the young pastor's expression that he found the laundry list of former parishes surprising.

"And now I am here," Roberto said, glancing at the roof of the car before leveling his eyes on the road again. "But why?"

"Don't you like it here?" Stewart asked, half-turning toward the priest.

"Do you?" Roberto asked with a quick glance at the young man in the passenger seat.

"I don't know," Stewart answered, folding his arms and settling back in the seat. Barns and pastures flashed past behind him out the passenger window. "I've only been here three months."

"Well, let's just say the city walls aren't built on carnelian," Roberto said with a frown that he was quick to wipe from his face. "Still, the countryside is full of God's handiwork. Look how beautiful the mountains are. Why did He have to put *people* here?"

"Are the people here so different?" Stewart asked, looking over one shoulder back at King City.

"No, no," Roberto answered and parked his car at the end of the paved mountain road. "Unfortunately, they're just the same. I'm the different one." He pulled on the parking brake and opened his door. "Let's walk."

The priest's quick pace left Stewart struggling to keep up at first. Roberto wondered why the young pastor kept his head down most of the time. Maybe he was concentrating on the wildflowers sprouting along the edges of the path. Roberto stopped, and Stewart almost smacked into his backside.

"Look," Roberto said in a low voice, pointing to three deer grazing near a tree further up the trail. Stewart stared at the animals, but Roberto looked back down the trail. The view from the side of the mountain reminded Roberto of how clean and ordered everything looked out the plane window during flying lessons. Lavender and poppies covered the base of the foothills. In the distance, another mountain range bordered the opposite side of the flat valley floor. Green squares of fertile fields lined both sides of a curving river that led to Castroville and the sea. Stewart turned to stare back at King City, which hugged the edge of the brown Salinas River.

"I don't know where I'll ever—" the young minister started, and Roberto turned back to face him. He saw the three deer look up with dark eyes and big ears. Stewart followed Roberto's gaze and watched the deer, startled by his voice, disappear into the brush in three quick leaps. "Oh, I'm sorry."

"It's not important," Roberto said with a shrug. "Finish what you started."

"Somehow I am supposed to raise $50,000 down there for a new church hall," the young man continued with exhaustion evident in his voice. It was an emotion Roberto understood. "Sometimes, it seems I've exchanged all my time in God's word and prayer for a lot of hard work."

"I felt the same at first," Roberto said, looking up at the mountain top and remembering. "So many times overwhelmed." Then he looked back at Stewart. "And now I've been put out to pasture. All my hard work must be traded for prayer and time in God's word." Roberto smiled at the twist of fate.

"They expect so much sometimes," Stewart said, nodding in the direction of King City.

"Only miracles," Roberto said with a laugh.

"Must we dream their dreams?" the worried young man asked with his lowered eyebrows pinched together. "Meet their angels? Receive their revelations?"

"Of course," Roberto said, knowing he had asked the same thing once. "They'll drop by for an hour on Sunday and see what we got. They have jobs, families, and an entire world system to operate."

"It would be impossible without—" Stewart started.

The wild cry of a small animal interrupted the young pastor. The noise grew to a scream, and at the crescendo, turned to silence.

"What was that?" Stewart asked, his eyes scouring one area of the mountain. "Do you think it's dead?"

"Oh, yes," Roberto answered with a certainty he tried to explain. "I've heard the sound before. It's the scream of death. Excruciating pain, then peace."

"I overheard the ladies in the church hall," the young pastor said, his memory jarred by Roberto's words. "They were talking about Mendoza murdering Esther Beabot. They knew all the gory details about a missing screwdriver, and how she screamed." It amused Roberto that Baptists gossiped just like Catholics. Stewart turned away from Roberto and looked up the hill.

"Do you know what that scream was for?" the priest asked, watching the young pastor's tired eyes.

"Expressing terror, I guess," Steward answered, sounding like he didn't understand the question.

"Maybe." Roberto's thoughts raced ahead. His words came out in a rat-a-tat style that seemed to help him express his thoughts fast enough. "Or maybe the body suddenly realizes death is coming. It screams to the spirit, 'Go, go, go. I'm trapped here. You go on without me.'" The priest glanced up the hill and then back across the valley. "Then the spirit is free to move on."

"But will the spirit know where to go?" Stewart asked.

"Maybe, if we do our job . . . "

"Or maybe in spite of it," the young pastor added.

"Maybe," Roberto said with a nod.

"You know, Mrs. Beabot's death exposed some ugly prejudice in my church," Stewart said. "Parishioners are condemning a whole race of people for Esther's death."

"Prejudice may lead to a greater injustice," Roberto said, recalling his anguishing encounter with Maria Consalvo. "The second murder at the Motor Court may be worse than the first. The police seem all too willing to consider Richardson's shooting of Hector Consalvo an accident. The timing couldn't have been worse for Hector's his family. Prejudice may be a blessing in disguise for you and your church."

"Quite a disguise," Stewart said, studying Roberto's face.

"Are there any Hispanics in your congregation?" Roberto asked in an attempt to explain.

"No, I'm sad to say."

"Then your church is united against a common enemy," Roberto said, spreading his arms wide.

"Somehow, I don't find that very comforting," Stewart said with a confused look.

"You would if your church community was torn in two," Roberto said with a sigh. He looked down toward King City and shook his head. "Half of my parish feels outraged over Mrs. Beabot's death, just like your ladies. The rest feel just as strongly about the murder of Hector Consalvo. Now, how do you teach them to love in one hour a week?"

"With help," the young man answered, looking up. Roberto followed Stewart's gaze skyward and signed himself.

"And lots of walking," Roberto said and then resumed his brisk pace up the trail.

The Sanctity of
the Confessional

"I HAD IMPURE THOUGHTS ten times," said the little voice in Spanish from the other side of the screen.

"Say five Hail Marys and go in peace, my son." Father Roberto answered in the same language with difficulty and stifled his yawn.

The door closed. The door opened again. More impure thoughts. It was a typical Saturday afternoon, hotter than Hades in that dark confessional box, and Roberto had yet to hear an original sin. Father Carlo was supposed to hear confessions for Spanish speakers, but he had vanished. Again. The door opened and closed once more.

"Father, I don't know what to do." The young lady's words in Spanish filtered through the screen, bypassing the standard format. It was enough to jolt Roberto awake.

"The Lord is understanding," Roberto said. He knew that true distress always spoke out of form. He continued in Spanish. "Let His Holy Spirit guide you."

"Father, you don't understand—" At that moment, a blast that sounded like a gunshot echoed from beyond the church walls.

"Go on," Father Roberto said, urging her on and dismissing the sound.

"I've seen something very important," she said in a halting whisper. "I should tell someone, but I can't. Will I be forgiven?"

"You must pray to God for the strength to do what is right," Roberto answered, testing the limits of his Spanish.

"If I tell, it will kill my mother," she said, her breathing sounding quick and uneven. Was she crying? He hoped not. It was difficult enough for him to counsel rational people in Spanish. Or any language. She seemed to compose herself for a moment, and then continued. "My mother's heart is very weak. She had to be taken to the hospital when she learned my brother was killed. The doctors say she must stay quiet and take medication every day to live. It would kill her if she knew I found the screwdriver in his closet." Roberto's suspicions were confirmed. It was Maria Consalvo. He wished he didn't know. "If I don't speak out, an innocent man may die. Whose life should I choose? My mother's or a stranger's?"

Maria Consalvo's agony touched Roberto. He knew that if her information remained concealed, Mendoza would pay for a murder that Hector Consalvo had committed. He also knew Maria would never forgive herself if she told the truth, and her mother died, even if there was no connection between her decision and the death. The sanctity of the confessional limited his options and formed the boundaries of his advice to her.

"Will your decision be best for everyone?" he asked her.

"I have no choice. My brother was my mother's only son. The truth would kill her."

"And what about you?" Roberto asked and wiped the perspiration from his forehead. "Will you be able to remain silent forever?"

"I don't know, Father," she answered, and he could hear the strain of truth in her voice. He had heard it at times in the confessional though not often enough. "Will the Lord forgive me?"

Roberto stopped to pray. He should have asked for wisdom to counsel her. Instead, he felt his soul begging that the cup she presented would pass from him to someone else. That someone else should have been Carlo. He was supposed to be hearing her confession, not Roberto. That thought made him angry, which in turn made him feel disappointed in himself. There were just some days he felt like the world's worst priest. He heard Maria sobbing on the other side of the screen. One of two innocent lives hinged on his reply.

He reviewed his options. If he refused to absolve her, it might change her mind, or it might make her burden heavier. He could pray for her, which he hoped would be enough. Roberto decided to show love through forgiveness and hoped that it would free her to do whatever was right. He cleared his throat and planned out his thoughts in Spanish.

"Go my child and pray," he told her. "Ask the Lord himself to speak to your heart. After that, if you still feel that the truth would kill, then you will be absolved of any sin. May the Lord give you the courage to speak the truth."

"Thank you, Father Carlo," Maria said in a whisper before she left. Roberto didn't correct her. It was better if she never knew who had really heard her confession.

The confessional door closed and then opened again. Roberto rolled his eyes and looked up. Couldn't God give him a five-minute break after a confession like that? Apparently not.

"Bless me, Father, for I have sinned." The man's perfect English startled Roberto.

"Si— I mean, yes. . ."

"My last confession was five months ago."

About Christmas time, Roberto calculated. It was difficult to concentrate after Maria's confession. The man's voice droned on.

"Father Carlo, I confess—" Another loud blast interrupted the man. The confessor paused and then continued. "I confess that I have said unkind things about Father Roberto." Roberto's stomach grew uneasy at the man's words, but he didn't interrupt. "Why does he want to change our church? He wants a stained glass window behind the altar. Why? The crucifix has always been there. I confess I am angry at Father Roberto, and now it is difficult for me to work with him. Father?"

"Uh-hum?" Roberto answered, not wanting to reveal his identity.

"I confess I have discussed Father Roberto's faults with many of my friends," the man said, and his voice climbed an octave. "I know that was wrong, but many of them agreed with me. Father, please pray for me to have a change of heart. I hate Father Roberto." The man let out a sigh that signaled to Roberto that he was finished.

"Not to worry so much," Roberto said, giving his best impersonation of Father Carlo's English. "Say five Our Fathers and an Act of Contrition."

"Thank you, Father," the man said, sounding relieved. "I'm glad I came."

"Your sins are absolved," Roberto said in a faint voice. "Go in peace." Another loud boom echoed after his words.

The door closed but didn't re-open. Roberto waited until the sound of footsteps faded away before peeking out the door. The church was empty. He deserted the confessional and slipped past the unoccupied pews. He stepped outside and locked the church door behind him. It was a relief to pull his key from the door and walk away. Just then, another explosion echoed from the back of the building. Roberto entered the rectory, charged down the barren hallway, and opened the back door.

Father Carlo was kneeling on the cement porch between a can of black powder and a miniature cannon. Roberto stood on the porch behind him without making his presence known. He watched Carlo reload the weapon and touch a lit match to the fuse at the back of the barrel. A loud bang sounded, and the cannon recoiled, rolling backward on its eight-inch, wooden-spoke wheels. The ball that soared from the foot long barrel blew a hole through a dying bush and the backyard fence. It stopped after denting the metal siding of the garage.

"Carlo, what are you doing?" Roberto asked, lifting his open palms.

"Do you like?" Carlo asked with a smile, looking up the back porch steps at Roberto. "I go to rummage sale at Presbyterian Church."

"You were supposed to hear confessions today," Roberto answered. Carlo's lack of concern still amazed him.

"Today?" Carlo asked, still kneeling. He signed himself and smiled. "Bless me, Father, for I have sinned."

"No!" Roberto answered, and he meant it. Carlo stood up, brushed the dust from his knees, and held his arms out wide in innocence.

"Truly, I forget, Roberto."

Roberto turned away and headed back into the rectory. He started to shut the door but poked his head back outside.

"Were there any calls for me?"

"You no want to know, Roberto," Carlo answered, smoothing back his thinning black hair.

"Why not?" Roberto asked, still feeling annoyed by Carlo.

"People are calling," Carlo answered, looking around the yard and avoiding Roberto's eyes. "So upset. The window. So expensive. They say they no want it. They are too much angry. Why you do this, they don't know."

"When will they come out of the dark ages?" Roberto asked, slapping his hands to his side and not expecting an answer. "I want to replace the crucified Christ with the risen one. It is part of the living Church—"

"Roberto!" The intensity with which Father Carlo said his name stopped Roberto. Carlo continued in Italian. "They don't understand yet. I understand you have a vision of bringing light into the church. I also know that David had a vision of the temple for the Lord, but it was his son who was allowed to build it, not him. It might not be the time."

"It is past time," Roberto answered in a loud voice, speaking in English. How could a priest like Carlo, one who couldn't even remember to listen to Saturday confessions, question him? "And I don't have a son. I will explain it again this Sunday. Hopefully, people will understand this time."

Roberto closed the door with a resounding thud and went to his room to lie down. He tried to relax, but the final two confessions he had heard still troubled him. Soon it would be time for evening mass and Fanny White's music. He had just started to drift off to sleep when Carlo fired the cannon again.

Feeling Flush

Tony was glad that he had landed the temporary position at Lopes Air Care in Castroville. It had allowed him to slip into a full-time seat when, as Bill had predicted, Lopes Senior had returned from his first vacation in 20 years and decided to retire. Sonny Lopes, the new owner, had made big plans for the business he'd inherited. That kept Tony's new boss busy, stealing accounts from other spray outfits and bragging about expanding into helicopters. Tony didn't care what Sonny did as long as the paychecks kept coming.

Dreary Castroville's entire social scene consisted of a lot of drinking, some wife swapping, and the annual Artichoke Festival. Patches had introduced Tony to some foggy weather friends at Clancy's Bar on the main drag near the airstrip. Bill had been gone three months before Tony had scraped together the down payment for a fixer-upper tract house on the edge of town near the beach.

One Friday evening, after escrow closed, Tony decided to surprise Della and arrive unannounced at Harmony Lane. He entered the front door at closing time. Laughter was echoing from the end massage room.

"Della?" he called, sauntering down the hallway.

"I'll be out in a sec, sugar," she answered. Tony stood outside the door of the last room and listened. He could hear the hissing of an aerosol can.

"Fuck the cleaning," he said, opening the door. "It's quitting ti—"

White foam hung from the walls. Messy white streaks crisscrossed the red rug. Tony stared at the massage table. It took a moment for him to untangle all the arms and legs. Della was sandwiched between two old men. One jumped up and grabbed a washcloth to hide himself. The other still lay on the table beneath Della. The pinned man shook the can of whipped cream and fired it at Tony.

"What the hell?" Tony shouted, jumping out of the line of fire.

"I can explain," Della said, sliding off her naked customer.

"Yeah, right," Tony said, slamming the door. He was out the front entrance and in his car before she could slip on a robe and reach the front door. Tony shifted into reverse and looked back once. Della was running toward his parked car. Her lips seemed to be calling his name, but he couldn't hear it. And he didn't want to. His boot slammed the gas pedal to the floor, sending his car backward out of the parking space until he hit the brake with a harsh squeal. He threw it into gear and sped off, ripping across the parking lot and bounding into the street.

Tony met Sheila at Clancy's the next night. She told him she was broke. She also told him she loved his blue eyes. Tony knew she wasn't great looking: her perfect hips and pretty breasts were offset by a long neck and big nose. Her limp hair was the color of dust, and heavy bangs shrouded her buggy, brown eyes, outlined in heavy black eyeliner. He decided he wasn't that interested, but he was horny, so he offered her a job as his housekeeper. She moved in the next day. It turned out she could make a great pineapple upside-down cake.

A week later, to his surprise, Sheila was still around. He lay sprawled on the ratty carpet of his living room floor, cleaning his new rifle and harassing Sheila while she mopped the kitchen floor. *Your Mama Don't Dance* blasted from a massive stereo in the corner. The music was so loud, Tony would never have known that the phone rang if it hadn't been for Sheila. She answered it, then handed it to him.

"It's some guy named Bill, calling from Arkansas," she said with a question in her voice.

"Far out," Tony answered. He jumped up, flipped off the music, took the phone from her hand, and stretched the long cord to sit down on the arm of his sorry-looking couch.

"Who was that?" Bill asked Tony, first thing.

"My live-in housekeeper," Tony answered. "Cool, eh?"

"What about Della?"

"She's history, Billy boy," Tony said. "It was never the same after she left her old man. Besides, I need a housekeeper. This hovel has three bedrooms." He looked around him. The place wasn't spotless, but it looked a hell of a lot better than it had before Sheila moved in. "The rooms are all so small, my new waterbed only fits in the living room." Tony glanced up at the round bed with its red crushed velvet upholstery covering half the floor space in the room. It was one of the few things he owned that he hadn't bought at a flea market.

"Your bed is in the living room?" Bill asked, busting up on the other end.

"Hey, it's the center of my life anyway," Tony answered and laughed. It was good to hear Bill's voice. Maybe he didn't understand Tony. Hell, no one did. Certainly not Sheila. But there was a bond there, a pilot's bond, nonetheless. "Where are you calling from?"

"I'm using a pay phone at the only watering hole in Flat Rock, Arkansas," Bill answered. Tony could hear country music whining somewhere in the background. "So tell me about the housekeeper."

"Not much to tell," Tony answered, draining a beer and dropping the empty on the rug. He reached into a bag on the floor, pinched the phone between his ear and his shoulder, and popped a fresh one. "She'd be perfect if she wore a bag on her head."

"Where do you find 'em, Tony?" Bill asked, sounding amused. "And why?"

"Can't live with 'em," Tony said, raising his beer and toasting his absent friend. "Can't live without 'em."

"Maybe if you were a little more selective," Bill said, showing his practical side.

"Those types require upkeep," Tony answered. In the kitchen, Sheila bent over to wring out the mop. Tony's eyes focused on her ass. "I'm looking for something low maintenance. That or no maintenance at all." Bill's tinny voice in the receiver broke his stare.

"So all she does is make the waterbed, I suppose?"

"Hey, all jobs have their benefits," Tony said with a shrug. "Some nights, she gets hers."

"You're a sick man, Tony."

"But well serviced," Tony said with a smile. He felt it was true. "So, when are you coming back?"

"Not for a few months," Bill said. Tony tried not to show his disappointment. He took some long swallows of beer and then burped. "Excuse you, asshole," Bill said before continuing. "I landed a spray job back here. I'm flying an old dog Cub. Right now, I have to fly every field in formation with my new boss, Farmer John Arbin."

"Have you scared yourself shitless yet?" Tony asked, pretty sure he knew the answer.

"Only every day," Bill answered, and Tony just nodded, knowing it was probably true. "I already put her down in a bean field once and cut a wire that took out the power in Flat Rock for half a day. And then—well, I always have to keep this roll of paper towels behind my seat to wipe the engine oil off the windshield. While I was flying today, the negative G's lifted them up, wrapped them around my head and sucked them out the window. I was yanking them from my face and trying to fly with a trail of paper towels flapping behind me."

"Oh, shit," Tony said. When he stopped laughing, he asked, "What did the boss say?"

"Same thing he always says. 'Gwon like that, boy, and the undertaker will be wiping yo' ass,'" Bill answered in his best southern accent. Tony laughed so hard, he almost fell off the arm of the couch. Then, his friend's voice softened. "Have you seen Cindy?"

"Once," Tony answered and took a sip. "She was at her new job in the mall. She could hardly wait to ask about you."

"All right!"

"Don't wait too long," Tony said, half hoping his advice might bring Bill back sooner. "She's a cutie, and she's got those big—"

"Don't remind me," Bill cut him off. "It's tough enough back here. Promise me you won't hit on Cindy while I'm gone."

"Not a chance," Tony said and smiled. Bill knew him better than he thought. "Besides, she wouldn't—"

"So you swear?"

"God, you got it bad," Tony answered with a laugh. "Hell, I swear. What are brothers for? You know what? I think I'm going to buy me a jeep. One of those British safari jobs with the tire on the hood—"

"Your three minutes are up, sir," the operator said. "Please deposit more change if you—"

"I'll call you again," Bill said, squeezing in the words.

"I'll be here, having a brew and banging the maid."

Over the next few months, Tony flew hard and drank heavy. Money came and money went, but that never bothered him much. Credit was just fine with him, and he tossed out all the bills that didn't say "Final Notice." He sold his ragtop to some fool and bought a jeep. The next month, he scored a Harley he had seen advertised in the local paper. He made the deposit with what should have been his car payment. He went straight from the bike dealer to Patches' ranch near Moss Landing, only a few miles from Tony's house. Patches had become a good drinking buddy in Bill's absence. The bike sat parked at the end of Patches' long driveway with the sun reflecting off the polished chrome.

"I always wanted a Hog," Tony said to Patches, who was standing beside him and admiring his new motorcycle. Tony folded his arms and nodded in the shiny bike's direction. "This one's almost brand new. It just has a tiny miss in the engine. I heard it on the way here."

"You?" Patches asked, leaning on his rake. "You can't even hear the alarm on your wristwatch."

"That's a high-pitched noise," Tony answered, dropping his arms and using his sleeve to wipe some dust off his new toy. "I've flown too many radial engines to hear those anymore. But engines, hell, they talk to me."

Tony rode it home, put it in his garage, and stripped it to the last nut. He spent the next two months putting it back together, when he wasn't flying, drinking, or fighting with Sheila. The day he finished and started it up, the motor purred like a lion.

"Come on, wench, go for a ride with me," Tony said, ducking his head in the kitchen and calling to Sheila.

He handed her the helmet he never used and mounted the bike wearing a tee shirt and jeans. She jumped on behind him. He counted on her body heat and a freshly downed six-pack to keep him warm. They flew down the back roads on Easter Sunday, dipping and swaying through the turns. The sweet scent of honeysuckle floated passed them on the breeze that kept his black curls from his face. Tony's smile grew wider when he darted between two cars on the highway, and Sheila held on to him even tighter. Nothing beat the feel of fifth gear vibrating between your legs and a pair of tits pressed into your back.

On the way home, Tony took the last corner near his house too fast and slid out on some sand. Sheila's arms left his waist, and she flew off, landing on someone's front lawn. Tony went down with the bike. The heavy motorcycle pinned Tony's leg to the pavement. Sheila got up with only minor scrapes.

"Tony, are you all right?" Sheila called and stumbled toward him.

"Hell, no, bitch," he said, his voice choked with pain. She could ask the stupidest questions. "Get this thing off of me."

It took all of her strength to budge the monstrous bike. He swore like a crazy man when she tried. She let go of it, and he heard a crack, followed by an electric shot of pain in his pinned leg.

"Mother fuck!"

"It's too heavy," she said, tears starting down her face.

"Don't just stand there, wench," he said. It even hurt to talk. "Go call for help, damn it."

"Only if you promise to marry me," she said. Sheila plopped down on the grass beside him and brushed sand from his black hair.

"What?" he asked, yanking his head away from her touch. "Are you fucking nuts?"

"You said you loved me," she answered, sounding wistful.

"What?" He closed his eyes and squeezed them shut, as if it would help block out the pain. "When?"

"Last night. In bed."

"Oh, hell, that doesn't count. I'd say anything in bed. I'm not going to fucking argue about this right now. Ah-h-h." He moaned and tried bracing the thigh of his trapped leg with both hands.

"But I'm pregnant."

"You're on the pill," Tony said, wincing through the pain. "Look, this hurts like hell—"

"I lied about the pill," she said, sounding like a little girl. "I thought you would marry me if I had your baby."

"You act as if I have morals," he gasped, looking at her in disbelief. "I'm an asshole, not a father. Now get me some fuckin' help here." He dropped his head, and it banged against the pavement, almost hard enough to knock him out. The pain nearly made him forget about his leg. He opened his eyes and saw Sheila running away. "Bring me back a beer," he yelled, and the effort made him suck in his breath and hold it, exhaling a little at a time. He looked at the bike and fought back tears. "Happy Fucking Easter, loser."

She never came back. Tony spent the next hour, moving the big bike an inch at a time and cussing at every shift of its weight. When he managed to free himself, he crawled to the liquor store on the corner and passed out cold in the entrance.

Love at the Mall

TONY LAY ON HIS COUCH in a full leg cast, drinking vodka straight from the bottle and popping pain pills. Patches had come by to visit, and Tony shook his fist at the taunting sounds of working airplanes overhead.

"Assholes," Tony said, looking in the direction of the engine noise above his house. "No flying, no sex, and no paycheck. I'm screwed." Tony picked up yesterday's tee shirt from the arm rest, threw it at the waterbed across the room, and swore at the pain the effort caused him. "Son of a bitch."

"You broke it bad," Patches said, looking around the unkempt room for a seat. Patches tossed the shirt on to a stack of albums near the fireplace and sat on the frame of the waterbed. Tony was immobile, Sheila was gone, and the junk was knee-deep.

"Open a window, would ya?" Tony asked Patches. "It's hotter than hell in here. And this thing itches so damn bad." He grabbed a straightened, wire coat hanger and slid it up and down inside the hard cast. "Ah-h-h, that feels so good."

Two days later, Tony couldn't take the frustration anymore. He had had enough of the heat and the 600-horse engines roaring over his house. It was a long way to his jeep in the driveway, but he was determined. After a twenty-minute struggle, he drove away with his cast propped up on the passenger seat. The ignition pedal felt strange under his left foot, but he got used to it by the time he reached Salinas and parked at the enclosed mall. He hobbled toward the entrance, dying to feel the air conditioning and to be shielded by its sound-proof insulation.

Inside, Tony limped on crutches toward the stationery store where Cindy worked. He entered the shop and noticed someone kneeling behind the showcase. Only the top of her head was visible with hair the same color as Cindy's.

"Hey, whatcha doing?" he asked.

"Stocking," a female voice answered. Her outstretched arm placed fancy pens and boxed thank you notes in the glass case.

"Just thought I would say 'hi,'" Tony said, removing one crutch and leaning against the display case in pain. "It's about all I can do since I broke my leg."

"Oh, no," she said, without looking up. "I'm sorry. How did you break it?"

"I dropped a motorcycle on it," he answered, trying to peek around the counter. Her voice sounded different. "Cindy?"

"She's at lunch," the girl behind the counter said. "I wish I knew how to do this right." She sat back in disgust and gathered small boxes of cards. Tony could see then it definitely wasn't Cindy. Whoever it was continued talking, her head down. "Should I give her a message?"

"Never mind," Tony said. He replaced his crutch and started to hobble away. "Well, you could tell her that Bill called."

"Bill?" the girl said, popping up with her arms full of boxes. "Are you Bill? She told me all about you."

"Oh, really?" Tony said and found himself smiling. It was as good as he had felt in days. He never could resist an opportunity to tease. "What did she say?"

"Well, I thought she said your hair was blond," the young girl answered, dumping the boxes all over the counter.

"Oh, that," Tony said, struggling to ruffle his curls.

Her wide, green eyes were now staring at Tony, and he imagined they could see colors no one else's could. To Tony, they were the eyes of innocence, blind to the obvious. There was a Disney quality to her naive expression, almost Tinkerbelle-like. Sandy wisps of short hair pointed toward her pixie face. Her boyish expression made her look very young, but he figured she must have been at least 18 to be left in charge of a store. At least he hoped she was. Even her clog-soled boots didn't make her very tall. She straightened her ivory tunic and tugged on the fringed, multi-colored scarf encircling her small waist.

"She never said you had a broken leg either," the girl said with a slight smile. "But she told me you write to her every week. It sounds so, I don't know, romantic. Like you might read poetry to her or something."

"Poetry?" Tony said. He thought she was joking. He changed his wicked laugh into a cough when he saw that she was serious. "She told you that?"

"Not exactly," she said, lowering her eyes and spinning one box in a circle on the glass counter top. "She told me you watched shooting stars together. Sometimes I think about that. About sitting in the dark with someone you, well, care about a lot and watching stars fall out of the sky. It almost makes you cry. But you know. You were there."

"Oh, I was there all right," Tony said. This time he really tried not to smile, but he couldn't stop himself. He also couldn't take his eyes off her.

"Was it cold?" the girl asked in a timid voice.

"Yeah, but—"

"But you never noticed, right?" she answered for him. "And you said to yourself, 'I'll remember this night for the rest of my life.'"

"Well, no—"

"Oh, you should have," she answered, speaking in a soft voice and clutching a box of note cards close to her chest. "It might never happen again."

"You're probably right," he said and nodded. What was going on here? What was there about her that was grabbing him? She was too sweet for him. And too nice, too sincere, too everything-good-he-could-think-of. He found himself ignoring the little voice that was telling him to leave.

"I'm probably wrong," she said, tossing the box on her haphazard pile. "That kind of stuff probably happens to other people all the time."

"Not really," Tony said, approaching her with a wince. The pain in his leg was killing him, but he still couldn't bring himself to walk away. "It never happened to me."

"What do you mean?" she asked, staring at him as if he had killed her dog. And worse yet, he felt as if he had. Think fast.

"I mean, I'm not Bill," he said, stumbling over the truth. He was just too entranced by her to come up with a good lie.

"But you said you were there," she said. He leaned on the counter, biting his lower lip to hide his pain. She backed away from him. Not the reaction he was going for.

"I was there," he continued, taking a deep breath. Fucking busted leg. Damn. Say something intelligent. "But you seem to know more about that night than I do. I'm Tony, Bill's friend."

"Oh, God, how embarrassing," she said, turning flush and dropping behind the counter again. "Oh, oh, I have to finish this. Excuse me." She reached up to grab a box of cards without looking at him. "I'll tell Cindy you were here. What did you say your name is?"

"Tony," he repeated. Don't blow this. "What's yours?"

"Angela. Please don't tell Cindy what I said," she added, peeking over the counter top. "It was so dumb."

"Not really," Tony said. He cocked his head and smiled. She blushed again. He winked. "Maybe a little."

"Maybe a lot."

Three customers entered, and Tony maneuvered away from the counter. He tried to think of a good reason to stay, but nothing came to mind. He hobbled out the door, looking back at Angela now and then until she was out of sight.

During the next few weeks, Tony found himself drifting back to the mall several times. He made sure his visits always coincided with Cindy's lunch hour. They lasted as long as he could bear to lean on his crutches.

He liked the way Angela blushed when she talked to him. She had told him she was 22, and he asked her out for a drink. She refused. He had even invited her to dinner, but she said she couldn't go. One day, three weeks after they had met, she agreed to have a cup of coffee with him on her break.

"I haven't gone anywhere except work lately," she said, sliding into the purple booth of the Bumbleberry Coffee Shop at the mall. "My father's very sick." Tony looked at her, and she looked away, staring at the pictures of wildflowers on the wall above their table. "My mother needs my help. I feel really sorry for her."

"Is it serious, what your father has?" Tony asked. It felt good to drop into the seat across the table from her. He rested one hand on his crutches for a moment before laying them down beside the booth.

"Yes," she answered in a light manner. Maybe she didn't like the old boy. Tony could understand that. But, at the same time, she didn't seem like someone who could be cold. "It won't be long."

"That's a bitch," he said. He tried to force his long cast under the table, but he had to leave it partially blocking the aisle. Damn thing.

"Yeah, sure. . ." she said, her eyes following the waitress.

"Is he dying?" Tony asked, not getting her reaction at all.

"I guess."

"You guess?" Tony asked, cocking his head and still not understanding.

"It's hard to explain," she answered, straightening the sugar packets in the holder. "My father, he never, you know, did stuff like a father. He wasn't around much. And when he was, I wished— This is all very hard on my mom."

"Was he mean?" Tony asked. A quick look of distrust in her eye told him he had better lay off the subject.

"You're a pilot, right?" she asked, folding and unfolding her napkin. "Do you like flying?"

"I love to fly," he answered, feeling a little off balance. Nine times out of nine, he could have cared less about someone's past, but now he was intrigued. "Look, if you don't want to talk about him—"

"I don't," she said, looking toward the exit. "Maybe I shouldn't have come."

"We can talk about something else," Tony said, hoping she wouldn't walk out. He would never catch her if she did. Not on fucking crutches. He went with her suggestion and changed the subject. "Flying is perfect. Especially in a one-holer."

"What's that?"

"That's when there is only room for one person, the pilot. That way, you never have to talk to anyone." What was he saying? Did he want her to think he didn't like to talk? He never remembered having this problem with Della or Sheila. Stupid stuff kept falling out of his mouth.

"He isn't the nice man everyone thinks he is," Angela said, keeping her eyes focused on the napkin she was shredding in her lap.

"I wish he would hurry up. My poor mom should fly a one-holder plane."

"One-holer," Tony said with a soft laugh.

"What?" she asked, looking up at him and killing him with her Disney eyes.

"It's a one-holer," he explained in a voice he didn't recognize. "Not a oneholder."

"Oh, sorry," she said with a shrug. "I don't know anything about airplanes."

"It doesn't matter," Tony answered and, for the length of her break time, he really meant it.

Two weeks later, Tony lay on his couch, propping his cast up on the arm of it and shooting flies with rubber bands. Patches dropped by to tell Tony that he was going duck hunting. Six weeks of inactivity was all Tony could stomach. He got off the couch and invited himself along.

"You can't duck hunt in a cast," Patches said with a laugh.

"The hell I can't," Tony answered, rolling off the couch and onto the floor.

"You don't even have a duck gun," Patches protested.

"I got something better." Tony reached beneath the couch and pulled out his newest purchase, something else he couldn't afford. "Look at this." He was sure the new rifle would impress Patches. A barrel had been mounted on the butt stock that was lying around in his car for the longest time. Patches studied it at arm's length, tugging on his gray goatee.

"Where did you get it?" Patches asked, handing the zebra-striped stock and barrel back to Tony.

"I already had the wood," Tony said with a smile. "A gunsmith mounted the barrel, but I didn't get a chance to test fire it before this happened." He knocked one end of the gun against his cast, stood up, and crossed the room, a crutch under one arm and a rifle under the other.

"How are you going to duck hunt with a crutch?"

"Hell, I don't need this," Tony answered, tossing the crutch on the waterbed. He pointed the rifle out the front window, taking a bead on the telephone pole across the street.

The next morning, Tony hunkered down in a duck blind beside Patches with difficulty. All went well until Tony actually knocked something out of the sky. He stepped into the marsh, too enthusiastic about retrieving his kill. His heavy cast sank in the soft bed of the pond. Cold mud oozed in the open toe and up his foot, trapping him like wet concrete. Tony fell, and the slime seeped in the top of his cast and down his thigh. He needed Patches' help to get out of the mud and back on dry ground.

When Tony finally got home, washing proved futile. He stormed out to the garage, followed by Patches. An hour later, he headed back toward the house, dripping with sweat and holding the remains of the cast he had sawed off his leg. He pitched the crumbling hunk of white plaster into the garbage can outside the sliding glass door.

"I'm flying tomorrow," Tony said, giving the garbage can a kick with his good leg.

"Shouldn't you see a doctor?" Patches asked.

"What for? I did the hard part." He brushed bits of plaster from the white thin leg beneath his torn pants and tried bending his knee. "Hot damn. Hand me the vodka."

Tony believed if he waited another minute to fly, he might explode. He reported to work the next morning, suffering from the most severe case of ground sickness he could remember.

"Where's your doctor's release?" his boss asked. Sonny stood up behind the desk in his dirty office, but he wasn't much taller standing than when he was seated. His oversized torso looked off balance on his squatty legs. Tony always wondered if his boss really had any knees under his pants. Sonny walked over and wagged a stubby finger in Tony's face. "I need that release. My liability insurance specifically—"

"Who do you think took off the cast?" Tony said and walked away, heading for the plane.

Tony never bothered going back to the quack. He figured he had saved the old boy a lot of hard work and himself a little money. His newly mended leg added an exaggerated swagger to his gait. His right leg swung out when he walked, as if it was longer than the other one. It seemed to be more noticeable when he was drunk, which was fairly often, though not often enough for Tony.

The season slowed to a crawl just when Tony needed money the most. Past due notices arrived daily. He tossed them in the trash. He dodged bill collectors and decided he had to do something fast to get some extra money. Piece by piece, he transported his motorcycle to Patches' old barn. After the last of it was gone, he broke the lock off his gate and kicked in the side door of the garage. He reported the theft of his motorcycle to the police and his insurance agent. A check arrived just in time to stall foreclosure on his house.

A month later, the county was chasing him to pay medical bills for Sheila's prenatal care. Tony went to Clancy's bar, rallying support for his defense.

"Look, I might have done it but not intentionally," Tony said to his compadres lining the bar. "She told me she was on the pill."

"You was framed," Bart said, lifting his glass. He was a permanent fixture at Clancy's since losing his job with AirRaid Ag and, worse yet, hadn't flown since O'Malley had fired him.

"Of course I was," Tony said, flattening his mustache with the palm of his hand. "Another round for my friends, bartender."

They all understood his side after he bought a few more drinks. He swaggered over to the jukebox and punched A-19, *Desperado*.

Money came and money went, and so did summer. Tony flew and drank and tried to forget. He was successful when it came to the paternity suit and the bills. What he couldn't shake was Angela, though he never told a soul.

For the longest time, she would only go to the coffee shop with him. She insisted her mother might need her and not be able to find her. Every time he pushed her for more, her eyes grew scared, and he backed off.

Tony never understood what the deal was with Angela, or her mother, or her dying dad. Her inaccessibility frustrated him. More than once he had sworn to himself he wouldn't see her again, but it was useless. The memory of her wide green eyes haunted him when he stared at the ceiling on long, lonely nights. He loved the way she looked at him, as if he was someone who cared. Four months after they first met, she agreed to let him drive her home from work, but only because her car wouldn't start.

"Stop there," she said, pointing to a two-story house. Tony parked his jeep and looked past her, out the passenger window.

"Is that your house?" he asked.

"No, I live on the corner," she answered, looking up ahead.

"Then what are we doing here?" he asked, putting his hand back on the ignition key.

"No," she said, pulling his hand away from the steering column. Her soft, electric touch made him want to kiss her. Still, there was an intensity in her voice that he couldn't disregard. "I don't want them to see us."

"Why?" Tony asked. He turned toward her and looked her straight in the eye. Hard as he tried, he couldn't read her.

"My mom will just worry," she explained and bit her lower lip. "And my father, he's worse."

"Sicker, you mean?" Tony asked, hoping he was right.

"No," she answered, looking away and twisting her shirt tail into a point. "If I come home with a guy, it's just worse."

"Would it help if I went in and met him?" Tony asked, not believing the words coming out of his mouth. He was offering to meet her old man? That was rich. The last time he had lied to a girl's father to get into her pants was in high school. He hoped it was a skill you didn't forget, like riding a bike or flying a stick.

"God, no," she answered. Angela opened the door and slid away from him.

"Wait," he said, grabbing her hand.

She stood on the curb in the dark, looking at him. Fear radiated from her eyes beneath the dome light. He felt her pull away, and he relaxed his grip. Her fingers slipped from his hand. She stepped back and glanced toward the corner house. The porch light was on. Tony let out a sigh and reached for the ignition key. She surprised him by popping back into the jeep. Her peck on his cheek made him feel like some eighth grader at a dance. Before he could say anything, she left and ran all the way home.

Days later, flying, waking up, or walking across the kitchen floor, he could still put his fingertips on the exact spot on his cheek. Twice he went to the mall and watched her from the menswear department in J.C. Penney. A week passed before he asked her out for coffee again. They walked across the mall to the restaurant, and he reached for her hand. A soft palm slid against his rough skin, and he couldn't wipe the smile off his face. For no reason, he picked her up, twirled her once, set her down, and walked on, holding her hand all the way to Bumbleberry's.

To Fly Forever

IT WAS THE MIDDLE of the day, but candles glowed in amber globes around Clancy's bar. The lighting suited Tony. The old TV's snowy pictures stayed tuned to a ball game that no one watched. Bill had returned. The two friends hugged the bar, shaking for drinks and shooting the shit. Tony listened to Bill talk about the flying, the heat, and the pecan pie. His young friend had picked up the flight time he had needed.

"I decided it was time to come home," Bill said, setting down his glass and giving Tony a suspicious look. "Especially when Cindy told me that you came by her store three times in one week."

"What are you saying, bro?" Tony said, arms out, pleading innocence he could never convey, even when it was true.

"Later, she told me about Angela," Bill smiled, scrutinizing Tony's face. "I met her, and, well, she's no Della."

Tony hoped the lighting didn't reveal too much. He had taken Angela to dinner and bought her flowers. She had caused him to do things he didn't understand, and now he could only laugh about it with Bill.

"I haven't even laid her," Tony said with a groan from his bar stool beside Bill. For a moment, Tony's face dropped into the crook of his arm resting on the bar. His mass of black curls hid his eyes. A second later, he sat up straight, shaking his head and stirring his drink. "I must be losing my stuff."

"Uh-oh, the 'L' word," Bill said, still watching his friend's face.

"Not me, Billy boy," Tony said, leaning back from Bill. "Never happen."

"Never say never."

"I'm serious," Tony said, lighting a cigarette and exhaling a long, slow stream of smoke. "Long term relationships suck. They make you do crazy things."

"Like what?" Bill asked, straightening his glasses and giving Tony a funny smile. He seemed to appreciate the chance to give Tony a hard time for a change.

"Get stable. Have kids. Grow old," Tony answered, twisting the ash from the end of his cigarette against the edge of the ash tray.

"That would be crazy to you," Bill said.

"Hey, we came here to celebrate," Tony said, lifting his beer in salute. "Here's to Sonny's new helicopter and our fixed wing seats. We'll be flying together, Billy boy."

"Leave the chopper to Sonny," Bill answered, clicking his glass to Tony's. "I'll take an airplane any day. Think there's money in helicopters?"

"Money?" Tony asked and took a sip. He licked the foam from his moustache. "No, but it's the future."

"If you go down in one of those things, you go splat," Bill said, slapping a flat palm on the bar. "There's nothing between you and the ground but a piece of glass."

"Ah, but what a view!" Tony laughed.

"Spare me," Bill said with a drunken grin. "Hey, it'll be great to work together."

"I'll drink to that," Tony answered and did. Bill accompanied him, one of the few people who could keep pace with Tony when it came to drinking.

Over the next few weeks, Tony and Bill worked like dogs together every morning. Angela and Cindy joined them in what began an endless string of lazy summer afternoons. In one of the first, Tony, Angela, and Cindy sat on Tony's back porch, watching the weeds grow while Bill made a beer run.

Tony clenched a fresh cigarette between his teeth and stood to fish a lighter from his pants pocket. He pulled out his silver case Zippo with a gold Great Lakes biplane on one side.

"That's pretty," Angela said, when she spotted it. "Where did you get it?"

"From a friend," Tony answered. He handed the lighter to Angela and shot a wary glance at Cindy. His glare was meant to keep

Cindy from mentioning that it had been a gift from Della. The way he tried to hide the origins of the lighter brought a confused look to Cindy's face. Cindy knew him well enough to know that he tended to brag about his other women, even to his other women. Tony's hard look bought Cindy's silence for the moment. He thought it might. Cindy had never been able to stare into his eyes too long. She looked away and kept quiet, focusing on the lighter in Angela's hand.

"It's very nice," Angela said, handing it back to him. Her fingers skimmed his palm, and the tickling sensation thrilled him.

"Thanks," he said. He started to slip it back in his pocket and then remembered to light his cigarette.

"How did. . ." Angela started speaking in a soft voice. Tony looked down into her wide, wondering eyes. A shy smiled glowed from her face from where she sat on the step of the back porch. She gripped the bare knees below her shorts, looking small enough for him to pick her up and whisk her away. "How did you know you wanted to fly?"

"I just knew," he answered, sitting down close beside her. He wished he could explain it better. How flying let him leave all the hurt behind. How flying had saved him. If he hadn't discovered flying, he would have been robbing banks for a living. "I just knew."

Bill returned, and it was brews all around. Rock and roll thumped from the stereo. Tony doused some T-bone steaks with whiskey and pepper. He opened the latest issue of Playboy magazine and crumpled up some pages to start the coals for barbecuing. Smoke billowed from Miss July, and the beer kept flowing. Later, they used metal knives to cut through the meat that swam in red juices on doubled paper plates.

Tony picked a dark, haunting record by Melanie and turned up the volume. Her scratchy, sweet voice cut through the cool night air. It was a switch from Tony's usual pick, Marvin Gaye. Tony had finished off his sixth brew by the time the meal ended. He brought out his new .44 magnum and showed Angela the massive, black revolver with a six-inch barrel.

"I want you to cut the cherry on this for me," Tony said, dropping beside her on the ragged sofa. Bill and Cindy sat on the floor across the living room, leaning against the waterbed frame.

112

"Do what?" she asked, leaning away from the gun in Tony's hand.

"I want you to fire it first," he said and smiled.

"I've never fired a gun before," she answered, watching him stand up again.

"You're starting with the best," Tony answered, taking her hand, pulling her from the couch, and leading her out the front door. Bill and Cindy followed.

The sound of rhythmic waves lapping ashore in the distance came from the beach at the end of the block. A moonlit field of artichokes lay across the road. Tony stayed next to Angela, who looked small and uncertain in the center of the driveway. Bill and Cindy watched while Tony put the heavy pistol into her hands, stood behind her, and supported her arms. Even with his help, Angela struggled to hold the heavy weapon out straight in front of her. Tony shifted her position until she was aiming at the telephone pole at the edge of the field across the street. He felt her finger trembling on the trigger.

"Just give it a little squeeze," he whispered into her ear and watched her face.

Angela squinted, turned her face away, and pulled the trigger. The echoing blast that followed stung Tony's ears and knocked Angela backward. Tony was happy to catch her, holding her longer than necessary and hoping his smile was hidden by the darkness. She seemed to welcome his embrace, brushing her cheek against his chest. He rested his chin on her head until she regained her balance.

After Bill and Cindy left that evening, Tony sat beside Angela on the couch, holding her hand. All the lights were off, and he played one song over and over, *Candles in the Rain* by Melanie.

The last of the coals glowed in the fireplace. Tony led Angela to the big round waterbed. She started to follow him and then stopped. He looked back at her, trying to read her expression in the darkness.

"I can't," she said in a whisper. She crossed her arms, as if holding herself together. She backed away from him until her back hit the wall. She slid to the floor in a small, trembling heap. He approached her and knelt down.

"What did I do?" he asked.

"It's not you. It's my father—" She stopped talking and looked at the floor.

Tony looked around the room, almost expecting to find Angela's father standing beside him. He turned back to her and cupped her face in his hands.

"He'll never know," Tony whispered in her ear and kissed her hair.

"He did things. . ."

She didn't explain any further, but her tears did. Another man might not have understood, but Tony had been a victim too, sexual prey for his foster parents. Her inability to describe the experience told him all he needed to know. Her father had violated the sacred promise a father must never break. The bastard. For some reason, the sexual exploitation of Angela seemed worse to Tony than what his twisted foster family had done to him. After all, that man was Angela's real father. Tony had not had foster sisters, and only now did he realize what would have happened to them if he had.

"It won't be like that," he answered. He took both of her hands and stood up, rising and lifting her with him. It felt as if she didn't weigh anything at all. He kept his mouth close to her ear, her hair brushing his lips. "I swear it won't be like that."

He removed the gold chain from her delicate neck, letting it crumple on top of the speaker. She touched his lips with unsteady fingertips. He kissed them as gently as he knew how.

Her body was as light and slender as any he had ever known. A fear that he might hurt her drummed in his head. She felt his curls, and her soft touch sent electric chills through his body. He directed her hands to his shirt buttons.

Light from the moon and passing headlights seeped through the battered curtains. Tony's clothing, and then Angela's, slipped to the floor a piece at a time. He pulled her with him into the water-bed. They melted into the churning blankets as one. Tony heard the singer switch to *Carolina In My Mind*, but it sounded far away.

After months of waiting, he felt his long body against hers, and it was sweeter than he had imagined. Tony wondered if he had died and gone to heaven, or at least purgatory. His lips pressed against Angela's, and her fears appeared to slip away.

Tony slid down between her legs and felt her relax. He kissed her inner thigh, holding her hips in his hands. He felt certain that a man's warm tongue had never licked her where his did. He felt inspired to make her feel something she had never felt before. Her body grew tense just before the small moan escaped from her lips. There was something about that sound that made him grow tense as well, but she couldn't have known that. His own ghosts had followed him to the waterbed, just when hers seemed to vanish.

His movements switched from coaxing to reckless. He sucked her breasts too hard before pinning her down with his whole body. Tony slid inside her with hard, sharp movements. He didn't want to know if he hurt her. He prevented her protests, pressing his lips against hers as hard as he could. Her hands gripped his shoulders, but the gentle pressure seemed laughable to him. She was trying to push him away. He wanted her more than ever, and his need grew frantic and brutal.

She struggled beneath him, turning her head to the side.

"Don't" she said with a cry. The word cut him to his soul, and he froze.

"Did I hurt you?" he asked, placing his elbows on either side of her face so he could lean close to her.

"Yes…"

"Angela, I'm sorry," he said, brushing hair from her soft cheek. "Believe me."

"No," she said, still trying to push him away.

"It happened to me too," he said, confessing what he didn't want her to know. Yet, he thought there was an outside chance she would understand. "I was just a kid. My foster parents did it to me."

Tony could tell that she wanted to push him away. It must have been the tears in his eyes that stopped her. He couldn't say any more. He just stared at her, his eyes trying to project a blue intensity that pled for her to stay. The lyrics in the song *The Citiest People* reminded him how unkind people could be.

"I'm all right," she said in a quiet voice.

"It won't happen again, I promise." He heard himself begging, and he couldn't believe he was doing it. "Angela, don't leave me." For moment, he didn't think she believed him. Her silence was killing him.

"I won't," she answered, and he dropped his head close to hers in relief. His temple touched hers, and since he couldn't say how grateful he was, he tried to portray the thought into her mind.

"I love you," he said, and a gentle stillness engulfed him. He wasn't sure if it was true, but it was the closest thing he could think to say that might describe what he felt. The words she said back to him made him soar.

"I love you too, Tony."

That feeling stayed with him for the rest of that night. And so did Angela. The next week, Angela left her mother's house, and her dying father, and moved in with Tony. Once she was with him, he didn't want her to go anywhere without him. Somehow, it seemed, she grew more naïve despite his influence, never losing the sweetness that attracted him. He knew Angela never understood his raw sense of humor or anything about flying, but somehow, she understood him. Nothing else mattered.

One foggy morning two weeks later, Tony reported to work, half asleep. He wandered into Lopes' rat-hole office at the airstrip. Bill was already there, waiting alone inside, standing behind the beat up desk and blowing his nose.

"Close your eyes, bro," Tony said, giving him a look before flopping on the dirty couch. "You're gonna bleed to death. How much did you drink last night?"

"Hartley killed himself," Bill said in a weak voice. The man with the dried apple face was dead. It was Hartley who had taught Bill to drink and fly a bar stool, long before Tony had shown up. Still, Tony was too tired to realize the effect Hartley's passing had on Bill.

"Bullshit," Tony said, realizing too late that it wasn't. Death wasn't something Tony liked to dwell on before he was awake. Or ever, for that matter. Giving it that kind of attention would make it possible. And right now, he didn't want death to be possible.

"I wish it was bullshit," Bill said, looking at Tony with a pained expression. "He hooked a hose to his car's exhaust and put the other end in the front seat with him."

"At least he had the guts to pull the pin," Tony answered without letting his eyes meet Bill's.

"Is that all you can say?" Bill asked, staring at Tony with fire in his eyes.

116

"What do you want me to say, Billy boy?" Tony lay back, crossing his arms behind his head and crossing his boots on the arm of the couch. Poor Hartley hadn't flown in years. In Tony's mind, it must have been a relief for the old boy to start the engine of that car.

"I don't know," Bill answered, sounding frustrated. "Say something more than that. Why did he do it?"

"Why didn't he do it sooner?" Tony asked, still staring at a knot hole in the plywood ceiling.

"You're an asshole, sometimes," Bill said, stomping across the room and shoving Tony's boots off the arm of the couch. "Hartley was a hell of a guy."

"Hartley was a pilot who couldn't fly anymore," Tony answered and stood up. His face was closer to Bill's than he had intended.

"Flying isn't everything," Bill said, walking away from Tony.

"Yeah, well, it's ahead of whatever's in second place," Tony answered, taking a step in Bill's direction.

"His funeral is Tuesday," Bill said, heading toward the door. "Just graveside services, if you're interested."

"They're going to plant him?" Tony asked, moving toward the door and blocking Bill's exit.

"Of course they are."

"Shit, don't ever let them put me underground, Bill," Tony said, wincing at the thought and walking away from the door. "I'd rather be barbecued and scattered."

"Oh, really?" Bill asked with a confused look on his face. He took his time releasing the door knob and turning toward Tony. "Scattered where?"

"The local dump," Tony answered, and then turned away. He headed back toward the couch, wishing he could just drop the subject. "It doesn't matter. There isn't enough left to hit the ground if you're over 1000 feet. I used to fly for a funeral home. You just turn the plane up on one wing, stick a sack full of ashes out the window, and rip the bottom off the bag." Tony gestured to show the moves of the plane, and then the bag. "With a little prop wash, everything blows into the atmosphere, and that's where it stays. When I die, I want my ashes scattered in the air. I want to fly forever."

"Fine," Bill answered, taking a step toward Tony. "You do that. Come Tuesday, I'm going to Hartley's funeral."

"Suit yourself, Billy boy," Tony said, collapsing onto the couch. "I could never bear to watch someone stick a pilot in the ground."

"Oh, sure..."

"No, really," Tony said, struggling to explain himself. As much as he hated the subject, he didn't mean to piss Bill off. "Look, if there's some right thing to say here, I don't know what it is. I didn't know Hartley like you did. You go for both of us. No hard feelings?" He hoped that was enough. Bill stared at Tony for a moment and then looked up, as if he could see through the roof to the sky.

"Yeah, OK," Bill answered.

"Great, let me buy you a beer," Tony said, rising again.

"Tony, it's five in the morning."

"So?" Tony said and watched Bill shake his head.

"You're one of a kind, Tony—thank God."

The day of Hartley's funeral passed. Bill went, Tony didn't. Other days passed as well. The fog only seemed to grow thicker. Tony would try to fly anyway, even though the visibility made it dangerous, if not impossible. Bill would wait on the ground and accuse Tony of taking unnecessary chances. In Tony's mind, flying, particularly cropdusting, was one long string of calculated risks. He liked to think of it as 99% boredom and 1% sheer terror.

It was a pisser to wait all morning in the fog to do a spray job, only to have the sea breeze kick in when it cleared. Tony knew the spray would drift to an adjacent field when the wind blew too hard. He had even watched it lift from one field and float to the next if it was too hot. Houses on the north side of a field demanded a north wind. Sometimes that came only after dark. To make matters worse, it was all commission. No spray, no pay. It was the worst part of the business, next to not flying at all. But when it worked, it was bliss.

ONE DAY IN AUGUST, Tony and Bill were waiting by the loading pit at the strip. The chemical stench that rose from the asphalt burned Tony's nose at first, but as time passed, he noticed it less and less. He sat on a five-gallon can of Phosdrin, whittling a miniature prop out of wood. Bill leaned against the office shack, watching the wind sock sticking straight out.

"Me and Angela are getting married," Tony said to Bill, without looking up. "Want to come?"

"You?" Bill asked, almost choking. "Married? You're shitting me."

"Why not?" Tony asked, looking at Bill and raising one eyebrow. "I've done it before. It's no big deal." Had he forgotten to mention that to Bill? Oh well. . .

"No big deal?" Bill said in disbelief. "What happened last time?"

"She divorced me," Tony said with indifference. He stopped whittling and looked up. "That wasn't so bad, but two months later, she kicked me out."

"You stayed after the divorce?"

"Why not?" he asked and started whittling again. He could remember his first wife, tall, blonde, really stacked, and angry at Tony most of the time. "She was still giving it away for free."

"You're disgusting," Bill said, but laughed.

"Hey, she thought so," Tony said with a shrug. He surprised himself. He could talk about it as if it had happened to someone else. At the time, the breakup hadn't been as easy as he tried to make Bill think it had been. He hadn't wanted to be the disappointment that he had been to her. In his heart, he believed it would be different with Angela. "Anyway, that was just a court house wedding. Me, her, and the janitor for a witness. I knew it wouldn't last. Angela wants a minister. She was raised with that stuff."

"What stuff?" Bill asked, folding his arms.

"Religion," Tony answered, checking the windsock. It was still stiff.

"Oh, that stuff. What did you tell her?"

"I told her that sounded bitchin'," Tony said with a shrug.

"Bitchin'?" Bill asked with a laugh. "I doubt anyone of the cloth would marry you."

"They'll marry anyone," Tony said, smiling. He studied the new little prop, stabbed it with a pin he had found and twirled it. "It's their job."

"You should call that priest," Bill said, snatching Tony's prop away. "That Italian guy. Remember? From the flight school. What was his name?"

"Robert?" Tony asked, ignoring his missing toy for the moment. He remembered the priest, and he remembered all the horrible landings. "Hell, he's Catholic. Besides, Angela knows some lady reverend that will marry us anywhere."

"Anywhere?" Bill asked, sweeping his arm out toward the dirty airstrip. "How about here?"

"No, not here," Tony answered, giving the place a once over. "Although, it's not a bad idea."

"Geez, Tony," Bill said, rolling his eyes.

"No… we thought it would be far out to get married at Patches' cabin by the river," Tony explained, staring down the valley in the direction of Arroyo Seco. "Actually, it's Angela's idea, but she's really excited about it, so why not?"

"That's it? 'So why not?'" Bill said. He spun the pin between his flat palms, and the tiny prop sailed toward the garbage can. Tony picked it up and started whittling again. "Tony, you're acting like you're deciding whether to have meat loaf for dinner."

"Hey, as long as it makes the woman excited," Tony said, dropping his hands and looking up at Bill.

"The little woman?" Bill teased.

"Ha, right," Tony answered, laughing and pondering the notion. "The little woman."

Parish Projects

"THERE'S NOTHING SPECIAL about dying," Father Roberto said, pointing to the huge crucifix on the dark wall behind the altar. "Everyone does it."

Roberto knew warm summer days in August didn't help the crowd listen to his homily. Almost no one occupied the first three pews. Most sat further back, shushing their kids, fanning themselves with church bulletins, and planning Sunday dinner. Attendance seemed sparser than usual, or maybe that was Roberto's imagination. Less formal parishioners were evenly sprinkled among the more stiffly clothed members. The latter were the ones who gave Roberto the most grief. Their version of Catholicism included the veneration of the saints, the sanctity of the Church, and all those mysterious Latin responses that they never understood but wished were still in use.

"Jesus' death on the cross was nothing special," Roberto said. The old guard's sleepy eyes popped open, and their backs stiffened. It had not been his intention to jolt them awake, but now that he had, he continued.

"Anyone will die if he is crucified. Too often we revere the cross. It would mean nothing if Jesus hadn't risen from the dead. Mohammed claimed to be a great prophet, but he died. Jesus died, but resurrected himself. Mohammed is still a very dead man."

Cold stares mixed with whispers of nervous laughter. He turned away from the podium, and then something else came to his mind. He turned back to face the pews again.

"It did not end on Friday," Roberto said, motioning again to the crucifix. Already, he could almost imagine the light streaming in

121

through the spot where he pointed. "Sunday came. Easter Sunday. We good Catholics still hang on to Friday. We need to tear down this cross and this dark wall. We need a window here. A stained glass window showing the risen Christ. Let there be light. Let us build it together and tell the whole story."

He replaced the microphone on the altar and sat in a chair, facing the people. His hands trembled in his lap. Thirty years of delivering Sunday messages, and it still made him nervous. He regained his composure and looked up.

Fire shot from the eyes of the older parishioners. The wife of the local produce baron glared at him. The good old boys, acting as ushers, whispered in the foyer. Roberto knew they had sent one letter to the bishop about their priest's "new ideas." They were probably taking notes for another.

Roberto finished mass and exited down the center aisle. The people sang a weak recessional hymn with the obligatory two verses. Roberto positioned himself at the rear of the church, waiting for the departing congregation. Each one shook his hand and left, as if he were a chimney sweep who would bring them luck. Only the newer members gave him anything resembling a genuine smile.

Roberto knew when the real talk would start. He had worked at enough parishes to know. He hurried to remove his vestments in the rectory, then jumped into his car, wearing civilian clothes. The restaurant across town was only five minutes away. He arrived and asked for a secluded booth. At first, he was disappointed with the comments he overheard through the plants from the party seated just after him. But, after their food arrived, they started talking about him, as he had suspected they would.

"Now he wants to knock out a wall," Mrs. Hardine said between bites of scrambled egg. Earlier, in church, Roberto had seen the produce baron's wife, wearing her faded red lipstick wider than her lips and black mascara dots around her watery gray eyes. She sat next to her husband and wore a blue pillbox hat with netting that teetered on her cheap, brown wig.

"Why does he always have to change everything?" asked the husband of the other couple.

"The boys and I have tried to tell him," Bob Hardine said, sounding exasperated. He unbuttoned the jacket of his well-tailored suit coat and loosened his tie. Roberto shifted behind the plants, out of sight. "Come out to the golf course on Wednesdays, Father, and we'll talk.' Do you know what he said? 'I don't play golf. Dogs chase balls.'" Roberto chuckled to himself.

"Perhaps if he were a little older, he would understand," said the pudgy, white-haired lady across from Mrs. Hardine. Roberto could see her between two leaves. Her flower print dress strained at the blue buttons near her sagging breasts. It was probably the warm weather that left her ankles swollen, and her flushed cheeks matching her fuchsia scarf.

"He's almost 60," Mrs. Hardine said. "That just shows you how young you stay in a profession with no worries." No worries? Roberto thought. Ah, if they only knew.

"What's this Ethnic Festival he's planning?" asked the good old boy facing Hardine. Roberto wondered how he fit in the booth. His prominent stomach rubbed against the table, accented by rainbow suspenders. "What's wrong with the annual rummage sale?"

Roberto had hoped they would be more accepting of his latest proposal. He was sick of church rummage sales. Everyone always donated the trash they didn't want and wouldn't help haul it away when it didn't sell.

"It's a lot of work for you—" the fat man's wife started.

"He has some grand notion of uniting the parish," Hardine answered. "As if *we* are going to socialize with the Mexicans."

"Not after what happened to Esther Beabot," the baron's wife said, dropping her fork. "It was cold blooded murder, and it makes me sick to even think about it."

Not Beabot again. Roberto wondered if people talked as much about her when she was alive. Now, according to everyone, she had been a saint. He wanted them to say more about the stained glass window.

"When is this festival anyway?" Hardine asked.

"The third Sunday in April," the man in suspenders said. "Same weekend I always hold the rummage sale."

"I think the Catholic Men's League might just sponsor a barbecue at the fairgrounds that weekend," Hardine said, looking around for confirmation of his brilliant idea. "We'll just see how successful his new idea is."

Roberto listened for a while longer, but they were on to talking about the new grocery store in town. He was disappointed that they were planning to subvert his Ethnic Festival, but he wasn't surprised. Maybe prayer would change their hearts, but he wasn't about to put money on it.

Roberto had to wait for them to leave before he could go. Back at the rectory, he carried the Sunday paper from the kitchen to the living room. Father Carlo rushed past him in the hall, almost dragging the wheels of his toy cannon over Roberto's stocking feet. Carlo parked the weapon by the front door and hurried out, carrying freshly ironed vestments. The funny little man was late for the noontime Spanish mass. Roberto stared after him and shook his head. It was time for Roberto to read himself to sleep. He headed for the recliner in the living room, took a seat, and opened the paper to see the headline.

BEABOT FAMILY DEMANDS
DEATH PENALTY FOR MENDOZA

Salinas' daily paper had just destroyed Roberto's plans for a peaceful nap. A cold sweat made him unable to focus on the details of the article. He recalled Maria Consalvo's confession about the bloody screwdriver in her brother Hector's closet. He threw the paper aside and decided to take a walk. The weather was warm, and he had only reached the corner of the church before a hushed conversation stopped him.

As usual, the Spanish mass overflowed out the church door. Roberto caught a glimpse of the young men lurking at the edges of the crowd. They wore white shirts and dark slacks. Their wet-combed black hair and their black boots shone in the fierce, noonday sun. They mentioned the death penalty, and he darted back behind the wall, out of sight on the cool, shady side of the building

Their attitude toward mass always amazed Roberto. It didn't seem to matter if they were inside or out, whether they heard the words of the priest or not. They were within ten feet of the church entrance for the majority of the mass. Roberto could almost follow their logic. Surely God knew all the pews were full, the heat was stifling, and Father Carlo was impossible to understand.

"They should have arrested that Anglo for killing Hector," Roberto heard an angry young man say in a whisper to his four friends. Roberto could look at the reflection from the window of a parked car in front of the church and see who was talking. He was close enough to smell the cigarette the speaker had lit. The young man leaned against the bright church wall and puffed his cigarette, switching from English to Spanish and back. "Hector was a cholo but a right-on dude."

"What was Hector doing that night?" the young Latino with the bolo tie asked the smoker. Roberto was relieved. At least they weren't talking about poor Esther Beabot. However, he wondered if they knew the truth about Hector.

"Hector was drunk and went to the wrong door," the smoker answered. "He wasn't doing nothing. Get drunk and die in this town. The pigs won't bother to write it down."

"They got Raoul Mendoza pretty fast," the tallest one said, jamming his hands in his pockets. "I hear he's getting the chair."

"Maybe not," the youngest one said. Roberto worried about the hope he heard in the young man's voice. Prospects weren't good for Mendoza. The young men might not know how angry the white parishioners, and the Baptists, were with Beabot's suspected rapist and murderer. But Roberto knew too well. "His trial starts tomorrow."

"You know he's going to die for it," the angry one said, tossing away his lit cigarette.

"Did Mendoza do it?" the youngest asked.

"I don't know," the tall one said. "My friend's sister says she was with him the night they say he killed the old lady." Roberto's hopes for an alibi for Mendoza rose, then fell. "But Blanca can't say nothing because she wasn't supposed to be with him. Her quinceañera isn't until next week."

"He didn't do it?" the young one asked. Roberto could hear the hope fading in his voice. "But why did they arrest him?"

"I don't know, man," the tall one answered. "Mendoza's a head. Maybe he was loaded. I don't know what he did."

"Two Mexicans got to die just because somebody robbed an old white lady," the angry one said. "That's a bunch of—"

"Sh-h-h," the one closest to the door said. "Communion. Come on." Roberto watched their reflection. The one guarding the door motioned for the others to follow him. They fell into a sloppy line that went nowhere for a few minutes. Roberto could see them standing tiptoed, trying to catch a glimpse of Father Carlo behind the altar rail.

"Are you going to the fiesta?" the tall one asked the others. Roberto was about to walk away but waited to hear the answer.

"I don't know," the angry one answered. "Are you?"

"Father said we should," the youngest said. Roberto frowned, wishing the young man might attend for a better reason. "Maybe I am. I guess so." The line moved forward a little, and the youngest one turned to the tall one behind him. "Are you?"

"I don't know . . ."

"I think I will," the one with the bolo tie said. "Do you know if it is true that they're taking down the cross behind the altar and making a stained glass window there?" Now they had Roberto's attention. He wished he could put his faith in the younger members of the parish, but they couldn't afford to tithe.

"That's what Father says," the one who had stood guard said.

"Anglos," the angry one said, shaking his head. "They do what they want to our church and never ask us." Their reflection showed them inching through the doorway and out of earshot. Roberto shook his head and walked away.

After the Spanish mass ended, Roberto headed into the church for a silent prayer. He had overheard too much. Sister Mary Teresa knelt in the first pew, her thick black hair hanging below the dark head covering of her habit. She had stayed to say a rosary after mass had ended. Roberto could imagine she would have been a pretty girl, but unlike him, she never wore street clothes. She was always clothed in her order's plain white blouse and navy blue skirt, both of which hung like sacks on her small frame.

Sister Mary Teresa always seemed to be in a hurry. She had described to Roberto how she had left her native India in a hurry, and that she felt she had been hurrying ever since. Despite all her rushing, he had noticed that she never failed to stop and talk with the children. He wondered how she liked King City. She was only 24, and it was the end of her third week living alone in the two-story convent beside the church. The museum of a building had once housed a dozen sisters who taught at the church's now defunct school. Sister Mary Teresa alone was now charged with organizing the children's weekly religious instruction.

Father Roberto left her to finish her rosary. He returned to the rectory and the newspaper he had tossed aside earlier. He had only opened it to page two before he heard the sister's voice.

"Father Roberto, Father Roberto," she called through the mail slot. "I need to talk to you."

Roberto dropped the newspaper on the floor to answer her call. He opened the door a fraction, and she breezed past him into the living room. Her long black hair beneath her head covering swirled behind her. A white headband framed her dark face, seeming so full of questions and seeking answers. Roberto knew he should have those answers but probably wouldn't. He could almost imagine a jewel hanging between her dark, fiery eyes.

"Have you made a decision?" she asked, speaking in a crisp, flat voice. Never pausing for a moment, she plucked his newspaper from the dark rug and folded it. He could almost feel her eyes scouring the plain room for flaws she could fix. The afghan was folded crooked. Books had been left stacked in an uneven pile on the end table. The window to the backyard needed cleaning. She had probably noticed it all.

"Decision about what?" he asked, eyeing the headline. At least she couldn't know about that.

"Lord, give me patience," she said, her black eyes scouring the ceiling. "The books. Catechism classes start next week. You said you would order the texts. Please don't tell me you forgot."

"Mama mia . . ."

"You forgot," she said, flapping the paper against her thigh in frustration.

"No, no, no," he said in three quick beats. "I remembered. I forgot to pick them up from the book store in Salinas. I'll get them this week."

"Tomorrow, you mean?" she said, folding her arms.

"Why tomorrow?" he asked. He didn't mind her rushing around, if that's how she wanted to live her life. He wasn't interested in being forced to live his the same way. There were other things on his mind. "Monday is my day off."

"You scheduled the catechism instructors' meeting for Tuesday."

"Oh, hell." He turned in a circle, then faced her again.

"Bless you, Father," she said, forgiving his swearing. "I will go. The bus leaves here at 9:00—"

"You can't haul books back on a bus," he answered.

"I can and I will."

"No, no, I'll do it." He changed to his priest-in-command voice, the one used to show that a parish problem had been solved, and an unquestionable decision had been made.

"You won't forget?" she asked, ignoring his tone of voice.

"Of course not," he snapped back.

"Do you feel well, Father?" she asked, her dark eyes zooming in on him. "You look, I don't know, a little pale. You are trying to do too much." She shook the newspaper at him for emphasis.

"I don't think so," he said, taking the paper from her. He placed it, headline down, on the monstrous Motorola TV. "I'm just worried . . . about the window. It needs to be done. The sooner, the better. It will build a sense of community in the parish."

"But Father, it's a lot of money. Nearly two-thirds of our annual budget."

"I can just see it," he said, looking out the dirty window. "It faces east to catch the morning sun. For evening masses, we'll have a spotlight outside."

"You must give the people a chance to adjust—"

"Time to reconsider, you mean." His humor wasn't improving.

"Time to raise money," she said, showing her practical side. She counted out her points on her fingers. "To decide on a design, find a builder, and get permits before—"

"Permits? Builders? Nonsense," he said, tapping his temple. "I know exactly what it will look like. Christ on Easter, rising on the hand of God."

"Father, I know what it is to have a vision," she answered, and her insight stopped him cold. "I know how hard it is to wait when working for the glory of God."

"If I wait for everyone to agree, nothing will ever get done," he said, throwing his hands in the air.

"Don't bulldoze your way through, Father," she warned, stooping to pick up a piece of lint from the floor and rising again. "Let the people help. Give them a chance to love you."

"This isn't a popularity contest," he said, walking away and keeping his back to her.

"I think you enjoy rejection," she said, and he could tell she had folded her arms by the tone of her voice. He turned to look, and sure enough.

"Maybe I'm used to it. My mother—" He stopped before sharing how his sister died, and how his mother pushed him away. His hands dropped into his pockets. "My mother had many children. I am the oldest. I'm used to acting on my own."

"You don't have to be alone," she answered. "Remember, this is a community builder." Her intuition unearthed the heart of the matter. She had done it with him before, and it was a trait of hers he found very unnerving.

"I'll get those books tomorrow in time for the meeting," he said, walking toward the front door and holding it open.

"Thank you, Father," she answered. She exited in a flurry, just the way she had entered, but paused on the front step. "I'll be around if you need help."

"I'll manage," he said, shutting the door without saying good-bye.

What God Has
Joined Together . . .

In ROBERTO'S DREAM, he was standing in front of a church full of people. Sister Mary Teresa stood in the side aisle, holding a sword. When she approached him, he noticed he too had a sword. She took his hand and led him away from the altar without saying a word. The people stared, watching them walk together to the side exit and out of the church. Roberto followed her to the rectory and down the long, barren hallway to his room.

They were both naked. He lay face down on the bed, and she stretched out on top of him, face down as well. Why couldn't he feel her breasts pressing against his back? Her arms and legs fit his body like a shadow. Her hands touched his, and an electrifying sensation streamed from her palms. The next instant, they had dressed and returned to the church where everyone had waited for them. He felt unclean lifting the host and blessing it for Holy Communion. A bell rang, like in the pre-Vatican II days, announcing the moment when the bread became the body of Christ.

He woke up. It was the middle of the night, and the phone was ringing. Father Carlo was supposed to take the emergencies, so Roberto let it continue to ring. The dream seemed too real to ignore. He realized he had had a spiritual joining experience with Sister Mary Teresa, even though he was sure he didn't like her. He was still half asleep, and the phone continued ringing.

"Carlo! Carlo!" he said, rolling out of bed and stepping into his office across the hall. "Hello," he said, mumbling into the heavy receiver. The glowing hands of the desk clock both pointed straight up.

"Is this a priest?" The desperate voice sounded deep and southern, maybe that of a black man. "I need a Catholic priest." Roberto's experience reminded him that people had a tendency to die at the least convenient times of the night. "You a priest?"

"I am Father Roberto," he answered, looking toward the dark hall for Carlo and hearing nothing.

"I need you to come to—"

"Now?" Roberto asked, rubbing his eyes.

"Right now," the voice answered in a quick tone. "It's one of the prisoners. He's going berserk and screaming for a priest. You got to come."

"Where are you?" he asked, fumbling with the switch of the desk lamp and reaching for a pencil.

"The county jail in Salinas," the man's voice answered. "They want the death sentence for him, and he's like to go bananas."

"Who is it?" Roberto asked and hoped he didn't know the answer.

"Mendoza is his last name. I don't know his first. You see, they brought him here . . ."

Father Roberto dropped his pencil. The man kept talking, but Roberto didn't hear him. He was paralyzed by what he had learned in Maria Consalvo's confession. Roberto couldn't involve himself. He knew too much. Carlo would have to go.

". . . so you got to come right now. Hello? Hello?"

"Yes," Roberto said in a weak voice. "Fine, fine. We'll send someone right away." Roberto dropped the receiver on to the cradle and stepped back from it. He raced to Carlo's room, flipping on lights along the way.

"Carlo?"

He opened the door and hit the light switch. The bed hadn't been slept in.

"Carlo?" he said, backing away.

The bathroom and living room were both empty. He rushed down the hallway and through the kitchen, dreading the worst. The door to the garage was ajar, and Carlo's car was gone. A map of San Francisco lay open on the kitchen table.

Roberto waited for half an hour, pacing and hoping Carlo would return. The drive to the jail took him another hour. He couldn't concentrate enough to pray very well on the way. How could he face Mendoza? He knew he wasn't the murderer. His dream about Sister Mary Teresa annoyed him. What power did she give him? Were they joining or was it all one big sin? Did she know Hector Consalvo was the real murderer? By the time he reached the guard house, he was blaming his mother. She had forced him to be a priest.

"I'm Father Roberto Ferentini," he said to the sentry after rolling down his car window. "I received a call—"

"Where you been, man?" asked the uniformed man.

"It's a long drive—"

"Go on up to the main office," the officer said, pointing to a three-story building glowing in the distance. "A sergeant will meet you there. Hurry. That boy's half-crazy. You're a priest. Maybe you can do something with him."

Once inside, heavy metal doors slammed shut behind Roberto. He followed the wide, square back of a uniformed officer down endless, silent hallways to the infirmary. The sound of their footsteps echoed from well waxed floors. The guard spoke, and his voice startled Roberto.

"Let me tell you," the guard said and inserted his key in the door. His tired brown face turned toward Roberto. "When this boy gets mad, the gophers hide."

Before he finished, Roberto could hear muffled shouts from the opposite end of the long room they were just entering. His escort crossed the room and unlocked the far door. Roberto heard Mendoza raging, sounding louder now that the door between them was open.

"Jesus, I don't want to die. Don't let me die. . ."

"Don't worry about going in," the officer said, standing at the door. "He's tied down good. Has been for hours. I'll go in with you, if you like. Of course, as soon as he sees my uniform, he'll get worse. I guarantee it."

"Perhaps I need to go in alone," Roberto said, wishing it wasn't true. He crossed the room with reluctance and eyed the doorway before entering.

"Fine, but I can't let you take those with you," the officer said, eyeing Roberto's rosary and Bible.

"But—"

"Sorry. County regulations. When you're ready to leave, just press the call button beside the door."

Roberto surrendered his blessed goods and stepped into a hospital-like room. The cold floor had alternating black and white squares of shiny linoleum, and the windows were barred against the night. The stale smell of perspiration and antiseptic hung in the air. Mendoza writhed on the only bed in the room, testing his restraints. He kept yelling as if he didn't know that Roberto, a priest, had entered the room.

"Let me go. Let me go. I never killed her. It's a mistake. I can prove it. Get this shit off of me. I never killed no—"

Mendoza stopped and stared at Roberto. The small young man had copper hair and two amateur tattoos on his face. One was a small cross, obscured by the young man's sparse goatee, and the other a teardrop near the corner of his right eye. Professional ink drawings of dragons and hearts stained his bare arms and chest. His clear, burning glare cut through Roberto, rising goose bumps on the priest's arms under his coat. After a cold, silent moment, Mendoza started screaming again, acting as if he never saw Roberto.

"God strike my baby daughter dead if I'm lying. I didn't do it. I never killed her."

"I believe you," Roberto said. His own voice sounded uncertain and weak, as if the words didn't want to leave him. He tried again. "I believe you."

"God take my newborn baby daughter," Mendoza continued yelling, ignoring Roberto's presence. "I swear by the Father, the Son, and the Holy Spirit that I never touched her. God strike me dead right now if I am lying—" The veins were bulging in Mendoza's neck and forehead.

"I know the truth," Roberto said, standing against the wall just inside the room. "I know you are innocent." Mendoza's first name jumped out at Roberto from the medical chart in a rack on the back of the door. "I'll listen, Raoul."

"No one listens," Mendoza said in a calm voice, then began yelling again. "They think I'm a murderer. I never killed her. I never went to that house."

"I know, I know," Roberto said, his palms pushing the air in front of him, face down. "Listen to me. I know you're innocent. God knows the truth—"

"I swear on my mother's grave," Mendoza screamed.

"It's a sin to swear," Roberto said, speaking in his rapid fire manner and taking a step toward the bed. Mendoza stopped ranting, turned his head, and stared straight through Roberto. The prisoner spoke to Roberto in a quiet, icy voice.

"It's a sin to hold an innocent man in prison," the restrained man answered. He enunciated each word, and his sudden calmness surprised Roberto.

"I realize it's wrong—" Roberto started, taking another step forward.

"I'm in jail for murder, and you tell me not to swear?" Mendoza said, still speaking in a soft voice, followed by a small chuckle. His odd mood swings convinced Roberto that the prisoner must be crazy. "You guys are all alike," Mendoza said in a normal voice, before returning to the raving man he had been before. "Even a priest of God doesn't believe me."

"But, I do—" Roberto said, walking to the young man's bedside.

"I never did it." Mendoza continued his rant. "I never killed her. I don't want to die."

"Raoul," Roberto said, raising his voice. "Raoul, I believe you."

"Let me go. Let me go. Get me out. Let me go."

Roberto felt helpless. He knelt on the cold linoleum and prayed while Mendoza continued yelling. When Roberto finished, he rose and removed a vial of holy water from his pocket. He approached the bed to anoint the young man's forehead. Mendoza threw his head from side to side, making Roberto's attempts impossible.

"I got to get out of here. They want to kill me. I never killed that old lady. I never went near her house or touched . . ."

Mendoza's screams continued. Roberto crossed the room and pressed the call button. He waited for the officer to arrive and wondered how he would have handled the situation if he had not heard Maria's confession. The officer arrived and escorted Roberto to the main gate. Walking alone, he passed through pools of light beneath isolated street lamps in the empty parking lot.

Once behind the steering wheel, he remained parked and stared straight ahead. The night was almost over. It was pointless to go back to King City. He would just have to turn around and drive back to Salinas for the catechism textbooks.

"Why, God?" he said in a whisper. "Why?" No answer came.

Roberto slumped against the driver's door in tears, closing his eyes and praying. He began to doubt his ability to keep the sanctity of the confessional that he had sworn to keep. If only Carlo could have come tonight, instead of him. If only a thousand things had happened. If only he hadn't been sent to King City. If only he had stayed at his last assignment. He had liked it there. He almost felt he had fit in. And even if he hadn't, he had had extra time to pursue something he had always wanted to try. Flying. If only he had been any good at it. Too bad he couldn't be more like his instructor, Tony, and know nothing about God, or Catholicism. No, his circumstances could never be that bad. At least, if all else failed, he knew there was a force wiser and stronger who could guide him. If only he could hear Him. Roberto tried to quiet his mind and just listen. After a while, he fell asleep.

Roberto woke feeling foolish and rumpled. The morning shift was arriving for work at the facility. He drove off in search of a donut shop where he could wait and drink coffee until the bookstore opened.

The Christian bookstore where Roberto had ordered the catechism texts sat between an all-night laundry and a liquor store. The bookstore opened at 9:00 a.m. The liquor store opened at 8:00.

Roberto stepped from his car, tired and preoccupied, and started toward the bookstore in a daze. He nearly walked smack into a tall man with dark, curly hair who was sauntering out of the liquor store. Roberto side-stepped the young man with two 12-packs of beer.

"Robert?"

Roberto looked back at the familiar face in unfamiliar surroundings.

"You don't remember me, do you?" Tony stood before him, wild haired, smelling of beer with a cigarette dancing beneath his moustache as he spoke.

TONY COULD TELL the exact moment when Robert remembered him. A winsome flash of recognition came over the priest's face.

"Tony?" Robert said. "Tony, how are you?"

"Couldn't be better," Tony said, throwing the beer into his Jeep. He opened one package and removed two cans. "You don't look so hot though. Sure I can't offer you a cold one?"

"No, thank you," the priest answered, shaking his head. "Really."

"Suit yourself."

Tony popped open one can and lifted his brew in salute to Robert before his first sip. Their reflection in the store window made an odd picture, even to Tony. He couldn't believe he was standing and talking with a priest in a collar in front of a Christian bookstore. Even odder, the priest was talking back to him, a guy in a Levi jacket having a beer for breakfast. Tony leaned against the fender of his jeep and rested his beer on the tire attached to the hood.

"Isn't it a little early?" Robert asked, nodding at the beer.

"You told me that you drink wine at 7:00 every morning," Tony countered and raised an eyebrow. "That must be the only good part about being a priest."

"That's not the same thing," Robert protested. He must have known it was pointless.

"Isn't it?" Tony asked after sucking foam from his moustache. "Maybe not. I ought the make you have one anyway. It's a special occasion."

Tony saw a look come across Robert's face, as if he were about to reprimand him. The look only made Tony's grin grow wider. Robert's face relaxed, and Tony knew that look too. He had seen it from almost every authority figure he had ever known. It was the look of resignation that always followed all efforts to "straighten him out."

"Special occasion? What special occasion?" Robert asked in his rapid fire form.

"I'm taking the plunge," Tony said. He realized the priest didn't catch his drift because Robert didn't congratulate him. "I'm getting married today."

"In a church?" Robert asked.

"In a church?" Tony said, mimicking him. He looked around the empty parking lot. "Listen to this guy."

"I just mean—"

"Jesus, don't you guys ever take a day off?" Tony asked, shaking his head. "No, not in a church. In Arroyo Seco." Tony nodded in what he thought was the cabin's general direction.

"Where?" Robert asked, looking at Tony and squinting from the sun. Tony stepped to one side, blocking the sun from the priest's face.

"I have a buddy with a cabin on the Arroyo Seco River," Tony said, taking a sip and remembering again what he was about to do. It made him smile to think of it. "Angela, the Mrs.-to-be, wants to get married outdoors."

"Angela?" Robert asked, leaning back against the fender of his car. "Is she Italian?"

"Not like you," Tony answered and laughed. "You might be relieved to know we are being married by a real you-know-what. Minister, I think."

"Not a Catholic wedding, huh?" Robert said, teasing him. "Too bad. A blessing will help. I'll say a prayer."

"You guys don't have a quota, do you?" Tony asked, standing up and taking his beer from its resting place.

"A quota?"

"Yeah. I mean, are you supposed to marry like so many people a month or something?"

"Not exactly—" Robert said, shaking his head.

"We could have you do it instead, if you're short this month," Tony said. He hoped Angela wouldn't blow it if Roberto happened to say yes. "I don't see what difference it would make."

"Not much," Robert answered with a smile. "Tell me, do you still fly?"

"Do I still breathe, you mean?" Tony answered, surprised the man had to ask. "Of course. I could never stop flying. I got a dusting job just after you. . ." Tony couldn't bring himself to say the word 'quit.' "Have you been flying?"

"Me?" the priest answered. "No, no, no. No time." It sounded like a lie to Tony's ear. But then, his hearing wasn't what it used to be.

"Busy, huh?" Tony said, then paused. "Too bad. If you're ever out by the airport, maybe we should go up again. Maybe." Tony regretted the words streaming out of his mouth

"I don't think so," Robert answered, and Tony felt a sense of relief. "I see cropdusters working every morning near King City. I'm happy just to watch."

"Really?"

"Yes," the priest assured him. "I remember what it feels like."

"You do?"

"Yes. Like making love," Robert answered with a smile.

"With a beautiful woman," Tony said, raising an eyebrow at the spunky little man.

"Your Angela, is she beautiful?"

"Yeah," he answered in a soft voice before opening his car door. He glanced from his wristwatch to the beer in his Jeep. "I better go or there won't be any refreshments at the reception."

"I wish you all the best," Robert said, pushing away from the car and offering his hand to Tony. His extended arm caught Tony off guard, and he paused a moment before shaking it. He let go too soon and turned toward his jeep.

"I'll need all the help I can get," Tony said, hopping into the driver's seat with a stiff leg. "So will my old lady. Look what she's getting." He spread his arms out wide behind the steering wheel with a fresh cigarette pinched in his white teeth.

"God's creation," Robert said.

"More like a free sample," Tony answered, starting his car. "Ciao, Robert." He threw it into reverse, gave a reckless wave, and roared away.

The Wedding

"I WAS CRAZY to agree to this," Tony said. He sat in the back seat of Bill's maroon Mustang with his bride-to-be. Bill and Cindy sat up front. Tony and Angela weren't feeling any pain. It was Cindy's idea that Bill, seeming the most sober, should drive them all to Arroyo Seco for the ceremony. Tony began having second thoughts before they passed the SeaMist Diner in Castroville. Ten minutes later, driving through the city of Salinas, Angela began to worry out loud.

"Maybe we are making a mistake," she said. Her index finger went to her mouth, but the nail was gone already. "We should have waited."

"Why does a minister have to do it" Tony asked. "It's not an exorcism." Tony's eyes locked on to the court house they were passing, and he pointed at it. "Bill, let's stop here. Look, there's a parking place."

"If you didn't want a minister, you should have said something sooner," Angela said, folding her arms.

"Get off my case," he answered. One look at her pretty face and his voice softened. "I want to do it."

"Yeah, I can tell," she said, almost in tears.

"Stop it, you two," Cindy said from the front seat. "It will all be fine."

Angela had invited all of her people to the wedding. It had been just three weeks since her father's funeral. Tony was surprised when her mother accepted, and when none of her other relatives did. He had invited none of his family, but Angela had sent invitations to his two foster brothers.

"I'm just so nervous," Angela said. "Everyone will be there. I'm afraid—"

"You invited *everyone*," Tony said. He dreaded seeing those two idiots again.

"I had to," Angela told him. "It's a wedding."

"You didn't *have* to invite my side," Tony said, pointing to himself.

"Of course I did," she said. "What if they found out?"

"We aren't that kind of family," Tony said. "I haven't seen Rusty in a decade. For Ray, it's been longer."

"What if they don't like me?" Angela asked and looked at Tony with a frightened gaze. He still couldn't resist those eyes, sparkling like a child's even when she worried.

"I don't like *them*," Tony answered. "So don't worry about it."

The Mustang followed the river down the valley, and they continued bickering. Thirty minutes later, they entered the dry foothills dotted with orange poppies, scrub oak, and cattle.

"Aren't you nervous at all?" Angela asked Tony, sounding hurt.

"Of course I'm nervous," he answered and leaned forward to tap Bill's shoulder. "Stop the car, Billy boy, and I'll get another brew from the trunk."

"No more until after the wedding," Bill answered. "We have to save what's left for the guests."

"Fuck the guests," Tony said, looking back at the trunk.

"Well, thanks a lot," Cindy said.

"Not you," Tony said. He was wishing he had bought an extra 12-pack for himself. He was pretty sure he was going to need it. "I mean, the hell with the other guests, if they can't enjoy a good party."

It seemed to Tony as if his nonchalant attitude was beginning to rub off on Angela. Even his worries faded away on the winding road to the hidden canyon. Marriage, ministers, and relatives didn't matter anymore to him. He was with a beautiful woman. Bill negotiated the deep ruts of the dirt road down to their destination. Tony was glad he wasn't driving. The bumps and groaning sound of the shocks stopped when they dead-ended at Patches' redwood cabin with the river rock base. The limb of a big sycamore still grew through one wall and out of the roof. The car rolled to a stop.

"I'm sorry I invited them," Angela said to Tony.

Tony wrapped his big arms around her, smothering her with kisses until she begged him to stop. He bolted from the back seat and stared straight up. He could feel the sun reflecting off the lenses of his black sunglasses, and he spread his arms out wide.

"Now this," he said, "is marrying weather."

"Let me show you where we should do it," Angela said, leaving the car and pulling Tony by the hand toward the creek.

"I'll do it anywhere with you," he said. He slipped his arms around her, pressing her back to his chest and kissing the back of her neck.

"I mean the wedding, Tony."

"Oh," Tony said, trying to sound disappointed. "Oh, well, OK."

Angela led them all down the sandy trail to a clearing ringed with sycamores and wild yellow mustard plants near the river's edge. Rushing water slipped over moss covered boulders near the canyon wall. Tony looked up, trying to see the woodpecker that drummed away in the highest tree beneath a powder blue sky. Angela, dragging him by one hand, pulled him to a wide, sandy spot by the water.

"Do you like it?" she asked, watching Tony's face.

"It's perfect," he answered in a quiet voice.

"The minister can stand on this big flat rock," she said, stepping on the boulder.

"Fine," he said, watching her childlike face grow bright with excitement. He was attempting to kiss her again when an approaching car drowned out the woodpecker.

"It might be the reverend," Angela said. She pulled away from Tony, leaving him puckered and off balance. "I have to change my clothes. Help me, Cindy."

"Of course," Cindy answered, starting to follow Angela and then looking back. "Bill, Tony, be sure to show the reverend the spot." Both women headed toward the cabin with Cindy talking a blue streak. "Have you got something old, something new, something borrowed—"

"Earrings!" Angela said, smacking her forehead. "I forgot earrings."

"Use mine," Cindy said, pulling them off and disappearing up the trail behind Angela.

"I don't have anything blue either."

Tony heard Angela's voice floating back toward the river. Both ladies were out of sight, but Tony could still hear their flurry of chatter. Bill and Tony began laughing at the girls before they were out of earshot.

The guests arrived in twos and threes, except Angela's mother, who came alone. Tony grew more anxious, pacing in front of the cabin and trying to stay out of the beer. His nerves were shot by the time the reverend was ready, a sturdy lady with short, short hair from an Episcopal church in King City.

Tony's brother Ray, tall, dark, and gay, arrived from San Francisco with his boyfriend. That was not at all how Tony remembered him. Tony's other brother, Rusty, arrived wearing a Panama hat and a muscle shirt with his girlfriend on his arm. He was tall too, but had sandy hair, which Tony didn't really remember either. They could have been two strangers. In fact, they were. He asked Rusty what he did for a living, and if he still lived in the Central Valley. His answer was short. 'No, I live in L.A. and sell drugs.' Tony nodded, not sure what to say. But he worked to smooth out their stilted conversation and found he liked them both more than he had thought he would.

Patches came too, since it was his cabin, and because Tony was thankful that he had been kind enough to stash the "stolen" motorcycle in his barn for the last year. Two loaders from Lopes Air Care and their girlfriends came for the beer. Some people from the cabin up the road wandered down to see what was going on. A fellow who no one knew showed up. He told great jokes, and the beer was plentiful so Tony wasn't worried. Total present and waiting for the ceremony to begin: 16 people and one Samoyed dog.

Tony was trying to sneak a beer from the ice chest when Cindy peeked out the cabin door. She instructed Bill to take Tony down to the river. The motley crowd followed them. Tony stood on the spot where the reverend directed from her perch on the rock. His hands started to sweat. He glanced up the path and waited. It took an eternity for Angela to come over the rise.

She had to be walking toward the clearing, but trees hid her from everyone's view, including Tony's. He waited at the end of the sandy path by the lady reverend in her flowery vestments. His eyes strained to catch a glimpse of Angela, watching the smiling faces of others who now could see her before he could. She came around the corner and down the path. Tony felt a hopeless smile cover his face. He knew it wouldn't go away no matter what he did, so he didn't even try.

Angela stepped into the sunshine in a long dress, looking like she just had walked out of a southern mansion. Tony noticed that the bouquet in her hands shook from nerves. But, damn, she was beautiful. A delicate orange ribbon was laced at her breasts beneath the square neckline of her cream colored dress. The orange velvet choker around her slender neck bore an ivory cameo. Sandy-colored hair peaked out in wisps beneath the wide brim of her translucent orange hat. The matching ribbon around its brim trailed down her back, and the train of her dress slid over the sand behind her.

To Tony, her approach seemed like that of a doe, hushed and graceful with wide, timid eyes. Her dress and hat dipped and floated with each step. The fluttering green of the sycamore leaves, the whisper of the river, and the lightness of her beauty burned into his memory. Tony knew then that drugs, time, and death could never erase that moment. He watched himself take her arm like a gentleman and guide her the last few steps. Robert's words echoed in his head.

"They hardly seem to walk at all. Just glide, like swans on water. The groom takes her arm, and they move toward me like one person."

Tony knew the wedding was not a mistake. Joy seized his heart and sent it soaring up past the upper most leaves of the trees and beyond the canyon walls. The reverend spoke, beginning the service, and Tony had the urge to tell her to shut up.

"Do you . . ." said a voice from somewhere. It floated to Tony's ears, and he responded.

"I do," Tony said.

"And do you . . ."

"I do," Angela said.

It proved difficult for him to slip the ring on Angela's trembling hand. When it was his turn, he had to steady her hand while she put the ring on his finger.

"What God has joined together . . ."

'Joined.' Robert talked about joining. Tony wondered if he was joining now with Angela. He felt a rush as if he were flying fast and low. It was nothing he remembered feeling at his first wedding.

"You may now—"

Tony didn't wait for permission. He took Angela into his arms and kissed her, long and deep. He was all that was holding her up, but it didn't bother him. He was willing to hold her up for the rest of his life.

And then it was over. They all walked back up the path to the cabin. The reception had started, but the dreamlike sensation of joining stayed with Tony for the rest of the day. There were lots of pictures and congratulations. In time, Tony found himself sitting on the front porch next to Bill, leaning against the river rock base of the cabin.

"Gimme a cigarette, Billy," Tony said. He stared up at the tree branch growing through the front wall. Bill lit two, passed one to Tony, and then laughed at the dazed look on his friend's face.

"The 'L' word," Bill said.

Tony could only look at his friend and laugh. It was undeniable. He spread his fingers wide on his left hand and stared down at the ring.

"Will you look at that shit?" Tony asked with the fresh cigarette clenched in his teeth.

"I don't believe you," Bill said, laughing at the grin on Tony's face.

"Hey, you're next, Billy boy. You're next."

TWO MONTHS LATER, Tony and Angela got a dog. Three months later, Bill and Cindy were tying the knot. They asked Tony to be their best man and Angela their matron of honor. During the wedding rehearsal at the redwood chapel near Cindy's parents' home, Angela's nervousness surfaced again, worse than ever. She had to lead the wedding procession down the center aisle, but she struggled to walk a straight line. The priest noticed her trouble and pointed out the center line where the two pieces of carpeting met. He asked her to follow that line, but she still had difficulty. As much as Tony tried to help her, it was useless.

Later that night, Tony welcomed his obligation to throw Bill's bachelor party at his house. He tried to find nude dancers or some girl to pop out of a cake, but they weren't readily accessible in Castroville. He settled for lots of booze and some borrowed porno movies.

Only Patches and a few of the guys from work showed up. After a few brews, they weren't even all that disappointed that the movies kept breaking. Bill spliced the film with adhesive tape, and Tony fooled with the projector while the guys made hand shadows on the screen. In the end, it wasn't worth the hassle. They all took turns holding the film up to a light bulb before giving up altogether.

By midnight, Tony noticed that everybody was pretty far gone. He stepped up on the raised hearth by his waterbed in the living room and delivered a toast to the groom.

"Here's to you, Billy boy," Tony said, gripping his beer can for stability. The more coherent guests gave a half-ass cheer. "It's a shame, but it happens to the best of us. And the worst of us," he said, pointing his beer can at himself. "Let me give you the same advice my old man gave me before I got married."

"Your old man wasn't even there," Bill said, half-seated, half-laying on the couch.

"Not this time," Tony said, protesting the interruption by waving his beer back and forth. "The other time. It was one of the six times in my life that I saw him."

"Must have been real good advice," Bill said, considering a sip from his beer, then putting it down.

"Here's what Old Dad told me," Tony started, wavering on the hearth. "'Son, show me a man who doesn't beat his wife or jack off his dog, and I'll steal them both.'"

"That is so sick," Bill said with a groan.

"Oh, yeah, I forgot the best part."

"Good, because I don't have a dog, and I'd never beat my wife," Bill said and laughed.

"Well, don't worry about the dog part," Tony said, shaking his head, "but you got to hit her where it doesn't show. Take the back of her head and put it right here," he said, clanging his beer can on the corner of the mantle. "That way, no one—"

Tony stopped talking. Even as ripped as he was, he realized he had exposed more of his dark side than he should. He wavered, then lost his balance, stumbling from the hearth. Right away, he remounted with a stiff leg and continued.

"And may all your ups and downs be between the sheets."

HONEYMOONS CAME AND WENT, and ups and downs were part of the job. Tony enjoyed the routine more than he admitted. Work days were short, and at 6:00, Angela had dinner on the table. One spring Tuesday, six months after his wedding, he came home in the middle of the afternoon and found Angela face down on the kitchen floor. The chilling similarity to his only memory of his mother haunted him as much as the fact that Angela could neither walk nor talk. He carried her to his car and headed for the hospital in Salinas.

Three days and nights passed, and Tony didn't eat, sleep, or leave her side. Angela slipped further away, unable to focus her eyes or make anything more than a pitiful cry. She remained on the fifth floor of the hospital for a week while doctor after doctor paraded through and reviewed her case. Each came up with a different diagnosis, worse than the one before, which some subsequent test disproved.

She was transferred to the psychiatric ward at County General. The latest guess? It was all psychosomatic. Again, Tony, Bill, and Cindy watched doctors come and go.

Tony had to credit Angela's mother. She refused to believe any of the doctors' conclusions and prayed for hours on end for her daughter. Tony watched doctors insert a tube down Angela's throat for feeding. That allowed Angela's mother to give her massive doses of carrot juice. Tony never figured out why she chose carrot juice, but he didn't stop her. He couldn't see where it hurt or helped Angela.

"I wish I could feed her some fucking carrot juice and feel useful, damn it," Tony said to Bill one afternoon, two weeks after Angela had fallen ill. His voice was too loud for the hospital coffee shop, but he didn't care. They both had a cup of coffee on the small table, but Tony could only stare at his. He flattened his moustache with his hand, and he could feel that he needed a shave.

"Maybe the guy with her now will know something," Bill said. "What kind of doctor is he, anyway?"

"He practices something called 'holistic medicine,'" Tony answered, thumbing the pages of a book he kept face down on the table. The binding edge was turned away from Bill, hiding its title.

"Are you reading the Bible?" Bill asked.

"Hell, no."

"I just thought maybe—"

"Well, you thought wrong," Tony snapped. He shouldn't have barked at Bill, but his patience was gone.

"Hey, Angela's mother could have slipped it to you," Bill said with an innocent shrug.

"Well, she didn't," Tony said, then lowered his voice. "OK, it's a book of love poems. If no one's around, I read them to her. I think she hears them. Hell, I don't know anymore."

Tony heard his name being paged and shot out the coffee shop. He met the doctor coming out of Angela's room. Cindy had been in the waiting room across the hall from Angela's room. Tony watched her rush to Bill's side when he arrived on the next elevator. Bill and Cindy walked over to join Tony and the doctor in the hallway.

"Are these your friends?" the doctor asked in a booming voice. Tony nodded. To him, the big man looked like Santa Claus in a suit, complete with his white beard, big stomach, and half glasses. The doctor looked back into Angela's room and then struggled to fold his arms across his big chest.

"It seems Angela doesn't want to get well," the doctor said, his booming voice threatening to wake half the ward.

"What do you mean?" Tony asked, fighting to restrain himself. "Why not?"

"She prefers to lie in that bed and be waited on," the doctor continued, still louder than necessary. Angela moaned, but the doctor only talked louder. "She enjoys the attention. In fact, it wouldn't surprise me a bit if she laughs when we walk away." Angela wailed again in a pitiful tone.

"I've had enough of your crap, pal," Tony said, looking up and down the hall and clenching his fists. Bill stepped forward to hold Tony back.

"What are you trying to do?" Cindy asked the doctor.

"Let's step into the waiting room," the doctor answered in a soft voice, nodding to his right.

"No," Tony said, starting toward Angela's room.

"Come on," the big man said in a whisper, grabbing Tony by the arm and pulling him into the empty waiting room. "Sit down, please."

"Why?" Tony said. He was in the waiting room but standing.

"I'm sorry I had to do that," the doctor answered, still whispering. He sat down in one of the chairs around the small coffee table. "I couldn't tell by talking to Angela just how alert she is. The things I said were designed just to elicit a reaction from her."

"So?" Tony answered. The doctor's explanation did not comfort him. But now, he wasn't shouting, and Tony strained to hear him.

"So, now I know she's 'home' so to speak," the doctor continued in a low voice. "I believe she has what we call 'locked-in syndrome.' It's as if she is locked in her own body and can't get out or respond normally."

Tony took a seat on the arm of the couch, putting his good ear close to the big man. Bill and Cindy sat down across the small room from them, near the coffee table covered with a fan of magazines.

"She's in there," the doctor said in a hushed tone. "Even if she doesn't have the muscle control to focus her eyes. She still hears every word that's said and still feels emotions. She can taste although she lacks the ability to swallow. She can tell hot from cold but can't pull away or reach out for either one."

"Is locked-in syndrome a disease?" Tony asked, not sure if he would believe the answer.

"No, it's a symptom."

"So, you don't know what's wrong," Tony said, dropping off his perch and sinking into the couch. Another in a series of dead-end diagnoses. He closed his eyes and sighed.

"No, but if we don't figure it out soon, she may die." That last word stabbed Tony through the heart. The doctor had spoken in a soft voice, but a sad cry arose from Angela's room. "I've requested a neurologist to examine her first thing in the morning. One thing is certain," he said and labored to rise from his chair. "There's nothing wrong with her hearing."

One for the Books

"CEREBRAL PONTINE MYELINOLYSIS." The words were spoken by a small, balding man with a wide forehead, who was the head of neurology at Santa Clara Valley Medical Center of San Jose, the nearest big city. He folded his stethoscope into the big pocket of his white coat. A pretty physical therapist with big glasses and long brown hair accompanied him. Tony stared at them both. The two of them waited for some reaction from Tony, Bill, or Cindy.

Tony and his friends had been stranded in the big city hospital waiting room, complete with its donated paintings and Styrofoam cups full of bitter coffee. They had been waiting for hours for the doctors to emerge and tell them something. The diagnosis now hit the walls of the big room, and the words echoed around unrecognized. Tony had the uncomfortable feeling that a bad dream was ending, and a nightmare was beginning.

"Are you sure?" Tony asked, straightening himself in the chair. For nearly a month, he had lived on soup, beer, and stale tuna sandwiches. His tired body had become accustomed to sleeping in waiting rooms, bedside chairs, and even hospital coffee shops.

"Positive," the doctor answered.

"So?" Tony asked. "What is that?"

"How it originates is a mystery," the doctor explained. "CPM sometimes develops on its own or can be precipitated by a blow to the back of the neck or lower brain, known as the pons area. In either case, it's extremely rare."

"How rare?" Tony asked, trying to read the doctor's expression, and failing.

149

"The number of documented cases is less than ten in this state. As you know, it's difficult to diagnose. Usually it's only discovered in an autopsy."

Tony dropped his head into his hands. All of his fight evaporated with the word 'autopsy.'

"Will she recover?" Cindy asked, reaching for Bill's hand.

"We can't be sure," the doctor answered, stabbing a pen at his coat pocket and missing. "Her age is in her favor. She's lasted longer than most. She'll be one for the medical journals if she does."

"It will take intensive physical therapy," the therapist said, removing her oversized glasses. "We have to train different nerves to function in the place of damaged ones. She has to relearn how to do almost everything."

"How long does that take?" Tony asked. It took all his strength to form the question.

"That depends on the patient," the therapist answered, sounding unsure. "It could be weeks, more likely months, possibly years."

"What's the average?" Bill asked.

The therapist and the doctor exchanged glances.

"I'm afraid only Angela can tell us that," the doctor answered after a pause.

"What do you mean?" Tony asked, rising from his chair.

"I mean, she's the first one to get this far."

"What about the others?" Tony asked.

"There are no others," the doctor said in a soft voice.

"Are you telling me no one has ever survived this?" Tony asked, stepping closer to the doctor. He hoped the answer wasn't what he thought.

"Not yet," the therapist said. "But for Angela, it might just be . . ."

"Oh, fuck . . ." Tony said. His shoulders dropped, and he turned away. Each piece of bad news left him feeling that Angela was slipping further and further away from him. Worse yet, there wasn't a damn thing he could do.

"Look," the doctor said, moving to stare into Tony's tired blue eyes. "We are going to put everything we've got into this."

"Yeah, right," Tony said in a whisper, raking his fingers through his dark curls.

"We aren't doing it for you," the veteran doctor said. "We aren't even doing it for Angela. There are careers that hinge on her survival. If you want to give up, fine, but—"

"Give up, my ass," Tony said, but the doctor continued.

"We have a precedent to set here, and we damn well plan to do it. This is big stuff in medical history. It's a once in a lifetime opportunity for our staff."

Tony learned to say cerebral pontine myelinolysis, and he learned to wait. Day after day, he made the 90-minute drive from work to the hospital. He spent every hour at her bedside, where his wife lay motionless, unable to speak or eat. Tony was too tired or worried to go home. He slept in the chair by Angela's bed and waited. He wasn't sure for what, but there was nothing else he could do.

Time passed, but nothing changed. He flew every morning and drove every afternoon. After three weeks, Tony gave away their dog and spent his first evening alone in their empty house, trying to figure it all out. He sat on the living room floor, downing a six pack, and cleaning his .44 magnum. A cold fireplace loomed on his right, tormenting him. It reminded him of his old man's words as much as Angela's silence.

"Show me a man who doesn't beat his wife . . ."

He couldn't remember hitting her. Had he been drunk? Maybe he didn't do it. No, he did. He must have. Other times, he had done things he couldn't remember. Friends once told him he pushed a piano down a flight of stairs, and he had seen the pieces scattered on the first-floor landing. He had once woken up parked 100 miles from home with his passenger door missing. What the hell had he been thinking? How could he have hurt her? Maybe it was the night he got tanked and decided he hated the color of the house. The next morning, Angela had told him he had taken a sander to the garage wall. He hadn't believed her until she had shown him the circle he had sanded in the paint, almost making a hole through the wall.

Tony pointed the unloaded gun at his head and thought about pulling the trigger. He changed his mind and aimed at the far corner of the mantle. He pulled the trigger, and it shocked him when a bullet whizzed past the hearth. It blasted through a wall of his house and in the neighbor's bathroom window. Luckily, they weren't home to hear the slug roll around in the bathtub. The next day, he told Angela about it. He tried to apologize. He meant to apologize for hitting her. Instead, he apologized for blowing a hole in the wall. She never moved or made a sound, except a pitiful cry when he started to leave.

Tony became the hospital's most consistent visitor. The staff allowed him to ignore visiting hours, and he knew he tried the patience of every nurse on the ward. They reminded him, over and over, not to sit on Angela's bed or to play the radio so loud. One sunny day, they found him carrying her to the window. More than once, they caught him smuggling in beer.

On Angela's birthday, he arrived with a bottle of red wine, a cupcake, and one candle. Tony stuck the candle in the cupcake and waited until no one was around before lighting it. He placed the flaming dessert on the sliding tray in front of Angela.

"Blow," he said, moving it close to her. Angela's expression didn't change, and her eyes stayed fixed on the candle. It burned down, and wax covered the frosting.

"Happy birthday, baby," he said, toasting her I.V. over and over until he had polished off the wine.

His behavior was appalling, but, for reasons he never understood, the staff didn't kick him out. They sometimes walked in when he was reading poetry to Angela. Like a fool, he would hide the book, even though it was too late, and they must have known. Other times, he would just rub her feet. He guessed that the nurses found it easier to let him adjust Angela's pillow or her body for her. Sometimes, she would whine, and the nurses would ask him why. He could tell them if it was the sun in her eyes or the pain from yesterday's shot. Somehow, he just knew.

He also learned how to strap her into a wheelchair and take her to therapy. He began his own attempts at eliciting some reaction from her. Every day, when he arrived, and again before he left, he placed his hand a hair's breadth from hers.

"Touch my hand," he said, over and over. "Touch my hand." But she never did.

Achievements made in therapy were so small, the therapist had to tell Tony what they were. He watched the woman through the glass walls of her office during sessions. During one, she rubbed Angela's lips with an ice cube, over and over.

"Why are you doing that?" Tony asked, peeking his head in the door.

"I need her to respond," the therapist answered. Her fingertips grew cold, and she switched the ice cube from hand to hand.

"Her lips are almost blue," Tony said in protest.

"I know," the therapist answered but continued. Angela moaned louder.

"This is crazy," Tony said, entering the room and pacing around. In frustration, he grabbed the handles of Angela's wheelchair. He would take her back to her room rather than let the therapist torture her. It wasn't like it was making any difference.

"Don't move her," the therapist said. "We never said this would be easy."

"You never told me you were going to freeze her lips off," he answered, starting to roll her away.

"Don't you want her to recover?" the therapist asked, grabbing the armrest of the wheelchair. She continued applying the ice cube to Angela's purple lips.

"What kind of stupid-ass question is that? Of course, I do."

"There," the therapist said, leaning back to rest for a moment. "Very good, Angela. Very good."

"What?" Tony asked, looking from the therapist to Angela and back again.

"She licked her lips," the therapist answered, as if that meant something.

"So?" Tony asked, wondering what her point was.

"So, it was a voluntary action," the lady answered. "Before she can eat, she has to learn to chew and swallow again. This is how it begins."

"Really?" Tony said, putting his face close to his wife's. "Do it again, Angela." She didn't respond.

"I doubt she will do it on her own," the therapist said.

"Use the ice cube," he said, and Angela moaned.

"I don't think she wants me to," the therapist said, turning the tables on Tony.

"Sure she does," he said, only to have Angela cry out again.

"I don't think so . . ."

"Give me that," he said, grabbing the ice cube from the therapist. Tony wheeled Angela around to face him and gave her a kiss she couldn't return. Then he traced her lips with the ice cube. "What a sexy mouth."

Angela moaned, unable to turn her head away in protest.

"How are we ever going to French kiss again if you can't do this?" he asked, licking his own lips with a quick tongue.

CINDY AND BILL visited twice a week, but they didn't notice Angela's minor improvements. What Tony and the therapist considered great strides, often seemed like nothing when Tony relayed them to his friends.

"If her lips are really cold, she can lick them," Tony said. Bill and Cindy seemed to wait for Tony to finish telling them the rest. He could tell they eventually realized that was the extent of her improvement.

"That's . . . great," Cindy said, half a second too late.

Inside, Tony felt defeated. Bill and Cindy brought a sucker for Angela on their next visit. They had hoped to tempt her to lick it by rubbing it on her lips. It didn't work. They forced Tony to go out to dinner when they could and offered to stay with Angela so he could take a break. He seldom accepted. He wasn't interested.

Tony continued to spend his nights in the bedside chair or on an unoccupied bed in the same room. The nurses scowled at first, then turned a blind eye. At the end of the second month, the night nurse walked in to find Tony asleep in bed with Angela. He heard her footsteps and kept his eyes closed. It surprised him when the nurse didn't raise a fuss. His body fit snug up against Angela's, like they were spoons in a drawer. His black curls against the bleached white sheets mingled with her sandy wisps. Tony held his breath. The nurse didn't even take Angela's blood pressure. She just scrawled some numbers on Angela's chart without turning on the light and left the room.

Angela's mother and Tony worked out an unofficial visitation schedule which allowed them to avoid each other. Tony went to work, and Angela's mother came to the hospital with her prayer group from church and carrot juice to pour down her daughter's feeding tube. She left when he arrived. Just as well. The last thing he needed was Angela's mother trying his patience. Her Sunday school attitude about the whole ordeal drove him crazy. They had gotten into it once, before they had worked out their uneasy truce.

"If it's God's will . . ." she had started.

"If it is, then fuck Him," Tony had answered.

Tony smuggled in more beer and grew more depressed. He thought about giving up. He wondered at times if he was only imagining improvement. Did he need to tie her as tightly into the wheelchair? Did her hand just move? Did she smile? Whatever it was that he thought he saw her do, Angela never repeated the act when he asked. He never knew how well she could see him. Deep inside, he believed she was conscious but with no way to break through and tell him.

SHORTLY AFTER TONY arrived one afternoon, a nurse took Angela for more tests. He left her room to wait in the coffee shop, his new second home. He wandered down the hall and pushed the call button. When the elevator doors opened, they revealed a lone passenger. A small, older man wearing a priest's collar. He looked pale, his forehead sweating.

"Robert?"

The man paused before giving an uncertain answer. "Tony?"

Tony joined him in the car. Both leaned against the handrail on the back wall. Tony studied Robert's face while the elevator doors closed.

"You feel OK?" Tony asked, inching away. "You look like you're gonna puke."

"No, no, no." Robert spoke a rapid denial before removing a handkerchief from his pocket to wipe his face. "I just hate hospitals. When I was a boy, my sister was very sick, and . . ." He put his handkerchief back in his pocket. "It's a long story. How are you?"

"I'm fine." Tony watched the numbers above the doors descend from 7. The coffee shop was on the first floor. "Well, I'm better than my wife anyway. She's been here for months."

"Sounds serious." Robert paused, then gave a half-hearted reply. "I could stop in and give her Last Rites."

"It's not that bad," Tony said. "At least I hope not."

"She doesn't have to be dying. It's really just a sacrament. The anointing of the sick."

"That's OK. Her mom's prayer posse has all the hallelujah stuff covered."

"Good to know." Robert nodded, sounding relieved. "How are you?"

"I'm hanging in there. Sorta. Accidentally shot a .44 through my living room wall, but other than that, I'm OK."

"That's not good. Still flying?" Robert asked, showing something close to a smile.

"Oh yeah. It's tiring driving between Castroville and here every day. Me and my car are both wearing out."

"I can't help with the car," Robert said when the doors opened at the first floor. "Maybe I can say a prayer for you."

"I'm not seeing the prayers from her mom's group helping Angela, but knock yourself out."

"Are they Catholic?" Robert walked out of the elevator, followed by Tony.

"Does it matter?"

"Not really." Robert looked past the candy stripers' station toward the waiting room. "I'm supposed to meet one of my parishioners here. They said I could wait by the front door since I wasn't feeling well in her room. She's been here several days for evaluation." Robert thumped his fist twice on his chest. "Bad heart. It didn't help that her son was shot and killed. Her daughter, Maria, had to attend a murder trial today."

"You Catholics are a wild bunch."

"Not usually. Anyway, Maria asked me to give her mother a ride home." Robert scanned the waiting room again.

"I was heading for the coffee shop." Tony took a step in that direction, then stopped. "They took Angela for some tests. Not that I could talk to her anyway." He shifted from foot-to-foot, wondering whether to walk away. He usually enjoyed having company to pass the time, but not a priest.

"Is she mad at you?" Robert guessed.

"Huh?"

"I mean, if she doesn't talk to you. . ."

"Oh, no. Well, yeah, probably." Tony took a moment to figure out how to explain. "She's been diagnosed with a locked-in syndrome. Supposedly she can hear and comprehend, but she can't move or show it." Tony almost told him his wife could lick her lips, but it didn't seem like a lot to show for being alive.

"Maybe you should forgive her?"

"I should forgive *her*?" Tony felt like he should have left when he had the chance.

"For being sick."

"It's not her fault." Tony said, jamming his fists into his jean pockets. "Maybe she should forgive me."

"Is it your fault?"

"I guess. Probably."

"Then maybe you should forgive yourself," Robert answered.

Tony looked at the small man. The priest had never worn a collar back when they had flown together. He felt grateful Robert hadn't asked why it was Tony's fault. Tony wasn't sure how he would answer anyway. Would the priest believe he couldn't remember?

"Forgive myself? Why?" Tony said, looking again with regret toward the coffee shop. "Forgiving myself won't make her forgive me."

"Forgiveness closes the gap." Robert stared at him long enough to make Tony look away. "When distance develops between two people, apologizing builds a bridge."

The elevator opened behind Tony. Robert looked past him, and Tony turned to follow his gaze. He saw a big woman in a little wheelchair being pushed toward them by an orderly.

"Not sure how I'll get her into the car," Robert muttered.

"Need a hand?" Tony asked.

"Please," Robert said.

Robert turned toward the woman. Tony knew Robert's smile was fake.

"Padre Roberto," said the woman in the wheelchair. Her smile seemed genuine. *"Gracias. Dios te bendiga."*

"She doesn't speak English," Robert whispered to Tony, then turned toward the woman. *"Ola, Senora. Mi coche est tu coche,"* Robert added, nodding toward his yellow car parked near the door.

The orderly pushed the wheelchair out the double doors. Tony followed him and Roberto to the vehicle parked in the patient-loading zone. When the woman stood up, the orderly retreated into the hospital with the wheelchair. Tony opened the passenger door while the woman clung to the little priest for stability. Each man took an arm and maneuvered the big woman into the car. The springs groaned when her full weight hit the passenger seat.

"Gracias, Padre," she said.

Tony lifted her legs into the car, the way he'd become used to putting Angela in a wheelchair.

"Gracias, Senor."

Tony lifted both hands to signal it was nothing, as if he had forgotten how to speak.

"Da nada, Senora," Robert said, then closed the passenger door and turned to Tony.

"Gracias—I mean, thank you, Tony." Robert fished his car keys from his pocket. "With my Spanish, it'll be a long ride back to King City." He rolled his eyes, then turned to walk toward the driver's door. "I hope your wife feels better soon. I'll say a prayer."

"What if she won't forgive me?" Tony asked, still waiting at the curb.

"Then forgive her for not forgiving you," Robert said over the roof of the car in his staccato style. "It's a start."

Robert waved, and Tony lifted his chin in acknowledgement. The little Italian slipped into the driver's seat. He started his car, tore out of the parking lot, and bounced out of the driveway into traffic, narrowly avoiding a school bus.

Tony walked toward the coffee shop, shaking his head.

"He drives like he flies."

ON THE FIRST WARM DAY of spring, Tony strapped Angela in her chair as usual to take her to therapy. He nodded and smiled at the head nurse at the nurse's station before he pushed Angela into the elevator. Once inside, his finger pushed the button for the ground floor. Therapy was on the fourth. The doors reopened, and he wheeled Angela out a side exit to the lush hospital grounds. He spread a blanket on the grass, untied her from the chair, and lay her down. He opened his book to a preselected page with a John Keat's poems and sat down beside her, reading in a soft voice.

"You say you love; but then your hand
No soft squeeze for squeeze returneth,
It is like a statue's dead—
While mine to passion burneth—
O love me truly!

O breathe a word or two of fire!
Smile, as if those words should burn me,
Squeeze as lovers should—Oh kiss
And in thy heart inurn me!
O love me truly!"

He waited for a response but received none. His body sank into the grass, lying face down beside her and dropping his head in the crook of his arm. After a moment, he raised himself onto his elbows and held her limp hand.

"Angela, say something for God's sake," he pleaded, recalling Robert's advice. "I'm sorry. I promise it will never happen again. I'd swear on a stack of Bibles if they meant anything to me. Look," he said, kneeling and pulling his wallet from his pocket. He held it open in front of her. "It's my pilot's license. On my license to fly, I swear I will never hit you again."

His breath remained locked in his chest, waiting for a response, but she didn't make a sound. He sighed and replaced his wallet. He rolled over on his back, lying beside her and watching a plane cross the sky, so high it didn't make a sound. His eyes caught the therapist in the fourth-floor window, staring down at them. Tony watched her check her watch. He was too tired to think of any good excuses. At least she knew they weren't coming for Angela's appointment.

After a while, his hand reached for the book again and turned another page. He continued to read to Angela without enthusiasm, rubbing his tired eyes. Later, he noticed her cheek was damp, but he could not imagine even one tear would ever stream down her pale cheek for him.

Tony snuck back in the building with Angela after the wind came up. They reached Angela's floor, but he lurked behind a wall, keeping her wheelchair out of sight until everyone had vacated the nurses' station. When they had, he hurried up the hall, looking behind him and pushing Angela in her wheelchair toward her room. He faced forward again and saw Angela's therapist heading straight toward them. She walked by, projecting a cold, clinical air. Tony could tell she was ticked.

"Hello, Angela," she said, passing them.

"Hi," Angela answered.

Back

EVERY STEP FORWARD was a small war. Tony could only watch. Making a fist, wiggling toes, or following the therapist's circling pen made Angela break into a sweat. Her speech was slow and deliberate, agonizing over one or two words at a time.

There were days Tony wished he could squeeze the rubber ball or balance between the parallel bars for her. A pattern developed that told Tony when Angela was about to make progress. He had noticed there was something about exhaustion that made Angela reach even deeper inside herself.

"Just try to move it," Tony said again.

The two of them were alone, she in bed and he standing beside her in that ugly but familiar hospital room. He placed the pen back in Angela's hand. It dropped to the blankets, and he picked it up again.

"You don't have to write your name, OK?" he said, placing her arm back on the piece of paper on her portable tray. "Just hang on long enough to make a mark."

Tony closed her hand around the pen again. Her eyebrows pinched together. He watched her try to send a message that her hand refused to receive. Her frustration echoed inside him. Angela began to cry, and the pen went flying to the floor. He picked it up again.

"You can," he said, pulling a lock of hair away from the corner of her eye. "I know you can. Just one more try."

She turned her head away and refused to watch. He folded her fingers around the pen and placed it in the writing position again.

161

"A mark, just a dot, and I swear I'll quit," he said, looking her in the eye. His stubborn intensity only made her cry louder. "Write 'Fuck you, Tony' in big letters. Come on, I deserve it."

She tried to ignore him, crying until tears soaked the pillow slip. He wiped her eyes and nose with a tissue and dropped into the bedside chair. Her arm remained frozen on the tray.

"Ah, bag it," he said with a sigh.

At first, Tony looked out the window, and stared at the ceiling in frustration. Her hand began to move, and he caught it from the corner of his eye. Angela bit her bottom lip. The tears stopped, and every muscle in her face tensed. Courage, for most people, was for life or death situations. Angela needed it just to make an ink mark on a page. She pushed her hand forward, pinched her eyes shut, and the pen wiggled between her fingers. Tony was on the edge of his seat, trying to hold back so he didn't break her concentration. A blue line began to appear on the white paper, and he couldn't contain himself any longer.

"That's it, that's it!" Tony said, jumping from the chair. "Hot damn!"

Angela's hand didn't stop, and Tony sensed another breakthrough moment. It was as if she had come far enough to know she could go farther. She crossed the top of the line she had drawn with a tiny mark before dropping the pen.

"You did it," he said. "You moved the pen. You made a mark." Her arm fell to her side, and Tony held up the paper. "Should we frame it and hang it up?" he asked, holding it against the wall.

"N-n-not . . . m-m-mark," she said, struggling to squeeze out each word.

"What?"

"Not m-m-mark," she said again. "T."

"Tea?" he asked, looking from the paper to her face. He didn't understand.

"M-m-mark is T."

Tony examined the paper in his hand. It was wiggly, it was ugly, but it was a T.

"A 'T,'" he said like a proud father. "You made a real letter." She gave him a lop-sided smile.

"T-t-t f-for T-t-tony," she said with effort. "F-f-fuck you, T-t-tony."

He turned her face to his. Tears blurred his view of her features, but he could see she was crying too.

"That's right," he said, laughing through his tears. "Fuck me."

She returned his joy with an otherworldly sound, her first attempt at laughing. He hugged her, then looked at the paper again.

"Son of a bitch," Tony said, sitting beside her on the bed and giving her a kiss. "I'll be damned. Or, maybe not." He thought maybe Robert's prayers might have made a difference. He placed his hand an inch from hers. "Touch my hand."

She groaned, but he didn't move it away.

"Come on, touch my hand," he encouraged her again. She had a long way to go, but she was so much better. Her fingers crawled over his, and he watched with a smile before bending over to kiss each one.

A WEEK LATER, Tony arrived at the hospital in a lousy mood. Sonny had ragged on his ass all morning at work, and the long drive had been slow and hot. He was passing the nurses' station when he noticed the closed door to Angela's room. The head nurse looked up from her paperwork.

"I'm sorry, Mr. Damascus," she said, looking over her bifocals at him. "You can't go in."

"What do you mean?" he asked. He rested an elbow on the corner of the counter but kept his eyes on Angela's door.

"It will only be a few minutes," she answered, averting her eyes from his and shuffling her papers. "Why don't you have some coffee?"

"I don't want coffee," he answered, standing up straight and backing away. "I want to see my wife. What's wrong?"

"Now, I told you it wouldn't be much longer," the nurse answered, still focusing on her paperwork. "Go down to the coffee shop, and I'll page you."

"No!" His angry word echoed, and he started down the hallway. Fear gripped him, thinking maybe something had gone wrong.

At that moment, Angela's door opened, and her mother slipped out of the room. She walked past Tony without a word and pushed the elevator call button.

"What's going on?" he asked her, and then shot another look at the head nurse. They both looked away from him. *Were they laughing at him?* He started down the hall, walking at first and then running full speed. His boots slipped when he attempted a sudden stop at Angela's room, and he went sliding past it on the slick flooring. He caught himself on the doorway.

What he saw stopped him cold. Angela was sitting up in a chair near the window sill that held a small vase of yellow flowers. Her mother must have dressed her in the soft pink robe she wore. Someone had washed and curled her hair and done her make-up, right down to the pink lipstick on her small mouth. Tony stared and didn't move. Angela smiled at the look on his face. He entered the room and closed the door behind him without a sound.

Much later, Angela would tell him that she had heard every poem he had read, even in the darkest days. She would cry again in frustration before her therapy ended. But that day, she smiled when he approached.

"Hey, gorgeous," he said, covering her mouth with his and smearing her perfect lipstick with a kiss. He pulled back and watched her struggle to speak.

"Hi, s-s-sexy."

Her gritty words brought him to tears. He knelt beside her chair, memorizing her face.

"God, it's good to have you back," he said, staring in disbelief.

"You," she said, then paused, summoning more words with difficulty. "You b-b-brought me b-b-back."

He cocked his head, not sure he understood.

"But what if it was all my fault?"

"You stayed." Her crooked smile said more than she could convey. "Th-Thank you."

Later, she would say he was the only reason she had come out of it alive. The experience changed her. Her new attitude seemed to say, "If I can survive this, I can survive anything." However, at that moment, she only had three words for him. She held up her palm.

"T-t-touch my hand."

Live a Little, Live a Lot

"ANOTHER ROUND for my friends," Tony said, looking to his right and left.

The noon hour bartender at Clancy's mixed the drinks for Tony, Bill, and Patches. They were the only patrons in the establishment. The man behind the bar knew about Tony's long overdue tab. Tony knew the bartender wouldn't have filled the order if it hadn't been for Angela's condition, and the fact that Patches was picking up the bill.

"To Angela," Bill said, raising his glass.

"To modern science," Patches said.

"To flying," Tony added.

"To flying," they all agreed.

"How's Angela?" the bartender asked Tony, who stood between Bill and Patches at the dark bar.

"Better," Tony said after his first swallow. "Much better. I pulled the curtain around the bed last night, and we had some great sex."

"In the hospital?" Bill asked, choking on his drink.

"I wasn't about to pay for a hotel room," Tony said, leaning both elbows on the bar and looking at Bill. "As if I could."

"What about the nurses?" Patches asked, leaning forward.

"They always get pissed, but—" Tony started.

"You've done it before?" Bill asked, setting down his drink and staring at Tony.

"Oh, sure," Tony said, taking a drink. "But now she's able to cooperate. Before, it was like making a corpse."

"You're a full blown pervert," Patches murmured over his Scotch. The short man stroked his gray, billy goat beard. Tony

165

guessed it was all that outdoor labor that gave Patches the weathered face of an older man and the body of a younger one.

"I'm just crazy about my woman," Tony said, finishing his screwdriver in a swallow.

"You're just crazy," Bill said, sipping a Manhattan.

"When's she coming home?" Patches asked.

"It's still a few weeks, but she's coming," Tony said, pushing his empty toward the bartender to signal a refill. The bartender picked up his glass and hesitated until he caught Patches' eye. Patches nodded, and the bartender mixed another drink for Tony. Tony ignored the slight. He needed the drink more than his pride. The jukebox across the room had stopped, so Tony went over and plugged in a quarter. His hand knew the exact location of E-7, *Whatever Gets You through the Night* by John Lennon. He walked back to the bar, still talking about Angela's improvement. "She can almost walk. Talks pretty good too. She better hurry. I don't know how much longer my old Jeep will hold together."

"How many miles does it have?" Bill asked.

"Shit, I don't know," Tony said, taking a sip from the fresh drink. "I disconnected the speedometer when I bought it. In the last four months, I would guess I've put on nearly 20,000 miles."

"I don't know how you fly, drive, and drink every day without killing yourself," Bill said. "I hope she gets home soon for your sake."

Tony knew he had been difficult to work with through his exhaustion, but Bill, and everyone else, had seemed surprised by his dedication to Angela. He'd been a little surprised himself, but he also knew he couldn't go on much longer. Her recent progress let Tony feel free to cut loose again, drink too much, and annoy the boss.

The following day, from 5:00 a.m. until noon, Tony and Bill sat at the air strip, waiting for the fog to break. It lifted only to have a north wind come up. They still couldn't work without the risk of drifting spray on to a neighboring crop.

They left and grabbed some sandwiches in Castroville but brought them back to the strip in case the wind dropped off. They headed back into the office, the only structure at the airstrip. Only one window, one door, and the pungent odor of chemicals made it less than enticing. Outside, a thin white coat of paint on the building's plywood walls was disintegrating from the salt air. Tony opened the door to see the exhausted couch, battered desk, and well-used dart board that furnished the ill-lit, 10-by-12 foot shack. Bill claimed the couch. Tony entered behind him and took a seat on the corner of the desk.

"Bush pilot," Tony said, resuming their usual distraction of listing great flying jobs. He unwrapped his sandwich, took a bite, and continued talking while he chewed. "I could do that."

"Fire bombing would be better," Bill said, pointing his sandwich at Tony.

"They get paid just to wait on the ground," Tony added. He knew several cropdusters who had switched to dousing blazes from old WWII air tankers. His eyes rolled at the thought. "We could be here all afternoon and not make a dime unless the wind dies off."

"Don't remind me," Bill said before taking a bite.

"Even then we won't make shit," Tony continued, allowing his long legs to dangle from the desk and his boot to kick the garbage can. He licked some mustard from one finger. His sandwich was balanced in his left hand, and he picked up a dart with his right. "I got 10 acres and you got eight. My 25 percent of the gross barely covers beer and cigarettes."

"Twenty-three percent," Bill said, reminding him of their real cut.

"Whatever . . ." Tony answered, flinging a dart at the board and missing. Sure, he would gripe about his profession—but only when he wasn't flying. Cropdusting was the only life he could imagine living, as long as the wind cooperated, and the work stacked up. Flying allowed him to make a couple hundred bucks before most people got out of bed in the morning and take the rest of the day off. Tony needed that kind of money right now, but chances of that happening weren't looking good.

"I don't see why Sonny makes us both sit out here," Bill said. "One of us could easily watch the wind alone."

"It's his fucking power trip," Tony answered, crossing the room to pull his dart from the wall and gather the others. He handed them to Bill. "Short people are like that. Hell, let's head over to my place for a couple of brews. He'll never know."

"Yeah, right," Bill answered, putting down his sandwich. "Sonny'll never know unless the wind dies down, and the work doesn't get done." Bill paused to take aim and threw a dart. It landed close to the bullseye. "These are both deadline jobs since they're close to harvest." He threw again. Bullseye. "It's now or never."

"Looks like never to me," Tony said, leaning forward from his perch to look out the low window. The tattered windsock was stiff, dancing back and forth. "Hey, how about airshow work?"

"Or flying stunts for movies," Bill added, tossing his last dart. Close, but no bullseye.

"We could get a couple of planes and put an aerobatic routine together," Tony said, dropping half of his stale sandwich in the trash.

"Let's put on a show in the old barn," Bill said, laughing and pulling the darts out of the board.

"Hell, it wouldn't be that tough," Tony said. "We've flown together long enough. You're good—"

"Thanks," Bill said.

"I'm great," Tony continued, staring out the window and past the windsock. "All we need is a gimmick, some hype—"

"And two planes," Bill said, always the practical one.

"There's two planes sitting right there," Tony said, pointing out the window. Two red-and-white Ag Wagons formed the small flight line on the strip. Both monoplanes sat tied down, side by side. They faced the sand dunes beside the strip that followed the river to the sea.

"They're not ours," Bill said, giving Tony a suspicious look.

"Details," Tony said. He popped off the desk, threw open the door, and gripped the door jamb overhead with both hands. He kept his back to Bill and watched the sun beginning to set on the sea.

"Hey, it's cold—" Bill started.

"I got it," Tony said, turning around. "Water-skiing. Come on." Tony threw his friend a jacket, and Bill followed him outside. He was halfway to the closest plane when he yelled back at Bill. "That's our gimmick." Tony pointed past the green reeds and brown pussy willows that lined the banks of the Salinas River. It was swollen wider than normal by recent rains.

"Water-ski on that?" Bill asked when he caught up to Tony.

"With the planes," Tony said, glancing over his shoulder to the Ag Wagons.

"They're not ours," Bill said again, but Tony had jumped up on the wing.

"Perfect," Tony called back over his shoulder. He pulled his helmet from the seat and slapped it on. "We'll make our mistakes in these, and then get our own." He opened the cockpit and heard the sound of Bill's boots running up behind him.

"Are you crazy?" Bill asked, reaching up and pulling him down from the wing.

"Look, it's easy," Tony said, smiling and explaining his idea with hand gestures. "Just get her level with the water, drop one wing a fraction until you get one wheel in—"

"You're out of your mind," Bill said, still holding Tony's shoulder.

"Then lower the other," Tony said, shaking loose Bill's grip on his coat and mounting the wing again. He looked back at his friend. "Come on, Billy boy. For God's sake, take a risk. Live a little." He slipped his long body into the cockpit with ease, and then leaned out the open side window. "If you're scared, just watch me once."

"I'm not scared," Bill answered, still standing his ground.

"Then let's go," Tony called back to him and started the engine. "Clear!" he yelled and closed the cockpit window.

Bill yelled something, but the sputtering engine caught, and Tony couldn't understand him. He taxied the plane toward the airstrip and looked out the side window at Bill, still standing by the other plane and growing smaller in the distance. The noise from the engine increased on the run up. Tony started the plane down the runway, passing beneath a low wire crossing the strip, lifting off, and banking left. His starboard wing pointed toward the sky just like the reeds in the river below him. Tony looked down and saw Bill racing toward the other plane. Tony circled and watched Bill's take-off, waiting for his friend to close in on him before heading upstream.

Tony followed the river, flying low with Bill chasing. Below, two wrinkled shadows of the planes skimmed over the water's surface. Bill pulled up on Tony's left wing and shook his head 'no'. Tony laughed and gave him the thumbs up signal before peeling off to his right with a roar.

Bill broke right also, and Tony could sense he was just a short distance behind him. Tony dropped altitude. Bill followed. Now traveling downstream, they both lined up on the river as if it were a row of crops. Ahead of Tony, the river rushed to meet the ocean. The sun slipped from the sky through purple and orange strands of clouds above the horizon. The bottom of the glowing orange orb just touched the sea.

Tony flew just above the water's surface, kissing the river with one wheel before pulling it up again. Barely a splash, he thought. He knew Bill was watching, maybe believing that was all Tony would do.

Tony stayed close to the water and dropped his right wheel again. It rolled on the river, creating a rooster tail of water beneath his wing. He dropped the other wheel and fountains spouted from both sides of the landing gear. He skied for a few moments before pulling up. His plane gained altitude, and Tony turned her back upstream.

Tony looked left to see Bill on his wing again. This time, Bill was pointing back to the strip. Tony smiled a shit-eating grin beneath his black moustache and pointed back to the river. He held two flat hands in front of him, palms down, indicating formation flight. Tony turned back and lined up on the river to descend on the water again. Over his shoulder, he saw Bill hesitate, then follow him in.

"Hot damn, it's show time," Tony said, the words lost in the noisy cockpit.

Tony knew Bill would be a great wingman. He had learned to cropdust by flying in formation. Not far behind, Bill mirrored Tony's movements. The two identical planes traveled a breath above the water in level flight, one in front, one in back, one a little to the right, the other a little to the left. Tony dipped his right wheel in, and Bill dipped in his left. They each pulled one wheel out and dipped the other. They returned to level flight, and then dropped altitude until both sets of wheels skimmed the water's surface. Fans of water gushed from both sides of each wheel of each plane.

"Fuck me dead," Tony said and pulled up. He looked over at Bill, who had come up beside him.

"All right," Bill mouthed and gave Tony a thumbs up.

They ascended together. Bill broke for the strip. Tony headed back up the river for another run or three. It felt so good to have the stick in his hand and his feet on the rudder pedals. Every woman he had ever slept with, including Angela, had told him they had seen him flying in his sleep, his feet fluttering below the blankets and his right hand wiggling back and forth.

Tony could have flown all day, but he knew he could get caught if he didn't return to the strip. After landing, Tony parked the plane next to Bill's. Bill had finished tying down his plane and was leaning against the shed. The propeller slowed, and Tony dropped open the window on the cockpit door.

"What a pussy you are," Tony called to Bill, and crawled out of the cockpit. His jump down from the wing sent shooting pain through his right leg. He kicked the chocks close to the wheels and sauntered stiff-legged toward Bill.

"It was a stupid thing to do," Bill answered, muttering more to himself than Tony. Bill pushed away from the building and walked past Tony.

"So why did you take off?" Tony asked, watching him walk by.

"Because I thought you might bust your ass," Bill said over his shoulder, still walking away.

"And why did you follow me in?" Tony asked, grinning and heading after Bill.

"I honestly don't know," Bill answered, keeping his back to Tony.

"Didn't you fucking love it?" Tony asked, grabbing Bill by the shoulder and turning him around to face him.

"Buzz off—" Bill said, shaking his hand away.

"You did," Tony said, pointing and laughing at his conservative friend. "I can tell."

"So what?" Bill said. He looked at Tony with an uncomfortable smile coming to the corners of his mouth.

"What do you mean, 'so what?'" Tony asked. "It felt so good, I thought I was going to come in my pants."

"I thought I was going to shit in mine," Bill said, laughing.

"Want to do it again?" Tony asked, half-turning back to the plane.

"Never," Bill said, walking off toward the office.

"What's the matter?" Tony asked, following his friend into the dirty white shack. "Scared?"

Bill turned and punched him in the stomach.

"Oh, come on, live a little," Tony said in a winded voice. He recovered and pushed Bill from behind.

"No thanks," Bill said, opening the door. He looked over his shoulder at Tony. "I'd rather live a lot."

"Hey, fine," Tony said, arms wide. "No hard feelings, right?"

"Oh, all right," Bill said.

"Great. Lend me five bucks, OK?"

Weeks passed, and Tony borrowed five bucks from Bill on several more occasions, not that he could afford to return the original five. In Tony's mind, Bill and Cindy led uncomplicated lives. They didn't have house payments, second mortgages, insurance, property tax, astronomical medical bills, heavy bar tabs, or even short term loans to repay. Tony did, not that he was paying any of them. He was just trying to hang on to the house until Angela got out of the hospital. He realized that he wasn't going to make it.

Tony covered the bullet hole in the wall with a calendar and hired a realtor. The "For Sale" sign went up a month before Angela came home. It sold in two weeks. Tony could have stayed until escrow closed, but both the power company and the phone company had shut off service. The new owners moved in and paid rent until the deal closed. The extra income went toward a down payment on another car, which gave Tony another payment he couldn't afford to make. He didn't have the heart to tell Angela.

"She's coming home tomorrow, and she still doesn't know I sold the house," Tony said to Bill one morning at work between loads.

"What are you going to do?" Bill asked and watched the swamper load more pesticide into his plane.

"Break it to her gently," Tony answered, waiting for the young man to finish Bill's load so he could start on Tony's. "I've got an idea, but I'll need your help."

"What can I do?" Bill asked.

"Could you loan me a few hundred dollars?" Tony asked. Then he added in a hurry, "Just until payday."

Tony could tell by the look on Bill's face that he could have asked for anything but that. Bill had been paying for their drinks and lunches. Tony had even borrowed Bill's car to go see Angela while his new one was being painted. The tank was empty when he had returned it.

"A few hundred?" Bill asked. He turned away to stare at the loader filling his plane's hopper, avoiding looking Tony in the eye.

"Sure," Tony said, walking in front of him and trying to reassure him. "I'll surprise her. I'll take her out for a nice dinner and get us some ritzy-titsy hotel room. After a night of record-breaking sex, I'll tell her about the house."

"I don't know . . ."

"Just until next payday," Tony said, walking toward his own plane. "That's only 10 days. I know you. You've got the first dollar you ever made. Give me a break, Billy boy. For Angela's sake."

"All right," Bill said.

Bill must have known he was making a mistake. Tony wondered if Bill had heard that others had loaned him money. He meant to pay all of them back. Soon. Of course, he wasn't drinking at Clancy's any more. They had told him they couldn't afford him. Still, Tony knew it wasn't like that with Bill. They were brothers. Bill loaned him $300. The next day, Sonny fired Tony.

It was his own fault. Tony had stuck a "Short People" album in the cockpit of the boss' helicopter. Worse, he had taped the drawing to it, showing with a hand flipping the bird and the words "Happy Fucking Birthday." Sonny had recognized Tony's neat penmanship.

The next afternoon, Sonny called Tony into the shack of an office between loads. It pissed Tony off that Sonny had interrupted him. He entered the office shack and flopped on the sofa, annoyed. The boss made it short and sweet.

"Hit the road," were the first words out of Sonny's mouth.

"Kiss my ass," Tony said, never moving from the couch.

"Why'd I ever hire a drunk like you?" The short man standing behind the worn desk put his hands on his hips and shook his head in disgust.

"Because I can fly better than any other scuzzball who ever worked at this flop joint . . . including you."

"That's not enough anymore, Tony," Sonny said, smacking a stack of papers down on the desk.

"Tough," Tony answered, staring at the ceiling. "'Cause that's all there is."

"Not anymore," Sonny said, walking from behind the desk. His fat fingers were tucked in his high belt, and his short legs moved as if he had no knees. "Not here."

"Why not?" Tony asked, jumping up to look down at him. He had two loads left on a deadline job, and the wind was threatening to come up. Precious time was slipping away. Tony could almost feel the money slipping through his fingers. It wasn't like Sonny to stop him from finishing a job. He could be such an asshole.

"A field man at the River Ranch said he saw you flying my plane and touching the gear on the water," Sonny said, his face turning red.

"You can't prove that was me," Tony said, stepping closer to get in Sonny's face. He could feel himself starting to melt down inside. He needed this job. Damn, that was weeks ago. Besides, for all Sonny knew, it could have been Bill.

"I know it wasn't me," Sonny said, and turned to look out the window. "I doubt it was Bill."

"Fine, asshole," Tony said, pacing. "I'm in the middle of dusting a field right now. You want to guess how much I've done?"

"Finish it and park it," Sonny said, walking back behind the desk. "I'll have your check ready this Friday."

Tony walked out and slammed the door behind him. He headed for the plane and threw a set of chocks back at the office before mounting the wing. Once in the cockpit, his engine started with a roar, and Tony took off as hard as he could while carrying a full load. He headed for the field, slogging through the morning air with the heavy load of sulfur dust. In his mind, he agonized over what had just happened. The bills wouldn't wait. Angela would be disappointed. That guy was a jerk.

"Fuck him if he can't take a joke," Tony said above the engine noise.

He flew inland until he reached the rolling landscape of the field he had started earlier that morning. The first few spray runs with the heavy plane were difficult. He struggled to soar just above the olive drab artichokes. Swirling prickly leaves and swaying thistle fruit passed below him. Cold air caught the wing tip curl and created ever-widening swirls of yellow sulfur dust behind him. The powder hung in the moist morning air before settling on the crop. A puffy yellow trail followed him into the sky at the end of each spray run. He closed the spreader at power line height and blew the sulfur dust back into the field with the prop wash.

The hopper grew emptier with each pass. He stretched the plane in the crisp cool air, and she felt new again. Tony knew he was pushing it. He climbed the side of a worn red barn before plummeting downward again. Hugging the ground, he made her swerve around telephone poles. A power line bisected his windshield moments before he shot beneath it. He swept through the border passes with a flair to catch the edges of the field. At last, the hopper was empty, and he knew he had to go back.

He felt a distinct, burning sensation, and he could almost imagine the red lines creeping across the whites of his eyes, a contrast to the blue. The stinging, sulfur dust, as fine as talcum powder, caused most of his tears. It seeped in through every crack of the breezy old craft. An aching hunch that he wouldn't be flying for a while made him shed a few more tears.

Tony headed back toward the strip, deciding on the way to get shit-faced as soon as possible. He came in for a landing, pondering various forms of revenge. Two favorites occurred to him. For the first, he aimed the propeller at the power line hanging across the middle of the runway. At first, the wire was horizontal in his line of sight, but he let it drop below the windscreen. It stretched taunt on either side of him before the prop sliced it. The electricity arced with a flash of blue light that would leave a black mark on the fuselage. The split wire formed black S's on either side of him before falling to the ground. With that maneuver, Tony cut off electricity to the airstrip. A satisfied smile accompanied his last landing.

His plane was rolling to a stop. The boss came surging out of his helicopter, the main rotor of the chopper still spinning. Sonny walked toward Tony's parked plane as fast as his short legs would carry him. Tony's worn leather glove grabbed the key from the plane's ignition. He hurried out of the cockpit, jumped off the wing, and walked straight past Sonny.

"Damn you, Damascus!!" Sonny yelled after him.

A chemical mix truck sat parked beside the dilapidated white shack. It contained a fresh load of pesticides, ready to be pumped into the hopper of the boss's waiting helicopter. Tony climbed the side of the truck, opened the hatch to a tank full of Diazinon, and dropped the key into the load. The milled piece of nickel silver was still fluttering to the bottom of the tank when Tony started his car and headed for the bar.

Heroes and Survivors

TONY DROVE his new sedan toward the airstrip, heading down the thin line of dirt followed by a cloud of dust. It was payday, and he had come to collect his check. He had parked and was walking toward the shed when he spotted Bill coming in for a landing. Tony thought about the $300 he owed Bill and wished he could keep his promise.

Tony slipped in and out of the strip before Bill could land. He peeled out without saying a word. In his rearview mirror, Tony saw Bill standing beside the plane, watching Tony's car pull away. I'll come back, Tony told himself. He returned an hour later. Bill was gassing up the plane between loads.

"Where'd you go?" Bill asked, jumping down from the plane's wing and returning the gas nozzle to the pump. He shot a glance over to the shack. "Sonny'll be pissed if he catches you here."

"Now doesn't that break my heart?" Tony asked with a surly vengeance, but couldn't summon his normal, nasty grin. He leaned against his car and squinted at the sun.

"You hungover?" Bill asked, locking up the gas pump.

"Hell, I don't know," Tony said, flattening his moustache with the palm of his hand. Bill's waiting plane looked tempting. "I haven't stopped drinking long enough to find out."

"Hey, things will change," Bill said and walked toward Tony. "Have you been looking for another job?"

"Not exactly," Tony said, looking around the strip. He was having a hard time looking Bill in the eye. "I have something better in mind."

"Like what?" Bill asked, glimpsing at the office door.

"I've been talking with Patches," Tony said, then paused to light a bent cigarette. The cigarette fit in the corner of his mouth, lifting one side of his black moustache. Bill looked him straight in the eye. Tony turned away, shielding his match from an imaginary wind. "He's always wanted to cropdust. We've cooked up a little plan."

"Are you two going into business?" Bill asked, keeping his eyes on Tony.

"We're talking," Tony said, staring across the river.

"And?" Bill asked. Tony felt Bill trying to drag the details from him. It was an odd sensation. He used to tell Bill everything. Now, there was something lodged between them that made Tony feel vulnerable. Something like $300.

"We might get a helicopter," Tony said, exhaling a slow, long stream of smoke.

"We?" Bill asked. He sounded hurt.

"Patches and I," Tony nodded. He lifted the cigarette to his lips and then lowered it. "Unless you want in."

"On what?" Bill gave an anxious look to the airplane, and Tony could tell he was worried about the wind switching.

"I'm coming into a chunk of change when escrow closes," Tony answered, examining the orange glow of his cigarette. He dropped that hand to his side and shoved the other in his front pocket. "Patches is letting Angela and me stay at the cabin, rent free. He's willing to pay half for a chopper, and I'll pay the rest plus do the flying."

"But you've never flown one," Bill said. "Go slowly on this." Bill's voice switched from hurt to genuine concern, and that made Tony feel worse.

"How difficult can it be?" Tony said with a quick glance to the shed. "Dickhead does it."

"True," Bill said in a quiet voice. "Hey, why did Sonny fire you anyway?"

"Uh?" Tony asked. Bill's question caught him off guard. Tony couldn't tell him the truth. "Hell, if I know. Wanted to do me a favor, I guess. After Patches and I start our new business in the other valley, we'll be a rich pair of mothers."

"If you're so rich," Bill said, "how about loaning me a couple of hundred?" Bill had mentioned the real reason for the awkwardness between them.

"No problem," Tony said, taking a drag, dropping his cigarette, and grinding it into the asphalt. "Soon as we get cranking."

Bill turned away, climbed up on the wing, and grabbed his helmet from the seat of the plane. Then, he paused and turned back.

"It's payday, Tony."

"That cocksucker deducted the wire from my check," Tony said, avoiding what Bill was really wanting to know.

"Are you saying you can't pay me back?" Bill asked, looking down at him from the wing. He dropped his white helmet onto his head but left the chin strap hanging. "Just say so because if—"

"I'll pay you back," Tony said, squinting as he tried to look at Bill. "Just not today. I don't have it."

"Sure," Bill said, jumping down from the wing.

"I can't," Tony said, following Bill around the front of the plane. There were things Bill didn't know. Maybe he wouldn't understand. "You know I would if I could."

"Yeah, right," Bill answered, walking at a quick pace toward the mix truck that held his next load of dust.

"Look, Billy boy, it's the truth," Tony said, walking behind him. "I had to tent the damn house for termites before the sale could go through. It took almost all of my check. In a couple of weeks—"

"Fine," Bill said, waving one hand in Tony's direction. "I don't want to discuss it."

"Hey, it's only money," Tony said, stopping and folding his arms. "I'll get it back to you."

"Just drop it, OK?" Bill said, entering the mix truck and slamming the door.

Bill drove the truck 20 yards and parked it close to his plane. Before he could get out, Tony climbed up on the wing and positioned the huge loading funnel over the hopper door in front of the cockpit. He pulled a lever that sent yellow powder streaming into the plane. Tony pushed the funnel aside when it emptied. Bill climbed up on the wing beside Tony, got into the cockpit, and snapped his chin strap tight. He reached for the ignition, but Tony didn't budge from the wing.

"I got a load to put out," Bill said and stretched his arm out of the plane. He grabbed the handle on the window and started to pull it closed.

"Terrific," Tony said. He forced a tired smile and remained perched on the wing. "Look, I just wanted to tell you, Angela's pregnant."

"Are you kidding me?" Bill answered, dropping the window and looking at Tony in disbelief. Tony wasn't sure how to react. He was still getting used to the idea himself.

"Maybe I missed my calling in life," Tony said with a laugh. "I should charge stud fees."

"Are you shitting me?" Bill asked, switching off the ignition.

"It's true," Tony said, combing his hand through his black curls and then shaking his head. "We're going to have a kid. God, I hope it's like her, and not me."

"The world can't take two of you, Tony."

"What if he is?" Tony asked, shrugging and forcing his hands into his pockets. "What if he's just like me?"

"I think you have to keep them no matter what," Bill said with a smile.

"God, the things I could teach him," Tony said, and his eyebrows jumped.

"Spare me," Bill said and paused. "You're not kidding, are you?" Tony shook his head. "What do the doctors say?"

"When they recover from the shock, you mean?" Tony said, leaning against the fuselage with one arm. "They figure it's OK. She's up and around, walking and talking, even driving a car. They figure there's no reason she can't have a baby."

"Hey, congratulations," Bill said, wiping his hand on a rag and offering it to Tony. Tony shook it and climbed down from the wing.

"Thanks," Tony said, looking up at Bill. "I always feel like such a hero when someone does that." Tony looked at his hand for a second before sliding it into his pocket.

"Get used to it," Bill said, looking down at him from the cockpit.

"Look, Bill, I'd like to do something really special for Angela. You know, take her out or something. Maybe you and Cindy could come along."

"Sounds good," Bill said, reaching out to close the window again.

"There's just one thing," Tony said, and then went for it. "Could you loan me a little money? Just 50 bucks."

"What?" Bill said, his head swiveling back to look at Tony.

"Just until—"

"Do I look like a fool?" Bill said, his voice growing louder.

"What?" Tony asked, throwing both arms out to his side.

"Go get drunk," Bill said, trying to start the engine, but she wouldn't turn over. "I've got work to do." He crawled out of the cockpit, preparing to prop himself.

"Hey, let me do it, Billy boy," Tony said, moving toward the front of the plane.

"No, thanks," Bill said, stepping in front of Tony. "And don't call me that."

"Why not?" Tony asked, taking a step back.

"I never thought you would do it to me," Bill said, holding one blade of the prop and looking over his shoulder at Tony. "You always did it to everyone else, but I never thought you would do it to me. You always said I was the brother you never had."

"You are, bro—"

"That's a load of crap," Bill answered, pulling the propeller once with all his strength. There was only a sputter. "You lied to me just like you lied to everyone else."

"Look, if the money means that much—" Tony started.

"It doesn't," Bill said, reaching up and grabbing the blade again. "It doesn't mean a damn thing, and neither do you." He yanked down hard, and the engine caught. Tony stepped away, and Bill scrambled onto the wing and into the cockpit.

"Look, I don't have it right now, OK?" Tony shouted over the engine noise. "Just wait. . ." He turned and ran to his car. Bill finished running up the engine, and Tony returned, carrying his rifle with the zebra-striped butt stock. "Take this," Tony said, holding it up toward the cockpit. "I'll give you the money when I get it."

"I don't want that ugly thing," Bill yelled over the roar of the engine. "Keep it. Keep the money. Don't fucking bug me anymore. Ever." Bill slammed the window shut and rolled toward the runway.

"Bill—" Tony yelled after the taxiing aircraft. It didn't stop. "Asshole."

Tony stood alone, watching Bill's take off. The plane launched from the end of the runway, and Tony swaggered to his car. He threw the rifle through an open window, and it dropped on the back seat. He opened the driver's door and sat down, staring at the empty runway. Bill wasn't coming back. He ran his hand through his hair, and then turned the key in the ignition. The engine whirred, sputtered, and went silent. He tried again but the weak battery only made a ticking sound.

"Son of a bitch," he said, jumping out of the car and slamming the door. "Damn!"

He pulled jumper cables from his trunk, lifted the hood of Bill's pickup parked beside him, and hooked the clamps to Bill's battery posts. As he expected, Bill had left his keys under the driver's seat of his truck. Most guys did at the strip, in case it needed to be moved while they were out working. He started Bill's engine.

The whole process of jumping his dead battery took about ten minutes. Tony slammed down both hoods when he finished and threw the cables back in his trunk. He was letting his engine idle when he spotted Bill coming in to land. He couldn't have put out a whole load of dust that fast. Something must have gone wrong.

Tony studied the plane. Bill's engine wasn't smoking. Nothing was on fire. The radial engine sounded fine to Tony's discerning ear. She seemed to fly all right. Tony's first guess was that a crew of farm laborers was working next to the field that Bill intended to dust. Maybe there was some doubt about which field to spray. Bill was now faced with the unhappy prospect of landing with a full load of dust.

"Serves you right, you S.O.B.," Tony said under his breath and chuckled to himself. He leaned back on the hood of his car, folded his arms, and watched Bill struggle with the tricky landing. "This is going to be rich."

Tony knew that most spray planes were designed to take off with a load, but not to land with one. He watched the lumbering plane descend with a feeling of justification.

The gear touched down on the dirt at the far end of the strip, inches short of the asphalt. Bill's placement was wise. He would need the entire length of the runway to roll the heavy craft to a stop. The wheels struck the lip of the pavement, and the plane launched back into the air. Tony started to smile, and then noticed the left wheel of the landing gear was dangling loose below the strut.

"Oh, fuck," Tony whispered, standing up straight.

Bill touched down again, and the broken left gear dug into the blacktop. The tail of the aircraft soared into the air above the cockpit. The plane plunged straight into the runway like an arrow, and the propeller ground into the asphalt. Momentum flopped the tail completely over the top. The plane skidded upside down and stopped, belly in the air. One wheel was still spinning, and the other hung broken and sideways. The canopy of the cockpit, now beneath the fuselage and pressed against the runway, started to collapse under the weight of the aircraft. Noise was followed by silence, which was followed by smoke.

Tony left his engine running and raced into the shack where Sonny was on the phone.

"Call the fire department," Tony said and grabbed the fire extinguisher from the wall.

"What are you doing here?" Sonny said, covering the receiver.

"Call the fire department, damn it," Tony said again. "Bill just crashed." Tony shot back out the door and ran to his car. He jumped in and pulled away, heading down the runway, fish-tailing with tires squealing.

"Get out," Tony said, driving toward the upside-down plane in the middle of the airstrip. He could feel his heart pounding, threatening to break through his chest. "Get out, Billy boy. Get out."

Small sparks started dancing in the spilled yellow dust around the downed plane. Tony remembered the full load of sulfur on board, now as dangerous as a hopper full of matchheads between two gas tanks. Sparks turned to tongues of fire.

"Get out, damn it, get out!" Tony said, pushing the gas pedal to the floor. He came closer to the crash site than he should have and slammed on the brakes. Smoke engulfed the plane, and flames began licking the fuselage around the engine.

"Bill-eeee. . ." he called, grabbing the fire extinguisher and leaping from the car without closing the door. His footrace to the plane continued in dream-like slow motion. "Get out!"

Black smoke accompanied the stench of rotten eggs and burning fuel. Tony raced toward the burning plane. It was crazy, but he couldn't stop himself. Through the flames, Tony could see something round and white emerging from the small gap that remained between the cockpit and the runway, where a window used to be.

Tony knew Bill couldn't move. He would be hanging upside down with his chin pressed to his chest, and his shoulders jammed against the asphalt. Breathing would be difficult. His legs would be above him. Blood would be rushing to his head. Smoke. The smell of smoke was everywhere. There were echoes of Hartley Bolger's voice in the air.

"I know a guy who went upside down. Didn't even get hurt. Then, he released his seatbelt and broke his shoulder when he hit the runway."

Break a bone if you have to, Billy boy. Just get out. Tony tried to portray his thoughts to Bill. Reach up, which is down, and feel for the ground. It's pressed against your shoulders. Bill released the shoulder strap, and Tony saw it hit the pavement, but Bill didn't budge. Another voice. An old boy from Mississippi that Tony used to fly with.

"Damnedest thing, that crash. I had to get out through the window, but I couldn't break the glass. Ended up kicking it out with my boot."

"The glass is already broken," Tony screamed, as if he were reading Bill's mind. Smoke, smoke. Oh God, don't let him burn.

"No-o-o," Bill said from the cockpit.

Tony heard it and moved closer. Bill was wiggling loose from the shoulder harness. In the next instant, he was squeezing himself through the small gap between the fuselage and the pavement. His white helmet poked out first, like it was coming through the birth canal. Sparks were flickering on the collar of Bill's jacket and at the ends of the blond curls that poked out beneath his helmet. Tony aimed the fire extinguisher at the back of Bill's neck, and then laid down a path of foam for Bill to follow.

"Get out, damn it," Tony yelled. Heat from the burning plane stung Tony's cheeks. "Keep coming, keep coming."

Bill clawed the pavement and kicked his legs, prying his way from the wreckage. Tony grabbed him by one arm and pulled him free, trying to point the fire extinguisher at the closest flames. Bill's chest came out first then his legs, minus one boot. His hand dropped from Tony's grasp, and Tony used both arms to work the fire extinguisher. Bill crawled past Tony toward the edge of the runway, trying to distance himself from the plane.

"Get away," Bill said, crawling by and tugging at Tony's pant leg. He was grasping for air and struggling to get to his feet.

"The plane," Tony answered, letting Bill pass and pointing the extinguisher at the wreckage. Bill, crouching, stumbled a few feet before dropping to his knees and crawling to the edge of the runway.

"Tony, it's full of gas and sulfur dust," Bill said, choking and gasping through his words. "Get back." The effort made him crumble to the ground. He knelt and braced himself with one hand in the dirt alongside the pavement. Flames tore through the twisted mass of metal he had occupied seconds earlier.

Tony fought the fire for a moment or two longer, like a madman pissing on a firestorm. Then, he threw the empty extinguisher at the blaze and ran to Bill just before the gas tanks exploded.

"Are you all right?" he asked, grabbing Bill by the shoulders and starting to pull him further away.

"Ah-h-h..." Bill said, grimacing with pain. "Don't touch me." Tony pulled his hands away. Bill grabbed his stomach and put his head down between his knees. Tony waited for him to either throw up or pass out. The fire burned through the fuselage, leaving a blackened metal skeleton.

"It wasn't your fault," Tony said, looking down on the back of Bill's white helmet. He turned to look at the landing gear, now black and pointing at the sky. "The gear broke when you touched down."

Bill forced his head up. He stared in the direction of the left wheel that dangled askew from the landing gear. He unsnapped his helmet chin strap and wiggled it from his head in pain. He tossed it as far as he could, a few pathetic feet.

"Let me help you," Tony said, starting to reach for him again.

"No—"

"Your lips are as white as chalk," Tony said, wondering if Bill was just pale or covered with sulfur dust. "I'll bring the car—"

"Don't."

"Come on, Billy boy," Tony said, looking back and forth from Bill to his car. "You can't still be pissed."

"I was so mad at you," Bill said, gasping for breath. "I forgot the fucking map of the field. I had to come back. Stupid, stupid. I nearly killed myself." He started to shake his head and then moaned from the pain.

"Look, Bill, I'm sorry," Tony said, kneeling next to him.

"Get away from me," Bill said, choking and looking up at him. Tears streaked his blackened cheeks. He pushed Tony away. "I never want to see your face again."

A fire engine came screaming up the runway, and Tony backed away from Bill, hugging his gut. Four firefighters leapt from the truck. Two of them grabbed hoses, and two more rushed toward Bill.

"Anyone else in the plane?" one fireman asked Bill. In the distance, Tony melted into the front seat of his car.

"No," Bill answered, collapsing. One fireman cradled him. Another ran for a stretcher.

Tony, feeling numb, started his car, turned around, and drove away, checking his rearview mirror. He pulled over on the dirt road to allow an approaching ambulance to pass. It screamed toward the heap of black metal in the middle of the runway. Tony's trembling hands steered his car down the road again. He pulled his car to a stop on the freeway overpass near the strip. Tony stepped out and looked back. The fire was doused, and the stretcher was being loaded into the ambulance.

A few moments later, the white emergency vehicle blew past him on the road, stirring up dust and tossing his hair around. It rifled down a straight road between lettuce fields toward the nearest hospital in Salinas. The lights were on, but the siren wasn't.

"Don't die, asshole," Tony whispered. "Please don't die."

At Least My
Mother Loves Me

ROBERTO PRAYED in his bedroom, mulling over the Catholic Men's League's latest complaint. Their list of grievances over the past two years included objections to the new song books, the updated candles, and the lack of hand bells. In particular, they opposed the new stained glass window. He stared at the simple cross on the wall, made from dried fronds from last Palm Sunday. Rumors surfaced daily of disgruntled letters written to the bishop. Roberto heard them from the office staff, Sister Mary Teresa, and even Carlo.

Roberto finished, signed himself, and headed for the living room, avoiding the local newspaper. Even so, he couldn't escape the subject that had dogged him more than the CML.

"He got the death penalty," he had overheard in the foyer before mass. "Deserves it too, the bastard."

"Mendoza is going to appeal the death penalty conviction," someone had said in the vegetable aisle of the grocery store.

Later that evening, it came to haunt him at his own dinner table. He was trying to choke down the leftovers that Carlo had heated for them.

"He pleaded innocent," Father Carlo said in Italian, from across the table. "The jury had only three Mexicans. The rest were white."

"I thought you were going somewhere," Roberto answered, dropping his fork with a clatter. Carlo never left when Roberto wished he would. "Didn't you say you needed the car?"

"Yes. True," Carlo said in English.

"You've taken it every night this week," Roberto said, shoving his half-eaten dinner away from him.

"It's the de Salvo sisters. . ." Carlo answered, sounding vague and playing with his peas. He looked like a child with his napkin tucked into his collar.

"Isn't that where you went last night?"

"They are very troubled," Carlo said and looked up. Tomato paste dotted his chin. "There is much worry in their family. The youngest sister thinks she may be . . ." His English failed him. He motioned a half circle from his chest to his lap.

"Pregnant?" Roberto asked, checking his memory. He could visualize the De Salvo sisters, all three so ugly it must have hurt. They had inherited prime farm land though, and Roberto had hoped they would be interested in donating to the window. "Is she married?"

"No, no. It is . . . It is no good."

"Maybe you shouldn't—"

"Without the church's support, I fear she will do a very wrong thing," Carlo said, his mouth full of food.

"Abortion?" Roberto asked. He got up and carried his plate to the kitchen, leaving it in the sink.

"Worse," Carlo's voice said from the other room. "She is constantly sad. She sees no reason to live. It is better that I go." Roberto returned to the room in time to see Carlo move the Parmesan cheese toward his coffee cup.

"Take the car," Roberto said, waving his hand. "Go, go." Carlo left without drinking his coffee.

Roberto stared at the door to the garage, long after it had closed behind Carlo. He didn't need the distraction of such petty affairs or Carlo's reminders about Mendoza. Let Carlo attend to the simpler needs of the church. He didn't speak English well enough to deal with the CML. At times, Roberto longed to confide in Carlo about Mendoza, but that would only have added to Roberto's burdens, the sin of defiling the sanctity of the confessional.

That evening, alone in front of the television, watching but not absorbing the newscast, he decided he needed a break. It had been ages since he had been away. He needed to go somewhere alone, away from murderers, stained glass windows, and stiff-necked parishioners. Some place he could forget about it all for a while. He needed to go home.

The office next to the living room was dark. He wandered in and switched on the light, finding the phone book, as usual, on the filing cabinet. One of the advertisers on the plastic cover was a travel agent in town. He knew they would be closed but noted the number and decided to call first thing in the morning.

ROBERTO'S EXHAUSTION carried over into the next afternoon. He went two rounds with Sister Mary Teresa over her objections to his new way of teaching catechism. A phone call from the travel agent interrupted them. The agent said she had found him an airline ticket to Italy at the end of the week. The long-awaited vacation would do him good.

Roberto went home for four weeks to forget everything and, for the most part, he did a good job. The days slid by with tranquility that refreshed him. There were dinners in the company of his elderly uncles, long talks with his mother at their old kitchen table, and ample samplings of the local wines. He attended daily mass at his childhood cathedral, enjoying the view from the rear for a change. His return to King City found him revitalized and ready for a fresh start.

"I hiked the hills I had hiked when I was a boy," Roberto said, during his first homily after his return. He stood before an ever-shrinking congregation, reveling in his renewed zest for life and God. Many of the old faces were no longer in attendance. The new ones weren't as numerous, but they seemed fresher and younger.

"I looked down on the same vineyards and ate dinner with cousins I never knew I had. I must have eaten more than usual. I feel it here." He smiled and patted his stomach hidden beneath his flowing white vestments. The parishioners listened, and a few even laughed.

"My mother cooked for me," he said, pacing the width of the altar.

The microphone attached to the neck of his garment squealed when he came too close to the choir's sound equipment. It coughed with static if he waved his arms, exposing the big bell sleeves of his vestments. It clicked and buzzed when passing aircraft radioed the tower of the Salinas airport.

"She is 90, but she still cooked for me," he said, wandering closer to the first pew. Those closest to the front of the church stiffened. "I had worried. Worried she wouldn't be well. Worried, that at her age, she might not even remember me. But she cooked dinner for me. We talked. I shared my personal experience of God with her. She shared hers with me." He walked back toward the altar area, took the two steps up to it with caution, and then continued.

"She wondered how I felt about my childhood. In anger, she had sent me away to the seminary. Later, she realized that was the wrong thing to do." He could almost see his mother's face when he spoke, and the vision of it made him sigh. "She told me she loved me. No matter how old you are, maybe the older the better, it's important to know your mother loves you."

"My personal experience of God says He is not in a book or a catechism. He's not in the kneelers, the communion rails, or the song books. He's here." The fist to his chest generated a wave of static from the microphone. "Before you know Him in the world, you must recognize him in your heart. Hopefully, the effect He has on your life will bless others.

"If your faith is alive, it will reveal love," he said, looking up at first, then across the faces in the pews. "Seeing my mother renewed me because I finally knew she loved me." He closed the holy book on the podium and sat down between the altar boys. In the silence that followed, he could hear a whispered voice from the second row.

"Only a mother would," the produce baron whispered. Bob Hardine's wife didn't bother elbowing him in the ribs. She had to know by now, after months of nudging, it wouldn't change a thing.

The boys in the back got up to start passing the collection basket. Roberto imagined they were taking notes for their next letter to the bishop. He watched their progress, swooping the basket on a stick down each sparsely populated row, coming toward the front at a measured pace. Sister Mary Teresa had told Roberto that half of the regular members now left town on Sunday mornings to attend mass in Greenfield, 12 miles up the road toward Salinas. The only part of the church filled to capacity was the rectory attic, jammed with the discarded communion rail and kneelers from the pews.

Father Roberto waited and mulled over his decision to dismiss Father Carlo from his position soon after he returned from Italy. To the parishioners, it must have seemed that Carlo was there one Sunday, and without explanation, gone the next, like the other items in the church. Some parishioners had murmured that he too might be in the attic. The lack of explanation about his departure became another conflict between the people and Roberto. He didn't think the truth would help them.

Roberto sat and looked out over the parishioners. Parents struggled with young children, but they weren't the only ones who agonized over Roberto's long homily. In the last pew, Roberto noticed a serious young man with glasses. While Roberto had been speaking, the young man had seemed to listen to every word that he had said. Perspiration had soaked through his well-ironed shirt though it was not a warm day.

RETURNING TO THE CHURCH had been hard. The young man with the serious face looked up. He wondered if the roof would cave in after his decade away. He had attended mass until his confirmation at age 13, then bolted. Three Sundays had passed. The roof had stayed above his head, but his anxiety remained.

Mass ended, and the priest took his place at the rear exit of the church. The young man noticed that not everyone felt inclined to shake Father Roberto's hand. Some seemed to regard it as a distasteful obligation. A few of the younger people looked uncertain. Bill wandered out of the church, passing the poster on the door for the upcoming Ethnic Festival. He felt some of that same uncertainty when Roberto offered his hand.

"Hello, Father," Bill said, controlling his nerves.

"It's a good morning," Roberto said in his rapid fire fashion. "Hardly any wind."

"A slight south," Bill answered, correcting him with a professional eye on the trees.

"For King City, that's good," Roberto said with a laugh.

"So I've noticed," Bill answered. The wind, friend and foe to the cropduster, had blown nonstop since his arrival in King City two months ago.

"You're new to town, aren't you?" Roberto asked.

"Fairly new. Does the wind ever stop?"

"Almost never," Roberto said. "What brought you to King City?"

Bill sensed Roberto eyeing him. The rumors about the Catholic Men's League warring with the priest didn't mean a thing to him. He was too new to care about the politics of the church. He was just new enough to believe he could find in the same church the answers that he needed.

"I took a job here as a pilot," Bill answered.

"In King City?"

"I cropdust," he answered in a soft voice. He decided not to mention the crash that had forced him to find another job, or his need for an explanation of why he had survived.

"Ah, cropdusting, like making lo—" Roberto stopped himself and gave a cold stare to the organist approaching him. She patted his elbow and walked away. The priest focused on Bill again. "I knew a cropduster once. Tony. Tony, um, I forget his last name. Do you know him?"

"I don't think so," Bill said, his green eyes looking away.

"Black hair, black moustache. Tony something. I wish I could remember his name."

Bill didn't answer. It was a new life for him and a new town. To him, Tony was dead. He nodded to Roberto and headed for his car. He would try again next Sunday.

ROBERTO SAID GOOD-BYE to a few more parishioners, but his eyes kept wandering back to a group of Catholic Men's League members standing near the edge of the church parking lot. Bob Hardine, the produce baron, was there, surrounded by what looked to be a quorum of the CML. The local jeweler, the hardware store owner, a teacher, and a banker flanked Hardine. Now and then, they glanced Roberto's way, but they seemed more focused on one man in particular. Abe Alvarez.

Roberto found it odd that Abe was with the group at all. The story was that Abe had applied for CML membership before he was elected Chief of Police, but his application had been denied. He would have been the first Hispanic member, if he had been accepted. The CML had invited him to become a member after he became Chief, but Abe had declined. Now they were talking to him as if they were all great friends.

A few more parishioners shook Roberto's hand, and he tried to be pleasant, but the informal meeting of the CML distracted him. The last of the parishioners filed out of the church. Roberto stepped just inside the doorway of the church by the dispenser of holy water. His green eyes remained fixed on the CML members talking to Abe. The big man with the wide forehead looked uncomfortable out of uniform. He was shaking his head "no."

Were they asking him not to support the Ethnic Festival? Roberto tried to read the expressions on their faces. The ladies that worked in the church office had each taken Roberto aside on separate occasions to whisper to him that the CML planned a barbeque at the armory on the day of the festival.

Roberto had noticed that Abe had been attending the English mass for the last several weeks. His wife had been attending the Spanish mass. Abe's wife was a devoted member of the Hispanic Catholic women's group, the Sisters of Guadalupe or Las Hermanas Guadalupe as they called themselves. Sister Teresa attended their activities. She had told Roberto that Abe's mother was ill, which is why the Alvarezes attended separate masses, so someone could be with Abe's mother at all times. Sister had advised Roberto to visit the elderly woman, but Roberto had asked Father Carlo to do it. Chances were good that it had never been done.

Roberto moved from the doorway to the small window beside the statue of the Virgin Mary. It offered a better view of the CML encounter with Abe. Roberto should have made the time to see Abe's mother. Visiting the sick was always difficult. He never felt he brought hope to them. It always reminded him of when his sister died, and how his mother turned away. The overall experience was one of pain, despite the solemn promise of his vocation to minister to the sick. Someone, anyone, would be better at it than Roberto.

The members of the CML were now showing a piece of paper to Abe and offering him a pen. Probably another letter to the bishop. That wouldn't go far. Roberto knew the bishop had cancer, not that Roberto had visited him either. The bishop was too sick to worry about missing communion rails and kneelers or opposition to a stained glass window in the smallest parish of the diocese.

A tap on the shoulder from behind startled Roberto. It was the small, bespectacled visiting priest who had come to celebrate the noon mass in Spanish in place of Father Carlo. Roberto changed his vestments and said a silent prayer of thanks before showing the new man around. Roberto's Spanish was atrocious, and he was grateful that someone would be presiding instead of him. After a quick tour, the new priest assured Roberto that he felt comfortable.

That left Roberto free to head back to the rectory and box up Carlo's remaining clothes and books. He headed up the walk, whistling, sure that he could finish the job in twenty minutes. Two representatives of the CML waited for Roberto at the other end of the walk by the rectory door. Lord, give me strength . . .

"Father, we have tried to be patient," Art DeVries said, the older of the two men. His opening comment, combined with the informal meeting that Roberto had witnessed, put Roberto's stomach in a knot before he reached the steps.

"Patience is a virtue," Roberto answered in his quick style and fumbled for his key. "Come in, come in."

Roberto entered the residence, followed by the hardware store owner Art DeVries and his younger counterpart, Larry Weeks, a high school math teacher. Stiff wooden chairs near an orderly desk were part of the cold furnishings in the bleak church office. Like most Sundays, it was devoid of the older ladies who usually answered the phones or made Roberto's tea.

"Sit, sit," Roberto said, a little delighted that he could offer them such uncomfortable chairs.

"No, thank you," Art answered just as the other man was about to take a seat. Larry stood up again and shoved his hands in his pockets.

"Glass of wine?" Roberto asked, starting toward the hall.

"No, Father," Art said in a firm voice. His strong hands suggested youth when Roberto compared them to his own. Yet the gray at Art's temples implied age when he stood next to Larry. His clear blue eyes seem wise and honest, but Roberto felt bad news was coming just the same. "You must bring back the communion rails. You can't ignore the people's feelings indefinitely."

"Feelings change," Roberto said, placing his missal on the desk. "Are you sure you won't have some wine?"

"Father Roberto," the teacher said, pointing toward the church. "Those railings were built by the men who established this church."

"Peter and Paul?" Roberto asked with a smile.

"The Hardine Brothers," Larry answered. He pushed his glasses up his prominent nose—a nervous habit—and continued. "The people of this church know how important tradition is to the continuity of a parish. However, when someone comes in and makes sweeping changes without regard for—"

"Tradition and continuity are fine," Roberto said, half-seated on the desk and crossing his arms. "I did not make up the changes written in the Vatican II documents. I was not even taught how to bring them to the people. My seminary training dealt with the old ways. This spiritual revolution is more difficult for me to accept than for you. It uncloaks mysteries I always accepted as indefinable. The people are no longer subject to an ancient ritual in a language they don't understand. They are participating in something living. Every good Catholic should understand *why* they stand and sit during mass, not merely conform like robots."

"But the rail?" the store owner and president of the CML asked.

"You shouldn't be fed like baby birds," Roberto answered, holding pinched fingers in front of him. "You should come forward, stand up, and receive your portion like an adult."

"It isn't the removal of the rail so much," Larry said. The teacher rubbed his fingertips together and looked around the room. Roberto assumed he was longing for chalk and a blackboard. "It's the way it was done. One Sunday it was there, the next—"

"I was blessed with unexpected help," Roberto answered, leaving the desk and removing his sweater. He stepped around the corner to hang it up and returned with a handful of flyers advertising the Ethnic Festival. "Would you mind distributing these?"

"You're not listening," Art said, slapping his arms against his sides and looking at the ceiling.

"Of course I am, but we cannot stay kindergarten Catholics forever. Take some posters." Neither man reached for the papers in Roberto's outstretched hand.

"Father," Art said in a quiet but firm voice. "The Catholic Men's League feels if you persist in this manner, we can no longer promise financial support."

"What do you mean?" Roberto asked, lowering the posters. This is what he had dreaded when he first saw them.

"Speaking as treasurer on the CML's behalf, we are asking for your cooperation," the teacher said, backing up Art.

"Cooperation?" Roberto repeated, feeling confused. "Of course. What do you need?"

"Reinstall the railing," Art said, sounding irritated.

"That's not cooperation," Roberto said. "That's regression."

"The people are not ready—"

"They never are," Roberto said, looking from one man to the other. "That's why there are leaders. One man steps forward. With God's blessing, the people follow. Maybe one of you—"

"You give us no choice," the teacher said.

"From now on," Art said, "all funds collected by the CML will be held in a separate account. Until you recognize that we, the people, have a say—"

"I realize that—" Roberto started.

"—our funds will be withheld."

"Fine, fine," Roberto answered, turning away. He evened the stack of papers in his hands with a few nervous taps on the desktop. They had planned to tell him this from the moment they walked in the door. He should have guessed. Still, he had hoped. He turned back to face the two men again, holding the posters toward them. "Hand out some of these. Put one in the window of your store. Take them to the school."

"What?" they both asked.

"For the unity of the parish. The Hispanic and Anglo communities must function like one body for this parish to survive."

"In order for this parish to survive, we need a priest who listens," Art said, using a stern tone Roberto didn't often hear. "Until then, you can display your own posters."

"I agree," Larry said.

"Do you agree because you are a member of the CML?" Roberto asked. "Or because you feel it is right?" He could tell by Larry's pause that he had made the teacher think. Maybe enough to think twice about holding the CML barbecue at the armory on the same day as the Ethnic Festival.

"Both, I suppose," the teacher answered.

"I understand. Is there anything else?" Roberto asked.

"Nothing else," Art said with a sigh. His companion reached for the door knob.

"In that case, excuse me," Roberto said. "I have posters to distribute."

Rumors of the Italian Stallion

ROBERTO HEADED DOWN the hall toward Carlo's old room even before the door closed behind the two men. He dropped the bright posters on Carlo's bed and began packing box after box. It was easier to lose himself in the simple task than to ponder what had just happened. The relief he had felt from his much-needed vacation in Italy faded. Soon Mendoza's fate would return to haunt him. His eyes landed on the miniature cannon in the corner.

"I'll ship his books and clothes, but not the cannon. Mama mia."

Noon mass was almost over before Roberto carried the last of Carlo's boxed belongings to the garage. Sister Mary Teresa came marching toward him while he was loading them into the trunk of his car. Oh, no. . . He heaved an exhausted sigh but couldn't avoid her. She entered the garage like a storm in a teacup. Her dark habit whirled in a petite flurry, and she waved some papers with one hand.

"These flyers . . . They're on every windshield in the parking lot," she said in a big voice, holding them close to his nose. He grabbed one and held it at arm's length. The messy photocopies were covered with someone's crude handwriting. There was a sudden gnawing in the pit of his stomach.

"They're all in Spanish," she said. "They mention Father Carlo, but I don't know what—"

"Come with me," Roberto said, starting down the driveway and talking back over his shoulder. "We need to find them all before mass ends."

"What's it all about?" she asked, following his rapid steps past the overflowing church to the parking lot. Roberto couldn't help noticing that the visiting priest drew a bigger crowd than he did these days.

"What it says isn't important," Roberto answered, heading into the parking lot at a crisp pace. "We must remove every one of these."

Sister Mary Teresa stopped in the middle of the parking lot. The white flyers were lodged beneath every windshield wiper of every car. They waved in the King City wind. Roberto began gathering them, one by one, and had five or six before he looked back at her. She hadn't moved. Her piercing eyes glared at him, and her hands remained glued to her hips.

"Sister, we have less than ten minutes," he said, walking back toward her. "We have to hurry." He turned to strip a flyer from the nearest car, and then moved on to the next one.

"Father, I own a Spanish-English dictionary," she said, still rooted to the spot. "How badly do you want my help?"

He glanced at his watch and looked at her, feeling frustrated. She returned his stubborn stare. He had to compromise.

"It's about Carlo," he said, approaching her.

"I know that much."

"And the de Salvo sisters," Roberto said, speaking softer and glancing from side to side. "It says they are agents of Satan who tricked Father Carlo."

"Nonsense."

"It claims that the de Salvo sisters forced him to be—" He looked around again before continuing. He had hoped to avoid this, the truth. "—to be their lover."

"What?" she asked, with her fawn-like dark eyes full of trust. "Everyone will know that's crazy. He was so shy, so humble, and his homilies were sacred."

Even she didn't know, Roberto thought. Carlo's eloquent Sunday messages had all been stolen from Homily Weekly magazine. He would leave her with her illusions.

"Yes, well. . ." Roberto started, checking his watch again.

"Why did he leave?" she asked.

The wind had picked up, threatening to spread the papers across the entire town.

"We'd better hurry," Roberto said, starting to turn away.

"Let them blow away like the chaff that they are," she said, sounding confident. "No one will believe it."

"Sister," Roberto answered, "Blanca de Salvo is pregnant."

She stared at him as if he had two heads, backing away in disbelief and bumping into a car parked behind her. A flier flapped from the windshield. She grabbed it and wondered at the foreign words. Roberto gave her one last sharp look before turning and grabbing more flyers from more parked cars. From the corner of his eye, he could see her moving from car to car until her hands were full. Roberto did the same. They met at the far end of the parking lot, out of breath.

"I don't see any more," she said, her dark eyes searching the cars. Roberto was doing the same. People began to swarm out of the church before he could be sure they had gathered them all. Laughing, waving, and chattering in Spanish, they started off to enjoy a blustery Sunday afternoon.

"We've done what we could," Roberto said, putting his flyers under his arm and reaching for hers. "Give them to me. I'll burn them."

"This is why you asked Father Carlo to leave, isn't it?" she asked, handing him the evidence. Roberto wanted to tell her 'no' but it was too late.

"I don't know if it's true for sure," Roberto answered. "He was always away, but that doesn't mean—" He let his thought end unfinished and started back toward the rectory.

"You could have told me," she said, following at his side. "You could tell the people of this church who really removed the kneelers and the railing. They blame you, you know."

Her uncanny ability to know what she couldn't know surfaced again. It was pointless to tell her anything but the truth.

"I had mentioned those things to Carlo," he said, still walking and hoping she would leave him alone. "In time, I would have done them myself. I wanted to wait until the people were no longer confused by the new song books and the other little changes. It was God's timing, not mine."

"They blame you for sending Carlo away," she said, staring at the flyers in his hand.

"That isn't important," he answered, shaking his head and avoiding her eyes.

"Are there other unimportant things?" she asked. She stopped at the steps to the rectory door. "Are there more burdens you share with no one? Life shouldn't be like that."

"God is there for me," he answered, walking up the steps and opening the door.

"I am here," she said, and he stepped inside. "Let me know if you ever need a live person to listen."

He turned and nodded, acknowledging her offer before closing the door. Inside the office, he dumped the flyers on the desk and stared out the window, watching her walk away. If only he knew how to accept her offer. . .

To Feel, To Fly

TONY STOOD ALONE wearing worn out jeans in a meadow of thick, blonde grass near Castroville. A long line of eucalyptus trees behind him defied the flat landscape. An April breeze rose from the ocean, skimming the surface of the slough to the west. Rust-colored pussy willows swayed in the knee-deep green water.

The state compensated Patches to convert his property into a duck preserve. A distant bridge separated Patches' wetlands from the salty harbor. The windows of his house faced the ocean where rugged, graceless fishing boats wobbled out to sea. A big barn nearby hid a motorcycle in parts, which Tony had stolen from himself.

Tony's blue eyes searched the morning sky, marking it with an imaginary grid, and checking each block one at a time. He was stone sober for the first time in weeks. His eyes focused on a black dot far away, and he cupped one hand behind his good ear. Whopping blades cut the air and he headed for Patches' house on the solitary dirt road that split the field. He started to run, but the pain made him settle for a brisk walk, his mended leg swinging out to one side.

"Patches," he called, poking his head in the front door. "It's coming."

"Now?" a voice answered from inside.

"Hurry," Tony said, leaving the door open. He headed back up the road, walking on the weeds between the wheel ruts. Patches followed 100 yards behind him.

Patches had mown a round bald spot in the grass in the center of the meadow. Together they had painted an orange X on the stubble inside a large orange circle. Tony pointed north and smiled. It felt like Christmas morning. Patches left the dirt road. A Bell helicopter swooped over the tree line, and Tony waved his arms at the craft hovering overhead. The aircraft paused above the orange X before it dropped in for a soft landing with dust and grass pelting Tony.

"Hot damn!" Tony said, not that anyone could hear him. He ducked his head and started toward the bubble of the chopper before the rotors stopped spinning. Inside, a busy man wearing a white helmet and blue flight suit secured the controls. Tony knocked on the thick glass and motioned for the pilot to open the door.

"Can you take me up in this sucker?" Tony asked before the transparent door was open all the way.

"What?" the pilot said in a loud voice over the diminishing noise of the rotor blades.

"I want a ride."

"I need a check first," the pilot answered, dropping his chin strap. "Then she's yours, and you can do what you want."

Tony hunched below the rotor blades and headed back to Patches.

"Did you bring the money?" Tony asked him, keeping an eye on the aircraft.

Patches pulled a check from his shirt pocket. He stared at the out-of-place helicopter in the middle of his meadow, and Tony snagged the paper from his fingertips.

"I'm going to get this guy to take me up," Tony said, heading back to the chopper before the pilot could unbuckle. He couldn't wipe the grin from his face. His outstretched hand pushed the check through the open bubble door. "Here's your dough. Take me up."

"Right now?" the pilot asked.

"I just bought a helicopter, and I've only got a week to learn to fly it. Let's go."

"Hey, I'm just delivering this thing," the pilot said, narrowing his eyes and creating a mass of lines on his dark, weathered face. "I'm not an instructor, pal."

"Good," Tony said. "I hate instructors. They're such cocky bastards." He forced his way onto the seat. "I just want to watch. Maybe ask a question or two. Where'd you learn to fly?"

"The military," the pilot answered, cranking her up again. "'Nam mostly."

"Perfect. I need low-level stuff. Think you can handle that?"

"No problem. You ready?"

"I'm always ready to fly," Tony answered, and clicked his seat belt shut.

The main rotors picked up speed, and Patches watched from beyond the painted circle. The helicopter rose and a whirlwind of debris forced Patches to turn away.

Tony felt the thrill of breaking ground anew. The chopper reached the tree tops. Patches grew smaller and smaller. They pivoted and headed over the slough. The big blade above Tony sliced the air while the engine behind him throbbed in his ears. His legs hung out in front of him, feeling exposed as though he were riding a Ferris wheel. The visibility and vulnerability of the bubble shocked him.

"Man, there's nothing out there, is there?" Tony yelled above the racket, sweeping his arm in front of him.

"Don't swing your arms in here," the pilot said in a loud voice. "You ever flown before?"

"Not in one of these." Tony launched into a barrage of his own questions before the pilot could ask him anything else. "How come you got so much left rudder?" he asked in airplane terms.

"Anti-torque. For the tail rotor."

"Opposite of an airplane," Tony said to himself. "You are barely moving that." Tony almost pointed to the stick between the pilot's legs, and then remembered the warning about not waving his arms around. He nodded to it instead.

"The cyclic," the pilot said, naming it. They soared over the harbor at Moss Landing. "If you move it, you've gone too far. You only think about moving it."

"How about that?" Tony asked, looking down. The pilot's left hand lifted a lever up and down like the parking brake of a car.

"The collective? Almost the same. Pull up for engine speed. Twist to adjust the main rotor pitch."

"Up for speed, twist for pitch. Up for speed, twist for pitch. Up for speed, twist for pitch," Tony said, parroting it into his memory.

So far, everything jived, he thought. For the past two months, he had not been on a drunken binge, contrary to what Patches and Angela thought. He had been on a fact-finding mission in all the local airport bars. Everyone who had ever been near a helicopter got free drinks as long as they talked. He had even found someone who would sign off on his helicopter rating—for a price. His brain was a storehouse of knowledge, but only now was his body experiencing how it felt.

The pilot slowed to a hover, backed up, and turned around. The maneuver was like nothing Tony had ever done or felt before.

"It's like being a virgin," he said, but the pilot couldn't hear him. Tony wanted to wallow in the feeling, but he couldn't. He had to pay attention to the pilot's moves, continuous and slight. The pilot scanned the highway until he spotted his friend driving toward Patches' house, their pre-arranged pick-up spot. They had to head back after a ten-minute flight.

Before they landed, Tony noticed Angela parking her car in the meadow. She must have finished their wash at the laundromat in town, and now she waited beside Patches. The helicopter set down, and the car they had spotted on the freeway headed up the long drive. When the rotors slowed, Patches started toward Tony and the pilot, but Angela stayed put. Tony reached over to open the door.

"How was it?" Patches asked in a loud voice. He surveyed with envy the piece of machinery he and Tony now owned.

"A hummer," Tony said, assuring Patches when the rotors stopped. "Stick spray booms on this baby, and we'll be two rich mothers."

"Think you can fly it?" Patches asked.

"Piece of cake," Tony answered, lying to hide his fear.

"Great," Patches said. "I can't wait to go up for a ride."

"Maybe tomorrow," Tony said, and the pilot laughed. He must have wondered where two nuts like Tony and Patches got enough money to buy a helicopter. Tony knew only a small portion of the escrow from his house sale was tied up in the deal. Most of that went toward medical bills. The lion's share of the down payment came from Patches, whose land served as collateral.

The pilot inspected the check once more before replacing it in his pocket. Patches, Angela, and Tony walked him up the drive. After a quick good-bye, he hopped into his friend's waiting car. The three of them watched the car leave, and then turned back to look at the aircraft.

"Now what?" Patches asked, standing next to Angela's car.

The helicopter with long, droopy blades waited motionless in the field. Tony was almost afraid to go back to her alone, but he had no choice. This was his bright idea. He started to walk away.

"Tony, wait," Angela said, reaching for his hand.

"Time to go for it," Tony said, pulling away. He grabbed his scuffed helmet from behind the bags of groceries in the trunk of her car. A look of panic crossed her face.

"Maybe you shouldn't," she said, holding his arm with both hands. He knew she tired easily now, though her pregnancy barely showed.

"I have to," he said, holding her jaw with one hand and kissing her pinched lips. "You're going to love this. I'll take you up for a ride. You'll see."

"I don't want a ride," she said, folding her arms. "Will you listen to reason?"

"It's just another flying machine."

"Wait—"

He left her standing by the car and headed back to the helicopter followed by Patches.

"She might have a point," Patches said, walking beside Tony.

"Don't you start," Tony answered. "Will you look at this? We got our own fucking helicopter. This is so bitchin'."

"It's something all right," Patches said, stopping short of the craft.

Tony walked all around it, dragging his fingers over every long inch of tubing and the blades of the tail rotor. He wiped oil off the engine, rubbed it between his fingers, and smelled it. Patches stood back and watched.

"Don't you want to touch her?" Tony asked Patches.

"I suppose," Patches said, approaching the craft. "Where?"

"Anywhere," Tony said with a laugh. "She's ours." With that, he lay down in the stubble and felt the warm underbelly of the chopper. He looked up and Patches was only a foot closer. "At least sit in the thing, would ya?"

"OK," Patches answered in a hesitant voice. He opened the door with caution and slid into the seat, being careful not to touch the controls. Tony jumped in beside him.

"Ready?" Tony asked, strapping on his helmet.

"Are you crazy?"

"Yeah," Tony said, chuckling in a devilish way before removing his helmet. "But not that crazy. One thing I learned from flying with that guy is that I need more time in one of these babies." Tony stroked the cyclic and let the tips of his boots rest on the pedals. Sure, it would be scary, but it would be damn fun too.

Patches left Tony in the chopper and headed back to the barn to work. Angela waited by her car until she saw Tony crawl out of the bubble. He could almost see the relief on her face. She turned away and started carrying groceries into Patches' house. Tony spent the rest of the day with the helicopter, though he never fired it up. After a while, it got too hot inside the craft. He moved outside, placing his helmet on the stubble for a seat and leaning back against the bubble. His bent knees held the owner's manual, which he read cover to cover, along with "The Basic Helicopter Handbook" that came with it. His reading began to unveil the engine to him, which only revealed half of the mystery.

That night at dinner, Tony and Angela ate at Patches place. Tony asked Patches for a couple hundred dollars over the meal Angela had cooked.

"For what?" Patches asked, spilling his beer on the slick red-checked tablecloth. He set down his mug between two cigarette burns. Patches' home décor had a definite bachelor feel to it.

"Parts," Tony said between bites of steak, not looking at Angela or Patches.

"What parts?" Patches asked.

"I think some seals are going," Tony answered, still chewing.

"Already? You haven't even gotten off the ground."

"Hey, if you don't think it's important. . ."

"It's not that," Patches said, pushing peas around his plate.

"Then you'll buy the seals?" Tony said, looking up and winking at Angela.

"I suppose."

"Great," Tony said, popping a fresh brew. "I'll get them at the airport tomorrow."

"You can't repair a helicopter," Angela said. Her chair scraped the linoleum, and she rose to carry her plate across the dark kitchen. "You don't know how."

"It's just basic maintenance," Tony said, cutting his steak, putting a piece in his mouth, and talking while he chewed. "Like changing the oil on a car."

"Oh, sure," she said. He could hear her sarcasm from across the room.

"I know what I'm doing," he answered. She dropped her plate on the counter, and her silverware bounced into the sink.

"No, you don't," she said and walked outside, slamming the door behind her.

"Prego!" Tony called after her.

THE NEXT MORNING, Angela headed for the cabin. Tony took Patches' money and went straight to the county fair. He was the first one in line for the sight-seeing helicopter rides. The old boy flying the Huey grunted 'hello' and Tony entered the craft. He insisted Tony pay before allowing him to buckle the seat belt.

"Here," the pilot said. He handed his passenger a white sack and stashed Tony's ten-dollar bill in his pocket.

"I don't need—" Tony said, starting to fling the sack aside.

"You want to fly or not?"

Tony flattened the bag under one leg, and then studied the bubble. He guessed that the man doing the flying was over 50. Half of an unlit cigar hung beneath his nicotine-stained moustache. Wild, wiry eyebrows shaded his tired eyes.

"Aren't you a little old for this stuff?" Tony asked.

"We'll see," he muttered, and the rotors started turning overhead.

Tony tried asking questions, but the old man only twitched his cigar. After a while, Tony didn't care as long as the asshole kept flying. They landed after the customary ten-minute ride. Tony handed him another ten bucks.

"Again?" the pilot asked.

Tony nodded, never breaking his concentration. His eyes remained fixed on the pilot's motions for another take off, ten more minutes of flying, and a second landing. He handed the pilot more money.

"Are you nuts?" the pilot asked.

"Hey, you got your money. Do me a favor. Just hover."

"What?" the pilot said. "Get out!"

"I gave you money," Tony insisted, keeping his seat belt buckled. "Fly me around again."

After their sixth landing, the line for the helicopter stretched halfway around the Tilt-a-Whirl. The pilot shut her down.

"Out, bud."

"I have more money."

"So do they," the pilot said, nodding at the people in line.

"But—"

"Get in line," the pilot said, pointing with his unlit cigar.

Tony bought a corn dog and a beer, and then stood behind a fat lady and her son at the end of the line. He waited in the hot sun all day and managed seven more rides, the last at twilight. By then, Tony noticed the tired man's shaky take-off.

"You should have hovered longer," Tony said without thinking.

"Get your own helicopter," the pilot said in a grunt.

Tony laughed and realized that he now knew how flying a chopper was supposed to feel. He didn't know everything, not by a long shot, but he might just pull it off. After all, flying had always been a matter of feeling to him.

Fighting to
Keep a Promise

TONY DROVE BACK to the cabin late after his day at the fair, at first feeling good about his progress. His thoughts turned dark during the hour-long drive when he thought about his finances. Patches was letting them live there rent free, not that they could have paid him. All of their money was soaked into a helicopter in the middle of a field 50 miles north.

Angela seemed stronger than before she got sick. Maybe it was the pregnancy. Now, unlike before, she had strong opinions about where their lives were going, and she voiced them more often. Several times she had told him that she didn't want him to fly the helicopter. He felt weak, no job, no money, and, no, he didn't know how to fly the helicopter. Yet. At times, it seemed as if he had soaked everything into her getting better without thinking about what would happen once she was well. Maybe it wasn't all that bad. Maybe he was just hungry.

When he arrived, Angela sat alone in the little riverside cabin. Her small frame occupied the end of one bench of the long picnic table in the kitchen. Above her, a 50-watt bulb with a tin shade cast a triangle of dim light. She glared at him through blurry eyes when he walked in the door. Her silent greeting annoyed him, and he stomped his boots across the wooden floor.

Two sets of dirty dishes remained on the table, food well-dried on the plates. The wine bottle, nearly full when Tony left that morning, sat empty in front of her. She pushed her short hair from her forehead and stared at her wine glass.

"Where have you been?" she asked, breaking her silence.

"At the fair," Tony said with a laugh.

"I was worried you were off in that crazy helicopter."

"What if I was?" He threw his jacket into the next room on an unmade bed. What had she been doing all day? He reached for the cookie jar by the sink, found it empty, and slammed the lid shut.

"I don't want you to fly it, Tony," she said, not looking up from her glass.

"Hey, it's no big deal," he answered, heading for the old fridge.

"You don't know how."

"I'll learn," he said, holding open the door and staring at the empty shelves.

"It's bad enough being here alone all day without you. If something happened to you in that helicopter—"

"Hey, you're not sick anymore," he said, slamming the door shut and whirling to face her. He was hungry, and there was nothing to eat. "There's no reason you can't go out by yourself."

"I like being with you. Where were you really?"

"You're on my case, woman."

"Good," she said, slapping her hand on the table and making the plates jump. "You need someone on your case." The wine was talking as much as Angela, but he didn't care.

"I seriously doubt that," he said, re-opening the old, round-cornered refrigerator door and removing a brew for dinner. "Who was here?"

"Why?"

"Someone was here," he said, glancing at the plates. He thought he had seen Patches' car pass him on the main road down.

"Maybe."

"Who?" he asked, kicking shut the refrigerator door and walking toward her.

"A friend," she answered, tracing the rim of her wine glass with a delicate finger.

"Who?" he asked again, only louder. He slammed down his beer and grabbed her by the shoulders to face him. "Who?"

"Bill," she answered, looking at him with spite.

"Bill?" he said, repeating the name and withdrawing his hands. That son-of-a-bitch. He picked up his beer and stared at the brown bottle. Bill would be attractive to her about now. He had money and a job. Just the stable sort that every woman wanted. Not some loser with a helicopter he couldn't fly. Tony turned the bottle in the light before downing it in consecutive swallows. "When did he leave?"

"Not long ago," she said in an arrogant tone and rose to put her glass in the sink. She wavered, struggling with her balance when she walked. "I told him I didn't want him here when you came home."

"Why?"

"Just because," she answered and wandered into the other room without looking at him.

"Why?" he asked louder, hurling his dead bottle into the waste basket in the corner. He pulled another beer from the fridge and bounced the twist-off cap across the countertop. He followed her into the next room, drinking as he went. She stood by the fireplace in the area that served as both living room and bedroom. "Why didn't you want him here when I got home?" he asked again, looking at the unmade bed.

"I'm just kidding, Tony" she said and picked up another log for the fire. Her eyes looked more faraway than normal. "It was just Patches." He grabbed her small wrist, and she dropped the wood. The rage that welled inside him burned his eyes. She wouldn't turn and face him, which made him madder.

"I asked you why?'" he said, raising his voice.

"Tony, I told you I was kidding. Now stop, you're hurting me."

"Why did Bill come here?" He shoved his beer onto the mantle of the river rock fireplace and gripped both her small hands in one of his, forcing her to look at him.

"He didn't."

"Answer me," Tony said, pulling her close to him like a rag doll. He had to know.

"I did answer you," she said, starting to cry. "He was never here. It was only Patches—"

"The hell it was," he said, looking back at the bed. "It was Bill, wasn't it?"

"No—"

"Wasn't it?" he said, even louder. He raised his flat hand over his shoulder.

"Tony, no." Her voice stopped him. "You promised."

She crouched to get out of his way and started to shake. He released his grip and she backed away. Her terrified eyes glanced from him to the door. He stepped in between her and the possible exit.

"You promised," she cried, her fingers covering her mouth. "At the hospital. Remember? Oh, God. . ."

"Why, Angela?" he asked, approaching her and speaking in a soft, tense voice. He struggled to maintain control, but he could feel himself losing it. "Why did you do it? Why Bill?"

"I didn't," she answered in tears, shaking her head. "I didn't—"

"God, I love you so much," he said, cupping her small face in his hands. She was so beautiful. "More than I thought I could. Why did you ask Bill to come here?"

"Tony, you're wrong—"

"You're mine," he said, stroking her face with a soft touch. Rage boiled inside him, just behind his clenched teeth. "I can't hit you. I know I can't hit you. But it hurts so bad. God, I wish I didn't love you so much."

"Tony, you're mistaken. Believe me," she said. Her words searched for a place in his heart beyond his hurt. "Bill was never here."

"Did you do it here?" he asked, glancing at their bed.

"We didn't—"

"God, I want to believe you, Angela."

He pushed her back up against the wall and ripped open the buttons on her blouse. He pushed the garment away and unsnapped her bra. His arm wrapped around her waist in a stranglehold and he cupped one breast in his hand.

"Did he hold you like this?"

"Tony, he wasn't here. Trust me, please . . ."

He turned, whirled her around with him, and dropped her on the bed. She stared up at him. He unzipped her jeans and yanked them from her. She looked too scared to move, but he couldn't stop himself. His fingers undid the buttons on his shirt, then his jeans. His clothes dropped to the floor. She grew more upset with every piece of clothing he removed.

"I never wanted anyone else to have you," he said, as if that would explain something.

"No one did," she said through tears.

He lay down beside her, trembling with rage. He traced his fingers over her body. The more he thought about it, the angrier he became.

"He saw you like this, didn't he?"

"No," she said in a whisper.

"My stepfather used to hit me," he said, his eyes wild and tearless. He could almost feel the strap on his back, smell the musty furniture, and see the tired drapes, always drawn and hiding his boyhood terror from the neighbors' prying eyes. "He told me he had to. He told me he loved me."

"Tony . . ."

"But I promised. Oh, God I promised you I'd never hurt you. I have to have you."

He rolled on top of her and slid himself up inside her. He grimaced, his faced racked with pain. She sobbed in silence, keeping her hands at her sides, unwilling to touch him. He grabbed at her breasts and buttocks, then released them. His rough hand turned her face toward him, and he pressed his mouth against her lips too hard. He stroked her with force, grabbing her shoulders and squeezing his blue eyes shut. His tears fell on her cheeks. He rushed to wipe them away and pretend they didn't exist. But they did, and it made him angrier to know he had been foolish enough to care so much. He stroked her harder and harder until his emotions peaked in one long and agonizing climax. Finally, his body rolled away from hers in exhaustion.

Tony lay still for a moment. With a start, he sat bolt upright and started searching through papers on the night stand. He leapt out of bed, grabbed his beer, and downed it. He pulled on his pants, opened the door, and stepped outside. The cold midnight air enveloped him.

"No-o-o," he said, crying into the night and hurling his beer bottle toward the rushing river.

He stepped back inside, slammed the door, and returned to the bed. Angela lay still, frozen with terror and pleading with her eyes. He stretched out beside her again, and his hand passed over her. She cringed beneath his touch. Still on his stomach, his hand grabbed the phone from the night stand near her head. He dialed like a crazy man, holding her down by laying his arm across her. His face was so close to hers that he was sure she could hear the expressionless voice on the other end of the line.

"That number has been changed to 555-4996. Again, 55—"

Tony disconnected and dialed again. It rang twice.

"Hullo—" a sleepy voice mumbled.

"Hello, cocksucker," Tony said. The other party hung up. "Son-of-a-bitch!" Tony redialed the same number.

"Hello," the same voice said, sounding angry.

"Hang up if you want, cocksucker. I'll just call back again."

"You're drunk, Tony," Bill said. At least he was awake enough to recognize his former friend's voice.

"Damn lucky for you," Tony said, one arm still holding Angela down. "Otherwise, I'd be at your house, blowing your cock off." Bill slammed down the receiver, but Tony called back.

"What do you want?" Bill said as soon as he answered the phone. Tony knew Bill had a real temper, when pressed. And he intended to press it.

"What do I want?" Tony asked. "What in the hell do you think I want?"

"Hey, unlike some people, I work in the morning," Bill said before hanging up again. Tony dialed again.

"Knock it off, Tony," Bill said when he answered it. Tony hoped he was waking up Cindy too. She should know what Bill had done with Angela.

"After what you did?" Tony said. "I ought to keep you awake all night."

"Sober up, Tony. What did I do to you?"

"Act like you don't know—"

"I don't, asshole," Bill said.

"Did you think I wouldn't know? I'm an old cheat. I know when my woman's been fucked."

"Time to dry out, fool," Bill said before hanging up again.

Tony redialed six or seven times, but it only rang and rang. Bill must have disconnected the phone. In the end, he slammed down the receiver in disgust. His tired eyes focused on Angela, still pinned beneath him.

"So, was he good?" he asked her, sounding almost calm.

"Tony, I tried to tell you—"

"Better than me?"

"Tony—"

"What was he like, huh? What did he do to turn you on?"

She took a deep breath and looked away. He forced her to turn back and look at him. His eyes couldn't seem to see her through his hurt, no matter how hard he looked. She stared from one of his eyes to the other, and then seemed to come to some kind of decision.

"He was gentle," she whispered.

"Oh, I'm sure he was."

"He was gentle, and he never hurt me," she said, her voice trembling.

"Did you want it that way?" he asked, his hand clamped around her jaw.

"I— I wanted to be held close. I wanted to be safe. I wanted you, but you weren't here. I'm sorry. You scare me."

He drew away from her in slow motion and sat up. His hand reached toward her face again, but he stopped when she flinched. He stood up and covered her with the blankets instead. His perplexed gaze stared down at her.

"I never loved anyone," he said in a soft voice. "Not like this. It scares me. I wish you hadn't done it, but I know why you did. I'll never know how to do it gently. You deserve that from someone. Too bad it can't be me."

He left the room and stood in his jeans, naked from the waist up, in a triangle of light on the kitchen floor. Bottles clinked in the refrigerator. He came back into the bedroom and set some beers on the nightstand. Without a word, he grabbed his shirt and buttoned it, slipped on his socks and boots and scooped his jacket from the floor. He grasped the necks of three beer bottles between the fingers of one hand.

"I'll be with the helicopter," he said in an empty voice. He didn't want to feel any more. Numbness would be a relief.

"Tony—"

"Don't come there," he said, heading for the door. He pulled his car keys from his pocket and looked back at her. The pain was driving him crazy. "I have a promise to keep. Don't make it any harder." He shut the door behind him with a soft click and headed for his car.

215

Balancing on a Broomstick

TONY SAT IN THE BUBBLE of the helicopter, reading a manual and not noticing Patches approaching. It was just after dawn, and the clean air of spring blew in fresh off the ocean. Patches slapped an open palm on the Plexiglas door. The sound startled Tony and sent a flurry of birds from the treetops at the edge of the property. Dew on the long grass had dampened Patches' pants legs during his hike through his field.

"When did you get here?" Patches asked after Tony opened the door. He tugged at his billy goat beard and checked his watch.

"Earlier than you," Tony answered, half stretching.

"I didn't hear you drive in," Patches said, looking at the instrument panel. "Hey, did you get the seals?"

"The what?"

"The seals. I gave you money for seals for the helicopter. Did you get them?"

"Oh, right," Tony answered, staring past Patches and across the field. He took a deep breath and closed his eyes tight for a moment. Sleeping in a helicopter was not comfortable. "Sure," Tony continued, looking at Patches for a moment and then back at the manual. "Put them in already, too. Really makes a difference."

"Good, I guess," Patches said, trying to read Tony.

"You got a long stake?" Tony asked, tossing the book aside.

"For what?"

"It's hard to explain," Tony answered, rolling his shoulders and stretching his neck. "I just need something to drive into the ground. You got one?"

"I suppose," Patches answered, looking over his shoulder at the barn. When Patches turned back, Tony was blowing warm air on his red fingertips. "You cold?"

"Naaa. . ." he lied, climbing out of the chopper. He unfolded his long body, taking time to stretch his right leg in particular. "Got some rope?"

"How much?"

"Oh, 15 to 20 feet should work," Tony said, going over the plan he had hatched in the dead of night. It was crazy, but it just might work. And, if it didn't, well, Angela wouldn't miss him, that's for sure. "It's got to be strong though."

"I have a long piece from my dad's old fishing boat. I can't say how strong it is."

"That'll work," Tony said.

"What for?"

"Let's get it and I'll show you," he said, sauntering toward the barn with Patches at his side. "Hey, is my old motorcycle still in there?"

"Somewhere, yeah. Why?"

"Just curious."

Twenty minutes later, they returned to the field with Patches carrying the stake and Tony carrying two lengths of rope. Tony pointed out a spot near the orange circle where the helicopter sat and asked Patches to drive the stake into the ground. Tony tossed the shorter rope into the bubble and lay down beside the helicopter. The straw of the mown field felt like a bed of nails on his back. He made quick work of tying the longer rope to one skid of the helicopter. When Patches finished, Tony tied the other end of the long rope to the stake. Patches leaned on the sledgehammer, out of breath. Tony grabbed the rope and pulled as hard as he could, the coarse twine burning his hands.

"Shit," Tony said, wiping his red palms on his jeans. He went back to the helicopter and found his worn leather flying gloves. His fingers filled the familiar gloves, and he used them to test the rope again. It held. He let go, feeling satisfied it would work and heading back to the helicopter.

"What are you doing?" Patches asked.

"Hell if I know," Tony said with a nasty grin. The only thing he knew for sure was what he had to do. He had to climb into the helicopter and not look back or he might lose his nerve. His bent head entered the cockpit, and his body slipped into the unfamiliar seat. He tried to ignore the knot in his gut.

"Wait!" Patches said, dropping his sledgehammer and running toward the aircraft.

Tony waved him away, shut the glass door, and fastened the seat belts around him. Patches pounded on the door, and Tony started laughing but didn't open it. He used the short rope and his teeth to tie his right forearm to his thigh. His right hand gripped the cyclic between his knees. Patches refused to leave until the blades overhead began to turn. He backed away, yelling something at Tony. Tony couldn't hear him, but he could guess what he was saying. He gave Patches a brave thumbs up and looked up. Who was crazy enough to think of putting spinning wings on the roof? This was going to be the ride of his life.

"Let her buck," Tony said, and the noise from the engine behind him grew louder.

Patches was backing away in helpless amazement. The last thing Tony remembered thinking was that Patches must consider him a crazy son of a bitch. The craft rose like a tethered bird, and Tony tried to move the controls as little as possible. The rope securing the chopper to the ground was pulled taunt, forcing her down to earth. He made the helicopter lift and drop without grace, and then rise again.

Next thing he knew, the chopper started pitching to the side. The blades of the main rotor came too close to the ground, but Tony managed to right her again. He struggled to set her down, breathing a sigh of relief when both struts were on the ground. What the hell was he doing wrong? Tony's jaw muscles flexed, his moustache twitched, and his shoulders were so tense, they touched his helmet. He waited a minute, added power, and took off again. She almost rolled over again before he managed another hard landing.

"Damn," he said. "This thing doesn't want to fly."

He checked the cyclic in his right hand between his legs and the collective in his left hand. He stared at his feet on the pedals and remembered in a flash.

"Opposite of an airplane. Left rudder, not right," he said out loud, referring to the anti-torque pedals which countered the thrust from the tail rotor. The blades were still spinning when he opened the door, pulled off his left boot, and flung it outside.

His next attempt showed a slight improvement. He went up and down harder than he liked, but at least he had stopped that rolling shit. After two more attempts, he saw Patches wander back toward the house. Tony knew how much money Patches had sunk into the helicopter. He didn't blame him if he couldn't bear to watch.

The rhythm of the engine lifting off and settling down, over and over again, rooted itself in Tony's ears. After half an hour, Tony got out and stood beside the chopper to take a whiz. His eyes glanced in the direction of Patches' house in time to see the curtains twitch on the kitchen window. Tony shook his head, zipped up, and jumped back into the helicopter to repeat the landing and take-off sequence.

For the rest of the day, Tony climbed out of the helicopter only for short breaks. He was afraid he would forget what he had just learned if he took time off. The sound was familiar now, but the touch, the sensation of flying that oozed control without abruptness, was what he was seeking. He was determined to find that feeling if it meant staying tethered to the ground for the rest of the week. It was five o'clock that evening before he climbed out of the bubble for the last time. He headed home, his clothes drenched in sweat.

The drive home was long, and he almost fell asleep twice. He stopped to buy a pizza. Back in the car, he turned up the radio and wondered how Angela would react when he showed up. She was probably dreading his return. At last, his car headed down the bumpy dirt road to the cabin. Dust settled around his vehicle when he parked. It took all his strength to open the car door. Only the sound of the bubbling creek broke the silence. His tired body stumbled out of the car and headed for the kitchen. It was empty. He wandered down to the water's edge. She was crouched beside the river at dusk, staring at the rushing current.

"Hiding?" he asked, standing on higher ground.

"Sort of," she answered, still squatting and dragging a stick through the sand.

"Hey, a promise is a promise."

She looked up at him, and he wondered why she ever married him. He knew he looked pretty raw, his hips at an angle and one hand shoved into the front pocket of his jeans. His black curls were pressed flat from sweating beneath a hot helmet all day. A bent cigarette dangled from lips buried beneath a black moustache. He inhaled and exhaled smoke before shoving his sunglasses off his face and closing his exhausted eyes. They opened and focused on her.

"Anything to eat?" he asked.

"Not much," she said. "Beans." Angela looked away from him to the water. "I didn't have any money."

"I brought a pizza home with me."

"You're kidding."

"No, really. It's in the car. Come on."

She stood and brushed sand from her backside. He headed toward her and she backed away. He could sense her reading his every move.

"Don't worry," he said. "I couldn't do anything if I wanted to. I'm wiped out." He flipped his cigarette into the river and started back toward his car. Angela walked beside him. From the corner of his eye, he saw her staring at his face. After a few steps, he put one arm across her shoulders to lean on her.

"I flew it today."

"How did it feel?"

"Same as my life. Like balancing on a broomstick."

Back in the cabin, he downed a beer and two pieces of pizza before collapsing on the bed, fully clothed. The last thing he saw was Angela staring at the flames in the fireplace and watching sparks escaping up the black chimney into the night. Next thing he knew, the crackling fire had died away. The lights were out, and Angela crawled in bed beside him. She couldn't move him to his side, so she had curled up in the vacant space available. She kissed his nose, and he grumbled.

Seconds later, his whole body went rigid. He dreamed he was flying the helicopter. His right hand gripped the cyclic, his feet pushed left and right against the pedals. The helicopter was out of control. Suddenly, Angela was beside him, taking his hand and placing it on her stomach. Was she trying to make him crash? Then, he realized, that part wasn't a dream. Something was moving in her stomach. The baby. Their baby. He fell back to sleep with his hand still on her stomach.

It was 2:00 in the morning when he grabbed her by the shoulders. She woke with a gasp, his angry eyes fixed on her. He pushed the covers off her and slid his hand over her nightgown.

"Damn him!"

"Tony—"

"Damn that son of a bitch," he said, leaning across her to grab the phone from the nightstand. The dial lit up when the receiver was lifted. He cussed while he dialed. It rang twice.

"Hullo," a sleepy voice said.

"I'm glad I woke you up, you bastard," Tony said, squeezing Angela tighter.

The line went dead, but Tony called back. He held Angela down with one arm, whispering "I'll kill him," while the phone on the other end rang again.

"I'm staying on you, brother," Tony said before the other party could speak.

"Give it up, Tony," Bill said, sounding weary.

"You'd like that, wouldn't you? You cold mother fucker. You were my friend."

"Tony, what is your problem?" Bill asked, sounding fed up.

"You dicking my old lady is my problem."

"You're full of shit."

"You think I don't know?" Tony asked, sitting up. "You think I'll forget? Like you forgot you were my friend? It doesn't work that way."

"You're drunk—"

"I'll ruin your season, Billy. You'll be so tired you'll fuck up when you're flying—" The line went dead. "Don't hang up on me, fucker."

Tony started to call the number again. Angela reached for his hand to stop him. It started to ring on the other end, and he pushed her hand away. The receiver was pasted to his good ear when Bill answered.

"Tony, knock it off," Bill said, oozing with anger. "I never touched Angela."

"Tony, stop," Angela said, pleading at his side. "Just stop."

"The hell you didn't," Tony answered. The whole idea was too much for Tony to keep inside. He'd lost it all. His house. His job. His best friend. And now, he believed he was losing his wife, and the baby she carried—his baby. And he didn't know how to stop it. It wasn't a big surprise. He should have expected it. Everyone he had ever cared about deserted him. But this time is was more than he could bear.

"You're hopeless," Bill said before slamming down the phone again.

Tony sat on the edge of the bed and redialed, but the other end just rang and rang.

"Answer it, asshole," Tony screamed at the receiver. "Answer it or I'll let it ring for the rest of the night." Eight or ten rings later, Bill lifted the receiver and replaced it. A dial tone buzzed on Tony's end of the connection. He slapped the receiver back into the cradle.

"Tony, he never—" Angela said, but he smothered her words with a violent kiss. She lay stiff beneath him, tears welling in her eyes.

"No," she said, managing to turn away from him. Her wet face left a damp spot on his cheek.

His hand wiped off the moisture, and he pulled himself away from her. Still dressed, he rolled out of bed, grabbed his boots, and yanked them on, hopping around in the process. The dark room left him searching for his jacket and growing frantic when he couldn't find it.

"The chair," Angela said.

Tony snagged it from the arm and headed for the kitchen. The shelves in the refrigerator were empty, not even holding the beer he craved, just a half-dead Coke. He slammed the door hard enough to knock an empty fruit basket off the top. Angela pulled the worn quilt up to her neck and shivered when he entered the room.

"I wish—" he said, making a quick, tight fist. "I wish I never made that damn promise."

He backed away from her, bumping into the chair and whirling to face it. His boot slammed against one leg of the chair, and it tipped over, causing Angela to wince and pull the covers around her even tighter. He hated losing his temper, hated that she was scared of him, and hated the thought of another man being with Angela.

The old wooden door slammed behind him after he walked out. The rev of the car's engine echoed off the canyon walls, and he roared away, bounding over the ill-kept dirt road too fast. In an hour, he would be back in Patches' field.

The pattern continued over the next two nights. Bill didn't get any sleep. Angela was crumbling from the stress. Tony never hit her, but he couldn't lie in his own bed without imagining what Bill and Angela did there. His temper would flare, and he would storm out before he did something he would regret. Patches would find him in the helicopter every morning. Tony would take off and land all day, still tethered to the ground.

Throughout the whole mess, only the helicopter brought him any joy. Anger and frustration had to be pushed aside when he climbed into the bubble. The machine required every bit of concentration he could muster. Patches watched for short periods of time, then walked away as if he couldn't bear to look. Tony knew what Patches feared because they were Tony's fears too. Tony might either crash their investment, kill himself, or both. To Patches credit, he never crossed Tony, though they hadn't exchanged a pleasant word in days.

On the third day, Tony practiced his tethered take-off and landing wearing both boots. He even untied his arm from his leg. The next day, he untied the rope from the skid. He sat in silence in the bubble, hoping he was ready. He set the blades in motion and breathed in sync with the swooping beat. The engine reached a certain pitch, and he knew it was time.

"For Angela," he said and lifted off.

No tether held him back this time. He jerked from a hover to forward flight after a wobbly but viable take-off. The ground pulled away below him and the eucalyptus trees loomed before him. He turned to avoid them. Below him, Patches stood in the middle of his field and shoved his fist into the air so hard both feet left the ground. Tony wanted to wave but didn't dare. It was not time to relax. Not yet. Maybe never.

Flying the strange machine for the first time was a struggle, but being airborne soothed him like it always had. He did his best to circle the flat meadow, feeling untouchable and free. Fly-me, fly-me urged the pulsing rotors, but he was afraid to go too far from the orange X painted on the stubble. He made one pass over the slough before deciding to try and land.

The chopper neared the X on the ground, and he could feel his angle of approach was all wrong. He aborted, hovering with his bottom teeth chewing his moustache. Horrid images of never being able to get down swirled in his mind. He kept circling.

"What if I'm stuck up here? Then what?" he asked, then answered himself. "I'll run out of gas, that's what."

He tried again, swooping toward the mown spot as if he were landing an airplane. Again it felt all wrong, and again he pulled out. His approach was nothing like that of the gruff pilot at the country fair. Tony visualized a Tilt-a-Whirl on the left of the X and a hot dog stand on the right.

He came in slow and attempted to hover just above the X. All of those forced, tethered landings took over when he reached the rope-length height. She sank to a hard, but safe, landing. Gangly and ungraceful, but a real, if jolting landing. He cut the power to the blades and fell forward, covered with sweat and ready to cry. Patches was running toward him, so he stuffed that emotion.

"You did it," Patches said as soon as Tony opened the door. "I don't believe it."

"Piece of cake," Tony answered, trying to sound casual, but he was too weak to climb out.

"Liar," Patches said with a laugh.

"Maybe," Tony said, smiling. "It was so sweet, Patches. It scared the hell out of me, but it was sweet."

"You going to do it again?"

"Of course. That's what flying is all about. Ninety-nine percent boredom and one percent sheer terror. In this case, maybe more than one percent."

One more time around the patch turned into six. When he made his final landing that day, he felt like he just might survive. He started the long drive home, stopping at the corner market to buy two steaks, a six-pack, and a cheap bouquet of carnations. He hopped back in the car, turned on the radio, and sang along with Joy to the World about some bullfrog named Jeremiah.

He began to hope. Soon, the business that he and Patches dreamed of starting would be off the ground. The money would roll in, and he would be in the chips again. Angela and he would have one high old time. He'd make damn sure of that.

He parked in front of the cabin at twilight, imagining the lazy, full moon nights to come with plenty of music and booze. Long, hot days, full of lying and flying. They would have it all—money, a baby, and no more hospitals. A light glowed in the kitchen window, and he couldn't wait another minute to tell her.

"Angela?" Tony called out, walking in the door. He put the steaks and a six-pack in the old refrigerator and took out a beer. "I untied her today. It was righteous."

He popped open his brew and hid the flowers behind his back before heading into the other room.

"I flew her around the patch seven times. That means seven successful land—"

He glanced around and realized he was talking to himself. Tony headed back to the kitchen. Dishes dried in the rack on the counter, and the air felt too quiet. He crossed the empty room and opened the door to start back outside, but stopped.

A white, folded piece of paper sat propped between the salt and pepper shakers in the middle of the table. He sat down his beer and the dying bouquet to pick up the paper. His name, printed in neat lettering on the outside, sent a chill up his spine.

"No," he whispered to himself, looking around.

He carried his beer and the note into the bedroom, slumping into the chair that faced the cold, black fireplace. After a long swallow, his shaking hands unfolded the note. Delicate handwriting delivered her message.

> Tony,
> Nothing ever happened with Bill. I swear it. I hoped you would believe me. I kept hoping things would get better.
> I'm sorry to leave you this way, but if I saw you face to face, I wouldn't do it at all.

I'm going with my mom to the Midwest. For my sake and the baby's, please don't try to find us. I love you so much I'm afraid I would come back to you. If I did, it might kill us both. Maybe this way, you can keep your promise.

My love always,

Angela

He read the note over and over. After two more beers, it landed crumpled up in the fireplace. He pulled it back out, smoothing it flat again on the arm of the chair. He refolded it and tucked it in his shirt pocket. His eyes focused on the silent phone on the end table. He dialed a familiar number, holding his beer in his dialing hand and the receiver with the other.

"Hello." A pause. "Hello?"

"Why did you do it?" Tony asked Bill, just above a whisper. "Why did you have to go and fuck with my old lady?"

"God, Tony, will you back off?" Tony knew Bill sensed something different in Tony's voice because Bill stayed on the line.

"Why, Bill?" Tony asked, his voice cracking.

"I didn't." Bill's simple answer wasn't one Tony could believe.

"She told me you did."

"But I didn't," Bill said again. Tony didn't want to believe he was telling the truth.

"You must have," Tony said, slapping his hand on one wall. "She wouldn't have left me if you hadn't."

"She left?"

"Don't act surprised, asshole," Tony said. The emptiness of losing Angela became an ache in his stomach. He bent forward, his arm across his waist. "Is she with you right now? Are you fucking her while you are talking on the phone to me? I hate your—"

"She isn't here. She's never been here. Tony, she loves you."

"The hell she does," he screamed. Nobody loved him. Bill should have known that, if anyone. "Why did you fuck her?"

"I didn't, damn it," Bill answered. "Never did and never would."

"Sure—" Tony said. His voice faded, and he bent over in pain.

"Look, I like Angela."

"A lot, right?"

"A lot more than you do."

"You don't know shit, asshole," Tony said.

"I know more than you think," Bill answered, sounding like a man who hadn't gotten a good night's sleep in a while. Tony had struck a nerve with his former friend. "I remember your advice. 'Hit them around the back of the head where it doesn't show.' What if I did fuck her?—which I didn't. At least I didn't beat her. I didn't put her in the hospital. I didn't nearly kill her. I don't know how you live with yourself, Tony. Angela is a wonderful girl who deserves a heck of a lot better than you."

"Bill—"

"Hang up and have another beer," Bill said, slamming down the phone.

Tony stared at the receiver with the buzzing dial tone still in his hand. He hung up hard and hurled the whole phone across the room. It crashed against the wall with a ringing bang. He sat down in the chair, and then slid to the floor on his knees, grabbing his gut and slumping forward. His attempts to muffle his aching sobs by biting the sleeve of his jacket failed. Tears, more painful than drops of blood, fell on the cold, stone floor. Near midnight, he climbed into bed and hugged Angela's pillow, but it wasn't enough to fill the empty pit in his stomach.

Reality is a Dream

"WHEN YOU FLY under a wire, you duck your head," Rand West said as the afternoon light warmed the room. Rand was Bill's new boss and the owner of Stardusters, Inc. in King City. Bill watched the show, silent, from behind the counter in the kitchen.

Bill had always worked at cropdusting operations that hid poison pails from inspectors and crumpled propellers from unreported accidents. Most of the operators he had worked for in the past had avoided the FAA and the press at all costs. However, Rand West had converted a single-wide mobile home into a comfortable office with his desk in the middle of what had been the living room. He seemed to thrive on being able to accommodate a constant stream of reporters and inspectors at his airstrip outside of King City. State of the art gas pumps and well-maintained toxic waste disposal units stood beside futuristic, enclosed loading systems at the far end of the runway.

Bill noticed that Rand flexed his bare forearms for the benefit of a pretty reporter seated on the leather couch across from him. He seemed to enjoy posing in a white flight suit behind his tidy desk. The gray in his temples lent credibility to the words he spoke.

"If you fly under a wire and over a barbed wire fence, you duck your head and lift your feet," Rand said.

"No kidding?" the young lady asked, crossing her legs to keep him talking.

"No kidding," he answered with his patented boyish grin and a wink. Bill could tell that he was driving for a full page spread. Later, the reporter's article would describe him as an accomplished pilot, 48, dapper and mature, with time in Navy fighter planes.

Bill's views on publicity were the opposite of Rand's. Rand benefited from having a sensible sort like Bill to oversee the day-to-day cropdusting functions at Stardusters. Bill presumed he had been hired to placate the farmers and allow Rand perform at more air shows.

Rand handled the public relations end since he loved seeing himself fly on the six o'clock news or anywhere else for that matter. Bill knew him well enough to know that Rand flew for a living because he lived to fly. Every form of flying that paid was fair game to Rand, from cropdusting, skywriting, and banner towing to spreading ashes for the local mortuary. The proceeds supported his true passion, aerobatic flying. Agrobatics, Rand called it, his own version of stunt flying that incorporated cropdusting techniques. He was a crowd pleaser at more than 30 air shows a year.

The first dozen times Bill had seen Rand practice agrobatics, his precision and lack of common sense had left Bill slack-jawed. The weeks had passed and Rand's constant buzzing above the airstrip had become as comforting as a mosquito in a dark bedroom. Bill had tried not to watch Rand perform, but he always did. Now, he felt sure that the female reporter, mesmerized by Rand, would ignore him.

"Cropdusting takes a lot of nerve, doesn't it?" she asked Rand, lowering her notebook.

"Nerve?" Rand repeated, changing his pose. Bill thought if Rand had had a silk scarf, he would have tossed it over his shoulder for effect. "No," Rand continued. "It's more like will power. Anyone can hold their fingertip on a football. Only a few won't flinch when the kicker kicks it. Almost anyone would run into a burning building to save a child. Only certain people can run in to save a couch. Skimming crops at 100 miles per hour six inches above the ground to kill bugs and weeds takes control. Blow a magneto at 100 feet. Watch the engine burn on the way down. Only a cropduster worries if someone sees him bounce on landing. He uses his will to suspend fear."

"So, cropdusters aren't just hot shots," she said. Bill almost laughed out loud when he saw that she was swallowing Rand's daring description.

"The public's image of the cropduster is one of a mad man who poisons field workers and pollutes the environment," Rand answered with too much sincerity. "In truth, the average cropduster just wants to help feed a hungry world." The woman knew good copy when she heard it and began scribbling in her notepad.

Bill slipped out the back door and busted a gut laughing as soon as he was outside. The Salinas River sat near the backside of the mobile home, and a worn path led around to the front of the office that faced the runway. Bill had to smile as he walked that direction. The way Bill saw it, Rand had forgotten to mention that most ag pilots are little better than flying prostitutes who work for two pimps, Flying and the Almighty Dollar. Their johns were farmers and that particular day, the strip was crawling with them.

Bill headed across the runway, where he would be needed to help with the day's festivities. The landing strip sat with the Salinas River to the west and the foothills of the Gabilan Mountains to the east. Stardusters' annual "Spring Thaw" celebration was hosted there every April and was now in full swing. Farmers and industry people feasted at the company's expense inside a big blue hangar beside the mobile home. The Thaw featured catered Mexican food and booze by the gallon. It gave local farmers a chance to clear up delinquent accounts and get ready for the new season ahead. It also provided Rand with an excuse to perform his aerobatic maneuvers and smile for the press.

"Soar Feat," Rand's red, white, and blue aerobatic biplane glistened in the middle of the runway. Bill wandered toward it, thinking about his two months at Stardusters. He still tended to sneak around corners when the media or government officials showed up. A pilot he had known once lost his license just because of an incriminating photograph. File footage of a cropduster could appear on TV whenever the local news anchor reported a case of pesticide poisoning. He didn't want to be someone's background cropduster.

Bill stopped when he reached the shiny plane, turned, and looked down the runway at the bright yellow workhorses he flew. They were larger than the aerobatic plane, the strong and able sort of craft that he felt comfortable flying. He knew Rand flew those too, but less and less these days. Still, Rand's style of flying had taught Bill a few tricks that improved his cropdusting.

In many ways, Rand's flying was similar to Tony's. They were both artists, crowd-pleasing. Bill thought of himself as more of a craftsman. He could fly well, but he tried to look at the bigger picture. It wasn't important to him to be seen as a pilot who could stretch a plane, the way it had been to Tony. In fact, Bill felt just the opposite. He never wanted to be a rivet popper. He never wanted to tax the engine unless it was unavoidable. The mechanics sometimes commented that his plane needed less maintenance than the others. His former bosses, even Sonny, liked the fact that he organized his work orders the day before he had to fly them. They had all liked his practical approach and remarked on his ability to discern the most efficient order to fly the fields. Bill had a knack for finding little ways that the company could realize more profit.

The yellow planes at the end of the runway may have looked unimpressive to some, but they were hardy, fixed-wing aircraft. After Bill's crash, Sonny had said he wanted Bill to stay. The problem was that his former boss had wanted to use the insurance money from the totaled plane to buy a helicopter. Bill had thought it might work at first and had even taken the lessons required to earn his helicopter rating. Rand and he had met at the helicopter flight school, where Rand was doing the same thing. Before the lessons had ended, Rand and he both had agreed that choppers just felt too squirrelly and that fixed wings were better suited to flying. Rand had offered him a job flying one, and Bill had accepted.

Bill's green eyes scoured the length of the runway, from the deserted loading area at one end to the hangars at the other, where the farmers milled around. It was comforting to him that there was not a helicopter in sight. Bill wasn't afraid to try something new. In fact, he liked to learn. In his own black-and-white mind, he divided the world into learners and non-learners. Into pilots who took risks and survivors who took calculated risks. Rand and Tony might have had a similar style, but Rand was a learner, and Tony wasn't. Well, he was, but it seemed to take a two-by-four between the eyes to get his attention. Tony had managed to move from the Della/Sheila phase to dating a sweet girl like Angela. After last night's phone call, Bill was pretty sure Tony couldn't make it last.

He tossed the chocks away from the aerobatic plane, thinking about how he and Cindy were a different story. She was a free spirit who complemented his down-to-earth soul. He appreciated the balance she added to his life. His world was black and white, but she understood shades of gray. As an artist, she had to. He was uncomfortable with those areas. Going back to church had seemed to make that more evident. He understood heaven and hell, but in-between areas of religion like purgatory, limbo, or reincarnation bothered him. The ideas still intrigued him, but he preferred the exactness of science. The concept of moving molecules around to make one chemical kill weeds and other kill bugs was more concrete. Science was something he appreciated because each hypothesis had to be proven. He preferred the objective to the impulsive. The craftsman to the artist.

Some of the swampers approached Bill at the edge of the runway and started joking about Rand's ego while waiting for the aerobatic demonstration to start. Just then, the boss emerged from the mobile home in his bright white flight suit. The lady reporter was on his arm. A small entourage trailed him to his compact plane, a Pitts Special with a powerful engine. Bill was forced to wait for the fanfare to subside before propping the plane.

Once the engine caught, Rand headed down the runway, gaining speed and taking off with a roll. The plane climbed and the engine snarled even louder. She flew straight into the air, climbing high with white tracer smoke billowing from the underbelly. The biplane fell out of the maneuver at the top, appearing to be out of control. A sequence of flat spins downward produced a coil of smoke winding around the vertical trail that Rand had made on his way up. He must have felt daring to complete 17 spins.

"Pull up, pull up," Bill whispered, watching and feeling tense. The red, white, and blue aircraft came out of the spins far too close to the ground in Bill's opinion, and Rand reoriented himself with some level flight before continuing. Rand's maneuvers exemplified the difference between them. Bill believed in saving for a rainy day. For Rand, the rain would never last. Bill's crash had made the prospect of death too real. Or maybe he was just getting older. Something was forcing him to look at the gray areas of life and learn to accept them.

Bill escaped the Spring Thaw early, while everyone else stayed to stare into the sky at Rand's chilling agrobatics. Father Roberto had finagled a promise from him to help disassemble the game booths that had been used earlier that day for the Ethnic Festival. In his pickup, Bill tossed his latest Civil War book from the driver's seat. All the waiting for the wind involved in cropdusting had caused him to become a book junkie. There were periods of history he felt close to, like WWII and the battles of 17th century mariners, but even those couldn't rival the connection he felt to the Civil War.

He left the dirt road of the strip, driving into town and arriving at the church in the late afternoon. It was a good thing he showed up to help. No one else had.

Roberto was working alone at the far end of the defunct Catholic school's playground. Weeds grew through the cracks in the bleached blacktop, and the paint had faded on the old free throw lines. The priest wore paint-splattered jeans and a dark sweatshirt that read "Father Knows Best."

"Need some help?" Bill asked, approaching from the far side of the deserted playground.

"Always, always," Roberto answered. He looked up and smiled at Bill. "Collect the folding chairs. There's a rack for them in the storage room behind the cafeteria." Roberto waved his hammer toward a large, vacant building.

The sun set, and the two of them worked side by side. They removed decorations and stored the disassembled game booths. They condensed all of the trash from the celebration into one large, green dumpster. Bill didn't ask why he was the only one helping, guessing that it had something to do with the disagreement between the priest and the CML.

"Come over to the rectory for a drink," Roberto said, when they finished.

"My wife—"

"Call her," Roberto said with a quick laugh. "Tell her you're with a priest. There's no safer excuse."

"OK," Bill answered, following Roberto behind the church, the shortest route to Roberto's front door.

The rectory seemed sterile and boring, just how Bill had imagined a priest's lifestyle. An empty bedroom sat to the left of the entryway with vacant bookshelves, a naked mattress, and a small cannon in the corner. Across the hall, uncounted ticket stubs from the festival games cluttered the office desk.

"Come to the kitchen," Roberto said, heading down the hall at a quick pace. "This way."

"Can I use the phone?" Bill asked, stopping just inside the front door.

"In there," Roberto answered, pointing to the doorway next to the office. Bill entered the small sitting room, furnished with a few rigid, unmatched pieces. The black desktop phone weighed a ton. Bill dialed and heard glasses clinking in the kitchen.

Bill stared beyond the television, looking into the backyard with the phone ringing on the other end of the line. An exhausted peach tree leaned on a broken-down fence in the fading twilight. Cindy answered, and Bill told her his whereabouts. The CPR class that she taught had just ended, and she had stopped by the house to grab a few things on her way to aerobics. She had become very health conscious since they moved to King City. Bill was sure it had something to do with her desire to get pregnant, but he approved. He enjoyed the fact that he was her favorite victim when it came to practicing her CPR technique. All that exercise made her look even better now than when they were first married. Plus, she still had nice boobs. It embarrassed him to think about that stuff in the priest's house.

"Vino," the priest said, entering the room with two glasses just as Bill hung up. "Good for the blood. You like red wine, don't you?"

"I'm afraid I like it too much," Bill answered, feeling awkward. It was always difficult to explain why he had quit. "I try not to drink it."

"Ever?"

"Not for the last four months."

"And you call yourself a Catholic?" Roberto said, with a smile.

"I call myself an alcoholic," Bill said in a frank manner. In his opinion, everyone was allotted a set amount of alcohol in life. Bill had consumed his share and maybe someone else's too.

"Surely, just one glass . . ."

"No thank you, Father," Bill said, keeping firm. He had attended a few AA meetings, but he wasn't the type to join a group. Drinking had ruined Tony's life and his marriage. That was all the inspiration Bill needed. "I've seen too many cropdusters take just one glass."

"Let me get you something else."

Bill protested but the priest insisted, pointing to the words on his shirt. Roberto left the room and returned from the kitchen, carrying a glass of orange juice. Bill accepted it with thanks.

"That other cropduster I knew . . . he liked to drink," Roberto said.

Bill knew who Father Roberto meant, and he regretted that he had lied to him about knowing Tony. The priest settled into a squeaking recliner upholstered in a sick green Naugahyde. A crooked, variegated afghan, handmade, hung over the back of his chair. Bill took a seat on the unyielding brown couch.

"You mean Tony?" Bill asked with a sigh. "He drinks like a fish."

"You told me you didn't know him," the priest said with surprise.

"Wishful thinking . . ."

"Say, 'Bless me, Father. I have sinned,'" Roberto said, eying Bill with curiosity. "Why did you deny knowing him?"

"I was angry at him. Really angry. Still am."

The priest waited. Bill felt as if he were in the confessional. He noticed that Father Roberto stayed quiet and just looked at him, using the power of silence the way some folks used words.

"I wouldn't have brought it up, but he's been bugging me," Bill said, twisting his glass in his hand, over and over. "Four nights in a row, he has telephoned in the middle of the night. I haven't heard anything from him for the last two nights. He was drunk and accusing me of . . . of stuff."

"Are you angry at him because he drinks?" Roberto asked, lowering his wine glass.

"No, I'm angry at him because he nearly killed me. Or at least, he nearly made me kill myself."

Bill left the couch and wandered over to the television. He gazed out the window while touching one of the rabbit ears antennas with his fingertips.

"He didn't repay a loan," Bill started, and then looked down at the glass of juice in his hand. "But it wasn't the money so much as the fact that he didn't respect our friendship enough to repay it."

"Maybe he couldn't," Roberto suggested, putting his wine glass down and focusing on Bill.

"Maybe he wouldn't," Bill said, whirling back to face the priest. "He always had money for booze."

"But it was only money," the priest said in a calm voice. "Nothing life-threatening."

"Oh, yes it was. On the day he should have paid me back, he came to the strip just as I was about to take off. Instead of repaying me, he asked for more money. He had done it to other people before, but I never thought he would do it to me. We were close at one time. Almost like . . . brothers."

"That's when it hurts the most."

"I told him I never wanted to see him again. I climbed into the plane angry. I took off angry. I couldn't even put out the load of sulfur I had because I had forgotten the map of the field. I returned to the airstrip and crashed on landing."

"Oh, no—"

"I know it wouldn't have happened if I had been thinking straight."

"You can't know that," Roberto said.

"But I do," Bill insisted, recalling the incident and trembling. Every time he retold the story, it made him feel like he was back in the plane, trapped and close to burning. "It was terrifying, Father. It's the main reason I came back to the church. The plane was on top of me. It started to burn. You know, I'd had dreams like that," Bill said, pacing without looking at Roberto. He walked behind the couch and dragged one hand along the top of it. "But in my dreams, it never went that far. The crash was like a bad dream, and I couldn't wake up."

"Reality is a dream," Roberto said, watching Bill wander around the room. "Don't forget the realm of God. Life on Earth is only the smallest slice of His realm. Just a little dream. The truth is, when you crashed that day, you woke up to a greater reality."

Bill felt stunned and struggled to comprehend the priest's idea.

THE DISTANT LOOK in Bill's eyes told Roberto that something about what he had said resonated with the young man. The telephone in the office started to ring. Roberto let it go for awhile, and then got up, went into the next room, and answered it. The caller asked Roberto if he was a priest. He almost said 'no.'

"This is Father Roberto," he said into the receiver, admitting the truth.

"I'm a correctional officer at Soledad Correctional Training Facility," the voice said into Roberto's ear. The call was from the state prison in the middle of the Salinas Valley. Roberto could guess what they wanted. The headlines had not been good for Mendoza. "An inmate here lost his death penalty appeal today. He wants to talk to a priest. To you."

"I'm busy right now," Roberto answered, trying to avoid his own nightmare.

"He's waiting for you," the officer said. "What should I tell him?"

"Tell him—" Roberto paused and lowered his voice to keep his dilemma from Bill. "Tell him I'll be there as soon as possible."

Roberto replaced the receiver with a quiet click and returned in a haze to the living room where Bill waited. He walked past Bill in silence, sinking into the recliner and growing pale before downing the rest of his wine.

"Are you all right?" Bill asked.

"Fine, fine," Roberto answered, noticing the words came out in a whisper.

"Perhaps I should go . . ."

"No, stay," Roberto said in an anxious tone. It was wrong, but he wanted to avoid meeting with Mendoza for as long as possible. "Stay for dinner."

"Sorry, Father, I can't," Bill said, looking at the clock on the wall. "I promised I'd be home. Maybe another time."

"Oh . . ."

"Are you sure you're all right?"

"Fine, fine."

Bill excused himself, and Roberto nodded, unable to leave the recliner. His guest showed himself out, and the door closed behind Bill without a sound. Roberto knew he would not be excused from the task he had dreaded. Both hands covered his face for a moment, then he rose and went to find his car keys.

The Other Woman

ROBERTO DROVE HIMSELF to the prison that night. He arrived to find the lights of the high security facility casting an eerie glow in the late evening fog. The priest doubted he could handle the convicted man's rage. He remembered how distraught Mendoza had been before the sentencing. It would be worse after losing his appeal.

A correctional officer led Roberto to a far wing of the prison. The echoing sound of Roberto's footsteps made him feel like the convicted man. Mendoza occupied a private cell at the far end of the ward reserved for all those who faced the same fate. Death.

A cold sweat dampened Roberto's forehead even before the opening gate echoed down the long slick hallway of D wing. A curious mix of ammonia and cigarettes stung his nose. The slamming bolt behind him carried a message as final as the sign above Dante's Inferno. "Abandon all hope, ye who enter here."

Less than half of the twenty cells held prisoners. Roberto heard no raging, just the sound of a distant radio and someone coughing. He reached the occupied end of the ward, and everyone rose to see who was arriving to disrupt the normal schedule. Dark eyes behind bars followed him as he passed. Most saw his collar and retreated unimpressed.

Mendoza sat in a quiet, bare cell at the far end of the hallway. He was a recent arrival, and none of his personal effects had been hung on the walls. The guard unlocked the door of Mendoza's cell for Roberto, opened it, and ushered Roberto inside. He promised to wait down the hall and closed the cell door. Roberto wanted to beg him to stay.

"Wave when you are ready," the officer said, locking the door behind Roberto.

Mendoza sat on the shadowy lower bunk. The harsh light of a bare bulb revealed a limp rosary dangling from his fingertips. His nails were bitten to the quick. The dark beads hung between the worn knees of his faded blue jeans. The slight man stood when the priest entered, and the two men shook hands. His overriding calm confused Roberto. Mendoza lacked the fire of the writhing, raging man that Roberto had once seen restrained in a hospital bed.

"Thanks for coming, Father," Mendoza said, keeping his voice low.

"Of course," Roberto answered. "I just heard your bad news."

"Yeah," Mendoza answered in a quiet voice, gazing at the ceiling.

Nervous fingers pushed his curly, copper hair away from his face. The teardrop tattoo by his eye seemed appropriate. His freckles had faded, and the cross tattooed on his chin stood out in the absence of his former scant beard. He dropped his dark rosary beads on the white pillow of his small bed.

"I believe you are innocent," Roberto said, regretting the clumsiness of his words.

"You should have been on the jury," Mendoza answered, turning away. Was he smiling? No, he couldn't be.

"Would you like to pray?" Roberto asked, rooted to his spot in the middle of the cell.

"In a minute," the young man said, pacing around the small priest. Roberto watched him, convinced that he detected the trace of a smile. "What makes you think I am innocent?"

"You said you were," Roberto answered, shifting his Bible from one hand to the other.

"Everyone in here says that," Mendoza answered with a laugh. "Do you believe all of them?"

"They didn't say it to a priest."

"They would. Most of them would anyway."

"Maybe . . ."

"No, Padre, you know something," the convicted man said, tapping his temple. "I don't know how you know, but you do. You can't con a con."

"It comes with the job," Roberto said, adjusting his collar. He would rather have Mendoza thinking his information came from God than Maria Consalvo.

"I didn't kill that bit—," Mendoza started, then stopped. "Sorry. That woman."

"I know," Roberto said, looking into the condemned man's eyes. They were supposed to be the windows to the soul, but in Mendoza's case, the drapes were drawn. Roberto couldn't connect with anything behind them.

"So why am I here?" Mendoza asked, still circling Roberto.

"I'm afraid I don't know," Roberto answered, following him with his eyes.

"I'll tell you," Mendoza said, stopping to lean back against the sink. His finger pointed toward Roberto, then he pulled it back, and folded his arms across his chest. "I didn't kill that woman in King City. I killed an old woman in Mexico. I robbed her for enough money to get to California. This is my confession, Padre. Believe me, I'm sorry I did it. Not for the right reason, but I am sorry."

If confession was good for the soul, Roberto's had just been reborn. One of the worst burdens he had ever carried was now lifted from his shoulders by the slight man in front of him. Mendoza had killed someone, just not the one he was convicted of murdering. Roberto had never believed in the death penalty, but something about the justice Mendoza would receive was logical.

"So, do your thing, Padre," Mendoza said, pushing away from the sink and holding his arms open wide.

"What?" Roberto asked.

"You know. Pray."

"Of course, of course," Roberto said. He opened his book and fixed his green eyes on Mendoza. "Repentance would be something to consider."

"I'll see if I can squeeze it in," Mendoza answered, crossing the cell to peek through the bars. "My schedule is a little tight."

"Let's begin with a prayer for your family," Roberto said, thumbing through the pages of his book and clearing his throat.

"What family?" the convict asked, tilting his head as he looked at Roberto.

"The baby."

"Baby?"

"When I visited you in the infirmary, you said you had a baby daughter. You swore on her life that you were innocent."

"I did?" Mendoza said, and laughed. He shook his head and looked at Roberto with something resembling pity in his eyes. "I was desperate, Padre. I would have said anything."

"Do you have any children?"

"I don't think so."

"Was there anything else you told me that wasn't true?" Roberto asked, feeling embarrassed that he had been duped.

"Probably," Mendoza said, still smiling. "If I think of it, I'll let you know." After a pause, he continued. "I probably said I was innocent. That's not exactly true."

"Not exactly."

Mendoza moved away from the bars and toward Roberto. The smile was gone. He stood so close to Roberto, he could have kissed him.

"I'm scared to die, Padre," Mendoza said, whispering in Roberto's ear. He backed away and dropped to sit on the edge of the bed. "I think it must hurt to stop breathing. I hold my breath and try to imagine it. I'll know soon, won't I?"

"You're a braver man than I am, Raoul," Roberto said. He reached out and touched his thumb to the condemned man's forehead. "In the name of the Father," Roberto said, drawing the shape of a cross. ". . . and the son, and the Holy Spirit. Let us pray."

Rumors

"BILLY BOY!"

"What?" Bill asked, sounding blunt. It had been over two months since Tony had called. Bill switched the wall phone in his kitchen from one ear to the other and leaned back against the counter.

"I'm in Castroville, having a brew," Tony answered. Music was blaring in the background. It didn't surprise Bill that Tony sounded drunk at two in the afternoon. "Come on up."

"No thanks."

"Come on. For old time's sake."

"No," Bill answered, uncrossing his legs and standing up straight.

"Man, no one ever gets off your shit list, do they?"

Bill didn't bother with an answer. Tony just didn't get it. He never would.

"I got some new kind of honey here."

"I bet," Bill answered, not impressed.

"Hey, Angela and I are separated. I'm on the prowl again."

"You were always on the prowl, Tony," Bill answered, checking the clock on the stove.

"We all have our vices. Some of us just enjoy them more." Then, Tony lowered his voice. "Tell me, have you heard from Angela?" Bill could almost imagine him standing at the pay phone in Clancy's bar. He probably had one finger in his bad ear, and his back turned to the new woman, whoever she was.

"No," Bill answered with a sigh. "Look, Tony, I'm really not—"

"She should have the baby in a few months."

"Yeah, so?"

"Come on up and have a drink, Billy."

"No, Tony," Bill answered, walking toward the base of the phone.

"Why not? You quit?" Bill didn't answer him. He didn't feel there was any point. "You quit, didn't you?" Tony said, his voice raising an octave. "How could you?"

No answer. He knew Tony wouldn't understand, not that it mattered.

"Next thing you know, you'll be going to church."

Bill hung up and went back to work in his garage. He didn't need phone calls from Tony to know what was going on with him. Tales about Tony had been circulating through the industry like bad news. Later that evening, Cindy and Bill bumped into Patches in the bar of a local restaurant. Patches told Bill about his failed business venture with Tony.

"I was a fool to trust Tony," Patches said, drinking alone at the far end of the bar. He was nursing a bourbon and soda, talking and shaking his head. "In the beginning, it was all frost work. Tony flew at night, using prop wash to keep the fruit from freezing. He worked nights and drank days. He kept trying to find Angela, but it was like she had dropped off the face of the Earth."

"I should never have agreed to be the mechanic," Patches continued. To Bill, it almost seemed as if he were talking to himself. "A blade came loose on take-off. Tony put it all back together— better than I ever could have—but then he bugged out. Now I have a helicopter rotting in the field behind my house, and his motorcycle rusting in my barn. There's no fool like an old fool."

Stories about Tony continued to surface. Bill attended the annual Agricultural Aviators Convention the following month. He had been crossing through the bar on his way to the banquet room when someone called his name.

"Bill, how are you?" The voice belonged to a fat man with strawberry blonde hair. He swiveled around on his bar stool. It was Red Ryder, a pilot who had flown for a company in Salinas back when Bill was just a swamper. "Hey, how about Tony, huh?"

"Tony?" Bill answered, trying to slip away. "Yeah, well, I haven't talked to him since—"

"Didn't you hear?" the big man asked Bill. Red dropped a fresh swizzle stick atop a tall pile beside his icy glass. "Tony was working for some outfit in the desert. I guess he got tired of the lousy mechanics and late paychecks. One night, he took a company helicopter and his .44 magnum, and flew across the state line. He landed on the roof of some whorehouse in Nevada. I'm not sure what happened—"

"I know," King Sharp said, an ag pilot on the neighboring stool. Bill knew that King, a seasoned pilot, flew for one of the desert operator's competitors. "I heard he stuffed some tart in the bubble with him, and then shot at her boyfriend on take-off. He could have been charged with a felony, but the other party was involved in drugs. They didn't want anyone to call the cops."

"Guys like Tony preserve the cropduster's image," Red said, lifting a fresh drink. "And that's not easy to do."

"To Tony," said King, raising his glass to Red's.

"To Tony," Red agreed with a smile.

They were laughing when Bill left, but to him, it wasn't that funny. It bugged Bill all through dinner and the keynote speaker. Maybe it was his crash. It always seemed to go back to that defining moment in his life. Bill had had a deeper respect for mortality since then. Tony was just a joke to the others at the table, but Bill knew where Tony was headed. If he didn't clean up his act soon, it was going to kill him. Bill didn't want that to matter, but it did. Overthinking everything was a habit he couldn't kick. He could almost hear Tony's voice saying, "Hey, live a little." In that respect, Tony had been good for him. Still, Bill's answer had always been the same. I'd rather live a lot.

SIX WEEKS LATER, Bill was about to drop off to sleep when the phone rang. He sat up with a start in the darkness and answered it.

"Billy! What's happening?"

"Oh, it's you," Bill answered in a quiet voice, too tired to care. He sat back, leaning against the headboard and pulling the phone into bed with him. His whisper still woke Cindy. She gave Bill a quizzical look, and he mouthed "Tony." She sat up and listened to Bill's half of the conversation. "It's late."

"I'm in Salinas at the airport bar," Tony said. He sounded the same to Bill. Drunk and lost. "Come on up, and I'll buy a round."

"No thanks, Tony."

"Come on. Be a pal," Tony said and paused, waiting for Bill's reply. Bill had nothing to say. "Come have a brew. I got a new old lady. She's a peach."

"You said that last time."

"I had to," Tony said and then lowered his voice. "She was listening. So is this one. Come on. What do you say?"

"Good night, Tony."

"Don't hang up." Tony's voice faded. Bill could tell Tony had put his hand over the receiver. Tony's muffled voice said 'Get me another drink, doll face' before he came back on the line. "Sorry, I had to get rid of the old bag. Listen, have you heard from Angela?"

"Not a word."

"The baby is due next month, you know."

"I know," Bill said, sitting up and getting ready to put the phone back on the nightstand. "Look, Tony, why don't you just lose my number, OK?"

"You can't still be pissed at me."

"Good night, Tony," Bill said and hung up. It took a while for Bill to go back to sleep. His anger at Tony was starting to fade, and sometimes he even felt a little sorry for him. That loser would never get his shit together.

A MONTH LATER, Bill heard another rumor that Tony was working for a big operator in the middle of the state and getting married. Bill didn't think his divorce could be final, not that such legal technicalities had much to do with Tony. Bill began to dread every new rumor. He wasn't sure how much longer Tony could last at the rate he was going. Later, Bill heard that Tony had been fired within weeks of starting the job, after getting caught in bed with the owner's wife. At work or social gatherings, Bill started leaving the room if Tony's name came up. He didn't want to know any more.

TONY, RED-EYED AND SHAKEN, had driven 50 miles, what he considered a safe distance, before entering the parking lot of a strip mall. The address he had looked up two days ago had a vacant stall in front of it. The faded name of the previous business, the Curl Up 'n'

Dye Hair Salon, still remained above the door. Tony parked, got out of his car, and squinted hard in the morning sun. It didn't help his headache, which could have been caused by the vodka or his former boss's round house punch. He studied the hand-printed sign taped to the glass door and tucked most of his wrinkled shirt into his too-loose jeans.

HARCOURT INVESTIGATIONS
Missing Persons A Specialty

Tony hesitated, and then placed his hand on the cold metal push plate of the door. It opened, and he walked up to the counter, still wearing sunglasses. The small man inside had his back to Tony, facing one of six computers, each the size of a refrigerator. The shopkeeper sneezed and pulled a large white hankie from his front pocket. The force with which he blew his nose lifted the wire frame glasses from his face. He turned around and the sight of Tony frightened him. Seven successive sneezes later, he blew his nose again. Tony waited until the man recovered.

"Who's the private eye?" Tony asked, his tired eyes scouring the sparse office.

"It is I," the young, balding man answered, folding his handkerchief with precision and replacing it.

"You?" Tony asked and raked his fingers through his hair. This was a mistake, but what other options did he have? None.

"Dalton Harcourt," he said, extending his hand. Tony only looked at it, and the nervous man allowed it to drop, unshaken. "How may I help you?"

"I need to find someone."

"Is this a missing person?" Harcourt asked, and a goofy grin spread across his face.

"Are you sure you're a private eye?" Tony asked, removing his sunglasses and lifting an eyebrow to examine the guy. Dalton appeared blurry in the painful, bright light. Tony's eyelids felt like sand paper scraping his eyeballs when he blinked. He should have passed on the third bottle.

"Sir, I have access to all the latest technology," Harcourt said, trying to sound confident and failing in Tony's mind. "Finding a missing person is merely a matter of entering the correct data. Take Bertha here," he said, massaging the side of one of the tall tape drives. "She has the name and address of nearly every registered property owner in the state of California."

"What if someone isn't in this state?" Tony asked, since Angela probably wasn't. At least, he didn't think she was, but what did he know?

"Then we might have to ask Gretchen, Alice, Ruth, or Gwendolyn," he answered, walking the line and nodding to each machine.

"Who's that?" Tony asked, pointing to the last one.

"Candace," Dalton answered, folding his arms with a smug look. "She's strictly for international searches. Now, exactly who did you want to find?"

"My wife."

"I see," Dalton Harcourt answered, bringing a scratch pad to the counter where Tony was leaning in agony. The nervous man clicked his pen five or six times before holding it poised above the paper.

"What's her name?"

"Angela."

Harcourt noted it, and then looked up. The lenses of his glasses looked as if they had not been cleaned in days. At least he had an excuse for blurry vision.

"Last name?" Harcourt asked and sniffed.

"I'm not sure," Tony answered, staring at the notepad with Angela's name. "I mean, she could be using mine, but I doubt it."

"We can work around that," Harcourt said, trying to reassure him. Tony felt anything but. "Do you know her social security number?"

"No . . ."

"Driver's License number?"

"No . . ."

"Does she own property?"

"I don't think so," Tony said, getting pissed at his own lack of knowledge.

"Are you sure this is your wife?" Harcourt asked, looking up from the notepad that still only had the word 'Angela' written on it.

"Damn straight," Tony answered, slapping his hand on the countertop. Harcourt started sneezing again and went into the hankie ritual.

"Do you know what part of the United States she's in?" he asked after he had regained control. "Or do we need to consult Candace?" He smiled an unnatural smile over his shoulder at the big machine.

"Somewhere in the Midwest," Tony answered. "Last I heard."

"That's fairly broad, sir. Could you narrow it down?"

"Nope," Tony said, lowering his eyebrows to scrutinize the young man. "That's all I know." Harcourt laid the pen beside the notepad and looked up.

"Are you telling me you want me to find someone named Angela in the Midwest?"

"Yeah."

"Well, I'm sorry, sir," Harcourt answered with a nervous laugh. "Even Alice, Gretchen, Ruth, and Gwendolyn can't do that." Harcourt ripped the top page from his note pad and wadded it up. Tony grabbed his wrist before Harcourt could toss it in the garbage.

"I've got to find her," Tony said, releasing Harcourt and slapping his wallet on the counter. "Twenty bucks. It's all the money I have in the world. It's yours if you can tell me where she is."

"Twenty dollars?" Harcourt asked with a laugh, backing away. "I couldn't find my own mother for $20.00."

Tony jumped over the counter and grabbed Harcourt by the shirt collar.

"Don't mess with me—"

Before Tony could finish, Dalton Harcourt started sneezing so hard that Tony had to let him go. Harcourt leaned against Bertha, reaching for his handkerchief. Tony wiped his damp arm on his own pant leg.

"I'm-I'm s-s-sorry," Harcourt said after he recovered. "Even if you had $200.00, you haven't given me enough information."

"I need to talk to her one more time," Tony said, staring at the small man. Harcourt shrugged, and Tony headed for the door.

"Wait—" Harcourt said, leaving Bertha. Tony looked back over his shoulder. "It might not be of any help, but the best thing you can do is contact a mutual friend. In most cases, it's more likely you will find her that way. This," he said, pointing at the wall full of machinery, "is a last resort."

"Yeah, I know," Tony said, putting on his sunglasses and walking out the door.

A week later, Tony took Dalton Harcourt's advice. He made a long distance call in the middle of the day.

"Hello," Bill answered.

"Uh, hello, Bill?" Tony started, watching an airplane on landing cruise down the runway. "It's Tony. How the hell are you?"

"OK," Bill said in a quiet voice, and there was a long pause. For a moment, Tony thought they had been disconnected. Then he heard Bill's voice. "Where are you?"

"Fuck if I know," Tony answered. He turned around in the cramped phone booth outside the small terminal building. His back was to the runway now with his finger plugging his bad ear. "Somewhere in Washington State. I'm flying helicopter for an outfit with a federal contract. We're spraying a national forest for grasshoppers." Tony wanted to ask a different question, but instead he said, "How's Cindy?"

"Fine," Bill said, and Tony could almost hear a smile in his voice. "She's pregnant."

"You're shitting me," Tony said, but Bill didn't answer. "No, I guess not. Uh, congratulations and, well, give her my best. Hey, look, are you still sore at me?"

"Does it matter?"

"I don't know," Tony said, glancing toward his parked car. "I guess not. I know I never paid you back, but you can still have the rifle."

"No, thanks," Bill said.

"Look, I'm sorry." Advice from Robert bubbled up in Tony's memory. "Maybe someday you can forgive me."

"Maybe. Don't hold your breath."

The line was quiet for a moment. Tony wasn't sure how much longer Bill would hang on. He blurted out his question.

"Do you ever hear from Angela?" Tony asked and held his breath.

"No," Bill answered, and Tony exhaled.

"Shit," Tony said, shaking his head and feeling a burning sensation in his eyes. "I'm probably a father by now. It's not that I haven't dropped a kid here and there along the way, but this one is different. I'll probably never know."

"I'm sorry, Tony." Bill sounded as if he felt some compassion. Maybe Tony's situation seemed more real to Bill now that Cindy was pregnant. Or maybe he just caught him on a good day.

"Hey, don't be," Tony said, trying to laugh. "Hell, I deserve it. She did the right thing. No kid needs an old man like me. Do you think she'll tell the kid about me?"

"I don't know, Tony."

"Yeah," Tony said, ready to hang up. "Me neither. Look, I know you quit drinking, so I just called to say I'm having a brew for you."

"Thanks. How's work?"

Bill's question surprised Tony. He shifted in the phone booth and adjusted the phone on his ear. It had been a long time since someone asked him how he was doing. It felt odd and comforting at the same time.

"Boring," Tony answered. "Just a bunch of trees. Miles of 'em. We're flying Hillers up here. They're great machines, but I swear I hear something wrong in mine. I can't figure out what it is. I've had the mechanic on it three times. He's about ready to shoot me. I'm about ready to take it apart myself."

"Shit, don't do that," Bill said and gave a little laugh.

"Ahhh, it's probably nothing," Tony said and smiled. He could imagine Bill's face. He would have been smiling and shaking his head just like he used to do back when they were close. Bill was the one guy who always understood that telling Tony to do something for his own good was pointless. "Hey, I could never hear that well anyway. Look, I got to get going, or I'll be late for work. Can I give you my work number?"

"I don't know, Tony—"

"Just in case Angela calls," Tony answered, getting the words in before Bill hung up on him. There was a moment of silence before Bill answered.

"Yeah, go ahead," Bill said.

Tony gave him the number. He was waiting for Bill to write it down when a woman's voice whined "Ton-ee" behind him.

"Thanks, and I'll catch you later, bro," Tony said, holding one finger up toward the tattooed woman with the dark hair and thick makeup.

"Later," Bill said and hung up.

Tony looked at the phone for a minute, took a deep breath, and replaced the receiver in the cradle without a sound. He left the phone booth, and the woman folded her arms and looked at him, as if she was pissed. He wrapped an arm around her shoulders and guided her to the airport bar.

For the rest of the afternoon and evening, his mind kept wandering back to his conversation with Bill. His former friend hadn't sounded too pissed. Maybe he wasn't angry anymore. Maybe, just maybe, Bill would contact him if Angela called.

Nowhere to Go

Old habits were hard to break. Tony woke up early, even when he was hungover. And he was definitely hungover. He found himself naked in an unfamiliar bedroom. A tattooed woman shifted under the covers beside him. His senses seemed to be slipping, and it was getting harder and harder to orient himself. She was still asleep when he left the bed, gathered his clothes from various parts of the room, and wandered into the kitchen of what he guessed was her house. He splashed cold water on his face in a sink guarded by towers of dirty dishes.

A noise behind him made him turn around in a hurry, water still dripping from his face. It was her cat, not her husband, and he breathed a sigh of relief. Maybe she wasn't married, but he didn't feel inclined to hang around and find out. Instinct or some dull memory led him to the front door, where he stumbled out of the small, country house smack dab in the middle of nowhere. His dull, black '63 Cadillac sat parked in the overgrown grass of the front yard.

"God, let me still be in the state of Washington and somewhere near the airstrip," he said and opened the driver's door.

He drove off heading away from the sun because it was easier on his eyes. In time, a freeway on-ramp appeared. He took it and popped a warm beer from a six-pack on the floorboard. The last stale donut in a rumpled box served as breakfast. He finished it and sent the box sailing into the back seat. A road sign indicated the airport lay in the opposite direction. He made a U-turn over the dirt median. It would mean his job if he was late again.

He arrived at the airport, where his chopper sat alone on the flight line. The others were already out working. He parked and caught his sorry face in the rear view mirror. His fingers raked through his black curls and then wiped the foam and crumbs from his dark moustache. With any luck, he wouldn't cross paths with the boss.

The control tower reflected in the dirty picture windows of Real Flying, Inc. Tony entered to find one clipboard remaining on the counter of the deserted office. It held a map and his work instructions for the day. Tony heard paper rustling and looked toward the john. The door was ajar with the corner of a magazine by the door handle and a pair of pants on the floor around a man's ankles. He picked up the clipboard without a sound and left, heading toward the lone aircraft. The swamper at the loading pad fueled the helicopter and mixed his load. The sound of his chopper lifting off brought the boss surging from the office, buckling his belt and zipping his pants. Tony pretended not to notice.

Mountains covered with trees surrounded the airport. Tony's map marked out a straight forward spray job in imaginary blocks numbered 46, 47, and 48 near an unnamed peak. He flew high above the uncivilized landscape. His only landmarks were fire roads, streams and ponds. Pointed pines of a brilliant green grew so dense that bare earth almost wasn't visible below them. Those branches hid thousands of millions of destructive pests.

Tony circled the junction of two dirt paths, deciding how to begin. The load of pesticides on board would last for miles. It was still early enough to be cool. Good flying weather yet the heavy craft acted a little sluggish, and it wasn't just the load. He noticed the same miss in the engine rhythm that had dogged him for the last few days. He added power, and then pulled it back.

"What the hell is that noise anyway?" he asked and cocked his good ear to the engine. After a pass or two, the chopper grew lighter. She flew fine, but something still sounded wrong.

He set his course in a straight line and followed the contours of the land, now and then making a rare turn. The flying was as easy as it got with fair weather and no wind. No wires to dodge, no people to worry about, and no delicate surrounding crops to harm.

The first load took half an hour. Tony headed back for his second one, knowing the boss would be waiting. The helicopter had just kissed the landing pad, rotors still whirling, when the owner approached the bubble in a running crouch. He jerked open the cockpit door, spitting nails.

"I hired you to fly, hot shot," the red-faced man yelled over the engine noise.

"Sorry," Tony said, stepping out of the bubble and brushing past his angry boss to look at the engine.

Wiry red and brown hairs in Jim Real's thick eyebrows seemed pinched together beneath his balding pink scalp. Real's livid, quick eyes and tiny black pupils burned into Tony's back. Tony turned around to face him. The straining shirt buttons at Real's bulbous stomach threatened to burst.

"I've warned you before," Real said, his baggy jowls trembling.

"I know. I know. I won't be late again. I had car trouble."

"You said that last time."

"I did?" Tony asked. His blue eyes, bloodshot and pain-filled, squinted at Real in the morning sun. "Well, it's the same car. It did it again."

"Your car is the least of your worries, pal," Real said, raising his index finger close to Tony's nose. "Give me one good reason not to fire you."

"Because I'm a good pilot?" Tony said, turning away and fixing his gaze on the engine.

"What use is a good pilot who can't show up on time?" Real asked, moving to be in Tony's line of sight.

"What do you want me to do?" Tony asked, speaking into the motor. "Buy a new car? OK, I'll buy a new car."

"I want you to lay off the sauce," the boss said, sounding sincere.

"Sure," Tony agreed without giving it any thought.

"I mean it."

"OK, OK," Tony said, wiping an oily fingertip on his jeans.

"This is your last warning, Tony."

"Yeah, thanks. OK," Tony answered in a calm, disinterested voice. "I really think the mechanic should look at this."

"A mechanic has checked it every day for the last three days," Jim Real said, throwing up his hands. "There's nothing wrong with it."

"It sounds funny," Tony said.

"Get your hearing checked. Look, if you don't want to fly it, let me know. I'll get someone else."

"Hey, it's not that serious," Tony said, backing off. He needed the job. "Just a little miss somewhere."

"All right. OK," Jim said, glancing at the engine. "If it does it again today, let me know. Are you losing oil pressure?"

"No," Tony answered, bewildered.

"Is it running hot?"

"No."

"You got power?"

"Yeah," Tony said, looking away from the sun. "She's a little sluggish when she's heavy but after that, she's fine."

"You let me know if it keeps up," Jim said before walking away. He wasn't such a bad guy.

Load after load, nothing changed. Tony flew over miles and miles of trees and never any bare ground. The annoying noise continued, but the aircraft flew fine. He tried to put it out of his mind.

By noon, he was breaking ground with the eighth load of the day. It was starting to warm up. His hangover and his memory of that morning were fading. Then, in his head, all of a sudden, he was explaining the tattooed woman to Angela.

It wouldn't have happened if she hadn't left him. It didn't mean a thing. Hell, he didn't even know if he did anything. All he could remember was the tattoo on her butt, saggy boobs, and his tires tracks across her front lawn. And why did it matter? He couldn't even recall the woman's name. He couldn't understand why he was driving himself crazy about it. It wasn't like he would ever see Angela again.

"Who was that wench?" he asked.

"Tower to Oh-Niner." The voice crackled over the radio through the headset built into Tony's helmet. "Repeat that, over."

"Negative, over," Tony answered before flipping the mike away from his lips. "Shit." He switched radio frequencies, tuning out the tower and picking up a local rock station.

He circled the forested area with the helicopter, searching over his right shoulder for the spot where he had finished his last load. It took a while to find the split tree he had noted as a landmark. Two long spray runs passed before the aircraft lightened, and she felt ready to fly again. The treetops passed just below his feet, but he kept his eyes on the horizon.

The flying was easy. It gave him too much time to think. Soon he was repeating the mantra he had tried to believe for months now. It's over with Angela. It doesn't matter anymore. What a fool, falling for her. Now, he could be with another woman, but all he could think about was how to explain it to Angela. How to say it meant nothing. How to prove she meant everything. How his feelings for her were driving him nuts. If only he could forget that she once meant everything to him. Was he crazy to believe there was a time when he meant everything to her?

That's when a harmonica solo started wailing through the static of Tony's headset. The tempo picked up, and the rhythm went straight to his heart and came out his hand. A plane would feel good right now. He realized he hadn't thought that in months. Maybe it was the music, or the time of day, or the complete solitude of flying all alone, miles away from anyone who cared. Something inside him said, 'Fuck this spray job. Just fly.' He began flying for flying's sake, and the singer from Blood, Sweat, & Tears wailed the lyrics from *And When I Die*.

And in that moment, he wasn't scared of dying. He wasn't scared of anything at all. The chopper skirted the taller trees, swinging left then right below the main rotor. She hugged the contour of the terrain. He knew he was doing a lousy job of spraying, but he was doing some mean flying. The whole machine moved with the beat of the music, dancing through the sky with a trailing mist. Two eagles were spooked from the tree tops, and they swooped around him in lazy circles. He auto-rotated the chopper to watch them, ignoring the singer's cries about troubles, heaven, and hell.

The birds soared overhead, watching him. Heaven? Hell? Pray? Maybe, if he was lucky, there was the purgatory that Robert talked about. If he was lucky. But he hadn't been lucky lately. He cranked the machine around to show the birds a trick or two, swinging the tail rotor left and right and feeling free.

Freedom was a funny thing. Now that he had it, he wanted to lose it. The aircraft rose and fell in quick, flared turns, the sort he used when spraying short fields. He shut off the spray nozzles, saving what was left of the load and doing some serious dicking around.

When he finished the load, he'd have to go back for another, and he wasn't ready to go back yet. A little more time alone in the cockpit. A little more cloud dancing. Maybe, just maybe, if he got enough, he would forget all about the way he had fucked up his life.

The song suggested dying naturally worked best, and it seemed as good a goal as any. The raucous beat of the music outran him. Tony chased the eagles, tail up, bubble forward, boring holes in the sky. He tipped the craft sideways, then righted it again to make lazy eights in the sky until the music slowed with wistful lyrics about carrying on.

Now, like most other days lately, he could only think of Angela. He wondered about the baby. Was it a boy or a girl? Would the child carry on? Would he ever know?

The engine bucked, smoothed out, and then lurched forward with a jerk. His leather glove tightened on the cyclic. Dumping the load would lighten the craft, but his job was already in jeopardy. He gained altitude and searched for an open spot where he could land. The engine sputtered, coughed, and bucked again. He opened the dump doors, dropped the load, and switched the radio channel. Losing the weight of the pesticide gave him some lift.

"Oh-Niner to tower," he said, keeping his voice calm. No need to let on he was scared shitless if nothing happened. "I'm having engine trouble. I'm coming back, over."

"Tower to Oh-Niner," the crackling voice acknowledged him. It made him feel better for a half second. "Where are you, over?"

"Smack in the middle of nowhere," Tony answered, louder than he wanted to. His head was moving back and forth, scanning the landscape for familiar terrain. Trees. All trees. The engine sputtered again, and then smoothed out.

"Tower to Oh-Niner, can you make it?" a tense voice asked.

"Fuck, I hope so," Tony answered, feeling the sweat trickling down his neck and soaking his back. He tried climbing for a half mile, thinking he recognized a distant peak. A clunking rattle started again, growing louder and louder with no airport in sight. He didn't have much time.

"Oh-Niner to Tower," Tony said into the mike. He couldn't hide the truth from himself any longer. "I'm not going to make it, over."

"Oh-Niner, give us your location."

"It's all trees down there," Tony said, now battling with the cyclic to keep her in the air. He managed to gasp out some position. "South, southeast of the airport, over."

"How far, over?"

"Too far."

"Rescue choppers are on the way."

Tony left the radio on, listening to his engine and fearing the worst. Trees, trees, and more trees. Nowhere to land. A final bang was followed only by the whoosh of air rushing past him. His eyes focused on the dropping needle of the altimeter. Every muscle in his body tensed, and his stomach churned. He bit his lip and struggled to keep himself together. He kept his glove clamped on the cyclic, even though there was no point.

"I'm going in," he said, the words escaping before he could stop them.

"We see you."

"I'm going in," he said again, the trees growing bigger and bigger. He could see the spot where he would hit. He closed his eyes and turned away. "I'm going in. Shit."

Time held its breath, and seconds passed like days. No lift, no speed. The controls were now useless. Tony was just along for the ride. Pine needles and branches surrounded the bubble, blocking out the sky. He heard tree limbs cracking and metal skids ripping away, followed by the scent of fresh pine. The craft flipped over, and Tony was upside down when the main rotors sheared off with a deafening sound. The force of the impact threatened to hurl him from his seat, but the shoulder harness yanked him back. It felt like his arms were being ripped from their sockets. The door fell away in slow motion.

"No-o-o," he cried, watching the sharp point of a shattered tree jab through the open doorway. It pierced his chest wall, and everything came to a sudden, silent stop.

"Go on," Tony's body screamed to his spirit. "I can't make it. You go on without me." Unbearable pain was followed by blackness.

Go where? his spirit asked, looking down at the twisted wreck.

"Go!" his body screamed again.

Tony left his rag doll body strapped to the cockpit seat, bleeding in the dirt and pine needles. The view changed. No longer was he in the middle of the trees. He was looking down on the tree tops, viewing his earthly self and the scattered ruins of the helicopter. Tiny tongues of orange flames began to dance in the dry foliage beside the wreckage. The jumbled remains of the aircraft and a pilot's body, his body, lie intertwined at the base of a thousand trees.

In the same instant, he heard an infant squeal the first cry of life from a hospital in the Midwest. The sound propelled him back to Earth and into his body.

"Go," his body said, with only a whisper of strength. Again his spirit rose to the treetops.

Go where? his spirit asked, looking down a long tunnel with no light at the end.

Tony watched from the treetops, following the whopping blades of the rescue chopper hovering over the crash site, which was marked by a line of smoke and a small fire. Two men in orange jumpsuits scrambled down a ladder which hung from the chopper door. Tony could see the emergency crew fighting their way through the trees and followed them in.

Tony found himself back in the cockpit in pain, surrounded by the sound of fire crackling and rotors beating overhead. A calm voice began to speak to him. The words weren't those of an old pilot, telling him to unbuckle the seat belt and get away from the fuel tank.

"It's a place," the voice said. Tony felt himself ascending again, and the pain went away. He could see a small, bare room with a single bed where someone was napping. The place wasn't familiar, and yet Tony recognized it, even though that was impossible. The sleeping figure was Robert, and Tony watched Robert's dream. Two translucent bodies seemed to mesh in the air above the sleeping man. The priest was joining with the pilot's spirit. Tony's spirit. In that instant, Tony believed the words he had only heard once before. "It's a place where people go who never learned to love as children."

Where is it? Tony's spirit asked, wanting to shake the truth from Robert.

A moment later, Tony was rushing downward, slamming into the Earth and back into the wreck, unable to breathe. A stranger was holding a thumb on his lifeless wrist.

"No pulse here," one rescue worker said.

I'm dead, Tony thought, caught in the moment between time and eternity.

"I've got one here," the second rescue worker said, feeling Tony's other wrist. The pain made Tony want to scream, but he couldn't breathe. A wince crossed his battered face, and then he went limp.

"Go," his broken body urged his spirit in thought. "Just go."

Where is that place, Robert? his spirit asked, soaring back into the sky.

Living, Dying, and Flying

BILL GOT THE CALL about Tony just after dinner. He hung up and stood in the kitchen, feeling light-headed. Cindy was at his side, waiting for an explanation.

"It's Tony," Bill said, moving again with a purpose. He grabbed his plate from the table and left it by the sink. "He's gone down." He picked up the phone again.

His phone call to Rand, asking for a few days off, turned out to be his flight to Washington too. Bill mentioned Tony's accident, and Rand said he had an air show in the vicinity. He warned Bill he'd have to hurry to meet him at the strip. Not only would Bill have to help fly, but he would need to find his own way back. Still, to Bill, it seemed to be a sign that he should go. Cindy followed him down the hall, watching him pull an overnight bag out of the closet.

"How bad is it?" Cindy asked, sitting on the bed and watching him pack.

"The doctors don't expect Tony to make it through the night," Bill said, darting into the bathroom to grab his shaving kit. He returned and tossed it into his luggage. "That's if he survives the surgery."

"How did it happen?" she asked.

"I don't know," Bill said. "Tony's boss didn't give me a lot of details." He continued packing with fury until he found himself turning in circles. A deep breath didn't clear his mind or help him focus. Cindy walked over to him, and her blue eyes seemed to be waiting for him to tell her more.

"I don't know why I'm going," Bill said, zipping the bag shut and lifting it off the bed. "That crazy asshole."

"Don't say that," Cindy said. "Not now."

"Ah, damn," Bill said, dropping his bag on the floor and hugging her. He stepped back and looked into her eyes. "My phone number was the only one in Tony's wallet."

"Go," she said. "He needs you."

"If he's still alive," Bill said. He grabbed his bag and headed for the door, taking a book with him at the last minute. Cindy stood in the front yard and waved. He rolled down the window. "I'll call when I can," Bill said and backed out of the driveway. She nodded, waved, and watched him go.

Bill made it to the strip in record time. Rand started the plane as soon as he saw Bill heading up the road to the strip. After parking, Bill grabbed his bag, ran across the runway, and climbed into the rear seat of the two-place Pitts, right behind Rand. He helped pull the canopy shut over them. A click of the seat belts and they taxied toward take-off.

"It'll be sunrise before we get there," Rand said, after he and Bill had donned headsets. They broke ground and the sun was setting. It would be a long, dark flight.

"As long as we make it," Bill said.

"Take her," Rand said, looking over his shoulder to Bill. "I need to check the sectional." Bill nodded and Rand relinquished control. His boss started unfolding the map in the front seat. "I can get us to Seattle. I don't know about finding some air strip in the middle of a forest."

"Get me as close as you can," Bill said. "I can always rent a car."

"I knew you knew Tony," Rand said. His head was down, studying the unfolded map. "I didn't realize you were close."

"Were," Bill repeated, staring straight ahead. "It was a long time ago."

"You know, I always wondered . . ." Rand started, then paused. "Did he really drop the key in the mix tank when Sonny fired him?"

"Yep," Bill said, glad he could answer without having to look at Rand. Tony would shit if he knew Bill was flying a Pitts Special right now. If he lived, Bill would have to thank him.

"And he cut the wire to the strip on purpose?" Rand continued, half-turning toward Bill.

"Yeah," Bill said, and for some reason, he couldn't help but smile.

"He's one of a kind," Rand said, looking back at his map.

"He sure was," Bill said and swallowed hard, realizing he already thought Tony was dead.

Most of the flight took place by the light of the moon. Tiny towns passed below like clusters of light, surrounded by stretches of darkness. Somewhere near the Oregon border, Rand, who had caught a quick catnap, took over again. Bill managed and hour or so of light napping before they crossed the next state line. He always felt uncomfortable sleeping in planes, even jetliners. It seemed like a bad habit for a pilot.

They reached Washington just before the sun rose. They followed a heading to the Olympic Forest, though Rand was still keeping open the option of landing in Seattle. It could be hard to find a tiny airstrip in unfamiliar territory. They searched the forested landscape, looking for some sign of the airport. Bill couldn't help but think that this was the last view Tony had before his crash. Just as they were about to give up, Bill spotted a helicopter lifting out of the trees.

"Over there," Bill said. "Eleven o'clock." Rand saw it too and made a banking turn in that direction. Bill radioed the tower, and Rand brought her in for landing, taxiing to the apron area in front of the Real Flying office. Bill gathered his carry-on luggage and hopped out as soon as the Pitts stopped. A World War II vintage fire bomber roared down the runway behind him. Helicopters were already taking off to start their day.

"I'll gas up and go on to Seattle," Rand told him. "I'm staying in the Holiday Inn by the airport if you need a ride back, uh, sooner than you think."

"Yeah, thanks," Bill said, reaching up to the cockpit to shake Rand's hand. "I can't thank you enough."

"Just get back to work as soon as you can," Rand said. "And give my best to Tony."

"I'll try," Bill said, wondering if he would get the chance. He stepped back and Rand started the plane again, heading down to the gas pumps.

Bill adjusted his glasses, picked up his bag, and walked toward the office. The sound of the bomber's engine faded behind tree-covered mountains, and Bill opened the door. Only one man was there, standing behind the counter and holding up the morning paper with Tony's crash on the front page. It was a visual Bill didn't need, but he found himself pausing to look at the wreckage anyway. That image, little more than twisted, burnt metal made him feel certain that Tony would never survive. He looked away, and then cleared his throat. The man lowered the paper.

"Excuse me," Bill said to the balding man behind the counter. "Someone called me about Tony Damascus."

"Jim Real," the man answered, laying the paper aside and shaking Bill's hand across the counter. "Bill, right? Sorry to meet this way. There was no one else to call."

"Yeah, I know . . ." Bill said, dropping his luggage. He shoved his hands deep into his pockets and stared at the runway through the dirty plate glass windows. "Where is he now?"

"Still at the hospital."

"Is he . . .?" Bill couldn't finish his thought.

"He was alive when I called about an hour ago," Real said, shaking his head. "They jump started his heart four times last night. They said they probably can't do it again. Too hard on the ticker. They'll make him comfortable, but, you know, no extraordinary stuff."

"Oh . . ."

"You want his helmet?" Real asked, pulling Tony's battered brain bucket from under the counter. Bill held his stomach and looked away.

"Just toss it," Bill said, avoiding Real's eyes. "You think I can rent a car here?" Bill looked toward the tiny terminal building, feeling doubtful.

"Take Tony's car," Real said, nodding to the faded black 1963 Cadillac in the first stall. "It's right there. I think he lived in it. Keys are probably still inside. It will be faster."

"You're probably right," Bill said, looking out the window. Rand went by on take-off.

"Nice machine," Real said, following the Pitts Special with his eyes.

"Yeah," Bill said, pick up his duffel bag. "I guess I should. . ."

"I'm not sure how well that thing runs," Real said, eying Tony's car.

"It'll do," Bill said, heading for the door. He turned back when he realized he had no idea where he was going. "Where's the hospital?"

"Two miles west. It's the only three-story building in town."

"Thanks," Bill said, closing the door and heading toward the Caddy. He removed two armfuls of empty beer cans from the car and dumped them into a nearby trash can. His overnight bag went sailing into the back seat through the open back door, and Bill noticed a hunk of wood under the driver's seat. He pulled the zebra-striped stock of the world's ugliest rifle from the floorboard. A $300.00 price tag hung from the trigger housing with Bill's name and address written on the back.

"You Tony's friend?" a voice asked, surprising Bill.

Bill stood up too fast, whacking the back of his head on the door jamb of the substantial old car. He turned around, rubbing the aching spot. A young man with a slight build stood on the dying grass beside the dusty path. He wore greasy overalls. His narrow face twitched, and he shifted from foot to foot, working a red rag in his dirty hands.

"Yeah," Bill answered, expecting the mechanic to say it was all over.

"I wanted to tell you we tried."

"Sure," Bill said, slipping behind the steering wheel. He found the keys under the driver's seat. He knew Tony had left them there, intending to return. It wasn't hard to sort through the ring. It only had two keys. He forgot about the mechanic until the young man spoke again.

"We went over and over that machine. I checked it myself. It ran like a jewel."

"Right," Bill answered through the open driver's side window. He didn't have time for whatever this guy's problem was. "Look, I got to go—"

"How did he know?" the young man asked, ripping the rag in two. Bill started the engine and put it in reverse. The mechanic stepped forward and gripped the car door. "Tony kept saying something sounded wrong, but how did he know?"

Bill slipped it back into park, and his hand dropped from the shift on the column. His eyes connected with the mechanic's, and he looked away from the young man's pain to follow a plane on landing.

"He had perfect pitch," Bill answered in a quiet voice, watching the plane go to the far end of the runway.

"But he could barely hear," the young man insisted.

"Yeah, I know. He just did that."

Bill avoided the young man's eyes and shifted the Cadillac into gear again. The engine purred. The body looked shabby, but Tony had restored the motor to perfection. The mechanic backed away. Bill spun the tires on the gravel for a moment and then headed for the hospital at breakneck speed. His eyes stayed on the road, avoiding the glove compartment or anything else that might carry some reminder of Tony. Instead, he switched on the radio in time for the mournful start of *American Pie*.

Bill switched it off before the lyrics mentioned dying and drove in silence until he reached the hospital parking lot. The engine went silent when he parked, and he pocketed the keys. The Caddy's door shut behind him with a solid thud, and he ran to the hospital entrance. Volunteers, ladies in pink pinafores, monitored the lobby. Their sunny information booth stood by a window near the gift shop.

"Dr. Sherman, please report to surgery," a nasal voice droned over the P.A. system.

"Tony Damascus," Bill said to the volunteers, speaking in an anxious tone.

An older woman flipped through her files. A nurse pushing a wheelchair passed them, heading for the exit with balloons floating above her. On board, a young lady carried a well wrapped, tiny bundle. A man and another nurse followed with flowers, gifts and a suitcase.

"I'm sorry, but he's in intensive care," the volunteer said to Bill. "Only family members may visit on even hours for periods of—"

"He doesn't have—" Bill said, then stopped. The suspicious volunteer with the pearl blue hair examined him over her bifocals.

"Are you a family member?"

"Yes," Bill answered and coughed.

"What relation?" she asked, her pen poised above Tony's card.

"Brother," he said under his breath.

"Pardon me?"

"I'm his brother," Bill said again, speaking louder. "Just tell me how to get to his room. Please."

The second volunteer told her partner that Tony was that young pilot who crashed almost 24 hours earlier. Bill could see that Tony's card listed no other visitors. The volunteers didn't question Bill about his relationship to the patient any further.

"Go past the elevator and to the left," she said. "ICU is just beyond the nurse's station."

Bill grabbed the green visitor's pass from her hand and ran through the lobby to the hallway. He stopped at the ICU nurses' station.

"Can I help you?" a pretty woman asked. She wore a white hat perched on her brown hair.

"I'm here to see Tony Damascus. He's in bed 1E."

"Are you family?"

"Yes."

"The doctor is with him now," she said, nodding toward the ICU entrance. "Go on in."

Bill approached the double doors beside the nurses' station and peeked through the window before entering. A sandy-haired man in a long white coat stood writing on a chart beside a bed. Blinking lights, pumping machines, tubes, wires and monitors surrounded that bed. Bill hoped it wouldn't be Tony, but the mass of black curls resting against the white pillow case left little doubt in his mind.

Bill took a deep breath and opened the door, entering the room in silence. If Tony was still alive, he may have arrived in time to watch him die. His halting footsteps echoed across the room, and he paused at the end of the bed.

Tony looked angry, even with his eyes closed. Deep purple marks covered his cheeks and dried blood stained a butterfly bandage above one eye. His neck looked bruised while deep cuts, light scrapes and more bruises coated his forearms. Needles inserted into each hand were taped to his skin and he was hooked to a ventilator. An array of clear and blood-filled tubes connected Tony to various bottles hanging overhead. Bill could only guess what injuries the blankets hid.

"I'm Tony's brother," Bill said in a quiet voice to the preoccupied physician.

"We were wondering when a family member would arrive," the doctor answered. He, like everyone else, never questioned the veracity of the claim. The doctor entered the latest numbers on Tony's chart before stabbing his pen into his coat pocket and putting the chart aside.

"I'm Bill," Bill said, offering his hand but no last name. "I just flew in."

"Dr. Chambers." The quick, small man with tired eyes shook his head. "Bill, I wish I had better news. To be honest, I am stumped that your brother is still breathing. People recover in different manners, but a pattern usually develops. Tony doesn't behave like any patient I've ever had."

"Somehow, that doesn't surprise me," Bill said. He kept his eyes focused on the doctor. It was too frightening and painful to look at Tony. "Tony never does anything the usual way."

"His prognosis is not good," the exhausted doctor said with a serious look. The doctor's tone of voice made Bill wish that his friendship with Tony had gone a different route. "He squeaked through two and a half hours of surgery last night. We restarted his heart four times. His left lung was punctured in the accident as well as one chamber of his heart. We pieced him back together as much as possible, but the odds of him surviving internal bleeding are formidable. His injuries . . . are endless," he said, picking up the chart as if the list were too long to remember. "Severe concussion to the left frontal lobe, fractured mandible— jaw that is— six broken ribs, all on the left side, a sprained right wrist, innumerable bruises and lacerations. The immediate risk is the damage to his heart plus his immobility which could cause fluid to build up in his functioning lung. Also, there's a possibility of a broken right leg, although that could be an old break."

The doctor finished the laundry list of injuries, and Bill looked, really looked, at Tony. There was no reaction to the doctor's grim diagnosis from Tony. Bill remembered then, staring at Tony's battered face, that even during the darkest days of Angela's illness, she could still hear. Her moans indicated that someone was home. Tony gave no such clues.

"Right leg?" Bill asked. The doctor's words had triggered a memory. "He broke it last year."

"Lucky fellow, your brother. Another plane crash?"

"Motorcycle," Bill said, shaking his head and keeping his eyes fixed on Tony.

"If he survives," the doctor said, "and that's a sizeable 'if', he won't have another plane crash unless it's in a commercial liner."

"What do you mean?" Bill asked. He stopped pondering the anger behind Tony's bruises to scrutinize the doctor's face.

"I mean his flying days are over. He might breathe unassisted. His heart might even beat regularly, but he'll never fly again. No doctor would ever sign off on his flight medical."

Tony raised a weak right hand. Bill and Dr. Chambers both turned in surprise. Tony grabbed a tube and pulled it away from the I.V. needle in his left arm.

"What the—" the physician said, rushing to repair the damage on the spot. Machines sounded alarms for a few seconds, which brought a nurse through the double doors. The doctor signaled it was under control, and she retreated. "Strange . . ." the doctor said, when all the gauges and lights returned to normal.

"Say that again," Bill said, sensing something.

"Strange?"

"No, what you said before that."

"He'll never fly again."

Tony's arm went up again, pulling at the wires of the heart monitor pasted to his chest.

"Grab his arm," Dr. Chambers said to Bill and the doctor restrained Tony's other hand. "Nurse!"

It wasn't hard for Bill to hold him down. Tony had no strength left.

"What brought that on?" the doctor asked, and the nurse appeared at his side.

"He's trying to kill himself," Bill answered. A fleeting moment of joy passed through Bill, and his heart jumped, knowing what he hadn't known since he walked in the room. Tony was there and as mean as ever. "You said he'd never fly again—"

Tony's weak arm muscles contracted once more before the heart monitor went flatline. At first, the doctor thought it was a loose wire. His thumb raced to feel Tony's wrist.

"No pulse," he said to the nurse.

"I'll call for the emergency team," she said, starting to hurry away.

"No, don't," the doctor said, and Bill's eyes fixed on him. He wanted to punch him. "It's too much. It'll kill him," the doctor said. "Let him go."

"No," Bill said. He just got there. He hadn't had a chance to even say good-bye. Or more important, I'm sorry. He needed a little time. "No, please, you've got to do something."

LESS THAN A WHISPER passed from Tony's lips.

Go, I'm stuck here. You go on without me.

Tony had become adept at leaving his body. During the previous night, he had watched from every corner of the room while men with high tech jumper cables raced in and jolted him back into his body. They didn't come this time, yet the ceiling seemed to be as far as he could go.

Go where? his spirit asked.

"A place for people who never learned to love in childhood," came Robert's familiar answer.

Tony was watching the terror mount in Bill's face.

"Tony? Tony?" Bill said to the empty shell in the bed. "Do something," Bill screamed at the physician. The passion in Bill's voice touched something inside of Tony. He cared?

"Let him go," the man in the white coat said, holding Bill by one arm and keeping his hand on Tony's wrist as a professional courtesy. "There's too much damage already. Just let him— wait. A pulse. A pulse. Damn, I don't believe it."

"Are you sure?" Bill asked, leaning over the rail and staring.

Tony felt himself being sucked back into the vacuum of his body and let out a moan that sounded more like Angela's voice than his own. With each return, he was more convinced he should leave for good. Now Bill's presence was holding him back, but he couldn't figure out why.

"It's faint but it's there," the quack was saying, watching the body, his body, in the bed. Tony knew he was talking about him. "I can't say how much longer he'll be here, but he's here. I wonder what brought all this on."

"Flying," Bill said, still leaning over the bed rail. It felt like Bill was yelling in his ear. "Tony, I'll take you up. Like Hartley, remember? I'll let you fly. Just don't die, damn it."

It wasn't the chance to fly again that held his spirit back. Tony knew that now. It was the fact that Bill would even care enough to yell at him. He couldn't sort through what was happening. His mind felt foggier than any hangover. For some reason, he needed to stay in his body a little longer, and it had something to do with Bill. He'd figure out the rest later, if there was a later. Now, he just wanted to sleep. Somewhere someone was talking, but he couldn't put the words together.

"I'll be damned," the doctor mumbled. "He died four times last night. Nearly a corpse. Now, the guy wants to live."

The Soul Knows

THREE LONG DAYS PASSED before Tony occupied a room on Level One, just a few yards from the intensive care unit. About noon on the third day, he spoke for the first time. The sound startled Bill, half asleep in the bedside chair.

"Robert," Tony said in a whisper. Bill jumped up and stood next to the bed, wondering if he had been dreaming.

"Tony?" Bill asked in a cautious voice. Tony's battered face turned toward him, and Bill leaned closer to hear his words.

"Get me out of here, Bill," Tony said in a gruff, breathy voice. Tony's eyes opened, looking like two slits in his swollen face. The restraints on his arms ensured he wouldn't pull out any wires or tubes.

"Soon," Bill answered to placate him, feeling his lie wouldn't matter.

"Now," Tony said in a harsh whisper.

"Not yet," Bill said, glancing toward the door. Where was the nurse?

"Where is Robert?"

"Who?" Bill asked, trying to gather some clue from Tony's expression.

"That dago priest."

"Father Roberto?" Bill said, and he felt as if he entered some bizarre episode of the Twilight Zone. Why would Tony ask that of all things? And, even weirder, he knew the answer. "He's in King City."

"Take me there," Tony said with a pleading tone Bill couldn't deny.

"Sure."

272

"Now," Tony said, and surprised Bill by making a fist with his restrained right hand.

"Not now," Bill said, shaking his head.

"I don't know how to die," Tony said in a voice as weak as his breath. Tears slipped from his eyes.

"Have you thought about living?"

"No," Tony whispered. His eyes closed, and, exhausted, he fell back to sleep. Six hours passed. Bill grabbed a bite to eat and returned. There had been no change. Tony hadn't moved. Then, at sunset, Bill was staring out the window and Tony woke again.

"Bill?" Tony whispered.

"Right here," Bill said, turning and walking to his side.

"Robert. Take me."

"Soon," Bill said, thinking Tony's eyes looked more focused.

"Now?"

"Not now."

"Damn," Tony said in a breathy voice. "When?"

"When you can walk," Bill answered, thinking it was a safe bet. If Tony ever walked again, Bill would escort him to King City with pleasure. However, that day, if it ever came, was a long way off.

Tony flexed his arms and legs, as if trying to move. His effort didn't strain the ties affixed to the railings of the bed. His head dropped back to the pillow, and he slept for four more hours.

Nurses came and went. Bill watched them change I.V. bottles and write down Tony's stats. The doctor read them, shook his head and said he wasn't hopeful. Bill tried to tell them that Tony had spoken to him, and they all smiled at him, saying that was good news. However, their expressions said they didn't believe him. Bill's tired body remained planted in the corner chair, half-sleeping through the hubbub of the hospital night shift routines. In the middle of the night, Tony stirred again, and Bill stumbled to his bedside.

"Bill?"

"Yeah?"

"Help me walk," Tony said without opening his eyes.

"It's nighttime," Bill said, too tired to explain more. "Go back to sleep."

"You got a beer?" Tony asked, still whispering.

"What?"

"Put a beer on the window sill," Tony said, now looking at the window. "I'll walk to it."

"In the morning," Bill answered, not sure if he or Tony or both were just dreaming.

The next morning, while Tony was still sleeping, Bill went to the corner store. He bought a beer for Tony and called Roberto from a pay phone. At first, the priest didn't recognize Bill's voice.

"Bill?" Roberto asked in a sleepy voice. Bill must have dragged him out of bed to answer the phone.

"Father Roberto, do you remember Tony?" After a long pause, Bill added, "The pilot?"

"Yes, Tony," Roberto said, sounding awake all of a sudden. "Of course, of course. In fact, I think I had a dream about him a few nights ago. Why?"

"I'm in Washington," Bill said, not sure where to start his explanation.

"Washington?"

"It's a state, Father," Bill said.

"I know that. Why are you there?"

"Tony crashed," Bill said, and the words burned his lips. He composed himself for a second before continuing. "The doctor here isn't sure how long he will live. Father, he wants to see you."

"I can't come to Washington," Roberto answered without hesitation. "Surely, a local priest can—"

"It has to be you," Bill said, switching the receiver to his other ear and focusing on the black pay phone as if some magic might come from it and help him. He could almost hear the words Tony said to him. "He says he needs to know how to die."

"What? I don't understand."

"I don't either, Father," Bill said. "He keeps insisting I bring him to you. What should I say?"

"Bill, the soul knows where it needs to go for healing."

"You think Tony has a soul?" Bill asked, glancing in the direction of the hospital.

"Everyone has a soul."

"I hope you're right," Bill answered, feeling anxious. "I should get back."

Bill said good-bye, hung up, and stepped out of the booth. He used his pocket knife to poke two holes in the bottom of the beer can. The contents of the upended can oozed down the drain near Tony's Cadillac in the parking lot. Bill hurried back to the hospital, carrying the empty beer can. He arrived in Tony's room to find the staff hooking him up to another machine.

"What's going on?" Bill asked the nurse, looking from Tony to her and back.

"He tried to get up," she answered, monitoring the I.V. "His good lung has filled with fluid. He needs the ventilator to keep him breathing."

"Is he dying?" Bill asked, searching her face.

"You'll have to ask the doctor," she answered without answering. "But if there is anything you want him to know, I would say it now." That statement hit Bill like an arrow in the heart. She started to leave and then stopped in the doorway. "Who's Robert?"

"A friend," Bill said, watching Tony motionless in the bed.

She left, and they were alone. Bill placed the beer can on the window sill like he had promised. His hands gripped the bed railings, and he watched Tony struggle to breathe. The extra machine suggested Tony was losing ground. The bruises on his face even seemed pale. Bill felt Tony slipping further and further away. Tears overwhelmed Bill for the first time since he had arrived. They dropped in tiny damp spots on Tony's sheets.

"I never believed you'd go down flying," Bill said, his voice wavering. "Cirrhosis of the liver. Syphilis maybe. Even a knife in the back from a jealous husband, but never flying. Never." He crossed his arms on the railing of Tony's bed and dropped his head on them. "You were so damn good."

Bill stayed in Tony's room, pacing and watching the monitors. He was afraid to step down the hall to call Cindy. She would be wondering what was happening. Their daily phone call had kept Bill sane. Now, he could only pace and hope. Four hours later, Tony's blue eyes opened and focused on the beer can. He couldn't talk because of the ventilator, but he motioned toward the beer with his eyebrows and his hand. Bill shook his head. Tony gave him the finger. It seemed like the first time Bill had smiled since his arrival.

Over the next several days, the ventilator came and went and came back again. Bill grew accustomed to its rhythm and the schedule of the hospital. His own agenda consisted of watching Tony sleep, copious reading, pacing to distraction, and sleeping in the bedside chair of the small hospital room straight across from the nurse's station.

Tony started to stay awake for longer periods of time. Bill booked a room at a cheap motel across the street. It was a relief to spend his first night there a week after the accident. He lay down on the bed and called Cindy, telling her that he felt Tony had turned a corner of sorts.

TONY FIXED HIS BLUE EYES on the container in the window during most of his waking hours. He needed it so bad, he could almost taste it. He dreamed he drank it several times, only to wake up and find it still on the sill. Bill was being a real prick about not handing it to him.

The bandages around his chest were tight and uncomfortable. Everything hurt. Blinking, breathing. Forget moving. Even the sheet against his skin felt like sandpaper. He was supposed to die, but he didn't. He couldn't. And he didn't know why. He sure as hell wanted to.

This made having a broken leg feel like a picnic. If he couldn't die, he wanted to get the fuck out of there. The only thing as constant as the pain was Bill's presence. The first few days, Tony wasn't sure if it was really Bill, or just a mirage. Later, he realized it was Bill, snoring in the chair, reading a book, or staring out the window. Tony didn't feel like playing nice guy. His bum lung made small talk out of the question. As shitty as everything was, it did help to see Bill. Just having him in the room was enough.

Eight days after the accident, the nurses made their first attempt to help him sit up. Tony wanted to stand, but when he tried to slip one leg off the bed, they put the bed rails up. Two days later, when they helped him out of the bed to stand, he tried to walk. He took two steps toward the beer but started to black out. Bill caught him before he fell and placed him in the bedside chair.

Pain and exhaustion helped him stay put. It all reminded him too much of Angela and the months she had been sick. Breathing was a full-time job, but he had no intention of staying put. He would find a way out, he would find Robert, and he would find out how to die. Thoughts of never seeing Angela again and never flying made him more determined. He began to formulate a plan, which he revealed to the doctor on his next visit.

"You can't keep me here," Tony said, in a gruff whisper to Dr. Chambers while he was taking his pulse. It was a good day. The ventilator was unhooked, but still parked in the corner of the room just in case.

"You'll be with us for a while, Mr. Damascus," Dr. Chambers said.

It only got worse once he knew what he looked like. Bill held up a mirror for him when the doctor left, and what Tony saw made him turn away. It wasn't encouraging to learn he looked better than he had. Bill informed him that his facial swelling had subsided somewhat, and his bruises had changed from deep purple to greenish-yellow.

Tony wanted to rip off the tight bandages that held his broken ribs in place. However, the splint that immobilized his wrist made that difficult. The following day, a nurse took out the stitches on the larger cuts on his arms, but the ones from surgery remained. Inverted bottles overhead still supplied him with medication and supplemented his hearty diet of applesauce, broth, and Jell-O. Even rice was too painful to chew with a cracked jaw.

He was still determined to leave and informed the doctor of that on his next visit.

"Tomorrow," Tony said in a weak voice.

"Leave here tomorrow and you'll die," Dr. Chambers said to him point blank. He stopped writing on the clipboard and looked from Tony to Bill and back again.

"Bullshit," Tony said, then paused to get more air. He continued in a halting voice. "I've been trying to die."

"Be reasonable—"

"Tomorrow," Tony said in a stubborn whisper.

"What happens next time you need a ventilator?" Dr. Chambers said, folding his arms. "Do you know what it's like not to be able to breathe?"

"I don't care," Tony said. Gasp. Gasp. "Sign me out tomorrow." Pause. "Do it or I'll rip every machine off me right now."

"Talk to your brother," the doctor said to Bill and walked out in frustration.

"Look, Tony—" Bill started.

"You just get me Robert . . . *brother*," Tony said.

"I called him," Bill said. "He can't come. Don't be a damn fool."

Tony stopped talking. It took him a minute to catch his breath. Had Bill explained to Robert that he wanted to die and just didn't know how? Maybe Bill hadn't really called him at all.

"What did he say?" Tony asked. He wanted to say more, but he didn't have the energy.

"He said, 'The soul knows where it needs to go to be healed.'"

What the hell did that mean? Tony didn't have the strength to argue with Bill or he would have. Maybe that was why they had been friends at one time. Neither of them was afraid of confrontation. Of course, for Tony, it was just a habit. Rebelling was a way of life, a way of surviving. For the first time in his life, he wasn't in survival mode. But what made Bill so confrontational? Tony figured Bill was just the kind of guy who would stand up for what he believed.

Two days later, Tony forced the doctor's hand by refusing treatment. Tony had signed enough papers for Angela to know someone had to authorize treatment. Without it, Tony's health insurance wouldn't release payment. Bill tried to intervene, but he didn't have power of attorney. Tony was just lucid enough to make his own decisions. Dr. Chambers signed Tony's release papers against his better judgment.

Bill found a clean shirt and some jeans in the trunk of Tony's Cadillac. The nurses helped Tony shower. Bill got a quick course in bandage changing and six different medications, each with a different timetable. Tony overheard the staff say that they hoped the antibiotics would prevent infections and the anti-coagulants would keep blood clots from forming in his lungs. Bill carried Tony's few belongings— some shredded clothing, Tony's wallet, and the beer can— down the corridor toward the exit. Dr. Chambers cornered Bill by the door and blocked Tony's wheelchair pushed by a nurse.

"You'll need a portable ventilator," the doctor said, shooting a last look at his former patient. Tony turned away. "You can rent one at a medical supply outlet for just a few hundred dollars."

"I don't have a few hundred dollars," Bill said, and the frustration in his voice was apparent to Tony. "I came here two weeks ago, expecting to go to a funeral."

"He won't last 24 hours outside the hospital environment," the doctor said, sounding cocksure to Tony that he could rattle Bill's cage. "Thirty-six hours tops. Get a portable ventilator or your brother is a dead man. He might be anyway."

Tony would have laughed at the doctor's attempt to intimidate Bill, but it would have been too damn painful. He'd seen Bill crawl out of a burning plane. A few words wouldn't scare him. They were cropdusters for Christ's sake. Their strange profession required an odd mixture of psychosis and ice in the veins. What the doctor would never understand, even if he had known them 100 years, was that you can't intimidate someone who enjoys squeezing planes under wires. No bully can faze someone who flies 100 mph, a foot off the ground, just for fun.

"He isn't my brother," Bill said and walked away.

A SLAM DUNK BY BILL sent the torn clothes from Tony's accident into the trash by the exit. The Caddy stood parked at the curb. Bill opened the wide passenger door, putting Tony's wallet in the glove box and setting the beer can on the ample dashboard. He turned around and looked at Tony.

The trip down the elevator had been the most exhausting thing Tony had done in two weeks. Now, stuck and helpless in a wheelchair, he watched Bill walking back toward him. He really wasn't sure where Bill was coming from and how far he would go. He might just drive him around the block and bring him back. He wouldn't put it past him. Tony knew Bill was the one person who could get him to Robert, but he doubted Bill's willingness. Without a word, Bill stepped behind him and pushed him out the front door of the hospital to the waiting car.

The sun stung Tony's eyes, and it hurt to squint, but the warm, fresh air felt good. He tried to help Bill maneuver him into the car, but he didn't have much to offer. His weak legs got him to a standing position beside the open door. Bill put him in the passenger seat with all the grace of an arresting officer, complete with the customary head duck. It was embarrassing to feel Bill lift his legs into the car and place his feet on the floorboard.

"I must be out of my mind," Bill said, standing by the open passenger door, staring down at Tony with a disgusted look.

Tony's wary eyes remained fixed on Bill, but, huffing and puffing from the exertion, he couldn't comment. Bill's right hand reached for the lever that reclined the seat. His left hand moved behind the headrest to control how far and fast the seat lowered. Tony knew Bill was going to make a good father. Helluva lot better than any Tony'd ever had. Helluva lot better than he'd live to be. Bill slammed the door and slipped into the driver's seat, shaking his head. Last thing Tony remembered, the Cadillac was cruising south on the highway.

BILL HADN'T DRIVEN five minutes before Tony fell asleep in the reclined passenger seat to his right. His ragged breathing was worrisome. It prompted Bill to exit at the first town they came to on the highway. The Cadillac was idling at a red light, and Bill noticed a gunsmith shop next to a medical supply center. He took it as a sign. He pulled over and parked without waking Tony. Bill got out and opened the back door, sliding the ugly rifle from under the driver's seat and carrying it into the gun shop. From inside, Bill stood by the window of the rustic store, keeping an eye on Tony.

"Ugly gun," the old gunsmith said, lowering his glasses to examine the weapon.

"Collector's item," Bill said, countering his skepticism. "How much you gimme for it?"

"Maybe $2oo," the gunsmith said, his heavy eyebrows resting on his nose.

"At least 400," Bill said, laying the gun on the counter and glancing over his shoulder at the car. "I wouldn't part with it if I didn't have to."

"Two-fifty," the old boy said, opening the chamber and checking the rifling in the barrel.

"Three hundred," Bill insisted. "It's worth a lot more."

"Two seventy-five," the owner said again.

"Three hundred," Bill said, holding firm. The man shook his head. Bill picked up the gun and started to walk away.

"All right, $300."

Bill didn't bother putting the money in his wallet. He just folded it in half, left the gun shop, and walked over to the medical supply store. The door closed behind him, and he grabbed the first clerk he saw.

"I need a portable ventilator," he said, flashing the wad of bills near the pimply-faced clerk's nose. "Now." The clerk ran back to the storeroom, and Bill stayed by the glass front door, watching Tony. The kid seemed to take forever.

"The operating instructions are a little complicated," the clerk said, carrying the device up the aisle and setting it on the counter. "They're right here on the side. Step one, make sure the machine—"

"Thanks," Bill said, dropping the money on the counter, grabbing the red metal box, and hurrying out the door. He was putting it in the back seat when the clerk came rushing after him. Maybe $300 didn't cover it.

"How much?" Bill said, reaching for his wallet and hoping he had enough.

"No, you forgot the face mask," the clerk said, glancing at Tony, still asleep. "She's all charged and ready to go, but you'll need to plug it in every couple of hours." The sight of his bruised face was enough to make him take a step back. "I can call an ambulance for you."

"Good thought," Bill said. "But no thanks."

Bill took the extra part from him and put it on top of the contraption in the back seat. The Caddy pulled away with the clerk walking back to the store and shaking his head. Bill took the next on-ramp to the highway and headed south again. They would probably cross a state line or two before Tony knew the rifle was missing.

They traveled in silence through light rain with the wipers making a mess of the windshield. Tony slept for several hours, never moving. Bill guessed that the exertion of getting dressed and into the car must have worn him out. The Caddy cruised along in light traffic, giving Bill too much time to think. Was he out of his mind? Would they make it? A sane man would turn back. Hell, a sane man would never have left.

The soul knows, the soul knows. Father Roberto's words haunted him. Tony's soul probably didn't know shit. At that moment, Tony woke up gasping for air. Bill pulled over, and the car slid on the muddy shoulder of the highway.

When they stopped, Bill got on his knees in the driver's seat, facing backward and hooking up the face mask. He flicked the on/off switch of the ventilator four times. Nothing. He banged on the side of the contraption. Still nothing.

"Damn it," Bill said, twisting to look at Tony, who was now turning blue. "Damn, don't do this." He tilted Tony's head back and reached into his mouth to clear his airway, like Cindy had always done when preparing to practice resuscitation on him. It didn't help, and Bill knew what he had to do. "Shit."

The fingers of his right hand pinched Tony's nose closed, and he tried to ignore the bruises he was squeezing. He took a deep breath, pulled down on Tony's broken jaw, and sealed his lips over his former friend's open mouth. Fucking moustache. Tony's hair smelled like hospital soap. Bill pushed air into his lungs and rested one hand on his chest to feel it rise, wary of the bandages beneath the buttons of Tony's shirt. Three forced breaths went in and came out. There would be no point in chest compressions. It would kill him. Maybe he didn't need them. Bill moved away from Tony and tried again to get the ventilator working.

The list of instructions for the device was a mile-long. Bill was only halfway through them when Tony started gasping for air again.

Bill turned back to the front seat, lost his balance, and knocked the beer can into Tony's lap. Bill flung the empty container into the backseat and clamped Tony's nose shut. The heel of his hand brushed against the bandage over Tony's eye. Bill couldn't think about it, or he wouldn't do it. Blow, pause, two, three. Blow, pause, two, three. Blow, pause, two, three.

Bill let go, twisted in the seat, and made a third attempt at starting the ventilator. The switch clicked up and down six times before he banged the side of the machine. It started. Bill pulled the elastic strap behind Tony's head and secured the face mask over his nose and mouth. He waited on his knees in the driver's seat, hoping that would be enough. Two long minutes passed before Tony began to breathe with some regularity.

"Don't ever do that again," Bill said, collapsing in the driver's seat, drenched in sweat. Tony watched him with wide blue eyes, unable to answer. Soon they closed, and Tony fell asleep. Another five minutes passed before Bill could convince himself to get back on the road.

The Long Road Home

"Bill?" Roberto's voice asked on the other end of the line. "Where are you?"

"In Oregon," Bill said, closing the door of the mini-mart's phone booth. He had to stop to charge the ventilator. Rain spotted the glass, dampening the bitter afternoon breeze that came straight off the ocean. Tony waited in the car, raising the seat to help himself sit up.

"Where?"

"Oregon," Bill answered, watching Tony. He shouldn't be sitting up. He'd only been off the ventilator for an hour. "It's a state."

"I know that," Roberto said, sounding offended.

"Tony's with me," Bill continued, squeezing his words in as fast as he could.

"He's better?" Roberto asked, sounding surprised at first, then relieved. "You see? The power of prayer—"

"No. He just wouldn't stay in the hospital. He insists he wants to see you, if he doesn't die first. We should arrive by tomorrow. Will you be there?"

"I have to be," Roberto answered, and his voice grew distant. "They executed Mendoza."

"What?" Bill asked. The passenger window was opening. This wasn't good.

"Nothing, nothing," Roberto answered in his quick style. "There's a funeral in the morning, and the new bishop is coming in the afternoon. I'll be here. Has Tony told you why he needs to see me?"

"He can't say a lot," Bill said. Tony had his braced right wrist out the window with the rain falling on his open hand. Idiot. "Sometimes he can't even breathe."

"Shouldn't he be in a hospital?"

"Yeah, but try telling him that," Bill said, unable to hold back his frustration. And another concern. "Father, what if he dies?"

"Let us hope he doesn't."

"But what if he does?"

"We can always give him a good funeral," Roberto said. His answer sounded too matter-of-fact for Bill. "Let's hope we can make him a happier man before then. Just bring him home."

"I'm trying," Bill said, hung up, and returned to the driver's seat.

Tony stared out the passenger window at the mini-mart. He felt raindrops tickle his fingertips. Bill entered the car after making his phone call, but Tony didn't take his eyes off the liquor bottles glittering on the top shelf in the store window.

"That was Roberto," Bill said, leaning forward to look at Tony.

"Will he be there?" Tony asked in a husky whisper, settling back into the seat and checking Bill from the corner of his eye.

"He has to be," Bill said, putting the key in the ignition. "He has a funeral."

"Could be handy," Tony said, turning to look at Bill. His sly grin seemed to annoy his driver. Tony looked at the dashboard and noticed something missing. "Where's the beer?" Bill just glared at him.

"If I drive you all the way there and you die, I'm going to be pissed at you."

"You're already pissed at me," Tony whispered, staring straight at him. It didn't seem necessary to avoid the topic any longer. Maybe this was something they should straighten out while Tony was still around.

"We need gas," Bill said, cutting him off and starting the car. He pulled forward to the pump.

Bill got out and stood next to the car, holding the pump handle. Tony stared at the bottles in the cluttered window of the gas station store. His head turned and his eyes focused on the glove box. It took an effort to lean forward and remove his wallet. He stuck his bandaged hand out the window and motioned for Bill to come toward him.

"Buy me some vodka, will you?" Tony asked, holding his wallet toward Bill.

"Not a chance," Bill said, turning his back. He leaned against the car and stared at the changing numbers on the gas pump.

"Afraid I'll wreck my health?" Tony said and laughed, breaking into a cough.

Bill didn't answer. So the hell with him. He could get it himself—or die trying, which would be even better. He reached across his lap with his good left, yanked on the door lever, and pushed it open with one foot. Bill stepped back and watched Tony struggle to stand up. He was staring at the vodka bottle.

"What the hell—" Bill started. "You'll never make it."

"Get it for me," Tony whispered through his pain, resting one hand on the roof of the car for support.

"No."

Tony eyed the gas pump in front of him. Why'd it have to be so far away? He reached for it with his left arm and took a step. The intense pain only made him more determined to reach the bottle. A Coke machine stood beside the store entrance. Four steps, Tony judged. Maybe five. Shit. After a rest, Tony pushed off the pump and headed for it. Bill kept both hands in his pockets, as if restraining himself.

"Don't be such a damn fool," Bill said, taking a step in Tony's direction.

Tony inched forward, then braced himself against the vending machine, struggling to breathe. The long pause didn't change much. The hell with it. He staggered through the doorway and leaned on the counter.

"Vodka," he choked, glancing at the row of bottles behind the clerk's head.

"Which one?" the clerk said, looking away from Tony's battered face.

Tony waved his hand, indicating any would do. The clerk grabbed the closest one, as if it would help him get the nut out of his store before he dropped dead on the floor.

"Four-fifty," the clerk said, and Tony opened his wallet. Four ones. Damn.

"Loan me. . ." was all Tony could manage. He didn't have the breath. The cigarette display case between them held him up.

"Maybe you should go," the clerk said, returning the bottle to the shelf.

Tony wanted to argue but couldn't. Sitting down—no lying down—would be better. He left without the bottle, moving back toward the car with a long pause at the Coke machine. He wasn't going to make it. Four more steps. He started for the passenger seat, collapsing just before he reached it and falling against the car. Bill jumped over the gas hose and grabbed him before he hit the ground.

"Lend me a dollar," Tony said between gasps for air.

"A dollar?" Bill said through clenched teeth, straining to lift Tony into the passenger seat. Tony was seated and Bill blew it. "Lend you a dollar? I'll tell you what. I'll lend you twenty," Bill said. He pulled his wallet from his pocket and threw two fives and a ten at Tony. "Get as many bottles as you can. Hit me up again when you run out, but don't give me any more crap about wanting to see Roberto."

Bill walked away to pay for the gas. Tony tried to get out of the passenger seat but fell back into the car. Bill was inside the store, waiting for his change. A sharp, stabbing pain, like a gunshot through his chest, seized Tony. Bill's money slipped from Tony's hand and fluttered to the floor of the car. His face in the rear view mirror twisted in pain. The agony of not being able to breathe gripped him. Bill's face appeared from nowhere, moving between the mirror and Tony. The seat started reclining or it felt like it was. Tony couldn't be sure. Bill was reaching past him into the back seat to turn on the ventilator.

"Come on, come on," Bill said, talking to either Tony or the machine. Tony heard a bang, and a rhythmic whooshing noise started behind him.

"You stupid son of a bitch," Bill said, fumbling to put the mask on Tony's face. He secured it and gathered Tony's long legs into the car. Blackness flashed across Tony's eyes, and then they refocused, staring at the roof of the car. The passenger door closed with a definite thud, and Bill raced to the driver's side.

"What's your trip anyway?" Bill asked, once again in the driver's seat and starting the car. "We're going to the nearest hospital." They bounded out of the gas station and into the street. "I'm dumping you there, and I'm going home. I've had it."

Tony shook his head 'no', unable to speak. The air oozed down inside his chest and into his lungs.

"Damn straight," Bill said, shooting a nasty glance at his passenger. "I'm not taking this anymore."

Bill would follow through on the threat. Tony knew that. There would be no answers from Robert. No instructions on how to die. He would never get to ask the priest about purgatory, or how to get there, or if love existed. He would never know why he lost Angela. Again Tony shook his head.

"Why shouldn't I?" Bill asked. Tony sat mute and wide-eyed, unable to explain and listening to the engine pick up speed. "You'd be there now if I knew where the next hospital was."

"Robert," Tony said, with a gasp after lifting the mask.

"Leave that on your face," Bill said, racing down the main street, looking around like his head was on a swivel.

"Robert," Tony said again.

"In a pig's eye."

The city limits led to a long stretch of coastal highway without towns or even villages, let alone a hospital. Rugged rocks lined the unforgiving coastline. Frothy white waves from a storm at sea pounded the shore. The sun set in the late afternoon darkness and gray clouds, tinged with orange, coated the sky. Tony watched the wipers sweep rain from the wide windshield with the easy rhythm of two metronomes. His breathing began to match the wiper's pace, and he pulled the mask from his face. He was willing to do whatever it took to die.

"No booze," Tony said, five miles up the road.

"Shut up and leave the mask on," Bill answered without looking at him.

"I promise."

"Sure . . ."

"Really," Tony said in a whisper. "I have to see Robert."

"Why, damn it?" Bill asked, now giving Tony a look that could kill.

"I'm not sure," Tony said, gasping between words. "He said there were angels." Air. More air. "Breaking ground felt like a miracle."

One breath. Another breath. "That sex was like praying." Inhale. Exhale. Inhale. "That there is a place . . ." Tony paused again, but not just to catch his breath. His faint voice continued, and he felt overwhelmed by embarrassment. "A place for people. Like me. When they die. A place where people learn . . ." Tony stopped. He didn't want to say it. He had to or Bill wouldn't keep driving. Big breath. ". . . learn how to love."

Bill slowed the car, looking at the side of the road. A big H on a blue sign marked a hospital exit one mile ahead.

"How does that happen?" Bill asked, looking back and forth between Tony and the exit.

Tony shrugged. "I'm flying blind here," he whispered.

"Why are you so bent on dying?" Bill asked, and his hand reached for the turn signal lever. "You could still live. Check into a hospital. Let yourself heal."

"I'll never fly again," Tony said from under the mask.

"So what?" Bill asked, slowing for the exit. "You'd be alive."

"No," Tony said, staring at the roof of the car. "I'd just be breathing, Billy boy."

Bill passed the turnoff and stayed on the highway, heading south. Tony woke up about midnight and opened his eyes. The ventilator was off, and Bill must have removed the face mask. Probably had to charge the battery for the next time, if there was one. Bill was staring straight ahead with the unwavering focus of a pilot in command. He didn't notice that Tony was awake and looking at him. They crossed over the California border under a full moon. Towering redwoods crowded both edges of the winding two-lane highway. Sagging branches, heavy with moisture, hung high above the road, filtering the stars. A fat drop smacked the windshield. Tony closed his eyes and listened to the rhythm of the engine.

"Why didn't you just pay me back?" Bill said under his breath in the darkness. Tony didn't let on that he was awake. "Why didn't you stay with Angela? Why did everything have to change?" Those were questions Tony wished he could answer. Questions he wished Bill didn't need to ask. Tony let them hang in the air between them and fell back to sleep.

BILL, DOG-TIRED, hit the wipers when the rain fell, but he never stopped driving. Tony continued to sleep, moaning now and then, or whispering things Bill couldn't quite hear. At dawn, he guided the Cadillac into a supermarket parking lot on the north side of the San Francisco Bay. It was a relief to set the parking brake. Bill stepped out of the car, stretched, and found a power outlet for charging the ventilator. Then, he walked over to a phone booth. His finger dialed his home number. The sun rose behind him and just the tops of the Golden Gate Bridge towers pierced the fog. He apologized to Cindy for waking her and asked her to have the spare bedroom ready.

"Tony's with me," Bill said with a glance toward the car. "He's pretty bad off."

"If the doctor's released him, he can't be—"

"Yeah, well, he sort of released himself," Bill said. His bent arm pressed against the glass of the phone booth, and he rested his forehead there. "He wants to see Father Roberto."

"Tony wants to see a priest?" Cindy asked. Bill hadn't thought of the irony in that request for days. "I don't believe it."

"Me neither," Bill said, glancing behind him to check on Tony through the windshield.

"Does he look bad, honey?" Cindy asked in a tentative voice.

"He looks bad for someone who's alive," Bill said, looking away from the car. "But not too bad for someone who should be dead."

"You sound tired," she said. "Just come home. I'll have the room ready. Drive careful."

"I will," Bill answered, ready to hang up.

"I love you," she added. Her words felt so good to Bill, he wanted to crumble on the spot and tell her everything. That there was a reason he was driving a crazy, dying man to see a priest. That Tony believed in purgatory, or at least some place he could go and learn to love. That Bill knew now why he wasn't mad at Tony any more. There just wasn't time to explain it all.

"I love you too, babe."

Bill hung up, picked up the recharged ventilator, and wandered back to the car. Tony was still out cold. Bill returned the machine to the backseat. Though unused for several hours, it loomed like an unwelcome premonition. He repositioned the face mask an arm's length from the driver's seat. His tired body ached for a cup of coffee, but the stores and restaurants were all closed. The town was still sleeping. To be safe, Bill practiced turning the ventilator on and off. It was tricky, but he had the hang of it now. His eye caught the empty beer can on the back seat, where he had flung it the first time Tony tried to die on him. He picked it up, got in the car, put it back on the dashboard, and headed south again. Next time Tony asked for a drink, Bill would get him one. What difference would it make now?

Two hours further south, the coastal road snaked into the past, winding through Moss Landing and passing Tony's old street. Bill looked down the empty, familiar road, but there was no point in stopping. The dark Caddy cruised on a little further, like a hearse moving down Castroville's deserted main drag. Bill shot a glance at Clancy's bar. They'd had some high times there. Damn, this was fucked. They reached the outskirts of Salinas next, and Bill headed to the airport restaurant. He knew he could get a quick cup of coffee to go. He parked, exhaled, and sat back to stare at the familiar runway. His eyes started to close. He gathered the money from the floorboard that he had thrown at Tony hours before and opened the car door

TONY WOKE UP when Bill shut the car door behind him. One look and Tony knew in an instant where he was, although he wondered if he was dreaming. He reached over and honked the horn to get Bill's attention before he walked away. Tony knew it was real life. The sound made Bill stop and walk back to Tony's open window.

"Sneaking a beer?" Tony asked in his whispery voice.

"Just getting some coffee," Bill said, looking from Tony to the terminal building and back. Bill's green eyes looked dead tired. "And charging the ventilator."

"OK, I'll have this one," Tony said, reaching for the beer can on the dashboard. It lifted too easily. He upended it, exposing the two holes in the bottom. "Oh, far out."

"Look, if you want a beer that bad, I'll get you—"

"Get me coffee," Tony said, opening the glove box and reaching for his wallet with effort.

"I'll buy," Bill said.

"Naaa, come on," Tony said, handing him his last four bucks. "Here. It's on me. Keep the change. I owe you more than that."

"Forget about the $300, Tony."

"I don't mean that," Tony whispered. "Hell, I offered you a great rifle. You won't take it." Bill looked away, as if he were hiding something. Tony wasn't sure what. "I'm talking about everything you've done since my wreck. I'll never live long enough to pay you back."

"Don't say that, damn it," Bill said, stepping back from the car and away from Tony's bandaged, outstretched hand. Tony opened his car door, as if he would get out and would force Bill to take the money, but the effort proved too much.

"Wake up, Billy boy," Tony said, sitting back in his seat. Bill could be so clueless sometimes. "I'm a walking dead man . . . who can't walk."

"I need coffee," Bill said, starting to close Tony's door.

Tony put his foot out and prevented Bill from closing it. Tony looked around the 'port. This was where it all started. In Salinas. It seemed like 100 years ago, but it had only been a few. There was no reason why Bill should bring him all the way back, but he had.

"Hey, Bill, why?" Tony asked.

"Because if I don't get coffee," Bill started, giving Tony a curious look, "I'm going to fall asleep at the wheel."

"I mean, why are you doing this?" Tony asked, waving his arm in a circle. "Coming up to the hospital. Driving me to Robert." There was more, but Tony was running out of breath. "You know what a prick I am."

Bill stared through the passenger window at Tony, then looked over the car toward the terminal. "You were my friend," he said, still not looking at Tony.

"Water under the bridge," Tony said in a whisper.

"OK, you're an asshole," Bill said, banging his fist on the roof of the car. "But you're the asshole who gave me every good thing in my life. You introduced me to my wife. You got me cropdusting. Hell, you're the reason I quit drinking and started going to church. So, what do you want in your coffee, asshole?"

"Gin."

"Serious?"

"No, just black."

"OK," Bill said, looking at Tony with distrust. "Don't move. Just keep breathing, and I'll be right back."

"No hurry," Tony said, reclining his seat halfway. It was obvious Bill didn't believe him because he started the ventilator and put the mask on Tony's face before leaving. Bill walked away, and Tony's eyes started to follow him but switched to look toward a growl in the distance. A Stearman rolled down the runway and broke ground. Ah, baby. . .

FOR BILL, the coffee made the last hour of the drive bearable. They sailed along, passing the last miles in silence on the straight highway that split the flat valley floor. Telephone poles flicked past between the road and crops at the highway's edge. Rows of lettuce and broccoli pin-striped the brown squares of earth. The long straight lines of plants joined at the foothills in the distance. Farm crews labored in the fields, bent in huddles of ten and twenty, their backs to the morning sun.

Near the outskirts of King City, a cropduster worked near the road. Bill could see Tony's eyes following the ag plane's dive into the field. The aircraft raced toward them and pulled up, turning just above the car. They both listened to the waxing and waning of the radial engine. Bill looked over at his passenger and thought he detected just the trace of a smile buried beneath Tony's black moustache. He had seen that sly look before, whenever Tony had spotted a woman he wanted in a bar, or had heard a good song, or had found a new gun. Tony's eyes were closed. A fist formed at the end of his bandaged wrist and wavered between his legs. His heels were anchored on the floor and his feet pivoted at the ankles, moving imaginary rudder pedals. He was flying.

Bill took the cloverleaf off ramp into King City, ignoring the fast food places begging at the roadside. Ancient sycamores and tidy homes built in the '50s lined both sides of Bill's street. One look at Tony made Bill drive past his own driveway and head straight for the church six blocks away. If he hurried, Bill thought, if he went straight there, right now, then they were going to make it. Tony was going to see Roberto. That's all Bill had promised. After that, well, he felt safe in thinking the rest was up to God.

That Dark Battle

A HEARSE WAITED at the steps of St. Peter's Catholic Church of King City. Tony leaned on Bill, who carried the ventilator under one arm. Bill said they should have walked over to the rectory, whatever that was. It was hard enough for Tony to make it to the church steps. He gasped for air, and Bill guided him through the big double doors.

Tony's tired eyes adjusted to the light. He saw Robert in flowing green robes step up to the pulpit at the far end of the long center aisle. There was the soft, magnified sound of the priest's fingertips touching the wafer-thin pages of a book of holy readings below the microphone. Behind the priest, a simple casket, lid closed, rested in front of the dark altar. Two small white flower arrangements graced the top of it. Tony scanned the sparse crowd attending the funeral mass. The sorry look of the gathering made Tony doubt Robert could say anything of comfort.

"Raoul Mendoza wasn't a regular member of our parish," Roberto started. Bill and the ventilator entered the back row first, followed with difficulty by Tony. He collapsed, as much as sat, in the seat closest to the center aisle.

The priest stopped, cleared his throat, and watched them settle into the last pew. Bill motioned for Tony to wear the ventilator. Tony shook his head. Bill slapped the face mask over his mouth anyway and turned on the machine, but it didn't seem to help. The battery light flashed, and the machine switched off. Bill pushed the power cord under the pew and searched for an outlet. Tony's eyes turned to focus on Robert. The priest fumbled with his notes for a moment before folding them and pushing them under the book.

"But being a regular member wouldn't have prevented Raoul's death," Roberto continued in a hesitant tone. He looked odd in his priest's garb. Tony had only seen him in street clothes and never in a church. It was the same guy, only smaller. "I would like to think it might have postponed his death, but it wouldn't have prevented it. So it is written in the Book of Ecclesiastes. 'No one can hold back his spirit from departing; no one has the power to prevent his day of death, for there is no discharge from that obligation and dark battle.'"

Tony knew that dark battle. He tried to listen, fighting for each breath and feeling somewhat shielded by the darkly clad mourners dotting the honey-colored pews. Quiet sobs escaped now and then, revealing a hushed pain. Bill returned and moved Tony and the ventilator to the far end of the pew, closer to the wall. After plugging in the device, he flicked the power switch several times. A few seconds later, the machine started its rhythmic pulse. The device allowed each breath to come with less effort. That made it easier to listen, but it didn't make Robert's words any easier to understand.

"In the New Testament, Peter writes that 'the gospel was brought to the dead as well, so that, though in their bodies they had undergone the judgment that faces all humanity, in their spirit they might enjoy the life of God.'"

Huh? Tony wondered if he was supposed to understand that.

"We all know certain people who serve as the salt of the earth," Robert said, his eyes now fixed on Tony. "The flavoring that enhances our lives. Their whole perspective on life is different. If God looked at us through Raoul's eyes, I wonder what he would have seen. One thing is certain. God didn't look at Raoul through our eyes. God saw far more than we did."

Tony didn't like Robert addressing him, which is what it felt like, not that anyone else seemed to notice. That, and exhaustion, led him to lie down in the pew and close his eyes. His ears however, remained trained on Robert's voice, and he tried to follow what was happening. After all, the service would have been for him, if it hadn't been for Bill and that damn breathing machine. Robert seemed to be talking like it was for Tony anyway.

"St. Eraneus said, 'The glory of God is man and woman, fully human and fully alive.' Think of it. The Glory of God. Man and

Woman. Fully human. Fully alive. Few people experience that full glory."

Glory? Tony's eyes popped open. So that's what religious people call it. He's talking about sex. In a church. At least he seemed to be. Tony wished he was looking at Robert's eyes right now, instead of staring at the wooden beams of the high ceiling. Sitting up would be too fuckin' difficult. Still, that twinkle Robert used to get when he talked about sex would give him away. H-m-m-m. Tony had never heard it described as glory before.

"We don't live in a risk-free society. The risks we take are what we remember the most. For a young man, Raoul's memory was full. Many of us live long, safe lives without much to remember."

Robert's words made Tony smile. He did remember the risks the most. Flying. Living on the edge. Falling for Angela. Maybe Robert remembered flying fast and low.

"My last talk with Raoul made me realize that he knew something most men never know. He knew he was dying. Most of us never understand the final mystery of death."

What if you are trying to die but can't, Tony wanted to ask. What then?

"If a man lives doing what he loves, he is happy. If he understands why he dies, he dies well."

Robert stopped talking, and Tony could hear him shuffling around in the front of the church. A long silence followed, interrupted only by an occasional sniffle from one section of the church and then another. Tony continued to lie in the last pew, breathing easier. Raoul, whoever he was, understood why he had died. Tony tried to guess what his own reason was for still living until he drifted into an exhausted sleep.

MASS ENDED twenty minutes after Bill and Tony arrived. Bill watched the mourners file out behind Father Roberto and the casket. It was hard to look casual, seated beside his bruised and sleeping companion, the ventilator's tubes coiling around the pew. Bill could feel his own lack of sleep catching up to him. Roberto popped back in after the church emptied.

"I must accompany the family to the cemetery," he said to Bill. His eyes followed the air tube from the ventilator to Tony's tortured face. "I'll be back as soon as I can." He hurried back out the door, robes flapping behind him.

Bill sat back and sighed. Tony's questions for Father Roberto would have to wait a little longer. The peacefulness of the empty church had a calming effect. He checked Tony's breathing again, then shut down the machine and removed the face mask, allowing Tony to stretch out and relax. The long drive made Bill ache to close his eyes for just a minute. He signed himself, said a short prayer, and felt himself sink lower in the pew. An hour later, Father Roberto woke him with a hand to his shoulder.

"You're back," Bill said in a soft voice, blinking and trying to sound like he wasn't half dead. He removed his glasses and cleaned them with his shirttail. The afternoon light set the stained glass windows aglow. Roberto stood in the center aisle, his ceremonial robes gone. The priest looked comfortable in slacks, a sport shirt, and sandals.

"You shouldn't have come during the funeral," Father Roberto said in a soft, quick voice.

"How could I wait?" Bill asked with a nod to Tony. Roberto's reaction seemed wrong. There had been rumors around the parish—rumors Bill had ignored—insinuating Roberto avoided ministering to the sick. The 24-hour window that Tony's doctor had mentioned was slipping away. Bill's whole plan was to get Tony the answers he needed, and then dump him at the nearest hospital, which was eight blocks away. The whispers that Bill and Father Roberto exchanged woke Tony.

"Robert?" Tony asked in a hoarse whisper. Was it really Bill talking to Robert, or was he dreaming? He tried to sit up on his own, but Bill had to help. "I made it?"

"You made it, Tony," Robert answered, moving into the pew in front of him. The priest sat sideways near the center aisle and leaned over the backrest close to Tony. "Tell me why you are here."

"I had to know some things," Tony answered with an awkward glance at Bill. "Things you would know."

"Bill, would you excuse us?" Roberto said.

"Sure," Bill said, looking stiff as he stood up, shaking his pants legs down, and adjusting his glasses. "I'll wait outside."

Bill's footsteps tapered off, and the front door closed behind him with only a soft click. Tony watched him leave, feeling uncomfortable in the foreign surroundings. Rows of small candles flickered through red glass containers behind the pews across the aisle. Statues of strangers with plastic flowers at their feet watched from different corners of the room. Robert's eyes remained fixed on Tony's, but the priest's hand, resting on the top of the pew, was trembling. He looked uncomfortable to Tony, which seemed odd. If only they could just be in a cockpit instead. . . Like before. But nothing now was like it had been before.

"I need to know about that place," Tony said, avoiding Robert's eyes and looking across the empty rows of pews to the front of the church. The guy on the cross up front didn't make him feel any better. Now that he had arrived, he felt a strange urge to leave.

"What place?" Robert asked.

"Where people learn to love," Tony said, frustrated with having to explain. "Purgatory. How do you get there?"

"You have to die first," Roberto answered, looking perplexed.

"I tried," Tony said in an exasperated whisper. "Five or six times. It didn't work. I kept coming back here." He lifted his hands to indicate here on Earth, but he didn't think Robert got it.

"Maybe you made it anyway," the priest told him.

"Made it where?" Tony asked. Now he was the one who didn't get it.

"To purgatory."

"Are you saying I died," Tony asked, pausing to breathe, "and went to *Earth*?"

"In a way."

"Oh, that's just great," Tony said, rolling his eyes toward the ceiling. "I didn't get it the first time I was here. What makes Him think that I'll get it now?"

Robert closed his eyes and folded his hands. Tony could see his lips moving, but he wasn't talking to Tony. The priest sighed and opened his eyes again. There was a long pause, and Robert seemed to stare right through him. Tony remembered that he used to do that during their flying lessons. He didn't like it any better now than he had then.

"Tell me, Tony, did you ever love anyone?" Roberto asked, shifting in his seat and looking away as if he was trying to remember something. His fingered drummed against the top of the pew. "Your father? Your mother? Anyone?"

"My mother died when I was little," Tony answered, and paused, mostly to catch his breath. "My father left when I was four. I felt a lot of things for my foster family. Love wasn't one of 'em." Now it was Tony's turn to look away. His eyes focused on the books in the holder in front of him. His hand reached for one, but it didn't feel right. He stared down at the beige carpet. This was a mistake. And a lot harder than he thought it would be. He didn't have the strength to find out what he needed to know. Maybe he hadn't thought this idea through all the way. For some reason, he had just assumed Robert would just answer his question even before he asked it.

"But there was someone else," Robert said, sounding as if he knew more. Tony didn't answer right away, but the priest seemed to know how to deal with that. His silence extracted the truth better than words. Tony thought about Roberto's assertion and tried to ignore the pain in his chest.

"I got married," Tony answered at last. "It didn't work out."

"Did you love her?"

"Angela?" Tony asked. Her name felt like broken glass on his tongue. "I thought I did, but I was wrong. I don't know how to love. That's why I need to get to purgatory."

"Shoot for heaven, Tony," Robert said, his thumb motioning upward. "Shoot for heaven." The priest paused, looked up at the ceiling of the church, and then back at Tony. He seemed to avoid looking at the ventilator. "I want you to think back. Did you ever do one thing for Angela that showed her you loved her?"

"I did a lot of shit that showed her I didn't." Tony could think of a thousand things. Believing she slept with Bill was probably the stupidest.

"Not one good thing? You never brought her flowers? Took her dancing?"

"Not really," Tony said, brushing back his curls and recalling a spring day a long time ago. "Well, maybe. Once I..., na-a-h..."

"Say it," Robert encouraged him with a twinkle in his green eyes. "I'm a priest. You can trust me."

"Yeah, right," Tony said, looking straight at him with disbelief.

"I'm serious."

"It's crazy," Tony said, shifting to relieve the pain from the bandages across his chest. It felt like they were getting tighter. "You'd laugh."

"Try me."

"I read her poetry," Tony said, and for the moment, he was glad he could only whisper. He turned his head and stared at the pale face of a female statue draped in blue. "Angela was sick. In the hospital. Remember?" Short answers were all he could manage. "She couldn't talk or move. Just listen."

"If she couldn't talk or walk away, she couldn't reject you," Roberto said. "She also couldn't accept you. It was safe, completely safe, like loving a baby."

"I s'pose," Tony answered, but Robert's analogy was more stinging than he knew. Did the priest know that somewhere there was a baby?

"Did she recover?" Robert asked.

"Yeah," Tony said, "but she took off. I don't know where. She wouldn't speak to me anyway. Even if I could find her."

"You're sure?"

"Damn straight," Tony said, right away. "I put her there. I hit her. She stayed with me anyway," he continued, stumbling over the words and letting his eyes drop from the statue. He tried to take a deep breath but had to settle for several shallow ones. "She got pregnant. I promised I'd never hit her again. She couldn't trust me. I was jealous. She did the only sane thing."

"Why were you jealous?"

"Because I loved her so damn much, and I thought she didn't love me. At least, I thought I loved her. I must have been wrong. I don't know how to love."

"I think you do," Roberto said, standing up.

"Bullshit," Tony answered, looking up at him. "She would be here today if I did."

"Tony, you never needed to die to learn how to love," Robert said, placing a hand on Tony shoulder. "You've already been to purgatory. You already know how to love. Now, you want to die because you learned to love."

"No—" Robert's words felt like a knife in his chest.

"It's true," Robert said. "Did you hear what I said in the funeral mass? 'No one can hold back his spirit from departing; no one has the power to prevent his day of death, for there is no discharge from that obligation and dark battle.'"

"Oh, that's just bitchin'" Tony said, gasping for air between thoughts. "Now what?. . . Look at me . . . I can barely sit up . . . Sometimes I can't breathe . . . For sure, I'll never fly again . . . I don't know if I can love people . . . I died and went to Earth. . . What the hell am I supposed to do?"

"Maybe you need to ask God."

"Don't bring Him into this," Tony said, gripping the edge of the pew for support.

"You brought 'Him' into this," Robert said. "You came to me, a priest. Every man must have his own experience of God. It's part of living."

"And dying?" Tony asked, his breathing growing more labored.

"I would imagine so."

"You imagine?" Tony wanted to swear, but he didn't have the breath.

"I'm a man, just like you. I don't know everything and I haven't died yet."

"Oh, shit . . . I'm trying to die or love or some damn thing . . . and all you can say is 'I'm only human.'" Maybe the pain would go away if he laid down.

"BUT I AM ONLY HUMAN, Tony," Roberto said, pacing as he spoke. He paused, turned his back to Tony, and faced the confessionals across the room. Roberto would have loved to have the luxury of telling someone, anyone, how inadequate he felt. The back of his hand went to his forehead to wipe away the moisture. He had never been good at this. It always reminded him of when his sister died, and how useless he had been. "You want to learn to love. I want to believe someone loves me, even if it's only my mother. I don't have all the answers. I don't even know how to make love to a beautiful—" Roberto turned back. Tony was lying down in the pew. He rushed into the pew beside him. "Tony? Tony, what's wrong?"

Tony lay on one side, gasping for air. His face turned blue and Roberto panicked. He backed away from him, turned, and rushed out the door.

"Bill!" he yelled down the silent street. "Bill!"

There was no sign of him. Roberto turned and stared at the church door. Years ago, he had stared at the closed door of his little sister's room. Stay away, his mother had said. You've done enough damage. Roberto reached through his memories, gripped the handle, and yanked open the door.

The face mask of the ventilator lay beside Tony's face in the last pew. Roberto fit it over Tony's head with trembling hands and flipped the on/off switch of the machine. No response.

"Mama Mia, Mama Mia," Robert said, spotting the long instructions. "Jesus Christo, Jesus Christo—" Bill barged in the door as the machine began pumping.

"Father?" Bill said, rushing forward.

"Bill, hurry," Roberto said, relieved to see him. "I think he's dying."

"Tony? Tony?" Bill said, charging to his side. Roberto moved away. Slowly Tony's blue eyes opened with a caged animal stare. "It's all right. You're all right. We're right here."

Tony closed his eyes and relaxed. Each subsequent breath seemed easier and easier.

"He'll need to rest here for a while," Bill said, looking up at the priest.

"Where were you?" Roberto asked, backing away.

"Sister offered me a cup of coffee. I was just in the convent for a min—"

"Fine, fine," Roberto said, holding the edge of the pew. "The new bishop is coming. I have to go."

"But—" Bill said.

Roberto backed away at first, then turned, and picked up his pace. His knee didn't get anywhere near the floor when he genuflected between the altar and the first pew. It didn't matter. The sooner he got away, the better.

Bishop to Pawn

Roberto, shaken by Tony's visit, experienced difficulty concentrating on parish matters. Today's visit from the new bishop during his first month in office didn't worry Roberto. A certain amount of public relations work went with the title. Roberto had known many bishops who considered their office only an unavoidable stepping stone on the route to becoming a cardinal. Small parish squabbles wouldn't matter to such a man motivated to climb to a higher station.

Roberto waited in the rectory, lamenting the postponed installation of the new stained glass window behind the altar. That would have impressed the bishop, but donations had slowed to a trickle. Roberto tried to remind himself of the importance of God's timing, but the sound of the doorbell broke his concentration.

The man dressed in black at the front door removed his fedora and shook Roberto's hand. The bishop had left his assistant waiting in a parked car.

"It's a pleasure to finally meet you, Bishop Matthew," Roberto said and led the bishop into the living room. "May I offer you some vino?"

"Not today," the bishop said, placing his dark hat on the television. He patted his thick, white hair back into place over his pink scalp, and his gentle gray eyes surveyed the cold room. Nothing about his grandfatherly expression told Roberto if he approved or not.

"Lunch first?" the priest asked, starting toward the kitchen. "The ladies from the parish have prepared a special—"

"As much as I would like to, I can't," the bishop answered, clasping his hands low in front of him. "I celebrated mass at the south end of this diocese this morning and must say mass again in the north end this evening. In the short time we have together, we need to talk."

"Of course," Roberto said, re-entering the room one slow step at a time. He nodded to the recliner and said, "Please have a seat."

The newly appointed leader of the diocese, the eminent Matthew Mahan, sat in the overstuffed chair covered by the crooked afghan. Roberto perched on the arm of the couch, unsure if he should sit or stand.

"Father Roberto, during the past year, the previous bishop was very ill," the bishop started, studying Roberto with a gaze that felt unsettling. "After he died and I was appointed, I found many matters had simply been placed on hold. So—" The bishop stopped for a moment and adjusted his sweater vest. "You see, there's a stack of letters and petitions in my office from your parishioners—"

"Oh, those," Roberto said and exhaled. He sunk into a seat on the couch.

"You know about them?" the bishop asked. His surprised expression seemed to question the extent of Roberto's knowledge.

"Of course, of course," Roberto answered, talking with one hand waving. "We have some parishioners who don't like the Vatican II changes in the mass. Dead wood mostly. Kindergarten Catholics."

"They are extremely upset," the bishop answered, cocking his head as if he needed to look at Roberto from a different perspective.

"They'll recover in time," Roberto said in his rapid manner, happy he could reassure his superior on such a simple matter. "Businessmen in this town have run this parish for years. When I stepped in and took over, they felt displaced."

"Displaced?" the bishop asked. "It's their parish, Roberto."

"True," Roberto said, leaning on the arm of the chair. It was nice to have someone who would understand what he was going through. Carlo had never been any help. "But they don't understand the laws of the church. Their ideas would surprise you. It's become a question of power now. I'm in control, and they don't like it."

"Were you in control when Father Carlo was here?" the bishop asked, probing another matter.

"I was the head priest," Roberto admitted, sitting up straight again. "But I didn't know anything about his indiscretions. Not until—"

"You should have known," the bishop said, leveling a gaze at Roberto that made him more uncomfortable.

"It was hard to tell anything with Carlo," Roberto said, hoping he could begin to explain the odd behavior of his former roommate. "He was an unusual man with some very unusual habits. His role was simply to visit the sick and preside at the Spanish masses anyway."

"You sound as if that's not important."

"What I mean—"

"Roberto, I've already had a joint meeting with some of your parishioners," the bishop said. Roberto crossed his arms and studied the bishop's face. His superior continued. "Members of the Catholic Men's League and the Sisters of Mary met with me over breakfast. We had a bilingual meeting—"

"They met with you together?" Roberto asked, standing up as he spoke. "In the same room?"

"Yes," Bishop Mahan answered, looking up and sounding a little confused by Roberto's reaction. "They were very cooperative. Leaders from both associations agreed that they cannot work with you."

"They agreed?" Roberto said, not believing his ears.

"Yes," Mahan answered, watching Roberto pace. "Is that unusual?"

"It's just that the Hispanics and whites . . ." No, that didn't sound right. "This parish has always been so divided."

"Perhaps that's just how you perceive it," the bishop replied, gesturing toward Roberto with an open palm.

"No, no," Roberto said, shaking his head.

"Roberto, I think a change is in order."

"I agree," Roberto said, starting to feel a little better.

"I feel it would be best if you were to serve the Lord in a different capacity." It wasn't the reply Roberto expected.

"It isn't my fault that this parish won't accept Vatican II," Roberto said, covering his heart with his hand. "I was taught in the old ways. After I left the seminary, all the rules changed."

"It happened to us all, Roberto," the bishop continued, pressing his fingertips together. "God isn't an old God. He is a forever God, always changing and always the same. Your parishioners' complaints aren't about Vatican II. They're about you. They have a problem with you. Have you ever been on an extended retreat, Roberto?"

"Why?" Roberto asked, taking a step back and bumping the coffee table.

"You could benefit from it greatly," the bishop continued in a calm, too calm, voice. "But only if you enter into the experience with an open heart. Two new priests will be here by the end of the week."

"So soon?" Roberto asked, moving toward the window. He faced the backyard and avoided the bishop's face.

"The people have waited long enough."

"How long will I be away?" Roberto asked, studying the dying peach tree in the backyard.

"You won't be returning here."

"But—" Roberto said, turning to protest.

"I'm sorry." The bishop tried to cut him off. But Roberto needed to explain.

"But the window," Roberto said, motioning toward the church. "The stained glass window behind the altar is an important parish project."

"If the people want it, I'm sure they will build it," the bishop sighed.

"They don't want it," Roberto said. "But they need it. They don't understand how much—" Roberto stopped himself. One look at the bishop's fixed gaze told him it was over. He took a deep breath. "How soon should I leave?"

"As soon as possible," the bishop said, standing and pulling papers from inside his coat pocket. "I've been in contact with your order and brought your new directives with me. You've been assigned to work in their parish library in Minneapolis. It's intriguing work . . ."

The rest of the bishop's words floated by without registering. Roberto tried to be gracious, but it was an awkward situation. The bishop didn't linger long, mentioning something about six o'clock mass in Salinas.

"I wish we had more time," Mahan said, lifting his hat from the television. "Will you be all right?"

"Fine . . . fine," Roberto answered, accompanying him to the front door.

"The blessings of God go with you, Roberto." The bishop put his hand on the priest's forehead. Their spirits joined, and the power in his touch almost floored Roberto. His words bypassed Roberto's ears and went straight to his spirit. "We do our best, Roberto. Sometimes a man struggles to do one job, when God has sent him to do another. You've done something here you haven't seen. I pray God opens your eyes and your heart to that hidden miracle."

"Thank you," Roberto said and watched him leave. What did he say? The bishop walked down the steps, put on his hat, and turned to look back at the priest.

"You have not failed, Roberto. Trust me," the bishop said.

Roberto watched the bishop leave, wishing he could believe his words.

Joining

BILL AND TONY left the church and got back into the Caddy. Bill started driving, and Tony was too tired to ask where they were headed. The car didn't stop until Bill pulled into the parking space outside the emergency room of the local hospital.

"I'll go get some help," Bill said and put on the parking brake. He opened the driver's door.

"Don't bother," Tony answered, looking at Bill, then at the doors to the hospital. "I'm not interested."

"All I promised was to get you to Roberto," Bill said.

"You did that," Tony said. "You're off the hook."

"Look," Bill said, giving Tony a frank stare across the front seat. "That doctor back in Washington said you wouldn't make it 24 hours—36 tops—outside a hospital."

"I said, 'you're off the hook,'" Tony said again. He reclined the seat and closed his eyes. "You can take off now."

"What?"

"I'm too tired to argue," Tony said, turning his head toward Bill. Tony had talked to Robert, not that Tony felt he had found out much. It was all he felt he needed. Now he could die. "You can just leave me here. I just need sleep."

"No fuckin' way," Bill said, stepping out of the car. "I'm going in and getting help. Let someone else handle your next respiratory crisis."

"I'm not signing anything," Tony said, just before Bill slammed the driver's door shut. Bill reopened it, leaned in, and rested on arm on the roof of the car.

"You know what pisses me off?" Bill asked. Tony started to answer, but Bill kept raving. "You never reach for that damn thing on your own." Bill pointed to the ventilator in the back seat. "I thought talking to Roberto would change that, but it didn't. But you know what? Tough! Maybe you didn't find out whatever it was you needed to know, but I'm too fuckin' tired to care." He paused and stared at Tony.

"That makes two of us," Tony said. Right now, Tony just wanted to sleep and getting rid of Bill seemed like the only way to accomplish that. He wanted to quit thinking about living, and dying, and never flying again. And what the hell love was or if it mattered. He had run out of ideas about finding the answers. "Just leave me here. If I change my mind, it's a short walk." Tony nodded toward the emergency room doors.

"Fine," Bill said, standing up and looking at the hospital. "Fine." He stepped back and closed the door. Both of his hands held the door shut for a moment, and he looked around the parking lot. He pushed away from the Caddy, and his arms dropped to his sides. One hand slid his glasses further up his nose, then he turned and walked away.

Tony watched him go. Bill had done more than he had ever expected. It had been a hell of a ride. Tony knew it took a lot of guts to just walk away. But maybe that's what real friends did. Maybe they just gave up when it was what the other person wanted. Maybe that's what he should do with Angela. Maybe he would always care about her, but, somewhere, on some other level, he would have to let her go. She would stay in his heart, in his head, but never physically in his life. He closed his eyes and hoped he could do that. The driver's door opened and closed.

Bill got in without saying a word. He turned the key in the ignition and drove them out of the hospital parking lot. Six silent blocks later, the Caddy pulled into a driveway and stopped. Tony sat up and looked at the neat, grey house with white brick trim and orange nasturtiums spilling over the front planter.

"Your place?" Tony asked.

"Yeah," Bill said, taking the key from the ignition and half-opening the car door. "We'll get a meal. We'll get some sleep. If nothing changes, I'll take you back. The hospital will be there."

"You don't have to—" Tony started.

"Yeah, I do," Bill said, sounding resigned and pushing open the car door. Cindy, wearing a blue maternity smock, rushed down the front walk. Bill stepped out of the car, and she threw her arms around him. Tony watched her face and felt then that there are just some things you don't walk away from.

They guided Tony into the house and past the living room that served as Cindy's painting studio. Cindy led the way, and Bill carried the ventilator. The guest room, soon to be the nursery, was at the end of the hall. Sun shone through the open white shutters above a window seat full of stuffed animals. The two of them eased Tony into a chair beside the bed with the blue flowered bedspread.

Cindy was more animated than he remembered. One thing about her hadn't changed. She still never looked him in the eye. She talked nonstop about making him a meal and how much healthier the food from other cultures seemed to be. There wasn't time to protest, not that he had the energy. He hoped he could handle what he smelled cooking in the kitchen. His jaw still didn't work too well. She put a TV tray in front of him and came back with a plate of eggs scrambled with turmeric, a cup of weak-looking green tea, and rice. All this without ever looking him in the eye.

He was pretty sure she was pissed at him, though she never said so. Maybe it was because Bill had stayed away so long, or the fact that Bill had returned with Tony instead of alone. Maybe it was all those late night phone calls, back when he was still with Angela. He gave up trying to figure it out. The rice was too difficult to chew, but the tea and the eggs went down better than he had hoped. Cindy helped Bill change the bandage around his chest, commenting on how much weight he had lost and his bruised face. Tony wondered how she knew. She wouldn't look at him. She even managed to force some of the pills down him that Bill and he had ignored during the whole car trip. Then, at last, Cindy turned back the covers, and, Bill, who looked half dead, helped him into bed.

He didn't remember falling asleep. When he woke up again, it was dark outside. Bill was asleep in a chair beside him, his feet up on an ottoman. The shape of the ventilator loomed behind him, silhouetted by the moonlight coming through the slots of the open shutters. He stared at the black-and-white portable TV in the corner that Bill had left on. The late news was ending and the late, late movie,

The Blue Max, was beginning. He watched some commercials and a flying scene before drifting off to sleep.

IN HIS DREAM, Tony was soaring through the clouds in a two-holer Stearman while Robert sat in the front cockpit, messing with the controls. They flew into the box canyon in Arroyo Seco near Patches' cabin. The priest insisted on landing the plane like a helicopter, and Tony grabbed the stick from him too late. Forced to land, Tony tried to taxi the aircraft up a hillside. Thick underbrush snared the wheels and brought them to a sudden stop.

Tony leaped out of the plane, but the priest refused to leave it. Tony headed off toward the cabin, searching for a tool to cut them free. A swollen creek encircled the redwood and river rock structure where Angela and he had once lived. Moss-covered boulders, giant steps apart, provided the only access to the cabin. Each time Tony moved from one to the next, he slipped and almost fell into the water.

He felt exhausted by the time he reached the cabin's island. He crawled across the sand, too tired to walk, and fell through the front door. The refrigerator door hung open, revealing no beer, just a saw. His tired eyes looked beyond the kitchen and noticed Angela in the bedroom.

She stood by the fireplace, wearing a long blue dress and bleeding from one eye. He edged toward her on his knees and reached up to wipe the blood from her face. It was a sweet, electric moment when his fingertips touched her soft cheek. A surge of power lifted him from the floor and sent him soaring across the room. He landed flat on his back on the bed, looking back at Angela.

Her clothes flew away. Her body slid on top of his. Their arms and legs aligned. He was afraid he wouldn't be able to breathe, but she felt weightless. Her breasts didn't press against his chest. The only sensation he noticed was one of bright energy, flowing through her into him in an endless stream. The power she seemed to transfer to him became more important to him than her exposed flesh.

Their faces touched at the temples, allowing her to project thoughts into his mind. He felt their spirits join, shattering disjointed images from his childhood. Leather belts ripped in two, lids sailed off boxes, and closet doors swung open. The strength that flowed through her brought him to his feet. Holding her hand, he took the saw from the refrigerator, and they ran from the cabin. She guided him to a bridge across the water.

Together they made it back to the airplane, but they couldn't find Robert. Tony kept thinking he still needed the plane. He sawed through the brush, working hard to free the aircraft. When he finished, he turned to tell Angela, but she was gone.

"Angela, Angela," he called in his loudest whisper. A fresh growth of foliage gripped the plane again. He sawed through it again with all his strength. His mouth opened to say her name, but no sound came out. The saw dropped from his hand, and he tried to head back to the cabin, but it was gone. A phone started ringing, but he couldn't find it. And then he heard Cindy's voice. Where did she come from?

"Hello?" Cindy said.

Tony's eyes opened and he wasn't at the cabin. Bill was in the chair beside him, waking up. Sun was streaming through the half-open shutters. Cindy's voice drifted down the hall, where both men now listened through a sleepy haze.

"What a surprise . . . Congratulations. When? . . . Boy or girl? . . . How big? . . . What's his name? . . . Oh, Angela, I'm so happy for you."

Bill sat up straight when he heard Angela's name. Tony's eyes were locked on the extension phone on the nightstand in his room. Bill handed it to him, and Tony grabbed it, hoping he wasn't too late.

"Tell Tony," Angela said, her voice trembling in Tony's good ear. "If you ever see him."

"He's had a terrible accident," Cindy said.

"Don't tell me," Angela answered, cutting her off. "I don't want to know anything about him. He just ought to know he has a son, that's all. I have to go now."

"Angela?" Tony said in his loudest whisper. "Angela, wait. We need to talk. Angela?"

ANGELA GASPED with recognition. She stood rigid in the kitchen of her mother's new apartment. Tony was whispering her name. She pulled the phone away from her ear. In slow motion, both of her hands replaced the receiver on the hook without a sound.

Angela's mother burst in the front door of the apartment. Angela's fingertips were still tracing the curve of the receiver, and she didn't look up at first. When she did, the older woman was side-stepping packing boxes in the middle of the small living room and heading for the kitchen. She dropped two bulging brown grocery bags on the kitchen counter and pressed one hand into the small of her back.

"I'm glad we're back in California," she said to Angela, pulling a head of lettuce from one sack. "You don't get produce like this in Iowa. Honey? What's wrong?"

"I had the strangest dream before I woke up this morning," Angela said. She walked away from the phone and stared out the patio window. "I was at the cabin. Tony was there—" The baby started to fuss in the bedroom. Angela walked away in a haze to attend to him without finishing her sentence.

TONY HEARD CINDY rushing down the hall after the line disconnected. She entered the room, and the dial tone was still buzzing from the phone in Tony's hand.

"What's his name?" Tony asked in a soft, distant voice, laying back and keeping his eyes on the ceiling.

"Nathan."

The phone dropped from his hand to the bedspread, and his bent arm covered his face. Nathan, he repeated in his head. Good name. Strong name. Damn, she had been so close.

"Listen, Tony—" Bill said, picking up the receiver and replacing it.

"Not now." Tony whispered. "Not now."

Bill and Cindy stood in the room for a moment, then they both walked away. What could they say? Tony listened as their footsteps and voices faded down the hall.

"If only she would talk to him," Cindy said in a quiet voice.

"If only . . ." Bill answered.

But Tony knew she was never going to talk to him. It was over now. It had been for a long time. He just didn't want to believe it. He didn't know how. If this was love, it was nothing like flying fast and low. Flying fast and low may have been thrilling, but there was still a sense of control. It was the ragged edge of control, the edge he was used to, but it was still control. Love didn't let you have control. It didn't let him control it. You put your heart out there and take it as it comes. It wasn't some guarantee of getting loved back, like he had thought it would be. Love was taking the chance that someone would break your heart. As crazy and painful as it all felt, there was a place inside him that was glad that it had happened. Angela would always have his son, like a piece of him that would always be with her. Nothing could change that. Maybe that was the part of love that didn't die.

Maybe it was the dream, or the phone call and the sound of Angela's voice. Whatever it was, he now knew what to do. No more lying around waiting to die and being a burden to his friends. He would go back to the place where it all fell apart. Maybe he would learn why. Or at least he could die trying.

It was a slow, painful effort, but he got out of the bed. He paused in the doorway, judging the number of steps to the front door. Bill was leaning against the archway into the living room. He stopped talking to Cindy and turned to look down the hall. Tony left the doorway of the bedroom and began to inch his way up the hall. He stopped in the entryway that separated the living room from the front door.

"I have to go now," Tony said, leaning his back against the wide front door. He needed the support, if only for a moment. Now that he knew where he had to go, he wasn't about to wait another minute. Maybe, just maybe, all the pain would end there.

"Go?" Bill asked. "Go where?"

"The cabin," Tony answered. "I have some unfinished business."

"Like hell," Bill said, placing his hands on his hips.

"You know, so far, I've been damn polite," Tony said, fighting to remain upright. "I haven't died on you. I let you strap that stupid machine to my face. It's time to let go, Billy boy."

"Leaving now would be suicide," Cindy said, struggling to rise from the middle cushion of the couch. "Are you crazy?"

"You know I am, silly girl," Tony answered with a sad smile and reached for the door knob. "As usual, I can't pay the bill."

"But you're getting better," Bill said, moving forward and pressing stiff-armed against the door. "It's been almost 24 hours since you needed the ventilator."

"I've waited long enough," Tony answered, not wanting to waste his energy. It would take all his strength to get back to the cabin, if he could make it.

"You don't know what you're doing," Bill said, refusing to move.

"I know all I need to know," Tony answered him. "I know I have a son I'll never see. I know I blew it with Angela. I know I'll never fly again. Right now, I wish I knew a little less."

Tony pulled on the door with both hands, showing more determination than he had in a week. Bill resisted at first but then moved out of his way.

"Thanks, bro," Tony said in a soft voice and stepped onto the front porch.

"No-o-o," Cindy said behind him. She started to follow him out the front door. Bill held her back, and Tony headed down the walk. She turned to Bill and cried, "How can you let him go?"

"Father Roberto said the soul knows where to go to be healed," Bill answered.

Tony shook his head at Bill's response. Like hell it does.

"You'll never make it to the cabin," Cindy said behind him.

Tony just kept walking. The big Caddy door took some work to open. Tony was about to get into the driver's seat. Bill hurried toward him and shut the car door before Tony could get in.

"I know what I'm doing, Bill," Tony said. He didn't want to argue, but he wasn't about to turn back.

"And who will you kill in the process, asshole?" Bill asked. "Look, maybe you want to eat it on the freeway," Bill continued, pointing in the general direction of the cabin. "That doesn't mean everyone else out there does. At least let me drive you to the cabin."

"I need to go alone," Tony said, resisting Bill's interference.

"I won't stay," Bill said, looking from Tony to Cindy on the front step. "Cindy can follow us in our car."

"As soon as we get there—" Tony started.

"As soon as we get there, I'll leave," Bill said.

The sun rose over the east hills, and the two men stared at each other. A morning chill rose from the dew-covered grass and beyond the houses, they heard a six-hundred horse engine working. Tony looked down the quiet, neighborhood street and then back at his determined friend.

"You swear?" Tony asked.

"On a stack of Bibles," Bill answered without blinking.

"Yeah, right." Tony didn't think it was enough. "How about on your license to fly?"

"That too," Bill said, never dropping his gaze.

Tony waited a minute and then stepped back from the driver's door. Bill helped him into the passenger seat, and then raced around to the driver's side. Cindy left the front door open and hurried down the walk. Tony knew the look in her eye. She wanted to stop them.

"I don't like it," she said, grabbing Bill's arm and keeping him from entering the car.

"Maybe he'll change his mind on the way," Bill said to appease her. But Tony knew he wouldn't. "Go get in our car and follow— Shit, the ventilator. I'll be right back."

Bill hurried back into the house, and Cindy watched him, then turned to look at Tony.

"Don't do this," she said, looking at him for a moment before looking away.

"Why is it you never look me in the eye?" Tony asked. His blunt question stopped her for a moment.

"Oh, Tony," she said, and he knew she wouldn't answer. He did the honors for her and looked away. Where was Bill?

"Because you scare me," Cindy said. Her answer surprised him, and he turned to look at her.

"Oh, I thought you just hated me," Tony said with a smile.

"I never hated you, Tony," she said, and for the first time, looked right at him. He could sense her blue eyes struggling to stay fixed on his. "All the women I ever knew who looked you in the eye—"

"He's taking this damn thing with him," Bill said, brushing past Cindy and opening the back door of the car. "Whether he likes it or not."

"I get it," Tony said to Cindy, and Bill gave him an odd look. Tony looked away.

Bill kissed Cindy and got in the driver's seat. She closed the car door for him, and he rolled down the window.

"Just follow us," Bill said. "Damn, you might need to get gas."

"I can do that," she said and sighed as if she had just thought of something else. "I just hate driving on that road down to the cabin."

"I'll walk up and meet you," Bill said, trying to appease her. "No sense ruining the undercarriages of two cars. Just follow me down there and wait up at the top of the last hill."

"I don't know—" she started to say. The phone ringing inside the house interrupted her. She turned to hurry and answer it. "I'll be right behind you," she called back to them.

Bill started the car. Tony watched Cindy head back toward the house. She stopped at the front door, turned around, and looked him straight in the eye. He let out half a chuckle.

"What?" Bill said, watching for traffic behind him.

"Nothing," Tony answered and reclined the seat.

Cannon Law

Packing wouldn't take Roberto long since none of the furnishings were his. Even the crooked afghan knitted for him would remain in the parish's possession. He emptied his drawers and cleaned, working late into the night. He stored his typewriter in its case and snapped shut his suitcases. Mementos from his desk drawer filled half of a small box. Two engraved wine glasses that marked the 25th anniversary of Roberto's ordination lay wrapped in tissue on top of the mementos.

The following morning, he began the time-consuming task of packing his large collection of books. He carried empty boxes from the garage into the house and pondered how to break the news to the parish members. His decision? Leave it to the incoming priest. In her own uncanny way, Sister Mary Teresa already seemed to know.

"Whoo-hoo, Father?" she said, holding open the mail slot of the rectory's front door. "Are you busy?"

He saw her dark habit and long hair through the Venetian blinds, but he chose to ignore her and finish boxing his books.

"Father? Hello-o-o," she called again. He had to answer.

"Hello, Sister," he said, opening the door without inviting her in.

"You were up late last night," she said. He didn't answer her, but it didn't seem to bother her. She brushed past him and entered the rectory. "I saw your light on early this morning just as I finished my devotional." Her dark eyes looked past him to the scattered books in the office. "Can I help?"

"That's not necess—"

"It's no problem," she said, squeezing her tiny frame by him. "Really."

"But—"

"When are you leaving?" she asked, assessing the situation. She pulled an empty box over to the bookcase and began filling it. He watched her for a moment, wondering how to stop her. Impossible, he decided, and resumed packing. She didn't seem to notice he hadn't answered her. "Are you excited about your new assignment?"

"I'm not sure," he grumbled, picking up another empty box.

"Wherever you go, I'm sure the parish will feel extremely blessed to have you."

"I wouldn't say—" he started, but she wouldn't let him finish.

"When I think of all the good things you've done here—"

"What good?" he asked, slapping a book on the nearby desk. The sound echoed through the cold, half empty house.

"Father, you can't be serious." Her eyes blinked at him in astonishment.

"I am," he said, picking up the book again.

"I don't know where to begin," she said, still pulling books from the shelves. It seemed impossible for her to stop long enough to tell him. She restacked the books in a box and then stopped on her way back to the bookcase. "The new catechism, maybe," she said, folding her arms as if to keep herself still for a moment. "I wish you had visited the classes. You would have known how exciting it's been for the children."

"I meant to visit," he mumbled under his breath. He wished he meant it.

"All the new ideas from Vatican II," she said, reaching for a paperback. She put one hand on her small hip and wagged the book at him. "No one but you had the courage to initiate those changes. Others found it easier to go on in the old ways."

"Maybe I should have too," he said, talking into his half-packed box.

"Oh, no, Father," she said, turning to resume the task at hand and talking at the same time. "You brought people to church that had been away for years. Some had never been before. They saw something new and accepting happening here. You gave them a chance to be a part of it."

"After I drove away all the others," he said, dropping into a swivel chair. He turned away from her, gazing out the window in the direction of the church.

"You're wrong, Father," she said, stepping between him and the window. "The ones who left grew too. You gave them a gift no one else could. Their faith was in place, but it needed to be re-examined. Don't you see?"

He shook his head, wondering where she got her ideas.

"Father, the whole parish now stands shoulder to shoulder, finally all pulling in the same direction," she said, both hands now on her hips. "You did that."

"United against a common enemy," he said with a weak laugh. He rose from the chair and skirted around her. There were more books than he remembered.

"They may see it that way for now," she said, turning to watch him. "But it's just a starting point. They will recognize that their power comes from being united. When they were divided, they couldn't accomplish anything. A sacrifice had to be made," she said, lowering her voice. Her piercing stare held him frozen for a moment. "Not every man is willing to sacrifice himself."

She said nothing more and returned to packing with diligence. Her perseverance forced him back to work. They packed the remainder of the books in silence, and the quiet allowed him to ponder her words. He carried the final box of books to the garage, and she followed him. The box just fit, and the lid of the full trunk closed with a thud.

"Many hands make light work," the nun said. The bright morning sun blazed outside the garage door. She stood in the driveway, her arms folded across her chest. Her shadow pointed to the convent behind her. "I'll miss you."

"It's nice to think someone will," he answered, but he didn't think she would miss him for long.

"Father, there are days when I think you are the prophet Jeremiah come again," she said, shaking her head with a sweet smile. "You seem tortured by a duty you cannot refuse. Someday, I hope you can do God's work in trust instead of suffering."

"Impossible," he said, thumping his fist to his chest.

"All things are possible," she said, extending her hand to him.

320

"Perhaps," he answered. The moment their hands clasped, he envisioned a bright, stained glass window depicting the resurrection. When he let go of her hand, it was gone.

"You need to take another look inside," she said. "You forgot something."

"What?" he asked, thinking now that she was probably right.

"I don't know," she said. "My mother always said that to me."

"Fine, fine," he answered, turning back toward the rectory. He looked over his shoulder at her and couldn't help but smile. "God bless you, Sister."

"And you," she said. She disappeared into the convent with a twirl of her skirt and five quick steps.

Roberto examined each room of the empty rectory. Saints and martyrs stared back at him from faded pictures on the dull walls. A black-barreled weapon on wooden wheels remained parked in the corner of Carlo's old room.

"The new tenants can deal with you," he said to the cannon.

He left the rectory by the front door and slipped into the church through a side entrance. The priest took a seat in the front pew and almost regretted he had removed the kneelers. The faint glow of sunlight through the narrow side windows strained to light the cavernous room. He stared at the dark altar.

"Let Your anointing remain here," he prayed, but his voice failed him. "Can this cup pass from me?" he asked. His whisper floated to the ceiling, and his eyes dropped to the floor. "If there was only a little light. But now . . ."

Roberto shook his head and then looked up. The thought that occurred to him was as crazy as firing a .44 magnum through your living room wall. He jumped up and dashed into the sacristy behind the altar. A stepladder, used for recent repairs, still leaned against the cabinet with the altar boys' clothes. He hauled the aluminum framed ladder out behind the altar and opened it near the back wall. Roberto climbed to the second highest rung and struggled to lift the crucifix from the dark wood paneling above the tabernacle. He carried it back down the wooden steps, struggling to keep from dropping it.

"We all have our cross to bear," he said, propping it against the sacristy wall.

He turned, raced back to the rectory, and flipped on the light switch in Carlo's room. The bulb popped and the light died with a quick flash.

"Light, light," he said, whispering under his breath and fumbling in the dark closet of the room. "Let there be light."

His hand found a small cardboard box containing a square tin can and a coil of waxy string in the back of the closet. He gathered them in one arm and dragged the cannon behind him by its small link chain. The weapon trailed him out the front door. The cannon wasn't heavy but getting it down the stairs was awkward. He set it down on the path by the bottom step, gathering his other items. One yank on the chain pulled it into the church. He turned and locked the side door behind him.

Some raw spirit led him to position the cannon midway down the center aisle and open the can of black powder beside it. He poured a small charge into the barrel and packed it down with the miniature ramrod attached to the weapon's carriage. His fingers removed three smooth cannon balls from the small box, each the size of a large marble. He wrapped each of them in a square patch of cloth and placed two in his pocket. One hand held the remaining ball at the opening of the cannon barrel. His other hand grabbed the ramrod and forced the ball down close to the black powder at the opposite end of the barrel.

Roberto lay down on his stomach behind the weapon, and then rolled the cannon forward a bit. His left eye trained up the length of the barrel. It needed to angle up just a little more to point at the middle of the darkly paneled wall behind the altar. He adjusted it and pulled out a small pocket knife, cutting a two-inch wick from the coil and inserting it into a small hole at the rear of the barrel. A book of matches from the prayer intention candles in the back of the church was all he needed. He hurried down the center aisle to get it and returned.

Roberto stood behind the small weapon and took a deep breath before opening the matchbook. He struck the match and the smell of sulfur stung his nose. The flame touched the small fuse, and it sizzled out of sight into the rear of the barrel.

"I anoint you in the name of the Father . . ."

BOOM!

The cannon recoiled backward, and he jumped aside. His eyes raced to find the point of impact. Light shone through a hole the size of his fist in the dark wall behind the altar. He rolled the cannon back to the initial spot, loaded it again, and lit the fuse.

"And the Son . . ."

Sizzle, sizzle, sizzle, BOOM!

Another hole. He loaded it once more and struck another match.

"And the Holy Spirit. Amen."

BOOM!

He ran forward to put his finger into each of the three holes he had blown in the wall but stopped before touching them.

"I trust there will be a window, Lord," he said, lowering his hand.

Roberto left the cross in the sacristy but returned the cannon and accessories to Carlo's room. His footsteps headed down the rectory hall one last time, and he closed the door to the garage behind him. His packed car was ready to go. He got in, slipped his key in the ignition switch, and backed out of the driveway with squealing tires. One window flew open on the bottom floor of the convent, and a waving arm reflected in his rear view mirror. His yellow Dodge Dart failed to make the stop at the corner. Roberto turned left and headed for the freeway, leaving King City behind.

Ghosts

Tony exhaled and relaxed in the passenger seat, staring at the roof of the Caddy. Was Bill going to try and reason with him for the whole hour-long drive to the cabin? The lecture only seemed to stop when Bill's eyes were searching the rearview mirror for Cindy.

"You're being unreasonable," Bill started again. Silence. "You should have told Patches." Silence. "There hasn't been a phone there since you left the place. You know that, don't you?"

"Back off, will you?" Tony said. He didn't want to discuss his decision. "And turn on the radio."

"I'll feel like shit if you die," Bill said, his eyes darting in Tony's direction.

"I feel like shit now," Tony answered. "Trust me. Never quit smoking, drinking, sex, and flying at the same time."

"You're making a big mistake," Bill said in an ominous tone.

"It wouldn't be the first," Tony answered. "Look, you did your best. You took me to see a priest, didn't you? Just drop it, will ya?" Tony said, ending the conversation by turning on the radio himself.

The station clicked on and Marvin Gaye began to sing, "Let's Get It On." Tony leaned back and closed his eyes. The big Cadillac glided down the freeway, and Tony pretended to fall asleep.

Ten minutes later, they approached the off ramp for Arroyo Seco and crossed back over the freeway. Tony looked out the side window and noticed a yellow Dodge Dart racing down the highway beneath them, heading north. The commercial ended on the radio, and the Who started singing *Behind Blue Eyes*.

"I should have had a white picket fence," Tony said.

"What?" Bill said. Tony's random comment seemed to interrupt whatever Bill was plotting to change Tony's mind.

"Angela would never have left," Tony said with a weak attempt to explain. "We didn't need a big house like yours. Just a white picket fence."

"A little fence would never have stopped her," Bill said. "That's not why she left."

"The fence doesn't do anything," Tony said. "But if I was the kind of guy who could keep it standing and painted white, she'd still be here."

Tony turned his face away from Bill, watching the power poles flash by in time to the music. Beyond them, the country road was flanked by green hills, dotted with scrub oak trees and red cattle with white faces. He couldn't tell if he ached from broken ribs or the song dwelling on empty dreams.

The hidden dirt road winding down to the cabin warded off intruders with deep ruts and muffler-bruising stones. Bill used Tony's old key to open the locked gate. They passed six other cabins, spaced well apart on the way. The potholes challenged the old Caddy's shocks. The canyon narrowed and a final, steep descent dead-ended at Patches' cabin. Tony's first glimpse of the rock and redwood hideaway made him smile. It still sat at the edge of a flat sandy plain by the river that carved out a path at the bottom of the canyon wall.

They parked beneath the old sycamore tree. A big limb still grew through the front wall of the cabin, just as it had on the day it was built. Bill turned off the engine and opened the door but remained rigid in the driver's seat. Tony could hear the stream splashing past in the distance and two birds quarreling in the branches overhead. The fresh smell of dirt and mint entered the car. An erratic squirrel with a bottle brush tail dashed into the open, then spun around and dived back beneath the underbrush near the river.

"You were right," Tony said, breaking the silence. "I couldn't have made it alone, but I needed to come."

"I'll wait while you look around," Bill said.

"That wasn't the deal," Tony said and opened the car door. He drew his long body out of the car with effort and stood staring at the sky. Bill took the keys from the ignition. He walked around the back of the car and offered them to Tony. They stood facing each other by the wide trunk of the faded black car.

"If you change your mind—"

"I won't," Tony said and pocketed the keys.

Bill looked around at the familiar wilderness. His silence told Tony he was listening for Cindy's car in the distance. A slight breeze tickled the upper branches of the trees.

"Use that thing, will you?" Bill asked, half turning away from Tony and nodding to the ventilator in the back seat.

Tony looked from his friend's face to the car window but refused to make a promise he wouldn't keep. He'd learned that much at least.

"Thanks for everything, Bill," Tony answered, but he found it tough to look at Bill's face.

"I meant what I said," Bill said, adjusting his glasses on his nose. "I'll take you flying. Just name the time."

"Sure," Tony said and couldn't resist winking. "Maybe next week, huh?"

"I can't stand here and watch you do this," Bill said, shaking his head. "I'm going up the hill to meet Cindy." Bill pointed his thumb over his shoulder to the road they had just come down. "She hates driving down that."

"Yeah, Angela did too," Tony answered. He stood up straight and offered his hand with the sprained wrist to his friend. "Take care, bro."

"You, too," Bill said, shaking Tony's hand gently. He let go and started to back away. The sun was in Bill's eyes, and he squinted at Tony, both hands shoved into his jean pockets. "I sold the rifle."

"No sweat," Tony said with a shrug. Bill nodded and looked down at the ground. One tear made a dark stain on his dusty, leather boots. They both saw it, but neither said anything. That was no surprise to Tony. They never talked about half the things that they should have. They wouldn't start now.

Bill turned away, his eyes downcast and focused on each uphill step. Tony watched him crest the rise and disappear beyond the trees before he walked to the other side of the car. Bill was the best friend he had ever had. And half of the time, he hadn't known it. Now, Bill had kept his final promise. After a few steps, Tony rested his bent arm on the roof of the car and his head dropped into the crook of his arm to hide his tears.

After a minute, he looked up at the cabin door, pushed himself away from the car and shuffled toward it. Dead leaves littered the sloping front porch. Tony's old key wouldn't turn in the lock. He found a rock close by and smashed it against the window pane nearest the door handle. Chiming shards of glass trickled down to the dusty wooden floor inside. He reached through the jagged hole and turned the knob.

The door creaked open on reluctant hinges. Dark contradictions revealed a room cleaned by a man. The refrigerator door hung open, racks empty. Dead flower stems leaned in a vase, surrounded by a circle of curled, brown petals on the table. Flower pots of hard dirt offered no nourishment to Angela's brittle house plants left to die on the window sill.

Dust swirled in the morning sun, now blasting through the open front door. Tony's eyes roamed from bright to dark, focusing on the changes. He entered and ducked beneath the tree limb that pierced the wall and grew up through the ceiling. The unread note he had left for Angela remained propped between the salt and pepper shakers. He crossed the kitchen and his footsteps echoed over the unswept floorboards. Stiff joints slowed his stilted gait, and his boots felt weighted. His hand clasped the door jamb, and he ached when he stepped down into the bedroom.

Black and brittle remnants of past fires lay cold in the charcoal belly of the river rock fireplace. A patchwork quilt with yellow knots of yarn still covered the double bed. Black plastic pieces of a broken phone remained in the corner. The broken bits reminded him of the anger he had once felt there. Now, he only felt a sense of loss so painful that he wanted to get away from it.

He shuffled across the room and opened the exterior bedroom door that faced the sun. A streak of light split the dark room. Out of habit, he reached around the corner of the building and found his old walking stick still propped in its usual resting place. He trudged down toward the river, leaning on the stick for support.

There was a certain spot by the edge of the stream that was etched in his memory forever. His footsteps stopped at a large flat rock, and, struggling to breathe, he looked back over his shoulder.

Angela, graceful as a swan, floated down the makeshift aisle in her wedding dress. So real, so beautiful, he held his hand out to her.

The vision vanished in an instant, leaving only sand and stones. He brushed his hand through his thick hair. His last peek in a mirror had revealed gray strands woven into his black curls and moustache.

A short path beside the river led him down to a small beach. Clear water flowed over moss green rocks and darkened the sand to a hard, flat finish along the shoreline. Tony pictured Angela there, still crouched at the water's edge. Half memory, half illusion, she stood up and turned to him, brushing sand from the back of her jeans. His last daylight recollection of her, a photograph frozen in his heart, appeared to move toward him.

"O love me truly," he whispered, remembering the words he had read to her so long ago. Speaking made the mirage fade away.

Tony turned back toward the cabin, knowing more ghosts awaited him. The warm sun excited the bees, and the air carried a whiff of honeysuckle. It was a good place to die. He tried to take a deep breath, but it only made him cough. It was all here at one time, then gone in a minute. All the mistakes he made. How he went from a husband and father-to-be, how the family he always needed slipped away in a foolish jealous rage. But at least he had known it for a moment. It was love he felt for Angela, and he knew now—too late—that it was love, because it was still with him. Unending. Isn't that what love is?

He remembered the inviting bed inside, but before he could reach his car, he was fighting for each breath. He leaned on the hood of the Cadillac, wondering if he could make it to the cabin door.

Another hallucination blocked his way. It was Angela again on the walkway to the front door, wearing clothes he'd only seen in a dream and carrying a baby. He gasped for air and walked toward the latest illusion. His hand moved to touch her, and he sank to his knees, waiting for the latest figment of his imagination to disappear. If he had to go now, he was glad he could go looking at her face.

"Tony?" Angela said. She knelt to touch his hand, and her familiar voice sounded so real. "What's wrong?"

"Angela," he said in a gasping whisper. He dropped his walking stick and fell to the ground. She touched the palm of his hand, and her fingertips felt warm against his skin. He closed his hand around hers, shocked to feel substance beneath his fingers.

"Tony!" Angela said, panicking. She was real. "Oh, God, Tony, don't die. Not now."

The fear in her voice made the baby cry. Tony's son's whimper gave him a reason to try. He touched her face, then pointed to the car, unable to speak or catch his breath.

"What?" she asked, looking at the Cadillac and then back at him. He couldn't answer. "In the car?"

She placed the baby beside him on the ground. His arm encircled the dark-haired child in the soft blue blanket. Angela threw open the car door and spotted the ventilator in the back seat. She dragged the apparatus from the car.

"How does it work?" she asked in a shrill, desperate voice. Tony tried the switches. He glanced at the mask. Her voice sounded far away. The warm bundle fidgeted at his side. The light went gray and the last thing he felt was a tiny hand encircling his smallest finger.

"Now what?" she asked, and his eyes closed. "No, Tony, no. Don't leave me. I don't know what to do. Tony? Tony!"

Tony had seen that tunnel enough times to know where he was, but this time there was a light at the end. It was as warm as freshly baked bread and as inviting as sleep. One step toward it and he knew this time he would never return. Its pure love promised no more pain, yet a powerful force held his body back, touching the smallest finger on his right hand.

"You can go on without me," his body said to his spirit.

Not yet, his spirit answered.

Tony hovered just above Angela's sandy hair. Her frantic pleading stopped, and the sound of heavy leather boots running got closer. Bill appeared at her side and began flipping switches on the machine. Tony watched him place the mask over his lifeless nose and mouth. The elastic band that held it in place snapped and broke. Bill pressed the mask against Tony's face. No movement rippled his ashen face, but Angela kept calling his name.

"Tony, Tony. . ."

Tony felt himself crashing back toward earth, drawn back into the vacuum of his empty body. The first gulp of air seared his lungs like swallowing hot coals. Pain overwhelmed him, but he struggled for another breath.

"I love you," Angela said in a whisper. Her eyes, the sparkling ones he had fallen into when they first met, were now cloaked with a layer of moisture. He gasped again, and the tears streamed down her cheeks.

Tony's eyes opened and then closed. The sight of Angela, the baby, and Bill burned into his consciousness. He reached for his next breath with all his strength. When it came, he fought for two more. He turned his head to see the anchor that brought him back. The baby's hand still gripped his finger between the second and third knuckle. When he could move his arm, he reached for Angela.

"You want to live now, asshole?" Bill asked, still gasping from his long sprint down the hill. He let go of the mask and stood up. "If so, hold that sucker to your face."

The useless mask balanced on Tony's nose. There was no way he could know if Angela would take him back, if Bill would ever get past what had happened between them, if his son would think he was a good father. He couldn't be sure of anything, but love wasn't about guarantees. It was about giving it a shot, making a choice and living with the decisions others made. Taking the risk that your heart could be broken and believing somehow it could be made whole again. Tony pressed the mask to his face with both hands, reaching for every breath that would give him a chance to find out.

"Get him to a hospital," Bill said to Angela and stepped away. "It's where he belongs. I can't help him anymore." He looked at his friend on the ground with a piercing glare. Tony nodded, glad to feel the earth pressing against his back and Angela by his side.

"If he were in a hospital, I would never have found him," Angela said, kneeling beside him. She cradled the baby and brushed Tony's hair from his forehead.

The soul knows . . .

The Daily Mail

TONY GLANCED OVER the letter he had just finished writing at the kitchen table. A few breakfast dishes were scattered nearby with left-over egg yolk drying to a crust. The letter didn't say all that it should, but he was never one for writing. He couldn't say why he was doing it now. Maybe it was the clear day, or the 600-horse engine he had heard that morning. Maybe it was because today was his fifth wedding anniversary.

Or maybe it was inspired by the postcard mailed to him in an envelope with no explanation. The front had an aerial view of a Catholic Church in Minneapolis. The reverse side was addressed to Bill. It said:

> Hi,
> I'm not good at staying in touch. My diocesan library duties keep me busy. I spend most days with books, not people. Maybe that's best, at least until they find a church that's ready for me.
> Yours,
> Father Roberto
> P. S. Say 'hi' to Tony.

TONY PUT DOWN the postcard and picked up the letter he'd just written.

> Dear Bill and Cindy,
> Thought I'd let you know we're making it. I never write letters. I got a job mechanicing. It doesn't pay shit, but what the hell. Angela's working too, at a bank. I'm sending you a picture of the house we're renting.

Nathan is on his fourth day care center in five months. They always say he's a troublemaker. (Where'd he get that?) By the way, Angela's pregnant again. You can't keep a good man down.

I never did pay you that $300 I owed you. I'm sending you a check, but don't cash it until the 15ᵗʰ, OK?

    Tony

P.S. I know I only owe you $300, but I figure saving my life is worth something, so I threw in a little extra. Besides, I might want to go up sometime.

TONY FOLDED the letter around his check for $301. He looked at the picture of Angela in a maternity top, him in a dirty white tee-shirt, and three-year-old Nathan, wearing a cowboy hat and boots. In the photo, his son was trying to balance on the cross bar of the white picket fence around their front yard. He had a stranglehold around Tony's neck. Tony slipped the photo into the envelope with the letter and sealed it.

"Angela?" he yelled, walking down the hall toward their bedroom. He stopped when he reached the entryway by the front door. "Do we have any stamps?"

"I don't think so," she called back.

"Never mind," he said and picked up a letter that had arrived from her mother. "I found one."

He headed for the kitchen, turned on the kettle, and waited for steam to come out the spout. The stamp looked brand new.

ACKNOWLEDGMENT

To all the cropdusters, living and dead, that I have known or heard stories about. There's a little bit of Tony in each of them and a little bit of each of them in Tony: Bud Atwood, Jerry & Steve Bernal, Harold Bingaman, Ted Best, Bill Blackburn, Johnny Broome, E.G. Brown, Steve Chaney, Jim Cheetum, Frank & Frankie Gomes, Joe Healy, Bud Henry, Wayne & Ryan Handley, Tim Hill, Bill Hubbard, Steve Johnson, Terry Johnson, Palmer Jones, Dennis Kirkpatrick, Keith Laudert, Richard Miller, Harold Oberg, Paul Oleas, Doc O'Neil, Lou Ortelli, John Pelham Burn, Gordon & Mark Plaskett, Charlie, Dick, & John Reeder, Red Ryder, Tom Shannon, King Sharp, Mike Silveira, George Smith, Joel Swatosh, Art Treganza, Sean Tucker, Jerry Wayne, Larry Wright

Luanne Oleas was born in Steinbeck's Salinas Valley, the setting for FLYING BLIND, where her husband worked as a cropduster. Her previous novel, A PRIMROSE IN NOVEMBER, a family saga, is set in England and France. Her upcoming novel, WHEN ALICE PLAYED THE LOTTERY, takes place in the Silicon Valley where the author currently lives with her husband and two cats.